DAWN OF THE CLANS

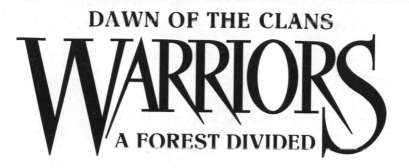

WARRIORS

A FOREST DIVIDED

WARRIORS

THE PROPHECIES BEGIN

THE NEW PROPHECY

POWER OF THREE

OMEN OF THE STARS

Book One: *The Fourth Apprentice*
Book Two: *Fading Echoes*
Book Three: *Night Whispers*
Book Four: *Sign of the Moon*
Book Five: *The Forgotten Warrior*
Book Six: *The Last Hope*

DAWN OF THE CLANS

Book One: *The Sun Trail*
Book Two: *Thunder Rising*
Book Three: *The First Battle*
Book Four: *The Blazing Star*

EXPLORE THE WARRIORS WORLD

Warriors Super Edition: Firestar's Quest
Warriors Super Edition: Bluestar's Prophecy
Warriors Super Edition: SkyClan's Destiny
Warriors Super Edition: Crookedstar's Promise
Warriors Super Edition: Yellowfang's Secret
Warriors Super Edition: Tallstar's Revenge
Warriors Super Edition: Bramblestar's Storm
Warriors Field Guide: Secrets of the Clans
Warriors: Cats of the Clans
Warriors: Code of the Clans
Warriors: Battles of the Clans
Warriors: Enter the Clans
Warriors: The Untold Stories
Warriors: Tales from the Clans
Warriors: The Ultimate Guide

DAWN OF THE CLANS

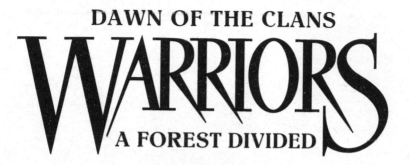

WARRIORS
A FOREST DIVIDED

ERIN
HUNTER

HARPER

An Imprint of HarperCollinsPublishers

Special thanks to Kate Cary

Library of Congress Cataloging-in-Publication Data

Hunter, Erin.

A forest divided / Erin Hunter. — First edition.

pages cm. — (Warriors, dawn of the clans ; #5)

Summary: As a cold, harsh winter approaches, the cats from the mountains prepare to divide into several camps, requiring each cat to decide where his or her allegiances lie.

ISBN 978-0-06-206362-5 (hardcover)

ISBN 978-0-06-206363-2 (library)

[1. Cats—Fiction. 2. Fantasy.] I. Title.

PZ7.H916625Fm 2015   2014005869

[Fic]—dc23   CIP

                                                                              AC

Typography by Hilary Zarycky

15 16 17 18 19   CG/RRDH   10 9 8 7 6 5 4 3 2 1

❖

First Edition

ALLEGIANCES

CLEAR SKY'S CAMP

LEADER

CLEAR SKY—light gray tom with blue eyes

LEAF—gray-and-white tom

QUICK WATER—gray-and-white she-cat

NETTLE—gray tom

THORN—mangy tom with splotchy fur

ACORN FUR—chestnut brown she-cat

KITS

BIRCH—brown-and-white tom

ALDER—gray-and-white she-kit

TALL SHADOW'S CAMP

LEADER

TALL SHADOW—black, thick-furred she-cat with green eyes

GRAY WING—sleek, dark gray tom with golden eyes

JAGGED PEAK—small gray tabby tom with blue eyes

DAPPLED PELT—delicate tortoiseshell she-cat with golden eyes

SHATTERED ICE—gray-and-white tom with green eyes

CLOUD SPOTS—long-furred black tom with white ears, white chest, and two white paws

LIGHTNING TAIL—black tom

THUNDER—orange tom with amber eyes and big white paws

HOLLY—she-cat with prickly, bushy fur

MOUSE EAR—tom with ears the size of a mouse's, missing part of one ear

MUD PAWS—tom with four black paws

KITS

OWL EYES—gray tom

PEBBLE HEART—brown tabby tom with amber eyes

SPARROW FUR—tortoiseshell she-kit

EAGLE FEATHER—brown tom

STORM PELT—gray tom with bue eyes

DEW NOSE—tabby she-kit with white-tipped nose and tail

RIVER RIPPLE'S CAMP

LEADER

RIVER RIPPLE—silver, long-furred tom

NIGHT—black she-cat

DEW— she-cat with a short, thick gray coat and bright blue eyes

WIND RUNNER'S CAMP

LEADER

WIND RUNNER—wiry brown she-cat with yellow eyes

GORSE FUR—thin, gray tabby tom

SLATE—gray she-cat

KITS

MOTH FLIGHT—she-kit with green eyes

DUST MUZZLE—gray tom-kit

ROGUE CATS

STAR FLOWER—golden she-cat with green eyes

SNAKE—gray tom

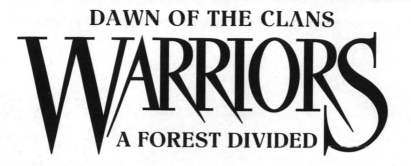

DAWN OF THE CLANS

WARRIORS

A FOREST DIVIDED

HIGHSTONES

THUNDERPATH

TALL SHADOW'S CAMP

THE FOUR TREES

WIND RUNNER'S CAMP

FALLS

RIVER RIPPLE'S CAMP

RIVER

THUNDERPATH

CLEAR SKY'S
CAMP

PROLOGUE

Cold mist pooled in the moonlit hollow. It swirled like water around the paws of the cats pacing restlessly beneath the oaks.

Clear Sky watched them from the edge of the clearing. Their pelts seemed to sparkle as though dusted with starlight. He shivered as he caught sight of Gray Wing, waiting at the far side of the clearing. *The dead outnumber the living,* Clear Sky thought, as he glanced toward the shallow mound at the edge of the hollow. Beneath the slow-settling earth lay the bodies of cats he had once hunted beside, killed in the Great Battle.

The spirit cats paused and glanced at him, then began moving once more, murmuring to one another in hushed whispers. Above them, the four great oaks creaked in the wind, their frost-whitened branches stripped clean by the cold.

Leaf-bare gripped the earth like a wolf holding prey. The earth felt like stone beneath Clear Sky's paws. Couldn't the spirit cats have summoned him to a greenleaf clearing, where warm winds could bathe his fur? After all, this *was* a dream.

A dark gray she-cat split from the others and padded toward him. "You came."

"Yes, Storm. I came." Clear Sky's heart ached with familiar

grief. How different his life would be now if he hadn't let her leave the forest when she was heavy with his kits. "But why have you called me here?"

Storm's gaze hardened. "We're growing tired of waiting."

Waiting? For what? Before Clear Sky could ask, bracken cracked on the slope. River Ripple was pushing his way through the frosty stems, his thick gray pelt silvered by the moonlight as he made his way down to the smooth earth at the bottom. Close by, Tall Shadow blinked near the roots of an oak. She looked surprised as though just awakening. Thunder's ginger pelt glowed in the shadows. The spirit cats must have summoned all the leaders to the dream.

Fur brushed the frost-wilted grass behind Clear Sky, and he turned to see Wind Runner slip silently past him. She had separated from Gray Wing's group. Had the spirit cats called her too?

Clear Sky shifted his paws uneasily. The living stood separately while the dead stood together. Were the spirit cats all that united them now?

"Well?" Storm's sharp mew jerked him back from his thoughts.

"What?"

"We told you to grow and spread like the Blazing Star. . . ." Storm glanced back at the living cats. "You haven't begun yet. Is fear holding you back?"

"Never!" Clear Sky puffed out his chest. "But how far can we spread? We already rule the forest and the moor. We recruit more cats whenever we can." He thought of how his own group had grown since the last dream.

"It's not enough!" An angry mew sounded beside Storm.

Clear Sky stepped back in surprise as he looked down and recognized the clear, bold gaze of a young cat he thought he'd never see again. The last time he'd seen this kit, her brown pelt had clung to jutting ribs. Hunger had killed her in the mountains before she'd ever left their mother's nest. Now she stood, chin high, eyes blazing. Her sleek pelt sparkled in the starlight; firm muscle showed beneath.

His throat tightened as he gazed at his younger sister. "Fluttering Bird!" he rasped. "It's you!"

"Of course it's me." Her yellow eyes blazed.

"I must go and speak with Thunder." Storm dipped her head and backed away, leaving Clear Sky alone with his sister.

"It's so good to see you—"

Fluttering Bird cut Clear Sky off. "Listen, you mouse-heart!"

Clear Sky stiffened. She was still a kit. How dare she speak to him like that? And yet . . . He frowned, puzzled. How long had she been with the spirit cats? She still looked like a kit, but she could see things he couldn't. His pelt rippled uneasily. Could his younger sister be *wiser* than him now?

She held his gaze. "There were still leaves on the trees when we told you to spread like the Blazing Star. You *talked* about it, but you've *done* nothing!"

"We've *survived*," Clear Sky argued. "Food is scarce and leaf-bare's here."

Fluttering Bird's ears twitched. "You should be thinking

of your kits and your kits' kits. Strength doesn't come from cowering in hollows and glades like frightened prey."

Clear Sky leaned over her, pelt bristling. "I *never* cower!"

"Then act!" Fluttering Bird stood her ground. "Follow your hearts! They will lead you home."

Clear Sky frowned. "You want us back in the mountains?"

"Not your *old* home!"

"Then where?"

"We can't make every paw step for you. That will weaken you all! We have told you all you need to know." Fluttering Bird's gaze scorched into his. "Now you must start thinking for yourselves."

Clear Sky stared past her, his gaze lighting on Tall Shadow as she shared words with Moon Shadow, Hawk Swoop, and Jackdaw's Cry. Wind Runner was with her lost kits. She nuzzled them, and he could hear her urgent purr throbbing through the cold night air. Her mew was sharp with grief. "My dear kits. Come closer. We won't be together for long."

Thunder paced to and fro, lifting his head eagerly as Storm padded to join them. Fox, Petal, and Frost crowded around River Ripple, their soft mews lost in the breeze. Gray Wing was several tail-lengths away, speaking with Shaded Moss and Turtle Tail. How separate they seemed. "We traveled here together," Clear Sky murmured, half to himself, "but now we don't even share prey." Sadness tugged in his belly.

"And who's to blame for that?" Fluttering Bird growled. "*You* turned against your own."

"That's not true!" he snapped back. "I've always done what

I thought was best! I tried to take care of my own."

"Then why do you stand here alone?" Fluttering Bird demanded. "Who do you have to care for you?"

Clear Sky swallowed, unable to answer her. Gray Wing seemed suddenly far away, the clearing stretching like a deep gorge between them. Thunder had not even met his eye since arriving in the hollow. Clear Sky knew they still silently blamed him for the battle and for taking One Eye into his group and nurturing him until he became a threat to all the cats. There was a time when they *wanted* to be near him. But he had driven them away. And now? Would any of them come now if he needed them?

He stared at Fluttering Bird. Was she *trying* to hurt him? "Why are you saying this?"

"You have followed your head, not your heart, Clear Sky." She flicked her tail. "Each cat here has a home waiting. Even you. But you have to find it for yourselves, and you must find it soon."

"How?" Where *was* home? How would they know when they found it?

"Follow your hearts." Fluttering Bird began to fade before his eyes. He stiffened. *Not yet!* The other cats were fading too, growing transparent as the dream began to disappear. The stars blurred above his head and the hollow grew hazy.

"Fluttering Bird!" Clear Sky struggled to see her. "Where should our hearts lead?"

Who do you have to care for you? Her words rang in his mind.

Did she want him to be close to his kin once more? Perhaps the only way to spread and grow like the Blazing Star was to join forces—be like a Tribe once more.

Darkness swamped him, and he blinked open his eyes.

He was back in his nest again. He gazed across the moonlit hollow where the forest cats had made their camp. His hackles smoothed as calm enfolded him. *I understand!* Fluttering Bird was trying to tell him how foolish he'd been to split from the others and mark out his own territory.

Determination surged through him. Wide awake now, he stood and crossed the clearing. He slipped past the brambles that shielded the camp, then bounded out into the forest. Starlight sparkled on his pelt as he glanced up at the sky. *I understand now, Fluttering Bird! I must draw the cats close—together once more—so that we can grow strong and spread like the Blazing Star.*

CHAPTER 1

Clear Sky yawned and stretched his forepaws until they trembled. He looked over the edge of his nest. A biting wind sliced beneath the arching root, which usually shielded him as he slept. It nipped his ears, and he narrowed his eyes against its sting as he gazed over the clearing.

Quick Water was crossing the camp, her fur fluffed up against the cold. A shriveled mouse hung from her jaws. Birch and Alder peeked out from beneath the low, spreading yew. Petal had made their nest beneath its dark green branches after she'd adopted them. Their own mother had been killed, and they hardly remembered her scent. Now Petal was dead too, taken by the sickness that had swept the forest before leaf-bare had come. Birch and Alder had nearly died, but the Blazing Star had saved them.

The Blazing Star. Clear Sky felt a pang of grief. If only Star Flower had told them about it sooner. It was the only healing herb that could cure the sickness. Now it shaped their future. He stood and shook out his fur as Alder and Birch hurried out to meet Quick Water.

"Is that for us?" Birch's eyes were hopeful.

His sister, Alder, dipped her head to Quick Water. "If you tell us where you found it, we could go and catch our own." The littermates were almost fully grown, lithe and fast and always eager to hunt. Clear Sky felt proud of the cats they'd become, and was pleased that he'd decided to let Petal take them in.

"Don't be squirrel-brained." Quick Water dropped the mouse at their paws. "We can share this one and hunt together later."

Alder and Birch blinked at her gratefully.

Clear Sky felt a prickle of worry as he watched them crouch close to Quick Water, taking turns to snatch a bite of the skinny prey. Prey was scarce. The sickness had killed much of it, and the forest was eerily silent, even for leaf-bare.

He shook the chill from his fur and hopped out of his nest. He'd wandered in the forest until dawn and had returned to rest, weary from the cold. The memory of the dream had followed him into sleep. Fluttering Bird wanted the cats to join together. They must be like the Blazing Star and gather like petals around the heart of a flower. He was sure of it. It made sense. If the cold had reached this deep into the forest, it would be bitter on the high moor. And with prey so scarce, the moor cats would surely freeze or starve if they stayed in their hollow. They'd be safer here, sheltered by the trees, hunting together, as Fluttering Bird had ordered.

He must tell them.

Perhaps they already know? For the first time he wondered what the spirit cats had shared with the others. Hope flickered in his belly. Perhaps they were ready to unite.

He slid out from beneath the root, its gnarled bark scraping his spine, and padded across the frozen earth.

Pink Eyes was crouching in the shelter of the spreading holly, squinting against the wind. Tiny flecks of snow swirled in the air and clung to his fur. Pink Eyes's tail twitched with annoyance and he drew his paws tighter under him.

Clear Sky nodded to him. "Where's Blossom?" he asked.

The old tom had arrived at the border with the tortoise-shell-and-white she-cat when the moon was only a scratch of silver in the sky, not long after the battle with One Eye.

"Still asleep," Pink Eyes answered, flicking his muzzle toward the holly bush. In the shadows beneath, Clear Sky could make out Blossom's pelt. When she was awake, the young she-cat hardly stood still. She was skittish and full of energy.

When Clear Sky had first met her, she'd been leaping for a dead leaf as it fluttered toward the forest floor while Pink Eyes sat a few tail-lengths away, his thin white tail curled neatly over two dead mice. He'd stood when Clear Sky had approached and had spoken before Clear Sky had a chance to challenge them for loitering near his border. "May we join your group?"

There had been a time when Clear Sky would have driven the two strays from his border—especially Pink Eyes, whose sight was so poor he couldn't see a bird in a tree—but these cats had respected his scent line and kept their hackles soft, and Clear Sky had learned that friends were better than enemies.

So they'd joined the group, and Clear Sky was soon glad that they had. Pink Eyes's weak eyesight had strengthened his other senses. The white tom could hear a mouse in the next glade and smell a rabbit through a patch of wild garlic.

Alder looked up from her meal, her splotchy gray-and-white pelt pricking where tiny snowflakes had settled along her spine. As she licked her lips, her gaze flashed toward Pink Eyes's twitching tail. Clear Sky saw mischief light up her eyes. She lunged and grabbed it, rolling onto her back. With a purr, she began pummeling it playfully with her hind legs.

"Hey!" Pink Eyes turned on her angrily. "Chase your own tail!"

"Why?" Alder froze, her paws in the air, and blinked at him innocently. "I'm not a dog!"

Pink Eyes glared at her. "And my tail isn't *prey*."

Birch padded to his sister's side, his ginger pelt bright in the weak morning light. "I just wish prey was so easy to catch," he said lightly.

The old tom snorted and marched away. He circled in a sheltered spot between the roots of an oak, then sat down and stared pointedly at Birch and Alder.

The brambles at the far end of the camp rattled. Nettle padded through the gap at one side. His thick gray pelt was damp. Acorn Fur followed him, a battered starling hanging from her jaws. Leaf padded after them, carrying a scrawny squirrel.

"I've never seen prey so scarce." Nettle padded past his campmates and stopped beside Clear Sky. "I don't know how we'll make it to newleaf."

Anxiety wormed in Clear Sky's belly. Alder and Birch were staring hungrily at Acorn Fur's starling. Quick Water's mouse clearly hadn't filled their bellies. *We must survive!* Clear Sky glanced through the trees. Was there more prey on the moor? Suddenly the boundaries he'd fought so hard to establish seemed to trap him. *We need to share what we have, not guard it.* Fluttering Bird must have known that.

"I'm going to Gray Wing's camp," he told Nettle.

Nettle's ear twitched. "Why?"

Clear Sky shifted his paws. Nettle had fought beside him to keep the boundaries they'd made. What would he say when he heard Clear Sky had suddenly decided that the cats should share their land and live as one group? He would understand once he knew that it was what the spirit cats wanted. But there wasn't time to explain now. "I want to see Jagged Peak's kits." This was true. He hadn't visited his brother's litter yet.

"The weather's closing in." Nettle glanced at the thick yellow clouds crowding the treetops. "There'll be heavy snow before the day's out, and if the wind picks up—"

Clear Sky interrupted. "I come from the mountains, remember? I'm used to getting snow in my whiskers."

Nettle shrugged. "It's your pelt." He glanced across the clearing as Blossom slid out from beneath the holly.

"Do I smell prey?" she asked brightly. Her gaze swiveled toward Acorn Fur.

Acorn Fur dropped her starling. "There's not much, but we can share."

Leaf laid his squirrel on the ground. "It'll do for now." His mew was cheerful, but Clear Sky could see worry darkening his gaze. The sooner he persuaded the cats they'd be safer working together, the better. He headed for the gap in the brambles. "Make sure Pink Eyes gets some food," he called over his shoulder. "His hungry belly is making him grouchy." He shot a teasing look at the white cat.

Pink Eyes stared stiffly ahead, as though deaf. Clear Sky knew his sharp hearing hadn't missed his jibe. Affection surged beneath his pelt. *Proud old fleabag!*

Blossom leaped onto a root beside Pink Eyes. "Do you want to share the starling or the squirrel?"

"I guess a bite of squirrel might be nice," the tom huffed grudgingly.

Purring, Clear Sky slipped through the bramble tunnel.

Outside camp, the wind was brisker. The branches above him swished in the breeze. He opened his mouth and tasted snow. It carried the stone tang of the mountains. Nettle had been right. A heavy snowfall was on its way. He hurried between the trees. The sooner he reached the moor cats' hollow, the better.

He followed the ridge until it dipped, then he leaped a fallen tree and climbed the slope beyond. Bare brambles snaked over the ground, and he had to watch where he put each paw. The ferns had withered long ago, but in their musty stumps Clear Sky could smell a hint of the forest's greenleaf lushness. Stiff bracken crowded the top of the slope. Clear Sky pushed through it, narrowing his eyes against the light as he neared the edge of the forest. He broke from the trees, ducking instinctively as he hit open country.

The icy wind streamed through his whiskers, and he flattened his ears. He glanced one way, then the other, tasting the air for danger. Dog scent clung to the grass, but it was stale, and he crossed the swath of withered ferns edging the woods and began to climb through the rough grass.

He paused as he neared a stunted thorn tree standing alone on the barren moorside. Beneath it, a mound of soil marked the grave where they had buried One Eye, the bloodthirsty rogue. The cats from moor, forest, and river had joined together to defeat him. Snow flecked the soil, and thrushes sang in the branches above.

He was a true ray of light.

Bitterness rose in Clear Sky's throat as he remembered Star Flower's words at the burial. How could she have been so deluded? One Eye might have been her father, but even she must have been shocked by his cruelty.

How could she have betrayed Thunder for him? Clear Sky snorted. He still couldn't believe that the treacherous she-cat had deceived his son.

The wind blew harder. Heather swayed ahead of him, and he hurried for its shelter, ducking among the brown bushes until he found a rabbit trail between the stems. He followed it, relieved to be out of the wind, zigzagging this way and that as he made his way up the winding path.

The heather gave way to a smooth grassy slope. In the open once more, Clear Sky spied the dip in the hillside where the moor cats' camp lay. He quickened his pace. Snowflakes streamed around him, falling thicker now.

Movement caught his eyes. A small flash of fur against the grass ahead made him freeze.

Prey.

A small rabbit was hopping toward the heather. Clear Sky dropped into a crouch and pricked his ears. Excitement surged through him as warm rabbit scent filled his nose. His tail twitched. He waggled his hindquarters, preparing to pounce.

Suddenly, the rabbit stopped and looked around, ears high.

Clear Sky froze.

The rabbit blinked, then bolted for the heather.

Now! Clear Sky surged forward. His paws rang on the frozen earth.

The rabbit fled. Fear-scent trailed in its wake. Clear Sky was closing in. He pushed harder against the frosty grass, fixing his gaze on the space in front of it.

Then he leaped. Stretching his forepaws, he landed squarely on his prey. It struggled beneath him. He was surprised at its strength. Quickly, he dug in his claws and sank his teeth into its neck. The spine snapped cleanly and the rabbit fell limp.

Clear Sky's mouth watered as blood bathed his tongue. He sat up and licked his lips. Should he leave his catch to take back to his own cats? He glanced toward the hollow. The moor cats might have greater need. And it would make a generous offering to Jagged Peak and Holly, in honor of their first litter.

He grabbed the rabbit's scruff in his jaws and carried it up the slope.

As he neared the moor cats' camp, he scanned the top of its gorse wall. Where was Tall Shadow? She was usually watching from her rock, scanning the moor with her solemn, wary gaze. He slowed as he reached the camp entrance. There was no cat guarding it. He pricked his ears. Had the weather driven them into their tunnels?

"We should wait for the snow to pass before we send out a hunting patrol."

Clear Sky heard Thunder's mew beyond the camp wall. Pride swelled in his chest. His son had grown into a fine tom.

"What if it lasts for days?" Gray Wing's mew answered Thunder.

"Let's worry about that when it happens."

Clear Sky nosed through the gap in the gorse.

Gray Wing turned to meet him, eyes round with surprise. "Clear Sky? What are you doing here?"

Clear Sky dropped his catch. "I came to visit Jagged Peak's kits." He glanced around the camp, a purr rumbling in his throat as he spied three kits tumbling across the grass at the far end of the hollow.

Thunder didn't follow his gaze. He was staring at the rabbit on the ground in front of Clear Sky. "Did you catch that on our land?" His amber eyes narrowed.

Clear Sky blinked at him. Only a few moons ago, they'd begun to grow close. Now he felt further from his son than ever before. "I—I brought it for Jagged Peak and Holly."

One of the kits squeaked excitedly. "I'm the fastest!"

Clear Sky saw a brown tom-kit struggle from his littermate's grip and race toward Jagged Peak, who was watching from the long grass at the edge of the hollow.

"No, you're not!" A tabby she-kit raced after him. The splotches on her pelt were like Holly's. White tips on her nose and her tail made her look as though she'd been dipped in snow.

"Wait for me!" A third kit trailed behind. His thick gray pelt and lithe frame reminded Clear Sky of Jagged Peak before the accident that had crippled his hind leg.

"Eagle Feather!" Holly stepped from the shelter of the long grass, and the brown tom-kit bundled into her. She scooped him up by his scruff and dropped him into the grass behind her. "Storm Pelt! Dew Nose! Back into your nest, all of you! It's too cold to be out."

Jagged Peak swished his tail. "They'll be warm enough so long as they keep moving."

"Let them play!" Shattered Ice called across the clearing. "It'll make them strong." The gray-and-white tom looked thin.

Mud Paws and Lightning Tail sat a tail-length away, sharing an emaciated mouse. Clear Sky could see their bones jutting beneath their fur.

Mud Paws looked up, chewing. "Check their tail-tips," he advised. "If they're frozen, it's time to stop."

"Let them have fun!" Sparrow Fur padded out from beneath the arching broom at the end of the camp. The she-kit had grown, but she was skinny, and her pelt dull. "If there *is* a snowstorm on the way, it might be the last fun they have for days."

Gray Wing kneaded the ground with his paws. "We really should send out a hunting party now."

"They might get caught in the storm," Thunder argued. "And Clear Sky has brought this rabbit." He nudged it with his wide paw. "The kits won't go hungry."

Clear Sky blinked. "Are they eating prey already?"

"They were born the new moon before last," Gray Wing reminded him.

That long ago? Clear Sky's thoughts flitted back to the dream. *We grow tired of waiting.* They had promised to spread and grow like the Blazing Star. He caught Gray Wing's eye. "We have to talk about what we saw." He scanned the clearing. "Is Tall Shadow here?"

"Pebble Heart's treating a scratch on her paw." Thunder nodded toward a jutting stretch of gorse. "In Cloud Spots's den."

"I can get her if you like." A mew sounded behind Clear Sky.

He jerked around. It was Owl Eyes. The young tom had broadened across the shoulders. His forehead was nearly as wide as Gray Wing's. "You've grown!" Clear Sky exclaimed.

"So has Pebble Heart." Owl Eyes stalked away and called into the gorse. "Tall Shadow, Clear Sky is here."

"I know." The black she-cat's familiar mew sounded from the shadows. "I can smell his scent." The bush quivered as Tall Shadow slid out.

Pebble Heart followed. "I'll put fresh ointment on it tomorrow," he mewed.

"Thanks." Tall Shadow stopped beside Clear Sky. "What do you want?"

Clear Sky hardly heard her. He was gazing across the snowy clearing. Jagged Peak nuzzled Eagle Feather near the edge. Pebble Heart followed Owl Eyes across the grass.

Sparrow Fur called to them from the broom. "Shelter under here!"

Gray Wing's gaze shone proudly as he watched. "She's so like her mother," he purred. "And Jagged Peak is turning out to be a great father."

Clear Sky glanced guiltily at Thunder. Would his son ever truly forgive him for driving him away? He looked back toward Jagged Peak, who'd crouched low to let Eagle Feather scramble onto his back. *Jagged Peak is a far better father than I was.* He shifted his paws, feeling the cold pierce his fur. *And Gray Wing raised another tom's kits while I wouldn't even raise my own.*

"Well?" Tall Shadow's sharp mew jerked him back to the present. "Why did you come?"

He met her eye. "I saw you in my dream last night."

"And we saw you." Tall Shadow tipped her head.

Clear Sky leaned forward, his heart quickening. "What did the spirit cats tell you?"

"To stop thinking and act," Tall Shadow told him. "That we've delayed too long."

"That's what they told me too!" Clear Sky trembled with

excitement. "They want us to join together."

"Join *together*?" Tall Shadow stared at him, eyes wide.

"Are you sure you heard them right?" Thunder tipped his head, curious.

"They told us to *spread*," Gray Wing snapped.

Clear Sky's belly twisted with frustration. *They've misunderstood the spirit cats' message.* "We'll be stronger together, especially with prey so scarce and bad weather coming." He lifted his face to the thickening snow. "We're more likely to spread and grow if we join forces."

Gray Wing narrowed his eyes. "But don't you remember what I said after the last dream? The Blazing Star has five petals, so I think we should split into five groups."

"We didn't agree on that," Clear Sky reminded him. "That's only what you think. I think the spirit cats want us to join together!"

Tall Shadow's ear twitched. "Lovely, it's another battle between the two of you," she growled. "When the time comes, I won't be joining your group. I want to make my own camp in the pine forest."

Clear Sky stared at her. "You can't!" His mind raced. What were they talking about? This was the opposite of what Fluttering Bird wanted!

"Tall Shadow's not the only cat who wants to move on," Gray Wing murmured.

Clear Sky jerked around to stare at his brother. "What do you mean?"

Gray Wing dropped his gaze. "There's been talk in the camp ever since the last dream. Not everyone wants to live on the moor."

"Come to my forest, then." Clear Sky pressed. Why were they making this so complicated? "It's sheltered there. With more cats, we can find more prey."

Thunder frowned. "I don't understand. You used to try to keep us out of the forest."

Clear Sky met his gaze. "I used to defend my borders," he admitted. "But I've changed. Now that I've spoken with Fluttering Bird, I know what—"

Gray Wing pricked his ears. "You saw Fluttering Bird?" His eyes lit up. "How is she?"

"She's well." Warmth flooded Clear Sky as he remembered his sister's sleek fur. "Better than she ever was in life."

"What did she say?" Tall Shadow asked slowly.

"She said we must each follow our hearts," Clear Sky told her.

"She meant we must find our own homes," Tall Shadow concluded.

"*No!*" Clear Sky flexed his claws in frustration. "Why would the spirit cats ask us to split up now? We'd be making ourselves vulnerable—especially after the sickness killed off so much prey. We must join together! The way we used to be. The way we should have stayed." His pelt grew hot. Gray Wing and Thunder were staring at him through narrowed eyes. Didn't they trust him? "Please come with me to the forest." He flicked his tail toward the other cats, half-hidden by the snow, which swirled across the clearing. "Every cat must come. It's sheltered there."

"No, Clear Sky." Thunder's growl cut to Clear Sky's heart. "After everything that's happened, we can't go back to how it was." His amber gaze sharpened. "Cats have died over the borders you created. Now you want us to pretend they were never there."

"But what about the spirit cats?" Clear Sky's mew was hoarse. *They're rejecting my plan.*

Gray Wing met Clear Sky's gaze. "They told us to spread and grow, and that's what we'll do."

"You should go home." Thunder jerked his nose toward the camp entrance. "No one's coming to live in the forest with you. If you want more cats to boss around, recruit some new strays."

Clear Sky swallowed. *What's gotten into Thunder?* Did he really believe Clear Sky just wanted to boss more cats around? Did he think he'd learned nothing?

Tall Shadow gazed anxiously into the wind. Flakes of snow whipped her face. "Perhaps he should wait out the storm. It's almost on us."

Clear Sky shook his head. He didn't want to stay. "I'll go," he growled.

Head down, he padded to the entrance. He had come to unite the cats. Now he felt further away from them than ever. How would he explain this to Fluttering Bird? He'd failed her. He pushed through the gorse, his paws heavy as stone. There must be some way to make the moor cats understand.

He flattened his ears as he padded out onto the open grass beyond the gorse. The wind was strong, the snow thick. It buffeted his fur, so cold that it felt like claws slicing through his pelt. Hunching low, Clear Sky hurried toward the heather.

I'll make them understand, Fluttering Bird. Snow battered his face. *I'll make them follow their hearts, I promise. We'll be together soon.*

CHAPTER 2

❧

Thunder watched his father disappear through the gorse. Guilt stabbed at his chest. *Was I too harsh?* He glanced questioningly at Gray Wing. "Should I make sure he gets back to the forest safely?"

Gray Wing didn't answer. He was gazing into the swirling snow, his thoughts clearly elsewhere.

Tall Shadow leaned forward. "Go," she murmured.

Thunder blinked at her gratefully and headed for the gorse. Pushing out onto the moor, he narrowed his eyes against the blinding snow. He strained to make out his father's pelt, and felt relieved as he spotted a dark shape moving ahead. Ducking low, he raced after it.

"Clear Sky!" The wind whipped his mew away. He pushed harder, digging his claws through the thickening layer of snow. Clear Sky disappeared into a swath of heather.

Thunder headed after him, ducking along a stale rabbit trail. He caught sight of his father's tail ahead. "Clear Sky!" Sheltered now, his call echoed along the heather tunnel.

Clear Sky stopped. "What?" He glanced back warily.

Thunder scrambled to a halt, his lungs burning from the cold. "I wanted to make sure you got home safely," he puffed.

"Is that all?" Clear Sky kept walking.

Thunder swallowed back guilt. "I know the moor better than you," he meowed firmly. "You could easily get lost in this storm."

Clear Sky flicked his tail.

Thunder followed. "I'm sorry about what I said."

Clear Sky didn't answer.

Thunder's belly tightened. *Why should I feel bad? He's the one who made the boundaries. Now he wants to abolish them.* He followed Clear Sky, flattening his ears.

The trail opened into a small clearing between the bushes, and Clear Sky halted. The wind gusted above the heather. Thunder's pelt pricked as his father turned to face him.

"I *don't* want more cats to boss around." Clear Sky's blue eyes glittered with hurt.

Thunder glanced at the ground. "Well, there was a time when you did," he mumbled.

"Not anymore." Clear Sky's shoulders drooped. "I just want us to be together, like we used to be. Fluttering Bird wants it too."

Thunder felt a surge of sympathy. Was his father still grieving for the young sister he'd lost? "What if you're wrong?"

"I'm not." Clear Sky gazed at him for a moment. He nodded toward a rabbit trail opening onto the clearing, then flicked his muzzle toward another. "Which one?"

Thunder brushed past him and ducked into the nearest tunnel. "This way." He led Clear Sky along the familiar track until it opened onto the hillside. Snow battered his face as he emerged, and he braced himself against the wind. It was bitter enough to freeze prey.

Clear Sky slid out beside him and stared through narrowed eyes. "Where's the forest?"

Thunder strained to see but the blizzard was thicker than fog. "If we follow the slope, it should lead us down to the forest's edge."

"I'll go first." Clear Sky pushed past him. "I know the scents of the forest better than you. I'll know when we're close."

For a cat who doesn't want more cats to boss around, you're awfully good at it. Thunder bristled but held his tongue and followed Clear Sky, keeping so close that his father's tail-tip brushed his nose. The wind roared in his ears. Cold pierced his pelt, and he fought not to shiver. "Maybe we should find a tunnel and take shelter till it passes."

"We're nearly there," Clear Sky called over his shoulder. "I smell fresh earth. The forest must be close." The gray tom quickened his pace. Thunder hurried after him, alarm pricking in his paws as his father's tail disappeared. "Clear Sky!" They mustn't be separated. Not in this weather. He blinked against the snow, relieved as he made out Clear Sky's pelt once more.

An angry roar exploded ahead.

Fear flashed through Thunder. *What is it?* Pelt bushing, he surged forward. "Clear Sky?"

A large, dark shape lunged toward Clear Sky from the blinding whiteness.

Clear Sky shrieked.

Thunder raced forward, the tang of blood hitting his nose, followed by the fierce stench of badger. His heart seemed to explode in his chest. "Clear Sky!" He heard the thump of hard muscle on the frozen earth, and the vicious snarl of the badger. Black fur showed through the storm; wide hindquarters bucked and trembled. The massive creature was pinning Clear Sky to the ground. Panic scorching through him, Thunder heard jaws snap.

"Let him go!" Thunder hurled himself at the badger's flank, digging his claws in deep. The badger shook him off and snapped again at Clear Sky.

Claws caught Thunder's flank as he fell against Clear Sky's desperately flailing hind legs. He jumped clear, his mind spinning. The badger was huge!

Thunder leaped again. Claws outstretched, he landed on the badger's spine. Biting hard into its pelt, he churned with his hind legs, but the badger only snarled and snapped again at Clear Sky.

He's killing him! Thunder was blind with terror and snow as his hind paw slid down the badger's leg. He felt his claws graze soft, wet flesh. The badger flinched and yelped.

It's wounded! Hope flashed through him. He slithered to the ground and sniffed out the badger's blood. Thrusting his muzzle close to its injured back leg, he clawed at the wound; then he clamped his jaws around it.

With a roar of agonized fury, the badger reared.

Run, Clear Sky! Thunder's gaze flicked toward his father, but Clear Sky was lying motionless on the ground. Thunder froze as the badger's head swung toward him. Swallowing, he backed away. He could taste the badger's blood in his mouth. He gagged. It was sour with infection.

A menacing growl rumbled in the badger's throat, and it leaped. Thunder dived to one side, rolling as he landed. He looked back to make sure the badger still had its gaze fixed on him, then raced across the slope.

The earth trembled as the badger pounded after him. Triumph thrilled beneath Thunder's pelt. The badger would never catch up to him. Especially with an injured leg. *I just have to lead it far enough away from Clear Sky.* He snatched a glance over his shoulder and glimpsed the badger's hulking shape following him. Bounding across the snow, he led the badger away. The wind whipped his ears as he pushed into the blizzard; then he turned and fled uphill, leaving the badger lumbering far behind. *Thank you, snow!* It would cover his tracks. Paws skidding, he made a wide circle and doubled back toward Clear Sky.

Please be alive!

Panic seized him. *Where is he?*

The snow that had hidden Thunder from the badger now hid his father.

Opening his mouth, Thunder tasted for Clear Sky's scent. Snowflakes landed on his tongue. His nose stung with the cold. "Clear Sky?" His call was barely a whisper. He dared not let the badger hear.

A moan sounded ahead.

"Clear Sky!" Heart soaring, Thunder spotted a shape on

the ground. "You're alive!" Reaching him, he dropped into a crouch. Clear Sky lay on his flank, his chest heaving. Thunder sniffed his pelt. He smelled the sour scent of the badger's blood. "Did it hurt you?"

Clear Sky blinked and struggled to his paws.

Thunder smelled a fresh wound. The snow was red beneath him.

"Where did it bite you?" Fear sparked through Thunder as he saw the fur at Clear Sky's neck clumped with blood.

"It's not deep," Clear Sky croaked.

"A badger's bite carries infection," Thunder warned him. "Let me get you back to the hollow."

"We're closer to the forest." Clear Sky stumbled as he spoke. His flank hit Thunder's.

Thunder dug his claws into the ground, supporting his father's weight. "Pebble Heart can treat your wound. He knows which herbs will stop it from turning sour." He felt Clear Sky heave a shaky breath. "Let's get out of here before that badger comes back."

"I don't know why you want to stay on the moor when it's riddled with badgers," Clear Sky grumbled as Thunder steered him up the slope toward the heather.

"There's a set in the forest too," Thunder pointed out.

"Far enough from the camp not to have them lumbering around, attacking cats."

Thunder was relieved to hear Clear Sky arguing. That meant his wound couldn't be too bad, though his father's paw steps were halting. He nudged Clear Sky on, anxious the badger might have picked up their trail. Snowflakes caught in his throat as he struggled to support his father. They stumbled uphill, the wind pushing them sideways.

Thunder was breathless by the time they reached the heather. Puffing, he guided his father into a rabbit run among the bushes. As the branches enclosed them, he relaxed. The badger couldn't follow them through here.

They reached the far side of the heather and emerged onto open grass. The snow had eased. Thunder could see the gorse wall of the camp and pushed his shoulder harder against Clear Sky's. "We're nearly there."

"It's my neck that's injured, not my mind," Clear Sky grunted.

"Or your tongue," Thunder growled back.

"Thunder?" Cloud Spots's mew sounded from the camp entrance. "Are you okay?" The long-furred black tom hurried across the grass toward them. His white ear tips and paws were invisible against the snowy moor. "I smell blood."

"Clear Sky was attacked by a badger," Thunder explained. Cloud Spots had been tending to injured cats since Thunder could remember. And he'd passed on his skills to Pebble Heart.

Cloud Spots fell in beside Clear Sky, pushing against his other shoulder.

"It's just a scratch," Clear Sky insisted.

"Even a scratch can turn nasty. Especially from a badger," Cloud Spots fretted. "But I have a good store of herbs." He lifted his chin and called to the camp. "Pebble Heart!"

The young tom appeared at the camp entrance, his tabby pelt standing out against the snow-blasted gorse. "Cloud Spots?" There was worry in his mew.

"Go and start chewing a poultice of marigold and oak leaf."

Thunder stiffened at the worry in Cloud Spots's voice. "He'll be okay, won't he?" He glanced at Clear Sky.

"Of course I'll be okay." Clear Sky straightened sharply, pushing the moor cats away, and marched into the hollow.

Thunder hurried after him into the snow-covered camp.

Tall Shadow darted from the long grass, shaking flakes from her spine. "I said go after him." Her ear twitched angrily. "I didn't say bring him back."

"We ran into a badger," Thunder explained quickly. "Clear Sky was hurt."

"Badly?" Tall Shadow glanced over her shoulder.

Gray Wing was crossing the clearing toward her, his paws kicking through the snow. "Is he okay?"

Cloud Spots was already guiding Clear Sky into his den. "He'll be fine."

Gray Wing met Thunder's gaze. "Should you have brought him back?" he asked anxiously. "He's already ruffled enough fur here for one day."

"He was attacked by a badger!" Thunder turned his tail on Gray Wing and followed Clear Sky into Cloud Spots's den.

Cloud Spots was easing Clear Sky onto his side. "Lie still so Pebble Heart can reach your wound."

Clear Sky huffed. "What a lot of fuss over a scratch."

Thunder wrinkled his nose as he padded across the sandy floor of the den. The tang of herbs filled the air. He noticed two nests at the back of the den, woven from heather branches and lined with moss. *How can Pebble Heart and Cloud Spots sleep in here with this smell?* Squinting though the half-light, he could make out wads of leaves stuffed between the gorse stems. "Is that your herb store?" he asked Cloud Spots. He was surprised the tom had collected so many.

"It should last us through leaf-bare." Cloud Spots's gaze was fixed on Clear Sky's neck as Pebble Heart carefully washed the bloodstained fur clean. "Is it deep?" he asked the young tom.

"No." Pebble Heart looked up. "A bit jagged, but that should help it close up easily." He twisted and grabbed a mouthful of dark sludge from beside him, then began to work it into Clear Sky's wound with steady laps of his tongue.

Clear Sky flinched. "Are you sure that will help?" he rasped.

Cloud Spots ran his tail along Clear Sky's flank. "The sting shows that the herbs are working."

Thunder sat back on his haunches, wondering how any cat had the patience to learn the name and use of every herb. "How long will it take to heal?" he asked.

"A few days." Pebble Heart stepped back.

Clear Sky struggled to his paws. He twisted his head gently, as though feeling for pain. "Thank you." He nodded to Pebble Heart. "That feels better already."

"I chewed some dock into the poultice," Pebble Heart told

him. "It will soothe the wound. When you get back to the forest, put some dock leaves in your nest when you sleep. It will ease the pain."

Clear Sky blinked gratefully at the young cat, then turned to Thunder. "See how well we manage when we work together?"

Thunder felt his heart grow heavy. Clear Sky was still trying to persuade him that the cats should join up.

He stared blankly at his father, searching for words.

Clear Sky spoke again before he could answer. "You saved me from that badger, and Pebble Heart has made sure my wound will heal. Imagine if we all lived in the forest?" His eyes grew brighter with each word. "We'd grow strong and spread, just like the spirit cats said."

"I don't think that's what they meant," Cloud Spots mewed gently.

Clear Sky turned on him. "How do you know? You weren't *there!*"

Thunder flattened his ears as he heard his father's temper flare. Perhaps Clear Sky hadn't changed that much after all. "Leave Cloud Spots alone," he murmured. "He just helped you."

Clear Sky's angry gaze flashed toward Thunder. "Why won't any of you *understand?* Fluttering Bird wants us to be together!"

Thunder felt suddenly weary. Fighting with badgers was bad enough. He didn't want to fight with Clear Sky too. He got to his paws. "Can Clear Sky take some fresh herbs home with him?"

Pebble Heart answered him. "I'll wrap the leftover poultice in a leaf for him."

"Thanks." Thunder headed out of the den. "I'm going to check on the kits." He wanted to make sure their nest was clear of snow.

Outside, a few flakes swirled around him as he crossed the clearing.

Jagged Peak was dragging a large piece of heather toward the far end.

"Are the kits okay?" Thunder called.

Jagged Peak dropped the branch and looked at Thunder. "We're moving them to a more sheltered spot."

Thunder caught up with him as he dragged the branch beneath the trailing broom. "Under here?"

Inside, a wide circle of clear earth sat sheltered by the dropping stems. Even stripped of their leaves they made a fine windbreak, and the snow hadn't made it through. Holly was near the back of the den, weaving heather branches together with her teeth. Eagle Feather, Dew Nose, and Storm Pelt were darting around her, pouncing on one another, tails flicking with excitement.

Jagged Peak dropped the fresh branch beside his mate. "Shattered Ice and Lightning Tail have gone out to collect more now that the snow's eased," he told her.

"We'll need moss to line it," Holly told him.

Eagle Feather scrambled onto her back as she crouched to spear another twig into the half-built nest. "I want a badger ride!" he squeaked.

Holly huffed with annoyance and shrugged him off. "Not now! I only have two pairs of paws!"

Thunder padded forward. "I'll play with the kits," he offered.

Holly glanced at him, relief glowing in her eyes. "Thank you, Thunder."

"*I'll* play with them too," Jagged Peak added quickly.

Thunder dipped his head. "We can both play."

Eagle Feather jumped onto his father's back. Dew Nose raced for Thunder and clawed her way onto his shoulders.

He winced at her tiny, thorn-sharp claws. "What about you, Storm Pelt?"

The gray kit was hanging back. "I want to help Holly."

Holly's ear twitched. "Go and play, dear."

"I promise I won't get in your way." Storm Pelt gazed at her solemnly. "I can push in the sticky-out bits." He reached up to the half-woven nest and tucked a heather sprig in with a nimble paw.

Holly purred. "Okay, then."

"Hurry up, Thunder!" Dew Nose curled her claws into Thunder's pelt.

"Careful!" Thunder gasped. "I'm not prey!"

Dew Nose purred as he pushed his way through the bushes.

"Hang on!" he warned as the trailing branches swept over them.

Dew Nose's paws tightened around his shoulders, and he purred, grateful that she was keeping her claws sheathed.

Outside, the clouds were thinning. The snow had stopped,

but the clearing was thickly coated. He waded through it, thumping his paws heavily against the earth like a lumbering badger, and trying not to think about the real badger he'd fought earlier. Dew Nose squeaked with delight and hung on harder.

Jagged Peak caught up to him. "Did I see Clear Sky coming back into camp with you?"

"Clear Sky?" Eagle Feather mewed on Jagged Peak's shoulders. "Where?"

"He's in Cloud Spots's den," Thunder explained. "We ran into a badger. He got a little scratch." He didn't want to frighten the kits.

"A badger?" Jagged Peak looked alarmed. "Close to the camp?"

Thunder shook his head. "Near the forest border. It was injured. I doubt it'll hang around long on the moor. Especially in this weather."

Jagged Peak was frowning. "If it was close to the forest border, why did you bring him back *here*?"

"He was injured—" Thunder began.

Jagged Peak didn't let him finish. "He's caused enough worry and gossip in the camp already! We don't need him stirring up more trouble." He stopped and shook Eagle Feather from his shoulders.

The tiny kit plumped into the snow with a squeak. "That wasn't long enough!"

Jagged Peak nodded toward the boulder at the other end of the camp. "Go and see if you can find some moss around the bottom of Tall Shadow's rock."

"But it's covered in snow," Eagle Feather objected.

"Then you'll have to dig for it," Jagged Peak told him firmly.

Dew Nose slithered down Thunder's flank and landed beside her brother. "Come on, Eagle Feather! Holly will be really pleased if we bring her moss." She bounded over the snow, sinking deeper with each jump. Eagle Feather plunged after her. "Wait for me!" They looked like frogs bobbing through water.

Thunder purred and glanced at Jagged Peak, but the gray tabby tom wasn't watching his kits. He was staring at Cloud Spots's den beyond the rock, his eyes dark with worry.

"Was he hurt badly?" Jagged Peak asked.

"Just a scratch," Thunder told him. Was someone other than Cloud Spots and Pebble Heart worried about Clear Sky after all? "Pebble Heart's just making sure it won't turn sour."

"So he'll be able to go straight home."

Thunder stared at Jagged Peak. "Don't you *care* that he was hurt?"

Jagged Peak dragged his gaze from the den. "It makes a change, I suppose," he snorted. "He usually *causes* wounds."

Thunder flinched, but didn't argue. Clear Sky had killed Rainswept Flower and banished Jagged Peak from the forest. He understood why the tom was bitter. But Jagged Peak's words worried him. He glanced around the camp. Tall Shadow was on her rock, gazing across the moor while the kits burrowed eagerly below. Mud Paws was emerging from the long grass at the edge, shaking snow from his ears. Dappled Pelt sat a few tail-lengths away, her ears twitching, while Mouse Ear stood beside her staring into the sky. "You said Clear Sky had caused gossip?" Thunder asked.

"You *know* Tall Shadow has been thinking about making a new home in the pines," Jagged Peak grunted. "And this weather has started everyone wondering whether living in such an exposed place is a good idea. Mud Paws and Mouse Ear said they were never this cold when they were strays. They could shelter in woods or by the river when the cold weather came."

Dappled Pelt padded closer. "We weren't even this exposed in the mountains!" she called. "We had the cave to protect us."

"But there's better hunting here," Thunder reminded her.

"There *was*," she agreed, "before the sickness killed half of it!"

Thunder's pelt pricked uneasily. "Do you *want* to move to the forest and become part of Clear Sky's group?" He could hardly believe it. They'd fought a battle to protect their life on the moor!

"Of course not," Dappled Pelt snorted. "But the moor's not the only place to live."

Thunder nodded slowly. River Ripple had his island. And Clear Sky's forest was not the only shelter nearby. The floor of the pine forest must be so sheltered by the thick canopy of needles that it never felt snow.

Mud Paws joined them. "I thought the spirit cats *wanted* us to move on."

"Spirit cats!" Mouse Ear puffed. "You don't believe that, do you? Dead cats talking to the living?"

Dappled Pelt blinked at the old tom slowly. "Thunder, Tall Shadow, and Gray Wing all saw them."

"Nothing but dreams." Mouse Ear tipped his head to one side. "They'd probably shared a rotten mouse before they went to their nests."

Thunder met his gaze with annoyance. "So you *want* to stay on the moor."

"I didn't say that," Mouse Ear snapped back. "I just don't intend to move because some imaginary cats told me to."

Jagged Peak swished his tail. "We have to settle this before everyone starts arguing."

Thunder blinked as Jagged Peak marched toward Tall Shadow's rock and leaped up beside her.

Tall Shadow reared in surprise. "Jagged Peak?"

"We need to settle where we are going to live before every cat starts fighting about it." The tom's mew rang across the clearing.

Holly's head poked out from beneath the broom. Cloud Spots's den shivered as Clear Sky pushed his way out.

Gray Wing crossed the clearing, his eyes round. "Jagged Peak? What are you doing?"

Thunder hurried toward the rock. Clear Sky's eyes were bright with hope as he stared up at Jagged Peak. Did Clear Sky think that his younger brother was about to agree with his plan to join together? Alarm twisted Thunder's belly. "Let's discuss this later!" he called to Jagged Peak. Did he have to make such a fuss while Clear Sky was still here? No one was going to join Clear Sky's group. Surely they could settle this without embarrassing the misguided tom.

Dappled Pelt stopped beside Thunder. "Let him speak," she murmured softly. "We've already put off this decision too long."

Mud Paws and Mouse Ear halted below the rock while Holly hurried toward them. Storm Pelt bounded after his mother.

She called to Eagle Feather and Dew Nose. "Come here, little ones!"

The kits were covered in snow from digging around the rock. A wad of moss dangled from Dew Nose's jaws. It trembled as she hurried toward her mother.

Holly swept her close with a paw and tucked her against her warm belly. She scooped up Eagle Feather too. Storm Pelt burrowed in beside them.

"We found moss for the nest," Eagle Feather mewed excitedly.

"Hush." Holly leaned down and licked the snow from his nose.

Paw steps sounded outside camp. A moment later Lightning Tail and Shattered Ice pushed through the gorse tunnel.

Shattered Ice blinked. "What's going on?"

Lightning Tail was holding a bunch of heather between his jaws. He dropped it and slid between Dappled Pelt and Mud Paws. "Is this a meeting?"

Jagged Peak gazed down at him. "We need to decide where we're going to live."

"At last!" Tall Shadow pummeled the rock beside her excitedly.

Holly curled her lip. "But I've just finished building a new nest!"

"I don't want to move to the pine forest!" Shattered Ice called. "It's as damp as a marsh in there."

"I don't want to stay here!" Mud Paws mewed. "We'll freeze to death by newleaf."

Mouse Ear growled in agreement. "I'm tired of hunting in rabbit tunnels!"

"I want to live near fresh water," Dappled Pelt called. "The water here tastes like peat."

Thunder stared in disbelief at the cats he'd shared a camp with for so long. Had they always been dissatisfied? Sadness jabbed at his chest. He'd grown up in the hollow. It was *home*. How could they abandon it? He stepped forward. "We can't leave the moor!"

"We'll starve if we stay!" Mouse Ear returned.

Clear Sky lifted his tail. "Let's do as the spirit cats ask. Let's be like the Blazing Star and gather like petals around the heart of a flower." His eyes shone. "Come live in the forest with me!"

Jagged Peak glared at him. "Do you think we're harebrained?"

"I'm not living anywhere near you," Shattered Ice growled. "And I'm not living under trees—I need to see the sky above my head."

"But trees will shelter us," Tall Shadow argued.

Thunder's thoughts spun. "How can we leave when we can't decide where to go?"

Jagged Peak padded to the front to the rock and looked around at the gathered cats. "Let's decide the same way we decided last time."

Thunder frowned. *Last time?*

Jagged Peak's gaze reached Gray Wing's and halted. "Remember?"

Gray Wing nodded solemnly. "Let's cast stones."

CHAPTER 3

Thunder *frowned as Jagged Peak and* Tall Shadow jumped down from the rock. *Cast stones?* What was Gray Wing talking about? "How?" he murmured to himself.

A warm muzzle nudged his flank, and he turned to see Dappled Pelt looking at him, her eyes sparkling. "We've done it before, when Clear Sky broke away from the group to set up his own camp in the forest—and before that, when he wanted to leave the mountains."

Gray Wing began to dig through the snow at the bottom of the rock. As he unearthed pebbles from the soil below, he kicked them out behind him. Jagged Peak scooped them into a pile while Tall Shadow hurried to the edge of the clearing and began to scrape a wide hole in the snow.

Pebble Heart and Cloud Spots slid from beneath the jutting gorse where they'd treated Clear Sky. The scent of herbs swirled around them, and Thunder noticed that Pebble Heart's paws were stained green.

Sparrow Fur and Owl Eyes nosed their way from the snowy grass at the edge of the clearing and padded toward the others.

Owl Eyes was yawning, and Sparrow Fur blinked sleep from her eyes.

"We're casting stones," Dappled Pelt called to them excitedly.

"Casting stones?" Owl Eyes sat down beside the tortoiseshell. "On what?"

"We're deciding where each cat will live," she told him.

Sparrow Fur's eyes widened. "Why *now*?"

Dappled Pelt glanced sharply at Clear Sky.

Thunder shifted his paws uneasily. The cats clearly knew that his father's interference had pushed them to make this decision. "We shared a dream of the spirit cats last night," he explained to Sparrow Fur. "They want us to spread and grow like the Blazing Star."

Sparrow Fur rolled her eyes. "We've known that for *ages*."

"Last night, they told us to hurry up."

Sparrow Fur tipped her head, curious. "Why?"

"We don't know." Thunder remembered the urgent tone in Storm's mew. Why were the spirit cats rushing them? Did they know something they weren't sharing?

"Thunder!" Tall Shadow's call shook him from his thoughts. "Help me clear this patch."

He bounded over to her and began to widen the circle she'd made by scraping away snow until soil showed beneath. He was still not exactly sure what she was doing.

When the patch was three tail-lengths wide, Tall Shadow traced a loop in the clear earth with a deft flick of her paw.

Then another and another until there were three circles marked on the ground. She lifted her muzzle. "Each cat must take a stone from the pile Gray Wing and Jagged Peak have made and place it in the circle that marks the place they wish to live."

Shattered Ice padded forward. "Which circle is which?"

Lightning Tail padded past him, carrying one of the heather branches he'd brought back to camp in his jaws. He dropped it and tugged off a brown sprig from the tip, then placed it in one of the circles. Then he put two more in the next so that the circles were clearly marked.

Tall Shadow nodded curtly. "Thank you, Lightning Tail." She addressed the cats once more. "The circle with no heather is Clear Sky's camp. The circle with one sprig is the pine forest. Two sprigs means the moor."

Dappled Pelt swished her tail. "What about the river?"

Lightning Tail blinked at her. "That's River Ripple's territory."

Gray Wing turned from the rock, his paws filthy from digging. "River Ripple must be included in our plans. The spirit cats chose to share with him as well as us."

"Okay." Tall Shadow drew a fourth circle on the earth.

Lightning Tail dropped three sprigs of heather into it.

Thunder tipped his head to one side. "What about the *fifth* petal?" If River Ripple was right, the spirit cats wanted them to separate into five groups.

Gray Wing nosed past Jagged Peak and stopped at the edge of the patch of earth. "There's Wind Runner's group."

When the sickness had reached the camp and killed one of her kits, Wind Runner and Gorse Fur had taken their kits—Moth Flight and Dust Muzzle—away from the hollow to make their own camp on the moor. There, Slate—a friendly rogue she-cat—had joined them.

Tall Shadow glanced around at her campmates. "Should I trace a circle for Wind Runner's group?"

"Of course," Shattered Ice meowed. "She's one of the five petals."

"No." Gray Wing shook his head. "She left for a reason," he reminded them. "She won't want any of us joining her."

Pebble Heart glanced toward the camp entrance. "Perhaps someone should get her. She should be part of this."

"One day she will be," Gray Wing told him gently. "But for now, she thinks she is doing the right thing for her kits by keeping to herself, and we should respect that."

Tall Shadow nodded. "Gray Wing's right. Wind Runner was always independent. She'll make her own decisions in her own time." She leaned closer to the patch of soil. "Four circles will have to be enough."

Mud Paws dipped his head. Mouse Ear nodded gravely. Cloud Spots sat down and wrapped his tail over his paws.

Sparrow Fur wove excitedly between Pebble Heart and Owl Eyes. "Can we choose *wherever* we want?" she asked.

"Of course," Gray Wing answered. "Turtle Tail told me we must each follow our hearts."

Thunder felt his tail tremble. Storm had told him that too. *But where does my heart lie?* He glanced across the clearing, aching suddenly with sorrow as he remembered playing kit games with Lightning Tail and Acorn Fur while Hawk Swoop watched fondly from her nest in the long grass. Could he really leave here?

Clear Sky pushed past Jagged Peak. "Our hearts belong *together!*" His eyes glittered wildly. Thunder felt a tug of pity for his father. Clear Sky was pleading for the cats to join him. *I've never seen him so desperate!*

Shattered Ice snorted. "Do you expect us to believe you?" He glared at Clear Sky. "Your heart has only ever led you toward power! You just want to be the only leader."

Thunder flinched as he saw his father shrink away.

Despair clouded Clear Sky's gaze. "Do what you want," he muttered. He slunk to the rock and crouched beside it.

Jagged Peak nudged the pile of pebbles with a paw. "Let's start."

Tall Shadow ducked and grabbed the first stone between her jaws. She dropped it into the circle with one heather sprig.

The pine forest. Thunder wasn't surprised. He knew that was where her heart longed to be.

Jagged Peak dropped a second stone beside it.

Thunder stared at him. "You too?"

Jagged Peak didn't answer him. He was gazing at Holly, a question in his eyes.

She padded forward. Eagle Feather, Storm Pelt, and Dew Nose watched as she took a stone and placed it beside Jagged Peak's. She lifted her head and blinked slowly at her mate. "The pines will protect our kits from the weather."

Jagged Peak purred and wove around her.

Eagle Feather scrambled toward them, kicking up snow. "But I like the moor!"

Holly bent and licked his ears as he reached her. "You'll like the pine forest too," she promised. "There'll be good hunting and lots of places to play hide-and-seek."

Clear Sky grunted beside the rock and tucked his paws tighter beneath him.

Thunder tried not to notice his father's disapproval. He glanced at the other cats. Who would choose next? His paws felt rooted to the earth. Should he follow Jagged Peak and Tall Shadow? Staying with the cats he knew best might be the wisest path.

He watched Gray Wing take a stone and place it beside Holly's.

You too? Thunder shivered at the thought of the dark pines. He could never live in shadow, with the sharp scent of pinesap tainting every piece of prey. He watched, his heart growing heavier as Pebble Heart, Mud Paws, and Mouse Ear dropped their stones beside Gray Wing's. Was every cat going to the pine forest?

He felt Dappled Pelt brush past as she padded to get a stone and watched, holding his breath, as she dropped it in the river circle.

Clear Sky leaped to his paws. "You're a cat, not a fish!"

Dappled Pelt blinked at him calmly. "We are choosing where we *want*," she meowed firmly.

Clear Sky frowned and sat down.

Thunder ignored his father's outburst. Choosing where to live felt hard enough already. His paws pricked as he stared at Dappled Pelt's stone. He should have felt relieved. He wasn't the only cat who didn't want to spend his life wading through pine needles. But watching his group split sent unease rippling beneath his pelt.

Shattered Ice followed Dappled Pelt, choosing the river. Then Lightning Tail took his turn. Thunder watched, his chest tightening. He'd shared a nest with Lightning Tail as a kit. The young tom and his sister, Acorn Fur, were like littermates to him.

Grasping a stone between his jaws, Lightning Tail padded toward the open patch of soil. He glanced at Thunder.

Was that a question in his friend's gaze?

Thunder looked away. *I can't help you decide. You must follow your own heart.*

Lightning Tail dropped his stone into Clear Sky's circle.

Clear Sky's ears pricked with interest.

Of course Lightning Tail chose the forest! Thunder was surprised he hadn't guessed. Acorn Fur had already moved there, and with Hawk Swoop and Jackdaw's Cry dead, he had no other kin.

Next, Sparrow Fur padded to the pile of stones and took one. Keeping her gaze low, she dropped it in Clear Sky's circle.

Thunder saw Gray Wing straighten.

"Sparrow Fur? Are you sure?" The gray tom stared at her.

She met his gaze and nodded. "I like it there."

Gray Wing didn't speak.

"I like the trees," Sparrow Fur insisted. "And I've always wanted to taste squirrel and . . ." Her mew trailed away. There was no mistaking the fierce grief burning in Gray Wing's eyes.

"You must follow your heart." He dropped his gaze.

Owl Eyes scampered past his sister and grabbed a stone between his teeth. He tossed it into the circle beside Sparrow Fur's and glanced at Pebble Heart. They were leaving their littermate. "Is that okay?"

"It's fine," Pebble Heart purred. "A Thunderpath may separate us, but we will always be littermates."

As Pebble Heart stepped forward to nuzzle his brother's cheek, Cloud Spots cast his stone into Clear Sky's circle.

Pebble Heart jerked around and stared at the long-furred black tom. His eyes glittered with alarm. "What will I do without you to guide me? How will I know which herbs to use?"

"You know them," Cloud Spots meowed simply. "I have nothing left to teach you. And it's better that we spread our healing skills between two groups. The pine forest cats will have you to treat their wounds. Clear Sky will have me." He glanced over his shoulder at Clear Sky. "He certainly needs someone to take care of his cats."

Clear Sky didn't seem to hear. He was staring at the four pebbles in his circle.

Thunder curled his claws into the ground nervously. While he'd been turning the question over and over in his mind, every cat had made their decision except him. "Well?" Clear Sky prompted. "Where will you choose, Thunder?"

Thunder glanced around at the cats he'd grown up among. Should he follow Gray Wing and Tall Shadow to the pine forest? Or Dappled Pelt and Shattered Ice to the river?

No. He knew what he had to do. He'd seen Clear Sky almost die earlier. Worse than that, he'd seen Clear Sky look uncertain. He'd watched his father plead. Deep in his belly, Thunder sensed a weakness in him that he'd never seen before. *He needs me.* Reluctantly, he padded to the stones and picked one from the remains of the pile.

He dropped it into Clear Sky's circle.

"Thank you, Thunder." His father's mew seemed to crack.

Thunder closed his eyes. *I've made the right decision.* Clear Sky was not the ruthless leader he'd once been. If his group was to spread and grow like the Blazing Star, Clear Sky would need help leading it. Thunder shook out his pelt, feeling relief wash through him like a fresh breeze.

The decision had been made.

And yet his heart pricked at the thought of the group splitting apart. Was this really the right thing to do? He imagined the hollow empty through the long leaf-bare, snow filling the deserted nests, the clearing growing wild with no paw steps to trample down the grass.

Mouse Ear wove around Tall Shadow. "I bet the pine forest has more prey than the moor."

Mud Paws lifted a black forepaw and began to wash it. "I can't wait to be out of this wind," he mewed between licks.

"Do you think River Ripple will teach us how to fish?"

Dappled Pelt's eyes were shining as she padded back and forth restlessly in front of Shattered Ice.

Sparrow Fur shuddered. "You *want* to get your paws wet?" She stared at the she-cat in disbelief.

"I want to learn how to *swim*," Dappled Pelt told her.

"It can't be harder than tunneling," Shattered Ice added.

Lightning Tail snorted. "I always suspected you were mouse-brained," he purred teasingly.

The cats seemed happy, but Thunder hardly heard them. Irritation pricked beneath his pelt as he watched Jagged Peak press close to Holly, the kits winding around their paws. Did he have to look so pleased with himself? Thunder stalked toward him. "Are you happy now that you've split up the group?"

Jagged Peak met his gaze, unflinching. "It's what the spirit cats wanted and you know it."

Thunder blinked, surprised by Jagged Peak's boldness.

"Things change, Thunder." Jagged Peak glanced back at his crippled hind leg. "Some of us are used to adapting. Perhaps *you* should get used to it too." He turned sharply, swishing his tail against Thunder's muzzle, and nosed Eagle Feather up onto his shoulders. "Do you want a badger ride to our new home?"

Thunder stared. Jagged Peak had changed. He'd become so certain of himself. *Should I begrudge him that?*

A pelt brushed his flank as Clear Sky stopped beside him. "Five cats will have to be enough." His gaze was fixed on the departing cats. "For now."

Thunder felt suddenly cold. There was icy determination in his father's mew. Perhaps Clear Sky hadn't grown weak after all. Had his anxious, pleading eyes just been a trick? "Do you still want them *all?*"

"Not *me.*" Clear Sky's blue gaze was calm. "Fluttering Bird."

Thunder shifted away. Perhaps it was best that the group was spreading itself across moor, river, and forest. No leader should command every cat. That was too much power to hold.

Clear Sky lifted his tail. "You'd better get ready to leave." Sparrow Fur and Owl Eyes were already pacing near the entrance. Beside them, Lightning Tail gazed wistfully across the hollow.

Gray Wing sat alone. The tom's golden eyes were dark with grief.

Thunder felt his throat tighten. "I have to say good-bye to Gray Wing," he told Clear Sky. He crossed the grass and stopped in front of his old friend. "I'll watch over them," he promised, tipping his head toward Sparrow Fur and Owl Eyes.

"It's like losing Turtle Tail all over again." Gray Wing's mew was thick. "I'm not ready to leave Tall Shadow, and Pebble Heart needs me. But how can I be separated from those kits?"

Thunder hated how hard this seemed to be for Gray Wing. "They're not kits anymore," he said softly. But he knew that although Owl Eyes, Sparrow Fur, and Pebble Heart were nearly grown, Gray Wing would always love them as a father.

"Anyway, you'll know where they are," Thunder soothed.

"You'll get to see them whenever you want."

"It won't be the same."

Thunder's heart twisted in his chest. *No, it'll never be the same again.* Around him, cats padded restlessly, their ears pricked and tails twitching with excitement at establishing their new homes. *I just hope we're doing the right thing.*

CHAPTER 4

As Thunder padded away, Gray Wing became slowly aware of the cold. The numbness that had gripped him since Sparrow Fur had dropped her stone in Clear Sky's circle eased, and he shivered, lifting his gaze to the two young cats at the gorse entrance to the camp. Owl Eyes leaped up to catch a stray snowflake. His eyes shone with excitement.

Gray Wing swallowed back grief.

Soft fur brushed his flank. He turned his head.

Pebble Heart was gazing at him with round amber eyes. "I've said good-bye to them. It's your turn now."

Gray Wing's paws felt like stone. How could he say good-bye? He'd never imagined they'd be separated like this. He glanced at the snow clouds glowering above the camp. Was Turtle Tail watching? Had she known this would happen when she'd urged them to spread and grow like the Blazing Star? Anger surged in his chest. "They're all I have left of her," he breathed.

"You still have me." Pebble Heart nudged him forward. "They won't leave until you say good-bye."

Did I make the right choice? Gray Wing wondered if he should be traveling to the forest. But how could he call the forest home? The hollow felt like home; it was where he had made his nest with Turtle Tail. It felt strange to be leaving it behind, but that was exactly what he had chosen. No cat had voted to stay in the hollow. *It will be empty now.* The thought was like a cruel claw of regret in his belly fur, but he knew he had to shake it loose. He knew he needed to stay close to Pebble Heart. From the start, the young tom had been special. He was a gifted healer and had dreams that were often uncannily true. A deep sense of duty pulled Gray Wing toward him. He couldn't ignore the feeling that the destiny of the cats was bound up with Pebble Heart's fate. *I must protect him.*

Gray Wing tried to take a deep breath to steady himself, but his chest was tight. Since he'd breathed the smoke from the forest fire, he often struggled for air. Now the chill of leaf-bare and the strain of leaving the hollow seemed to crush his chest like a stone. He closed his eyes for a moment, pulling in a shallow breath, then headed across the camp.

"You look excited," he meowed as he neared Sparrow Fur and Owl Eyes. Too late, he realized he'd made it sound like an accusation. "I mean . . . you look happy. You must have made the right choice."

Sparrow Fur met his gaze anxiously. "We didn't mean to hurt you."

"I'm not hurt," Gray Wing lied.

Owl Eyes blinked at him. "You're wheezing."

"It's just the cold." Gray Wing lifted his chin. He looked from Sparrow Fur to Owl Eyes, suddenly surprised by how grown-up they looked. Their soft kitten fluff was gone. Their pelts were sleek. Delicate muscle showed beneath. Sparrow Fur had the same pretty markings as her mother's tortoiseshell pelt, and Owl Eyes had his mother's lean, lithe shape. "Will you remember Turtle Tail, even in your new home?"

"Of course we will!" Sparrow Fur's mew was sharp. "We'll *never* forget her."

Owl Eyes's tail trembled. "I can still remember her scent."

Will you remember it even in the musty dampness of the forest? Gray Wing swallowed back a sigh. "Your mother was a brave cat," he meowed, "and kinder than any cat I've ever known. She'd be proud to see you face your future with such courage."

Owl Eyes tipped his head. "Will *you* be proud of us too?"

Gray Wing leaned forward and touched his muzzle to Owl Eyes's head. "I will *always* be proud of you." He licked Sparrow Fur's ears. "If you ever need me, come and find me."

He turned, struggling to breathe as sadness swamped him. Slowly, he walked away, feeling their gazes hot on his pelt.

"Come on, you two!" Lightning Tail's breezy mew rang out behind him. "Let's go!"

"Shouldn't we wait for Clear Sky?" Sparrow Fur called back.

Clear Sky padded from beside the rock. "I'll catch up." He stepped into Gray Wing's path. "I'll look after them," he promised.

Gray Wing narrowed his eyes. His brother had seemed so desperate when he'd begged the cats to join together. And the badger attack had clearly shaken him. But now his chest was puffed up as usual. And yet Gray Wing thought he saw a trace of fear darken the tom's blue gaze. He suddenly realized that he'd never seen his brother look scared before. It unnerved him. What was he scared *of*? He tipped his head thoughtfully. "Are you okay, Clear Sky?"

"Of course!" Clear Sky shook out his pelt.

"Are you still worried about what Fluttering Bird said?" Gray Wing understood the power their dead sister's words must have had on Clear Sky. He alone shared the guilt of her death. If only they'd hunted better or longer, she might not have died. *But we were young,* he reasoned. And yet—

"I'm not *worried*," Clear Sky insisted. "I just wish the other cats had listened to me."

Gray Wing didn't argue. Clear Sky would never stop wanting to tell everyone what to do. He'd learned long ago that arguing with his brother was a waste of breath, and right now he had little breath to waste.

"Are you sure you won't come with us?" Clear Sky urged.

Gray Wing shook his head. "I have been through so much with Tall Shadow; I can't leave her now. And Pebble Heart needs me."

Clear Sky dipped his head. "Very well." He headed toward the gorse entrance. It still shivered where Lightning Tail, Sparrow Fur, and Owl Eyes had charged through.

Jagged Peak and Holly were herding their kits toward it. They stopped to let Clear Sky pass. Jagged Peak looked over his shoulder. "Come on, Gray Wing. It smells like more snow is on the way. The sooner we reach the pines, the better."

Tall Shadow padded forward and scooped up Dew Nose in her jaws.

Dew Nose wriggled like a caught fish. "I want to walk!" she squeaked.

"It's a long way," Holly told her. "And the snow outside camp is probably deep."

Eagle Feather stuck his nose in the air. "No one's carrying me!"

"What about a badger ride?" Mouse Ear called.

"All the way?" Eagle Feather glanced excitedly at the burly tom.

"All the way," Mouse Ear purred, crouching.

Eagle Feather scrambled onto his broad shoulders.

"Can I have a ride too?" Storm Pelt asked shyly.

Mud Paws trotted toward him. "Climb up!" He nosed the kit up onto his back and waited while Storm Pelt straddled his shoulders, clinging on with his small paws and squishing low into his thick fur.

Dew Nose squealed louder, churning her paws with annoyance. "I want a ride too!"

"Okay." Tall Shadow put her down and leaned low to let her scramble onto her back.

Gray Wing longed to help, but he knew he needed to save his breath. Jagged Peak was right: there was a scent of fresh snow in the air. The chill of it pierced his chest.

Dappled Pelt and Shattered Ice were talking in low voices beside the gorse wall of the camp.

"What if River Ripple sends us away?" Dappled Pelt asked.

"If he does, we can join another group." Shattered Ice looked at Tall Shadow. "You'll take us in, won't you?"

"Of course!" Tall Shadow purred. Dew Nose was fidgeting on her shoulders.

"Come on." Jagged Peak was the first through the entrance.

A panicked look flashed in Pebble Heart's eyes. "What about my herbs?" He glanced toward the jutting gorse. It trembled, shaking snow from its branches, and Cloud Spots slid out. He held a wad of leaves in his jaws.

He crossed the snowy grass and dropped it at Pebble Heart's paws. "Take these. They'll keep you going for now. There are plenty of herbs left for you to get later." Pebble Heart blinked at the black tom gratefully. "What about you?"

"I'll make myself a fresh bundle." He began to turn back to his den, then paused. "There may even be better herbs in the forest."

Pebble Heart nodded, his eyes lighting up. "And the pines."

"I'll come and tell you if I find anything new," Cloud Spots promised.

"Me too."

Gray Wing saw them exchange a look so warm, he felt a sudden flash of jealousy. Pebble Heart was clearly fond of the tom who had taught him so much.

"Perhaps we should meet regularly to share what we've learned," Cloud Spots suggested.

Pebble Heart nodded eagerly. "Next new moon? At the four trees?"

Cloud Spots swished his tail. "I'll see you then." He

disappeared back into his den.

"Come on, Pebble Heart," Gray Wing called to the young tom. The others were already filing out of camp.

Pebble Heart picked up the bundle of herbs in his jaws and hurried through the tunnel after Mouse Ear. On the tabby's back, Eagle Feather squeaked as the branches scraped his spine, and he burrowed deeper into the tom's fur.

Gray Wing paused as he reached the entrance and looked back at the hollow. It was eerily quiet. Only the scuffing of Cloud Spots's paws as he rummaged in his den broke the silence.

Heart heavy, Gray Wing nosed his way through the gorse.

Outside, snow had dusted the moor. The heather rocked as the wind swept across it. Dappled Pelt and Shattered Ice were already heading toward the river. They seemed small under the great, yellowing sky.

Holly, Mouse Ear, Mud Paws, and Tall Shadow followed Jagged Peak over the grass. The tops of the pines showed in the distance, beyond the crest of the moor. Pebble Heart was running to catch up.

"Hurry, Gray Wing!" Jagged Peak called from the head of the group.

Gray Wing stopped, his nose twitching. An unfamiliar scent was tainting the snow. Rogues had passed this way, by the smell of it. And they'd lingered by the camp entrance. There was a dent in the snow where they'd sat. Why hadn't they introduced themselves, as most rogues did, out of curiosity if not suspicion? Unease pricked at Gray Wing's pelt. He thought he knew the scents of all the rogues who crossed the moor. But not these. *What does it matter?* They were *leaving* the hollow. Gray Wing scanned the moor. Wind Runner's camp was nearby. Memories of One Eye flashed in his mind. If strange rogues were hanging around, her kits might be vulnerable. He decided to investigate. "I'll follow your paw prints!" he called to Jagged Peak. "I'm going to scout for prey." There was no need to alarm the kits.

"Don't be long!" As Jagged Peak answered, Gray Wing sniffed the snow. Tracks led toward the river: Dappled Pelt's and Shattered Ice's. Another set led toward the forest: Clear Sky's cats. A third set carried the smell of the strangers. Gray Wing followed them downhill into the wide swath of heather. As the branches closed over his head, their scent grew stronger.

Two cats.

He slowed his pace. He was still struggling to breathe deeply. He didn't want to meet these strangers face-to-face when he felt so weak. But curiosity, and worry for Wind Runner's kits, drew him on. He pricked his ears as a growl echoed ahead.

"I don't have time." There was a snarl in the tom's voice.

An anxious mew answered it. "But I don't *want* to go by myself."

A shriek of pain sliced through the heather.

Gray Wing froze.

"You're not a kit anymore!" the first voice snapped.

Gray Wing crept forward until he saw daylight ahead. The heather tunnel opened into a clearing, and Gray Wing spotted the ringed tail-tip of a tabby flicking over the snow.

Quickly he turned off the trail and pushed his way into the tangle of bushes. He moved slowly, slithering between the rough branches like a water snake moving through reeds. They crackled around him, their stems brittle with cold.

"What's that?" He heard the stiff mew of one of the cats and froze.

"Probably a pheasant or a rabbit."

"Prey?" Excitement edged the she-cat's hiss.

"We'll eat later," snapped the tom. "You need to follow those cats."

Follow those cats? Gray Wing stretched his ears. He slithered forward as lightly as he could until he was close to the edge of the heather, hoping its dusty scent would mask his own. Through the spiky branches he could make out the two cats.

A broad-shouldered brown tabby faced a black she-cat. Both were scarred, their ears nicked at the tips and their fur crisscrossed by old wounds. The tabby's front legs were marked with a slash of white, his ears were torn, and half his whiskers were missing. The black cat's tail was short, squared at the end as though half had been lost in an accident.

How does she balance with half a tail? Gray Wing squinted through the heather. The black cat looked young, despite her scars; her muscles were taut. The tabby's flanks sagged with age, but experience glinted in his eyes, and Gray Wing noticed his long claws flexing as he talked. He'd be a formidable enemy, Gray Wing guessed.

The tabby went on. "I want you to follow them. Find out

where they settle. I knew they'd leave this barren piece of land eventually. I need to know where they make camp, where they hunt, their habits, their weaknesses, everything!"

"But why, Slash?" The black cat's mew quavered.

"Don't be such a mouse-brain, Fern!" The tabby lashed out with a paw and caught her across the ear.

Fern ducked away, a low whine in her throat.

"Just do as I tell you!" Slash hissed. "Watch and wait and report back to me."

"Why can't you come with me?"

Gray Wing wondered why Fern wasn't happy to be away from her vicious companion.

"I've got other fish to catch." There was menace in Slash's tone. "Don't let me down, Fern. Star Flower betrayed me, and she's lucky I let her live. I won't be so soft with you."

"I won't let you down," Fern promised quickly, pressing her belly to the ground like a frightened kit.

"And don't let them see you!" Slash showed his teeth. "When the time comes, I want to see the surprise on their soft, kitty-loving faces for myself."

"I'll be like a shadow," Fern mewed.

"You'd better be, or you *know* what I'll do to you."

Gray Wing saw Fern tremble as terror shone in her gaze. "I—I know, Slash."

"Good." Slash straightened, then stalked away across the grass.

Fern watched him leave, the terror in her eyes hardening to hate.

Gray Wing's tail-tip twitched uneasily. These rogues were going to be trouble, and yet their alliance was based on fear. *That is their weakness.* He kept still as Fern padded away. The black she-cat was heading across the slope, no doubt aiming for the Thunderpath and the pine forest beyond. He waited until Fern disappeared behind a wide clump of gorse, then wriggled out from the heather. Shaking crumbs of leaf from his pelt, he scanned the moorside. How long had Slash been roaming their territory? He talked as though he'd been watching the cats for a while. And he knew Star Flower. He must have known her father, One Eye. Gray Wing's paws pricked. These rogues were like poisonous weeds. One Eye had been killed, but Slash had grown in his place. Frustration flashed beneath Gray Wing's pelt. *Will we never find peace?*

He ducked back into the heather. He had to catch up to the others without bumping into Fern. He followed an arcing route around the gorse and slid from the heather near the top of the moor. From here he could see rolling countryside sweeping toward the mountains and, ahead, a steep sharp slope down toward the Thunderpath. Shapes moved over it. Jagged Peak and the others! Bounding forward, Gray Wing hurried to catch up. He paced himself, trying to ignore the stabbing in his chest, which was tightening more as the wind chilled. Flakes of snow began to whip his flank. A thick fall was closing in, already swallowing the distant mountains. By the time he reached his friends, he could hardly see a tail-length ahead.

"Gray Wing, is that you?" Pebble Heart's voice called

through the storm. Gray Wing followed it, relieved to see the young tom and his campmates. The kits were still clinging to Mouse Ear, Mud Paws, and Tall Shadow. Snow coated their pelts.

"There'll be shelter in the forest!" Jagged Peak called.

Holly answered him. "We have to cross the Thunderpath first."

The acrid tang of the black trail touched Gray Wing's tongue. It must be close. How would they cross it when they could hardly see past their whiskers? He wove past Mouse Ear and Mud Paws and fell in beside Jagged Peak. "Perhaps we should find cover and rest before crossing."

"No." Jagged Peak kept his gaze fixed forward. "We're going to keep moving until we reach the forest. There'll be prey there and shelter, and the kits are cold and hungry."

Gray Wing narrowed his eyes against the snow. Jagged Peak was acting like their leader. But he was right. They were close to the Thunderpath, and the pines lay just beyond. It might be a waste of time to scout the slope for somewhere to hide when they were certain that shelter lay ahead.

The wind roared in his ears, growing louder, until Gray Wing realized that it wasn't just the wind.

He froze. "Watch out!"

As he spoke, huge eyes blazed through the snow. He cowered, blinded by their glare. A monster was pounding toward them.

"Get back!" Jagged Peak tugged Holly and scrambled backward with a yowl. He pushed Gray Wing against Tall Shadow.

Dew Nose squeaked with terror as the monster roared past a tail-length ahead. Its massive black paws showed through the blizzard before it thundered away into the storm.

"That was close." Jagged Peak straightened. He glanced back at the others. "Is everyone okay?"

"Yes." Gray Wing was impressed by Jagged Peak's calmness. He checked the kits. They clustered together, tails bushed, while Pebble Heart and Tall Shadow crouched beside them.

"Was that a monster?" Eagle Feather gasped.

"Yes, dear." Holly reached up and nuzzled her kit on Mouse Ear's back. "We have to be careful."

"We will be," Jagged Peak growled. "At least we know where the Thunderpath *is*."

Gray Wing stared into the blizzard. "We can't cross it *now*."

"Yes we can." Jagged Peak stepped forward, then stopped. "The last monster made the ground tremble before it reached us." He shuffled his paws until they were deep in the snow. "I can feel when one's coming and warn you."

Holly blinked at him. "You can't just stand there!" she gasped. "What if one veers off its path and hits you?"

"It won't," Jagged Peak told her.

He's like a different cat. Gray Wing glanced at Tall Shadow. She was staring at Jagged Peak in surprise.

She caught Gray Wing's eye. "I've never seen a cat so changed."

Gray Wing nodded. "I was thinking the same thing."

Holly jerked her head around. "It's amazing what a little *love* can do."

Was that reproach in her mew?

Gray Wing felt a flash of guilt. Had he been too hard on his younger brother when all he needed was a little kindness?

Holly lifted her chin and padded to Jagged Peak's side. "I trust you." She touched her muzzle to his cheek, then called to Mouse Ear and Mud Paws. "Get the kits across when Jagged Peak gives the word."

Mouse Ear nodded and padded to where Jagged Peak marked the edge of the Thunderpath.

"Wait," warned Jagged Peak. "The ground's trembling." Gray Wing saw him stiffen. "Get away from the edge."

As Mouse Ear backed away, Jagged Peak stood his ground. The wind's roar became a monster's howl. Gray Wing held his breath as its eyes lit Jagged Peak. Horror scorched through him as the black paws of the monster loomed from the snow. But Jagged Peak hardly flinched as the monster hurtled past.

Gray Wing struggled to take a breath. Snow froze his mouth and made his chest burn.

"Now!" Jagged Peak called.

Mouse Ear and Mud Paws raced past him, the kits squealing. Gray Wing watched, trembling, as they disappeared into the blizzard.

"It's still safe!" Jagged Peak yowled.

Tall Shadow leaped forward. Holly raced after her, Pebble Heart at her heels.

"You too!" Jagged Peak glared at Gray Wing through the snow.

Gray Wing could hardly find the breath to answer.

Jagged Peak ran toward him. "Are you okay?"

"It's hard to breathe in this snow," Gray Wing rasped.

Jagged Peak pressed against him. "Lean on me." Gray Wing felt the tom's strong shoulder against his flank. He rested against it, suddenly weak.

"Come on," Jagged Peak urged gently. "I can't feel any monsters."

Gray Wing focused on his paws, trying to sense vibrations in the earth, but he couldn't tell whether the ground was shaking or his legs. He glanced at Jagged Peak. His brother's gaze was fixed calmly ahead. *It must be my paws. I can't be this weak. My campmates need me!*

Jagged Peak shouldered him forward. "Just keep moving," he grunted. "Once we're in the shelter of the pines, you'll get more air."

Gray Wing didn't answer. He stared ahead, thankful for Jagged Peak's strength. With faltering steps he padded forward, letting his brother guide him. The snow was smooth beneath his paws, the ground hard as stone beneath it. They must be on the Thunderpath. He struggled to hurry.

"It's okay," Jagged Peak reassured him. "The path's clear. Take your time."

As snow whisked past his muzzle, Gray Wing felt dizzy. "I can't do it," he gasped.

"You're going to have to!" Jagged Peak growled darkly. "I can feel the ground trembling."

Gray Wing tried to drag in air, his paws slithering beneath him.

"Hurry!" Jagged Peak shoved his shoulder harder against Gray Wing's flank and half lifted him onward.

Gray Wing heard the roar of a monster. Lights flashed through the snow. The world seemed to tumble as Jagged Peak hurled him forward.

We're going to die!

Gray Wing rolled, the snow soft beneath him, and slid to a halt. The monster's howl ripped through his ear fur. Stones and ice chips blasted his pelt. Acrid smoke filled his nose. And then there was just snow.

The monster was gone.

"Jagged Peak?" Panic ripped through his pelt. "Jagged Peak!"

"I'm here!" His brother's mew sounded triumphant in his ear. "We made it! I can see the trees."

Weak with relief, Gray Wing let Jagged Peak nudge him to his paws and staggered blindly forward. Dark shapes swirled in front of him, darkening more until eerie silence enfolded him.

The snow had gone. The wind had dropped.

Am I dead?

Blinking open his eyes, Gray Wing gazed around. Tall trunks soared around them. Beneath his paws he could feel a soft bed of needles.

"You made it!" Holly raced from between the pines and pressed her cheek against Jagged Peak's.

"Of course we did." Jagged Peak nodded to Pebble Heart. "Gray Wing's having his breathing trouble again."

Pebble Heart dropped his bundle of herbs. "I can smell coltsfoot in here." He unrolled the wad of leaves with his nose and picked out a dull green sprig. "It's dried from greenleaf, but it should still work."

Gray Wing smelled the familiar scent of the herb. Relief flickered in his belly. Pebble Heart held out a stalk between his teeth, and Gray Wing took it. "Thanks." He chewed it carefully to release the juices from the dried old stem before swallowing it.

"Let's rest here for a while." Tall Shadow shrugged Dew Nose from her back.

Dew Nose squeaked as she landed. "The ground feels weird!"

Eagle Feather and Storm Pelt leaped down from Mud Paws and Mouse Ear.

"It's all springy!" Eagle Feather bounced across the thick covering of needles.

"It must be a tail-length deep!" Storm Pelt shuffled his paws into the brown needles until they disappeared. "Look! I've got no paws!"

Gray Wing sat down, his chest loosening as the coltsfoot began to work. "Thanks, Pebble Heart," he murmured.

"I just hope there's more in this forest." Pebble Heart scanned the trees.

The tall, straight trunks were cracked, like ancient prey dried in the sun. Shadows pooled between them. Here and there, dense patches of brambles crowded their roots. Gray Wing looked up. The sky was hidden by thick branches, green even in leaf-bare. Their tips leaned and creaked, stirred by the blizzard howling above them, but they stood firm, their roots dug deep into the peaty earth.

"What do you think?" Tall Shadow followed Gray Wing's gaze upward.

Gray Wing whisked his tail over the needle-strewn earth. A sharp tang of pine cut through the thickness in his chest. He felt strength return to his paws. His shoulders relaxed. "I think I'm going to like it here."

"Should we make camp?" Holly called.

"Where?" Tall Shadow glanced around.

Gray Wing stiffened as Slash's order to Fern flashed through his mind. *I need to know where they make camp, where they hunt, their habits, their weaknesses, everything!* Had Fern crossed the Thunderpath yet? Was she nearby now? Gray Wing strained to see through the shadows, looking for a flicker of movement. Why couldn't Fern have an *orange* pelt? It was too easy for her to hide here.

"Gray Wing?" Tall Shadow was searching his gaze anxiously. "Is something wrong? Your pelt's pricking."

"Nothing's wrong," Gray Wing told her quickly. There was nothing she could do about Slash's spy. Why spoil a pleasure she'd looked forward to for so long? "Is the forest as good as you imagined?"

Tall Shadow purred and padded around the base of a pine, her paw steps no more than a whisper on the needles. "It's even better." She pricked her ears. "The wind sounds so far away."

"I can smell squirrel," Mouse Ear meowed happily.

"Should we hunt?" Mud Paws looked at Jagged Peak. Gray Wing blinked in surprise. Mud Paws was treating him like their leader.

Tall Shadow sat down and gazed between the trees. She didn't seem to have noticed, or if she had, she didn't seem to care. Her green eyes shone. Her black pelt melted among the shadows as though she'd become part of her new home already.

"Tall Shadow?" Jagged Peak called to her. "Should we hunt?"

"If you like." Tall Shadow shrugged.

Holly's gaze followed her kits, who were scrambling over tree roots, their noses and tails twitching with excitement.

With a leap, Dew Nose hooked her claws into the bark and dangled from the trunk. "Look! I'm climbing."

"Don't go too high," Holly warned.

Pebble Heart tasted the air. "Maybe we should find somewhere to build nests before we hunt."

"Let's split up," Jagged Peak suggested. "I'll hunt with Mud Paws and Mouse Ear. You, Holly, and Tall Shadow can take Gray Wing and the kits and find somewhere to rest tonight."

Take Gray Wing and the kits! Gray Wing felt a prick of resentment. Jagged Peak was talking like he was one of them!

Storm Pelt tipped his head. "Why can't Gray Wing hunt with you? He's a great hunter."

"Gray Wing's not as fast as he used to be," Jagged Peak answered.

Holly nodded. "He'll be safer if he stays with you."

Eagle Feather puffed out his chest. "I'll look after him!"

Jagged Peak looked fondly at his kit. "Gray Wing will be grateful to have such a strong kit watching over him."

Gray Wing flattened his ears. "I don't need *anyone* watching over me!" he snapped at Jagged Peak. "Just because you saved my life doesn't mean you get to treat me like a useless kit!"

Dew Nose bristled. "Kits aren't useless!"

Tall Shadow stepped between them. "I'm sure Jagged Peak didn't mean anything, Gray Wing," she soothed.

Jagged Peak dipped his head. "Of course not. But we all know that the fire damaged your breathing. You're not the cat you used to be."

Anger surged though Gray Wing. He flexed his claws, wondering if he had enough breath to scratch his young brother's ears. How dare he?

Tall Shadow flicked her tail. "Perhaps you should hunt, Jagged Peak," she suggested diplomatically.

Gray Wing frowned. Love hadn't made Jagged Peak confident; it had made him arrogant! "Be careful," he muttered. "Don't forget that you don't know what's out there." *Perhaps I should warn them about Fern and Slash.* This wasn't the perfect home they believed it was. There was danger lurking in the shadows. Then he glanced at Tall Shadow, worry darkening her gaze for the first time since she'd set paw in the forest, and swallowed back his anger. He wasn't going to spoil her moment. "I'm sorry."

He'd warn them about Slash when the time was right. Perhaps he wouldn't need to. He might be able to find Fern and talk to her. The rogue didn't seem to be a bad cat. She was just scared of Slash.

Gray Wing felt suddenly tired. They hadn't even found a new camp, and trouble was already stalking them. "Come on." He heaved himself to his paws. "Let's find somewhere sheltered to build nests."

As they set off, Eagle Feather scampered ahead. "Can I have my own nest?"

"When you're older," Holly called after him.

Gray Wing scanned the shadows beyond the kit warily. "Stay close, Eagle Feather. Until we're sure it's safe here."

CHAPTER 5

✣

A blustery wind shook the branches overhead. Thunder tucked his forepaws closer to his belly.

Beside him, Clear Sky huffed. "Are you cold?"

"No," Thunder lied, bunching his muscles to hide his shivers.

They were sitting at the edge of a small clearing, not far from the camp, watching Acorn Fur train Owl Eyes and Sparrow Fur how to hunt in their new woodland home. Clear Sky wanted to see how well his recruits were adapting to forest life.

Thunder bushed out his fur. The sharpness of the leaf-bare chill had eased in the past days, but snow clouds had turned to rain, and dampness dug deep into his thick pelt.

It wasn't raining now, but the trees still dripped from the last downpour. Fallen leaves were matted into wet clumps, making the forest floor slippery.

"Try again, Owl Eyes." Acorn Fur had laid a dead mouse near the edge of the clearing. "You need to reach it in one pounce. There are no second chances in the forest, with so many hiding places for prey."

As Owl Eyes crouched behind the roots of an oak, Thunder saw that the gaze he fixed on his quarry was anxious.

Sparrow Fur paced back and forth impatiently a tail-length behind him. "Hurry up!"

Acorn Fur glanced at the brown she-cat with annoyance. "Keep still, Sparrow Fur. Let your brother concentrate."

"I want a turn," Sparrow Fur complained.

"The mouse isn't going anywhere," Acorn Fur told her.

"It'll be shredded by the time I get to stalk it." Sparrow Fur ducked her chin sullenly.

"Owl Eyes needs to practice." As Acorn Fur spoke, a withered leaf dropped from a branch above them and pattered onto the wet ground.

Owl Eyes's gaze flicked toward it.

Acorn Fur whipped her tail-tip at him. "Don't look at the leaf! Focus on the *mouse!*"

Owl Eyes gasped. "Sorry!"

Thunder felt a jab of pity for the young tom. Owl Eyes's last pounce had sent him slithering past the mouse, his paws skidding on the muddy earth. If Acorn Fur made him any more nervous, his next pounce wouldn't be much better.

"It's good that he's so alert," Thunder said, standing. "You have to be wary in the forest. It's not as easy to spot danger as on the moor."

Acorn Fur bristled. "But he shouldn't take his eyes off his prey every time a leaf falls!" she snapped. "He'll never catch anything."

Owl Eyes peered up at the shivering branches. "I'll get used to it," he promised. His pelt was twitching nervously. Thunder could see that he still wasn't comfortable living beneath a tangled canopy of branches.

Thunder crossed the clearing and stopped beside Acorn Fur. "He's young," he murmured into her ear. "Remember how long it took you to learn your hunting crouch." He winked teasingly.

"I learned it quicker than you," she retorted.

"*And* quicker than Lightning Tail," Thunder reminded her.

She purred and turned back to Owl Eyes. "You'll be able to tell the difference between a falling leaf and a stalking fox before you know it," she reassured him. "For now, concentrate on the mouse. I'll warn you if I smell danger."

Sparrow Fur snorted. "This is taking forever!"

Acorn Fur called to her. "Why don't you see how many different scents you can detect while you wait?"

Clear Sky grunted. "Counting scents is for kits." He marched across the clearing. "Give her something better to do! Let her hunt *real* prey." He stopped beside the dead mouse and kicked it, sending it rolling across the forest floor. Owl Eyes never took his eyes off it.

Acorn Fur shifted her paws uneasily. "But she doesn't know how to hunt in a forest yet."

"And she never will if you don't let her practice." Clear Sky nodded to Sparrow Fur. "Off you go! Catch something for the other cats."

Sparrow Fur's eyes lit up. "Great!" She turned and headed past the bramble.

"Wait! You don't know what's out there." Acorn Fur beckoned to Owl Eyes with a flick of her tail. "We'll come with you!"

Owl Eyes was still staring at the dead mouse. "Should I pounce first?"

"Leave the mouse." Acorn Fur's pelt pricked. "We'll collect it on the way back."

Thunder saw the reproachful glance she flashed Clear Sky as she passed and gave her a sympathetic shrug.

Clear Sky didn't seem to notice. He was gazing between the trees, narrowing his eyes. "Someone's coming."

Thunder pricked his ears as Acorn Fur herded Owl Eyes and Sparrow Fur past the bramble and into a swath of bracken. Paws were pounding over the forest floor toward them. He tasted the air. *Lightning Tail!*

His friend burst from under a low jutting branch and skidded to a halt on the wet leaves. "Where's Acorn Fur?"

"She just left."

"Is she still training Sparrow Fur and Owl Eyes? I promised I'd help." Lightning Tail glanced around. "Which way did she go?"

Clear Sky snorted. "Through the bracken. Can't you smell her?"

"All I can smell is wet leaves," Lightning Tail meowed. "How do you ever sniff out prey around here? I can hardly taste my own tail when I wash."

"You'll learn how," Thunder promised. He was only just getting used to it himself. He'd lived in the forest before but had forgotten all he'd learned after moons on the moor. There, the wind had carried only fresh scents. Here, smells gathered and mingled, catching on bushes and lingering on tree trunks. The whole forest tasted musty with decay.

Lightning Tail nodded to Thunder. "Do you want to join us?"

"No, thanks." Thunder stared through the trees, wondering what was beyond the steep rise sloping up toward a thickly brambled crest. "I thought I'd explore my new home." He flicked his tail toward Clear Sky. "Do you want to come with me?"

Clear Sky jerked around. "Come with you?"

"I thought you might want to keep me company."

Clear Sky narrowed his eyes. "Are you planning to show me around my own territory?"

Thunder tipped his head, suddenly uneasy. "That's not what I meant. I just wondered if you wanted to come along—"

Clear Sky cut him off. "It's time I patrolled my borders." He lifted his tail. "Perhaps *you'd* like to keep *me* company."

Thunder's pelt itched with frustration. Why did Clear Sky have to make everything a battle? *He is the leader,* he reminded himself. *Let him lead.* He dipped his head. "I'd be honored."

Clear Sky marched from the clearing. Thunder followed.

Lightning Tail leaned forward as Thunder brushed past. "Does he argue about everything?" he whispered.

"Yes," Thunder hissed back.

Clear Sky could be obstinate. But they knew that already. Thunder just wished that he were better at guessing what was going to make Clear Sky's hackles rise. Dealing with his father was like picking his way through a briar patch—he never knew when he would step on a thorn.

Lightning Tail nosed Thunder's flank. "You've got more patience than me."

If only that were true. "See you later, Lightning Tail." Thunder hurried on, weaving through a crowd of slender birch trees, following Clear Sky between the trunks. Water chattered beyond. They were heading for a stream. By the time Thunder caught up, Clear Sky had leaped the brook and was crouching at the far side. Thunder stopped at the edge and watched as Clear Sky leaned down the steep bank and began to lap at the water.

The stream had been empty until the snow had melted; now it washed his paw tips and glittered beneath the bare branches as it snaked away between the trees. Thunder bent low and drank too. It was more refreshing than what he found on the moor, where the streams were sluggish, the peaty earth making the water taste like smoke.

He lifted his head, his chin dripping, seeing that Clear Sky was now pacing the far bank. "Are you ready?" his father asked.

After Thunder jumped the stream, Clear Sky nodded toward a gully that cut through the forest. "There's a huge oak along there. Beyond it, the forest stretches to Twolegplace."

"Show me." Thunder waited for Clear Sky to take the lead, then fell in behind him.

He followed his father over a rise, then hopped after him into the gully. It rose steeply on either side, muddy from the recent rain. Slippery roots snaked beneath Thunder's paws. Clear Sky moved easily between them, his pale gray pelt no more than a shadow in the gloom. Thunder was aware that his own orange pelt glowed. His paws slithered. He stumbled over a root, landing awkwardly as another tripped him. He was used to the wide smooth expanses of the moor. Even the rabbit trails between the heather were well worn and easy to navigate. The uneven path here unbalanced him, and he found himself concentrating so hard on where to put his paws that he didn't see the bramble stem hanging across the trail. It snagged his ear and he gasped with pain.

Clear Sky paused and turned his head. "Are you okay?"

"Just a bramble." Thunder glanced at the land rising beside them. The earth looked smoother up there. And there were no brambles. Why did Clear Sky insist on picking his way along this treacherous gully?

"Can't you go any faster?" Clear Sky called.

"I'm doing my best!" Irritation flashed beneath his pelt. *He's doing this on purpose.* His father clearly wanted to show how easily he moved through his terrain.

Clear Sky quickened his pace over the root-tangled trail.

I'm not playing your game. Thunder leaped up the steep bank of the gully and climbed the smooth slope. Shadowing Clear Sky's route, he kept to higher ground. A swath of bracken crossed his path and he pushed his way in, relishing the tug of the scratchy stalks as they scraped his pelt.

Clear Sky was waiting at the other side. "You're supposed to be following me." He stood on the slope, his blue eyes cold.

"I was, but I kept stubbing my paws."

"You've clearly forgotten how to move through a forest."

Thunder ignored his father's condescending tone, point-edly glancing up the slope. A huge tree towered at the top, stretching high above the canopy. "Is that the oak you were talking about?"

"Yes." Clear Sky swished his tail and bounded toward it.

Thunder leaped after him. Clear Sky dug his paws in harder to keep himself in the lead. As they neared the top of the rise, red fur flashed across ahead of them.

Clear Sky slowed to a halt, every hair on his pelt bristling.

Thunder smelled his father's fear-scent and stopped. Alarm shrilled through his tail. He unsheathed his claws as leaves swirled in their path. Was it a fox?

Tiny paws skittered over the forest floor, and a red squirrel leaped from the ground and scooted up the oak trunk.

Thunder rolled his eyes. "I thought it was a *fox*!"

Clear Sky's pelt was still bushed. "Don't be dumb!" he snapped.

Thunder glanced at his father out of the corner of his eye. *Then why did you look so scared?*

Clear Sky snorted. "Stop looking at me and watch where you put your paws. I don't want you stubbing them again." Lashing his tail, he marched past the oak.

Thunder followed, glancing up as the squirrel disappeared between the crisscrossing branches. Raindrops splashed down onto Thunder's muzzle. He shook them off and followed Clear Sky.

The ground beyond the oak sloped down to a glade. Thunder's heart sank as he saw brambles crowding the bottom. He could see a clear route skirting them—a trail through wilted fern stumps. But Clear Sky charged down the slope, heading straight for the brambles. Flattening his ears, Thunder followed.

Clear Sky hopped neatly among the damp stems.

Thunder winced as prickles grazed his paws, until at last the brambles thinned. Through the trees he could see the rain-washed red roofs of Twoleg dens glinting in the weak sunshine. He slowed, smelling unfamiliar scents.

Clear Sky kept moving.

"We're not going near there, are we?" Thunder stopped beside a yew bush.

"We might find some kittypet recruits." Clear Sky halted and turned. "Fluttering Bird wants us to spread and grow, remember?"

"But *kittypets*?" Thunder remembered Tom, the kittypet father of Turtle Tail's kits. He'd stolen them just to make Turtle Tail suffer, and she'd been killed trying to rescue them.

"Are you scared of them?" Clear Sky challenged.

"Of course not!" Thunder glared at him. "But they can't hunt or fight. What good are they to us?"

"We can train them."

Thunder hardly heard Clear Sky's words. Paws were scrabbling over leaves close by. He pricked his ears. Something was moving beyond the yew.

"Listen, do you hear that?" he hissed at Clear Sky.

Clear Sky whisked his tail. "It's probably a squirrel. We can hunt it on the way home." He headed toward the Twolegplace.

"We should catch it now." They'd already missed one today. Had Clear Sky forgotten it was leaf-bare? They couldn't afford to ignore prey.

"Then go catch it," Clear Sky called back.

Thunder ducked under the yew. Its dripping branches scraped his spine. Through its tangy scent he could smell more than squirrel. A second scent touched his nose—a familiar smell. His hackles lifted as he heard the crunch of tooth on bone. Dragging his belly over the cold wet earth, he peered out through the fronds on the far side.

A golden she-cat was bent over a dead squirrel. From its scent it was freshly caught. Thunder unsheathed his claws. This cat's tabby markings, and her white chest and paws, were so familiar they made his heart ache.

He slid from under the yew and glared at her. "Star Flower."

Star Flower turned, gazing at him with luminous green eyes. "Hi, Thunder. What are you doing in the forest? I thought you were a moor cat."

Thunder bristled. "What am *I* doing?" Didn't she realize she was hunting on Clear Sky's territory? "How can you show your face here after—"

She cut him off. "After what?" She tipped her head, her gaze steady. "After you murdered my father?"

She was talking about the rogue cat called One Eye, who had taken over Clear Sky's territory by force, viciously attacking any cat who disobeyed him. The cats of the forest *had to stop him!* But Star Flower had loved her father, despite his obvious faults. *Just like I loved her,* he thought.

He no longer had feelings for her, though. He was nearly sure of it.

"It wasn't like that," Thunder insisted.

"Really?" Star Flower swished her thick tail and turned back to her squirrel.

Thunder stared at her, bristling with indignation. If they hadn't stopped him, One Eye would have killed every cat on the moor.

Star Flower glanced at him. "Do you want a bite?"

Heat flashed beneath Thunder's pelt. "A bite? Are we allies now? Don't you care about *anything*?"

Star Flower lifted her head, her green eyes glimmering. "I care enough to forgive you."

"Forgive *me*?" Thunder snorted. "You're the one who betrayed us!"

"And you're the one who helped kill my father," Star Flower replied steadily.

The yew rustled behind Thunder.

"That wasn't my son's fault." Clear Sky pushed his way through the branches. "If you want to blame any cat for One Eye's death, blame me."

Star Flower's gaze flitted thoughtfully over Clear Sky. "You're the cat who took my father in, aren't you?"

Thunder threw her a warning look—Clear Sky wouldn't

want to be reminded of his mistake. He blinked with surprise as Clear Sky dipped his head.

"Yes, that was me."

How can he be so polite?

Star Flower's hackles softened. "That was kind of you." She brushed past Thunder and stopped a whisker from Clear Sky's muzzle. "Would you be kind once more and take *me* in?"

Thunder stared at her.

"It's hard for a loner," she went on, her mew silky. "I know you don't trust me, but you should. I was loyal to my father to the end." Her gaze flicked briefly toward Thunder. "Isn't that *true* loyalty?"

Thunder swallowed back anger. *Is she saying I'm disloyal for leaving Clear Sky all those moons ago?* He watched his father nervously. Would Star Flower's honeyed words work on him? Relief washed his pelt as Clear Sky shook his head.

"I can't let you join us," he told her. "Your father hurt a lot of my cats. They wouldn't thank me for bringing you back to camp."

Star Flower blinked slowly at Clear Sky. "And what if your cats told you they didn't mind?" she asked softly. "Would you take me in then?"

Clear Sky shook his head and turned away. "I can't," he growled. "Not after what your father did."

Thunder saw anger flash in Star Flower's eyes.

"Thunder, please!" She turned toward him. He tried to avoid her bright green gaze, but it hooked him. "It's going to be a long leaf-bare." There was fear in her mew. "I don't know if I'll make it through by myself. Now that One Eye is dead, I have no cat to help me hunt."

Thunder forced himself to look away, feeling Star Flower's desperate gaze burning through his pelt. Was he wrong to punish her for her father's sins? She was alone now. Without One Eye to bully her, perhaps she could be trusted. Perhaps she'd simply been one of his victims. Thunder felt his heart twist. "Clear Sky!" He called to his father. "Maybe we should give her a chance."

Clear Sky glanced over his shoulder. "She's One Eye's daughter!"

"That's not her fault!" Thunder knew better than most that a cat didn't have to follow in their father's paw steps. Star Flower's glossy pelt brushed his flank. Energy sparked through him like lightning. Her scent was so familiar, so warm. His mind whirled. He had to persuade Clear Sky to take her in. He couldn't leave her to starve. "You wanted to bring all the cats together!" he called. "Why not Star Flower? She was one of us once."

Clear Sky's blue eyes narrowed.

"Fluttering Bird wanted us to unite so we can spread and grow." Thunder pressed. "The more cats we have, the stronger we'll be."

Clear Sky glanced at Star Flower's squirrel. "I guess she can hunt."

"I can!" Star Flower snatched up the squirrel.

Clear Sky turned away, his tail twitching. "Bring her along. *You* can explain it to your campmates."

Purring, Star Flower followed Clear Sky past the yew.

Thunder walked behind her, his belly tightening. *You can explain it.* His paws pricked nervously as he pictured Lightning Tail's expression when he led Star Flower into camp. *He'll think I've gone crazy.*

CHAPTER 6

❧

Gray Wing dropped into a hunting crouch. High above him, faint sunlight filtered through the canopy and striped the forest floor. His tail twitched with excitement as he saw a lizard dart from beneath the fallen tree. He shifted his weight. Pine needles crunched like snow beneath his paws. As the lizard skittered from its hiding place, Gray Wing leaped.

Needles sprayed as he landed. His paws slid clumsily, but he hooked the lizard's tail with a foreclaw and darted ahead to give it a killing bite. It lay dead at his paws, and he sniffed its scales. They were a strange texture, smooth and slimy, unlike the prey Gray Wing usually hunted. *River Ripple eats them,* he told himself as he lapped at the blood welling at the lizard's neck. Its flesh might feel weird, but its blood tasted just like that of any other prey. Holly's kits might have fun picking at it.

Gray Wing straightened. The tightness in his breathing, which had been bothering him all morning, hadn't eased even when the sun's gentle leaf-bare warmth had melted the dew from the forest. The fresh tang of pine seemed to tickle the inside of his chest, making him cough and wheeze. He remembered feeling much better in the fresh winds of the moor and, for a moment, felt a sudden longing for his old home that was like a blunt claw snagging at his belly fur.

You live here now, he told himself. As he bent to pick up the lizard between his teeth, pine needles swished behind him.

He tensed.

Fern?

He'd seen no sign of the half-tailed she-cat since they'd arrived in the forest nearly a half-moon ago. But that didn't mean she wasn't lurking among the unfamiliar scents and deep shadows of the pine forest.

He turned, unsheathing his claws.

"Hi, Gray Wing." Pebble Heart padded toward him.

Gray Wing's fur smoothed. "It's you."

Pebble Heart's whiskers twitched teasingly. "Were you hoping I was Slate? She said she might visit today."

"No." Gray Wing shifted his paws, wishing that Slate *were* the only outsider who came here. He looked forward to seeing the dark gray she-cat from Wind Runner's camp on the moor. She had visited the pine forest several times since they'd arrived, to see how the cats were settling into their new home; she'd offered advice where she could. It had been Slate who'd suggested they make their camp between two wide swaths of bramble near the heart of the forest.

"It'll be easy to defend," she'd told Tall Shadow.

Tall Shadow had looked surprised. "Against what?"

Slate had shrugged. "Dogs. Foxes. Twolegs. These woods are like any territory. You'll need a safe heart in your new home."

Tall Shadow had looked crestfallen, and Gray Wing had stepped forward. "Tall Shadow has been dreaming about this for a long time." He caught Slate's eye. *Don't spoil her happiness here.*

But Tall Shadow had lifted her chin. "You're right, Slate," she meowed. "I've been foolish, trying to imagine that danger won't find us here. Of course we should be prepared. Show us the brambles. We'll build a camp where our kits can play safely."

They had built the camp, working hard for days among the prickly stems to shape the swaths into a fierce ring of thorns no intruder would dare penetrate. They'd threaded stems together, twining bush with bush until brambles encircled a wide, needle-strewn clearing.

Gray Wing could see it now, beyond Pebble Heart: a dark tangled mass, sheltering in the shadow of the pines.

"You're wheezing." Pebble Heart's observation shook him from his thoughts.

"My breathing used to ease by sunhigh." Gray Wing glanced ruefully at the sun glittering through the tops of the pines.

"Come back to the camp," Pebble Heart ordered. "I've got some fresh coltsfoot."

"You found some?" Gray Wing blinked with surprise as Pebble Heart began to head toward the brambles.

"It's the last of the season, protected from frost beneath a holly bush." Pebble Heart slowed to let Gray Wing fall in beside him. "Next to the Thunderpath."

"You went to the Thunderpath by yourself?" Gray Wing's

belly tightened. "You shouldn't—"

Pebble Heart silenced him with a look. "I'm not a kit anymore. You don't have to protect me all the time."

Gray Wing hardly heard him. There was a pain in his chest, like countless thorns were piercing his insides. He stopped and tried to draw breath, but couldn't.

"Gray Wing?" Pebble Heart turned sharply.

Panic whirled in Gray Wing's mind. He sank onto his belly, stretching his neck as he gasped for breath. The world began to spin around him. Pine needles swished beside his ear, and he felt Pebble Heart's paws pummeling his flank. He closed his eyes and tried to let go of the fear that gripped him. *I'll be okay.* Slowly he began to relax as Pebble Heart worked his way along his side, kneading his chest and then his back until Gray Wing's breathing eased.

"Thank you," Gray Wing rasped.

Pebble Heart turned to leave. "I'll bring you some coltsfoot."

"Wait!" Gray Wing heaved himself to his paws. "I can come with you." He didn't want to seem as helpless as prey.

"Your breathing's been bad since we came here." Pebble Heart gazed at him gravely. "I think you should eat coltsfoot each morning."

"Do you have enough to spare?" A long leaf-bare stretched ahead. "What if another cat needs some?"

"I've picked plenty, and there are still some dried leaves back in the hollow." Pebble Heart pressed his shoulder to Gray Wing's. "Are you ready?"

Gray Wing nodded and padded forward, trying not to lean too heavily on the young tom. *He's taking care of me now.* It seemed a lifetime ago that he'd rescued Pebble Heart and his littermates from Twolegplace. Yet it was hard to let go of the protectiveness he felt for Turtle Tail's kit. Should he warn him about Fern? And about Slash, who'd sent her to spy? *Not yet.* There'd been no sign of Fern since they arrived; perhaps the rogue had never come to the pine forest. Gray Wing hoped that she had used her chance to escape Slash and run—far away from here.

"You go first." Pebble Heart stopped in front of the bramble tunnel that led into camp.

Gray Wing ducked and padded through.

Tall Shadow and Jagged Peak sat near the far end of the clearing, their heads bowed in quiet conversation. Holly was rearranging her nest's moss lining while the kits tumbled in the pine needles behind her. Mud Paws and Mouse Ear were sharing tongues in the shadow of the camp wall.

"Hi, Gray Wing!" Mouse Ear looked up. "Did you catch anything?"

My catch! He'd left it behind. "A lizard," he croaked.

Mouse Ear hopped up and padded closer, stopping beside Gray Wing. "Can cats *eat* lizards?"

"River Ripple does," Gray Wing told him.

Mouse Ear wrinkled his nose. "I guess we can't be choosy." He tasted the air. "Where is it?"

"I left it outside camp."

Dew Nose turned from her game. "Can we go and get it?"

She glanced excitedly at Eagle Feather and Storm Pelt.

Holly straightened. "Only if Mouse Ear goes with you." She looked across the clearing to the tabby tom. "Is that okay?"

Mouse Ear purred. "Of course." He swished his tail happily as the kits charged toward him. "Which one of you is going to carry it back?"

"Me!" Dew Nose pelted for the bramble tunnel.

Eagle Feather was on her tail. "Not if I find it first."

Mouse Ear waited for Storm Pelt to catch up. "While those two are racing around," he whispered to the solemn young kit, "*we'll* find it, and *you* can carry it home."

Storm Pelt's whiskers twitched and he trotted toward the camp entrance.

"Don't let them out of your sight!" Holly called.

Mouse Ear flicked his tail as he ducked into the tunnel. "I won't."

Pebble Heart was already at the far side of the clearing, squeezing beneath the brambles. He wriggled out a moment later, a soft green leaf hanging from his jaws.

He hurried back to Gray Wing and dropped it onto the damp ground. "How are you feeling?"

"I've felt better." The pain was gone but Gray Wing's chest was still tight. He was relieved to see the coltsfoot. Crouching, he began to chew on the leaf stalk, its familiar bitter tang bursting over his tongue.

"I'll bring one to your nest every morning," Pebble Heart promised.

"I'll come and get it," said Gray Wing, with a jerk of his

nose. Irritation prickled in his belly. He knew Pebble Heart was only trying to help, but he hated being treated like an invalid. Was this how Jagged Peak felt when the cats made allowances for his lameness?

Pebble Heart shrugged. "Okay."

Gray Wing chewed another mouthful of coltsfoot and, feeling his chest loosen, sat up. He nodded toward the small hole under the bramble that Pebble Heart had gotten the leaf from. Beside it was Pebble Heart's nest, hardly more than a heap of pine twigs lined with moss. "You must be cold sleeping there," he observed. "We should build you a den."

"I'm no colder than any other cat." Pebble Heart pointed his muzzle toward the nests dotted around the edge of the clearing, twig piles like his own. Gray Wing's lay beside Tall Shadow's, a few tail-lengths from Mud Paws's and Mouse Ear's. Holly and Jagged Peak had made a large nest on the other side of the clearing where they could wrap themselves around their kits and keep them warm.

Gray Wing narrowed his eyes. "If we unravel the longest bramble stems and pull them away from the bush, we could use them to weave shelters around our nests."

Holly pricked her ears and padded closer. "That's a good idea," she meowed. "I worry about the next snowfall. There's no broom of gorse here to shelter under."

Pebble Heart met her anxious gaze. "I was planning on digging out earth beneath the brambles. I thought I could hollow out a den that way."

"Yes!" Gray Wing felt excitement rushing beneath his pelt

as his breathing returned to normal. "We could dig sleeping hollows and weave bramble stems over them. The sooner we make this camp into a real home, the better."

"Great!" Holly nodded eagerly. "Which side of the clearing do you think would be the most sheltered for the kits?"

He didn't need to taste the air to know where the coldest wind blew—he'd spent enough nights shivering in his nest. He nodded toward the far end of the camp. "The bramble wall over there will keep off the leaf-bare breezes." He lifted his nose toward a hole high in the canopy. Weak sunlight filtered through. "And you'll get sunshine, which will burn off early frosts."

"Pebble Heart." Mud Paws limped across the clearing toward the young tom. "I wrenched my shoulder chasing a squirrel yesterday. Do you have anything to ease the stiffness?"

Pride swelled in Gray Wing's chest to see how the cats were beginning to rely on the young tom for help. He hoped Turtle Tail, up among the spirit cats, could see how important her kit had become to his campmates.

"A comfrey lining in your nest should help," Pebble Heart told the brown tom. "But I'll need to go out and search for some. I've only collected coltsfoot and nettle so far."

Go out? For the last half-moon, Pebble Heart and the rest of the cats had stayed close to camp. But now Gray Wing's ear twitched with worry. Fern could be out there. Maybe Slash, too. Pebble Heart seemed to sense Gray Wing's concern, and he glanced at Mud Paws, who instantly gave a nod.

"I'll come with you," the brown tom offered. "Four eyes are better than two."

Relief washed Gray Wing's pelt. "Stay together," he warned.

Pebble Heart flashed him a questioning look. "Is something worrying you?"

"No." Gray Wing meowed quickly. "But we don't know our new territory yet. It's better to be safe than sorry."

Pebble Heart narrowed his eyes, but Mud Paws was already heading for the entrance.

"We'll be fine," he called over his shoulder.

"Don't worry so much, Gray Wing," said Pebble Heart with a flick of his tail. "It's not good for your breathing. We know how to look after ourselves."

Gray Wing watched Pebble Heart trotting after Mud Paws and tried to ignore the anxiety worming in his belly. He nodded to Holly. "Let's see if we can start weaving a shelter for your new nest." He headed toward the far end of camp, Holly at his side.

As he passed Tall Shadow and Jagged Peak, they looked up from their conversation.

"What are you doing?" Jagged Peak eyed Holly.

"Gray Wing's helping me build a den for the kits."

Jagged Peak's fur rippled along his spine as he padded forward. "They're *my* kits," he meowed sharply. "*I'll* build their den."

Holly moved aside as he pushed between her and Gray Wing. "Gray Wing says this end of the camp will be warmest," she told him.

Jagged Peak didn't answer, but began sniffing around the bramble wall.

Gray Wing backed away. If Jagged Peak wanted to take charge, why argue? Dew Nose, Storm Pelt, and Eagle Feather *were* his kits.

"Let me know if you need some help," said Gray Wing, giving Holly a polite nod. Turning, he noticed Tall Shadow gazing at him. She looked uneasy. Before he could ask if anything was wrong, the camp entrance rustled loudly. A familiar scent touched Gray Wing's nose.

"Slate!"

The amber-eyed moor cat was padding into camp. She dipped her head low to Tall Shadow. "I hope you don't mind my visiting."

Tall Shadow padded from the edge of the clearing. "We're always pleased to see you."

Gray Wing hurried toward Slate. "How are Wind Runner and the kits?"

"They get bigger every day!" Slate purred. "They're desperate to explore outside the camp, but Wind Runner won't let them." She lowered her voice. "I think Gorse Fur thinks a little fresh air will use up some of their energy, but Wind Runner just sticks out her tail and frowns. There's no arguing with her."

Gray Wing's whiskers twitched with amusement. Wind Runner had always been certain she knew best. It made her a fierce mother, but a strong one. The kits were lucky to have her.

"Why don't you come and visit?"

"The moor?" Slate's question took Gray Wing by surprise. He imagined the fresh wind rippling through his fur and pictured the wide-open expanse of heather and peat. His heart ached to be back there, but he shook his head. "I can't leave my campmates. Not while we're still settling in."

"Not even for a short while?" Slate gazed at him softly. "You haven't met Reed and Minnow yet. You'd like them." Reed and Minnow were rogues who had joined Wind Runner's group at the end of leaf-fall.

Longing tugged in Gray Wing's chest.

Tall Shadow flicked her tail. "Why don't you go, Gray Wing? We can manage without you."

Gray Wing shook his head. Perhaps if he hadn't overheard Slash and Fern, he'd go with Slate, just for a day. But he couldn't leave his friends when he knew that danger was stalking among the shadowy pines.

Mewling sounded outside the camp. Small paws pattered over the forest floor.

"Let *me* help carry it!" Dew Nose's mew sounded indignant.

The brambles rustled and Storm Pelt charged into camp. His eyes shone as the lizard dangled from his jaws. Eagle Feather and Dew Nose burst in after him.

"I would have found it first," Dew Nose squeaked. "But Eagle Feather kept getting in the way."

Mouse Ear padded after them. He nodded to Gray Wing. "Storm Pelt just followed your scent trail and went straight to it, while these two were running around in circles."

"We were not!" Eagle Feather puffed out his chest.

Mouse Ear purred. "Go and put it on the prey pile, Storm Pelt." He nodded toward the empty patch at the edge of the clearing. "Though it's not much of a pile right now."

Gray Wing flicked his tail. "We should send out a hunting party."

Mouse Ear met his gaze. "Do you want me to go?"

"Take Holly and Jagged Peak with you," Gray Wing told him.

"I can go too," Slate offered.

Tall Shadow stepped in front of the moor cat, her tail twitching with annoyance. "Jagged Peak and Holly are busy right now. And Slate has her own group to hunt for." Her angry gaze scorched Gray Wing's pelt.

He tipped his head, puzzled. "But the prey pile's empty. Jagged Peak and Holly can work on their den later. And Slate has hunted here for seasons. She can show them the best places to find prey."

Jagged Peak's gray fur flashed at the corner of his vision.

"What's going on?" The tom padded confidently toward them.

"Gray Wing's organizing hunting parties," Tall Shadow growled, straightening up. "I don't think it's your place to make such decisions."

Gray Wing bristled. "Mouse Ear offered," he pointed out. "I just didn't think it was safe for him to hunt alone."

Jagged Peak lifted his chin. "Tall Shadow's right," he

meowed. "You gave up leadership. You can't try to take it back now."

Shock flashed through Gray Wing's pelt. "I wasn't—"

Tall Shadow huffed. "You've been giving orders ever since you returned to camp!"

Gray Wing blinked at her. "I'm only trying to help."

"I'm leader here!" Tall Shadow snapped. "I brought us to this place."

"But . . ." Words dried on Gray Wing's tongue. He knew how much coming here had meant to Tall Shadow. He'd supported her decision and come to help her build a safe home. He'd spent every day watching out for Fern and Slash. He just wanted to keep his campmates safe.

"I'm sorry, Gray Wing." Tall Shadow's mew softened. "But you've looked after the cats long enough. You're not as strong as you used to be."

She thinks I'm weak! Gray Wing lashed his tail as she went on.

"It's time you let stronger cats take charge. You're not our leader anymore."

"I'm just as strong as any cat!" Gray Wing hissed. "How dare you say—" He stopped. A familiar scent was drifting through the brambles. His pelt bushed.

Fern!

He pricked his ears and heard pine needles swish beyond the camp wall.

That rogue is spying on us.

He raced for the camp entrance.

"Gray Wing?" Slate called after him.

"Don't go!" Tall Shadow's mew was sharp with worry. "I was only thinking of your health."

Gray Wing flattened his ears as he scraped through the bramble tunnel, opening his mouth to taste the air. It was definitely Fern. He scanned the shadowy forest floor. A dark shape darted past a pine tree and ducked into a clump of bracken. The mouse-hearted rogue was running away.

Gray Wing raced after her, hackles raised. Tall Shadow had no idea about the dangers lurking in their new home. *I'll show her that I'm not too weak to protect my campmates!*

CHAPTER 7

❧

Which way had Fern gone, Gray Wing wondered. The rogue's scent was still fresh, but he'd lost sight of her. He strained to see between the shadowy pines, stiffening as he spotted movement ahead.

Moving quietly over the pine needles, he followed. The black she-cat was weaving between the trees. It would be easy to catch up. Then he could drag her back to camp and show Tall Shadow that he wasn't too weak to look after his campmates.

Gray Wing frowned. Why wasn't Fern running? Hadn't she realized she was being followed? Curiosity itched beneath his fur. What was the rogue up to?

Dropping low, he kept to the shadows, treading as lightly as prey.

Weak sunlight seeped into the forest ahead. Gray Wing felt the faint rumble of a monster shake the ground. They were approaching the Thunderpath where it sliced through the trees, separating the pine forest and Clear Sky's woods. Fern's pelt showed against green as she slid out onto the side of the Thunderpath. Gray Wing paused and peered between the trees.

Fern crouched at the side of the Thunderpath, scanning the dark trail. A monster growled, its wide white flank flickering beyond the trees as it neared. Gray Wing curled his claws into the earth, his heart quickening as Fern darted onto the Thunderpath. The monster's eyes glinted in the sunlight. It was nearly on top of her.

Watch out! Gray Wing held his breath as Fern pelted across the dark stone. She leaped for the far side a moment before the monster thundered past.

Gray Wing raced forward and peered from the trees just in time to see Fern's tail whip past an oak into shadow. A howl pierced his ear fur. The ground shook beneath his paws. Gray Wing froze as another monster roared a tail-length from his nose. Wind whistled in its wake. Grit spattered his flank. His chest tightened as its bitter stench swirled around him.

As the monster thundered away, Gray Wing raced across the Thunderpath. Blood pounded in his ears as he leaped for the edge and plunged through a clump of bracken. Stopping, he caught his breath. Would he ever get used to the Thunderpath?

The stench of the monster fading behind him, he forced his hackles down and scanned the forest. The musty scent of fallen leaves filled his nose. Which way had Fern gone? He scouted between the roots of an oak. *There!* Her paws had passed this way. Nose low, he followed her trail.

The rogue cat had veered toward the edge of the wood, clearly making sure to avoid Clear Sky's camp. Was she heading for the moor to meet Slash?

Roots arched from the ground. Brambles spilled from between trunks. Gray Wing picked his way past them, dodging to avoid prickly stems. Fern was following a zigzagging trail, but she was staying inside the tree line. Gray Wing paused. Why hadn't she broken cover and headed onto the moor? He could see its grassy slopes beyond the trees. Wasn't that where she'd last spoken to Slash?

He frowned. Her path was heading toward the four trees. Was Slash meeting her there?

Gray Wing pushed on, ears pricked. He stumbled over a root, grimacing as pain shot through his paw. Thorns snagged his pelt as he staggered against a bramble. He decided to cross the moor to the four trees—it might be farther, but it would be easier that way.

He swerved and headed for the slope beyond the trees, ducking out of the woods and pushing through bracken. As his paws touched smooth grass, wind billowed through his fur. It filled his chest, clean and cold, its rich peaty scent so familiar he felt dizzy with joy. He bounded up the slope and skirted the heather toward the four trees. He moved quickly here. The ground blurred beneath his paws; air filled his chest. His heartbeat quickened and his whiskers streamed against his cheeks. As the slope steepened toward the top of the hollow, Gray Wing slowed. In the woods below, Fern would be picking her way through the undergrowth. He crossed the final stretch of grass to the rim of the hollow and gazed back across the moor. There was the dip—no more than a cloud shadow—where the hollow lay.

Was it still deserted? Were other creatures sheltering there now?

He narrowed his eyes, wondering if he could see Wind Runner's small camp. But the heather clearing where she'd made her home was hidden between the dips and rises of the moor. She had chosen well.

Gray Wing dragged his attention back to the hollow.

The bare branches of the four oaks showed dark above the rim. Beyond them the sun sank toward the distant horizon, burning orange in a pale blue sky. Gray Wing could feel dew gathering on his fur. He shook it out and shivered.

Below, the great boulder rose at one end of the hollow. Was Fern there already?

He padded forward and nosed his way down the bracken-covered slope. Slowing as he neared the bottom, he narrowed his eyes and scanned the clearing.

He stiffened as he spotted Fern's black pelt. She was crossing the clearing, her belly close to the earth, her stumpy tail twitching excitedly. She was stalking something.

Gray Wing tasted the air. There was no sign of Slash's scent. And Fern's attention was focused on her quarry.

Had she just come here to hunt?

His pelt prickled with hope. This was his chance to talk to her and find out why Slash had sent her to spy on his campmates. Ducking low, he slid through the last few stalks of bracken and padded softly into the clearing.

Fern was watching the grass at the far edge. She lowered

her chin and waggled her hindquarters, so intent on her prey that she didn't twitch an ear as Gray Wing crept across the clearing toward her.

"Fern?"

The black rogue spun with a hiss. Fear flashed in her eyes and she reared, unsheathing her claws.

"I'm not here to fight." Gray Wing stopped a tail-length away. He could smell her fear-scent.

"What do you want?" Fern eyed him warily.

"Don't you recognize me?" Gray Wing circled her, giving her a wide berth. Fern dropped onto all fours and turned, keeping her gaze fixed on him. "Why should I?"

"You've been spying on us for the past half-moon," Gray Wing told her.

Fern's eyes widened with horror. "You're one of the cats from the forest!"

Gray Wing rolled his eyes. She wasn't much of a spy. "Haven't you even learned our scent yet?"

The fur lifted along Fern's spine. "All I can smell in that place is sap and stagnant water."

Up close, her pelt looked dull, so thin that ribs showed beneath. *She's half-starved.* "It must be hard to find prey in such a stench," he commented.

She backed away. "I'm just not used to hunting alone. And prey is scarce since the sickness."

"Did Slash usually hunt for you?" Gray Wing watched her gaze, seeing fear flash sharper as he mentioned Slash's name.

"He helped," she said defensively. "So what?"

"But now he's left you alone," Gray Wing pressed. "You look pretty hungry."

Her eyes glittered. "I wouldn't if you hadn't interrupted me. I was about to make a kill!" She glanced ruefully at the grass. "My mouse has probably gone by now."

Gray Wing flicked his gaze along her skinny flanks. "You look like you need more than a mouse."

Fern lifted her chin. "I can take care of myself!"

"I can help you hunt," Gray Wing offered. "Like Slash used to."

Fern narrowed her eyes. "Why would you do that?"

"Because you're starving."

Fern stared at him.

"Slash is a bully," Gray Wing went on. "He's no better than One Eye."

"How do *you* know Slash?" Fern asked suspiciously.

"I saw him talking to you, on the moor."

Fern seemed to shrink beneath her pelt.

"You shouldn't let him push you around," Gray Wing told her.

"What else am I supposed to do?" she wailed. "If I don't do as he says, he'll kill me."

Gray Wing padded slowly closer. "It doesn't seem fair. He's left you to starve." He jerked his muzzle toward the empty clearing. "I don't see him looking out for you. What if I was a dangerous cat? You look too weak to fight. And you're lucky you made it through Clear Sky's territory unnoticed—my brother doesn't think much of spies."

"I didn't have any choice!" she snapped. Her gaze darkened suddenly. "You won't tell Slash you've seen me, will you?"

"Why would *I* talk to Slash?" Gray Wing asked, leaning closer.

Fern backed away, trembling.

"I'm not going to hurt you!" Did this cat believe all toms were as bad as Slash and One Eye?

"Then leave me alone!" Hissing, she batted a weak paw toward him.

Gray Wing easily ducked out of the way. "You need food. You're as weak as a newborn kit. Wait here while I hunt." He hurried across the clearing and dived into the long grass at the far side. Opening his mouth, he tasted for prey, his tail-tip flicking excitedly as he caught a musky scent. Sniffing his way along its trail, he saw the bracken twitch in front of him.

He dropped into a crouch. A small, brown shape moved between the stems. It was rooting among the fallen leaves. *Mouse!* Bunching up his hind legs, he leaped and slammed his paws onto the startled creature. It fell limp beneath him, giving up without a struggle. Quickly, he nipped its spine and carried it back to Fern, who was crouching in the clearing where he had left her. She hadn't tried to escape.

She really must be as frail as she looks.

He dropped the mouse at her paws. "Eat this."

As Fern gobbled it down, the scent of mouse blood touched

Gray Wing's nose. His belly rumbled. He hadn't eaten today.

As the last morsel disappeared, Fern licked her lips and sat up. "What's your name?"

Gray Wing stared at her. "It's Gray Wing."

"Thank you, Gray Wing," she said. She looked down for a moment, then back up at him.

Gray Wing shrugged. "I need you to do something for me in return."

Her eyes flashed with fear. "What?"

"Try to persuade Slash he's wasting his time with us," he told her.

"How?" she frowned.

"I don't know." Frustration itched beneath his pelt. "Tell him that we've made a strong camp. That we're dangerous. That he'd never win a fight with us." Gray Wing gazed at her. "Just convince him."

Fern tipped her head. "Slash would never believe there are cats he couldn't beat," she muttered bitterly. Her eyes suddenly lit up. "But I might be able to distract him."

Gray Wing leaned closer. "Distract him?"

"I could tell him you've been hunting beyond the pines. Once he hears you've found a fresh, new source of prey, he'll want to see it for himself—he's always been greedy."

"How will that help?" Gray Wing narrowed his eyes.

"It'll give you time to prepare," Fern told him. "He's going to make his attack soon. You need to make your camp as strong as you can, and practice fighting. When Slash comes, he won't come alone."

Gray Wing shivered, dread hollowing his belly. Slash sounded just like One Eye. "What about you?" This scrawny rogue could hardly hunt for herself.

"I'll be okay," she promised.

"You should stay here for a day or two," Gray Wing suggested. "You don't need to spy on us anymore, and there's prey here. Catch as much as you can and grow strong."

Fern nodded. "I will."

Gray Wing searched her gaze. Could he trust this she-cat to keep her word? Did she have the courage to lie to Slash and send him searching beyond the pines for prey that didn't exist?

She stared back at him, hope glistening in her gaze.

He realized he had no choice but to trust her. "Good luck."

Turning, he padded to the slope and headed toward the moor. He wanted one last look at it before he returned to the pines. He wove between the brambles and climbed over the top. The moor was bathed in evening sunshine. Above, the sky was streaked purple as the sun slid behind the trees. Gray Wing padded across the grass, which felt soft after the needle-strewn floor of the forest. A brisk, chilly wind lifted his fur and pricked at his flesh. Breathing deeply, he drew in the familiar fragrance of heather and stone.

Rabbit scent touched his nose. Excitement tingling beneath his pelt, he scanned the slope below. A young rabbit was hopping across the grass. It was heading for a burrow—a dark opening in the grass a few tail-lengths ahead. Could he catch it before it dived for cover?

His belly growled.

He charged forward, pounding down the slope. But the rabbit heard his approach and scampered away quickly, the white tip of its tail bobbing over the grass. As it closed upon its burrow, Gray Wing leaped. He soared through the air, his forepaws outstretched, and landed square on the rabbit. He clamped his jaws around its neck and killed it with one bite.

Joy flooded his chest as the scent of blood washed his muzzle. The rabbit's body was warm and he took a bite.

"That's not fair!" A tiny mew made him jump. He sat up, his mouth full.

A ginger tom-kit was marching across the grass toward Gray Wing. He was thin-faced and skinny even though, from the width of his shoulders, he looked older than Eagle Feather and Storm Pelt.

"That was my mother's catch!" the kit spat. "She was stalking it." He glanced over his shoulder. A dark shape was sliding from the heather.

Gray Wing tasted the air. A she-cat. He watched her approach, her tail low, her ears flat. She was a splotchy ginger-and-black tabby and even skinnier than her son. A ginger-and-white she-kit followed, her steps faltering. *They're half-starved, too! Just like Fern.* Gray Wing glanced at the rabbit, then pawed it toward the tom-kit. "Take it," he told him. "I didn't realize it was your mother's catch."

The she-cat stopped as she reached him. "You caught it. You keep it." She shooed the tom-kit away from the rabbit with a paw. "We don't take food from strangers."

The she-kit caught up to her mother and pressed, trembling, against the tabby's flank. "Can't we just take a bite?" She gazed at the rabbit with wide, hungry eyes. "If he *wants* us to share."

"No." The tabby she-cat hushed her sharply. "We catch our own prey."

Gray Wing dipped his head. "I've been lucky today," he told her gently. "This is my second catch. Please take it."

The tabby met his eye cautiously.

"Your kits are growing and prey is scarce," Gray Wing urged. He puffed out his chest. "I don't need it as much as you."

"It's a trick, isn't it?" The tabby's gaze sharpened.

"No." Why was this cat so wary?

"I've met your kind before," she growled. "You don't care if weak cats starve—you just want me to take it so you have a reason to start a fight."

Gray Wing noticed the shredded tip of one ear and a scar across her black muzzle. His heart twisted in his chest. "I won't hurt you," he promised. He glanced at the ginger-and-white she-kit. She so was frail. *Like Fluttering Bird.* "I had a sister who died of hunger," he told the tabby. "I would never let another kit die."

The she-kit's eyes filled with horror. "Are we going to die? Like Bramble?"

"No, dear." The tabby nuzzled her daughter's ear. "Bramble

was always sickly. We'll be fine."

Gray Wing wasn't so sure. This tabby looked too weak to hunt. She'd never have caught the rabbit before it disappeared into its burrow. "What's your name?" he asked her.

"Milkweed." She nodded to the ginger tom-kit, then her she-kit. "This is Thistle and Clover. Their sister, Bramble, died yesterday." Emotion glistened in her amber gaze.

"Then eat." Gray Wing leaned down and grabbed the rabbit in his jaws. He tossed it toward her and it landed at her paws.

Milkweed held his gaze, still wary. "You're one of those cats from the mountains, aren't you?" There was accusation in her gaze. "Ever since you came, there's been less land to hunt on and more mouths competing for food."

Guilt sparked beneath Gray Wing's pelt. "We came here because we were starving in the mountains," he explained. "That's where my sister died. We didn't come to steal your land or your food—only to share it."

"You've set the rogues against each other," Milkweed snapped. "Now every cat is fighting for prey."

"That's because the sickness killed so much of it," Gray Wing argued. *And because rogues like One Eye and Slash take pleasure from making other cats suffer.*

"Yet you'd share this catch with us?" Milkweed's nose was twitching. The scent of the rabbit must have been driving her wild with hunger.

"Yes." Gray Wing sat down and curled his tail over his

paws. "I'll stay here and watch over you until you've finished."

"Please, Milkweed?" Clover looked at her mother with pleading eyes.

Thistle padded toward the rabbit, his mouth open to draw in its warm scent.

"Okay." Milkweed crouched beside it and ripped a lump from the rabbit's flank. She dropped it at Clover's paws and tore off another lump for Thistle. Once they'd begun eating, she took a mouthful for herself.

Gray Wing turned away and let them eat in peace.

His belly rumbled. This was his second catch of the day, and he still hadn't eaten. He shifted his paws uneasily. Prey was scarce, but starving cats were not. Had the moor cats and forest cats really caused this suffering? *We only came here because we were starving.* Was there any way to help cats like these? He shook out his fur as an idea flickered in his mind.

Spread and grow like the Blazing Star.

"You should go to Clear Sky," he told Milkweed.

She looked up from the rabbit, blood staining her chin. "Clear Sky?" Fear flashed in her eyes. "He killed my friend Misty—he doesn't care for rogues like me."

Gray Wing's pelt rippled uncomfortably. "He took in Misty's kits."

Milkweed snorted. "That was nice of him. Perhaps he'll take in mine after he's killed *me*."

Gray Wing flinched. "Clear Sky's changed," he promised. "He wants to bring all cats together now in peace. He wants his group to grow and spread. Some of my friends have gone to live with him. I'm sure he'll take you and your kits in."

Milkweed grunted and returned to her meal.

"Just tell him Gray Wing sent you. Tell him I told you to come to him for food and protection."

Milkweed carried on eating.

Perhaps I should take these cats back to the pine forest. He frowned. Would they be safe there? The cats still had to find the best places for prey and learn new hunting techniques. And Fern sounded certain that Slash would attack. Clear Sky's forest would be safer.

Thistle sat up and licked his lips. "My belly hurts," he mewed.

Gray Wing gazed at him sympathetically. "That's because it's not used to so much food. Next time, chew more slowly."

Clover lifted her head and burped. "I feel warm now."

Milkweed straightened. "Thank you." She stared gratefully at Gray Wing.

"Go to Clear Sky," he urged. "You won't survive out here alone."

Milkweed wrapped her tail around Clover.

"Please can we go?" Thistle's eyes flashed with excitement. "I want to be a forest cat. I heard Clear Sky's cats train how to hunt and fight. If we go there, he might teach me to be the strongest fighter in the forest. Then we would never have to be scared again."

Milkweed gazed at him fondly, then glanced at Gray Wing.

"Do you promise he won't hurt us?"

"I promise." Gray Wing dipped his head.

Milkweed looked down at the rabbit carcass, then headed across the slope. Clover trotted after her, tail high, while Thistle snatched a final mouthful.

"Hurry up," Gray Wing prompted him. "Your mother needs you."

Thistle met Gray Wing's eye solemnly. "I'll protect her," he promised, then scampered over the grass after his family.

Gray Wing stood and watched until they reached the bracken edging the woods. His heart ached as they disappeared between the trees. *Please, Clear Sky, take them in.* He glanced toward the distant pines, then looked across the moor. Beyond its rose-tipped crest, the setting sun would be drenching Highstones. Longing filled his heart, and he broke into a run. Charging up the moorside, he dodged through swath after swath of heather until he emerged at the top. Beyond, he saw the wide, flat boulder that jutted out over the steep drop down to the Thunderpath. He hurried forward and climbed onto it. The smooth, wind-chilled stone stung his paws as he padded across. He lay down and hung his head over the edge and gazed across the rolling fields that stretched toward Highstones. They'd traveled that way from the mountains.

What would Stoneteller have said about the lives they'd made here? There was much to be proud of: new kits, new homes. As his belly rumbled once more, Gray Wing wondered if he should hunt again. But he couldn't drag his gaze from Highstones shining golden in the dying sunshine. What would Stoneteller have thought of the battles they had fought and the deaths they had caused by coming here? As the sun sank behind him and Highstones disappeared into shadow, Gray Wing closed his eyes and let sleep draw him deep into dreams.

CHAPTER 8

Gray Wing opened his eyes. Scents swirled around him, thick with memories. A chill nipped his ears with a cruelty he'd forgotten.

Water thundered behind him, and he turned to see the waterfall that veiled the entrance of his old home from the crags outside. Light shimmered through it and rippled over the cave walls.

"Hello?" His mew echoed in the deserted cavern. He scanned the dimples in the wide stone floor where his Tribemates had made their nests, which were empty but for twigs and leaves lying shriveled in each hollow. "Where are you?" Worry pricked Gray Wing's pelt. He stretched his ears, listening. Far away, he thought he heard faint mews. Distant paw steps scuffed the stone, but he could see no cat.

Had his Tribemates traveled beyond his vision? Were they spirit cats now?

"Quiet Rain! Snow Hare! Where are you?" His heart lurched as guilt scorched his pelt. He should never have left them. Had they starved without him? "What have I done?"

Purring rumbled at the back of the cave.

Hope flashed in Gray Wing's heart. He peered eagerly into the shadows and caught sight of a tail whipping away into the tunnel.

He hurried after it, blinking as darkness swallowed him. His paws ached on the freezing stone. His whiskers brushed the walls, and his tail snagged on the jagged roof. "Who's there?" he called anxiously into the blackness.

Suddenly, the tunnel opened around him and he emerged into a cave lit by moonlight, which seeped through a hole in the roof. Sharp claws of rock jutted up from the stone floor and down from above. Some touched, like paws meeting, and they glistened as water trickled down them. It pooled on the floor, sending light flickering against the walls.

An ancient white cat watched him from beyond the pools, her tail twitching softly behind her.

"Stoneteller?" Gray Wing blinked. Was she all that was left of the Tribe?

She didn't answer, but touched one of the pools with a forepaw, sending ripples shivering across its surface.

Gray Wing padded closer. "I'm so sorry," he began. "I never stopped to think how the Tribe would survive without us."

"Hush." Stoneteller lifted her green gaze to meet Gray Wing's. "You have nothing to apologize for."

"But the cave!" Gray Wing wailed. "It's empty! And it's my fault. If only I'd stayed—"

"Gray Wing." Stoneteller's mew was firm. "You cannot decide the fate of every cat. You do not hold power like that."

"Then why did you bring me here?" Surely it was Stoneteller

who had summoned him to see the empty cave. "What's happened to the Tribe?"

Stoneteller looked down into the pool as the ripples faded. "All will become clear soon enough," she murmured. "For now, you must let go of the past. The future is the only thing you can change."

A shriek jerked Gray Wing awake. He blinked at the dark valley stretching below him. The mountains beyond Highstones were no more than shadows against the starry night sky.

The Tribe! He jumped up. *Where are they?*

The shriek sounded again. It tugged him from his thoughts.

The moor was bathed in moonlight, the grass turned white by frost.

"Back off!" He heard a vicious yowl from beyond a patch of gorse. Gray Wing recognized it at once.

Slate! He leaped from the stone and charged over the top of the moor, skidding on the grass as he swerved around the gorse.

Slate was backed against its sharp spines. A fox snapped at her hind legs, then her muzzle, its sharp teeth glinting in the moonlight. Slate hissed and shrank deeper against the thorns. Blood darkened her pelt. Eyes blazing, she slashed at the fox's face with a forepaw, but it dived for her tail.

She whipped it clear just in time. The fox's jaws slammed shut on thin air. Yelping with rage, it lunged for her neck.

"Leave her alone!" Gray Wing plunged forward, pelt

bushed. Snarling, he leaped onto its back.

Caught by surprise, the fox staggered and fell. Gray Wing clung on, digging his foreclaws in hard. He could feel bones through its mangy pelt. Cats were not the only creatures starving on the moor.

Slate growled. "It tried to take my prey."

Gray Wing caught the scent of fresh-kill through the fox's stench. He turned his gaze to meet Slate's. The fox bucked beneath him, with far more strength than Gray Wing had expected. Hunger had clearly made it bold—and desperate. It jerked back its muzzle to snap at Gray Wing's neck. He felt his fur rip. Pain scorched through him. He let go with a shriek and slithered to the ground, struggling to find his paws on the frosty grass.

The fox turned on him. Its stinking breath bathed Gray Wing's muzzle as its savage jaws opened for a killing bite. Then fur flashed at the edge of his vision. With a yowl, Slate sent the fox tumbling backward.

Gray Wing leaped to his paws. Slate and the fox were tumbling over the grass. Muscle thudded on earth as they grappled with each other. The air shivered with their screeching. Gray Wing hurled himself at them as the fox's jaws clamped shut on Slate's ear.

Hissing with rage, he shoved the fox away. He heard Slate shriek in pain, but he was on his hind legs, batting the fox backward, swiping with one paw after another. He felt its fur rip beneath his claws until the fox's muzzle was wet with blood. The fox's eyes flashed with anger. With a yelp it turned and fled, streaking across the grass like a shadow.

Gray Wing turned to Slate. "Are you okay?"

She sat, her head low, her flanks heaving. "It got my ear."

Gray Wing rushed to her side. The tang of blood filled the air. It welled on Slate's ear, and he could see the tip had been ripped away. "It'll heal," he soothed.

His own pelt felt damp; his neck fur was drenched with his own blood. "Foxes don't normally fight that hard for prey," he growled. "I thought it would run when it saw there was two of us."

Slate was still panting. "Thanks for coming." She lifted her head, pain darkening her amber gaze. "But what are you doing on the moor?"

"I'll explain later." Gray Wing was too dazed by the fight to think up a good reason for being here. He couldn't tell her about Fern—their conversation had to remain a secret while Slash threatened her. If word got out that she'd spoken to him, the vicious rogue might kill her. "Let's get you back to your camp. You're bleeding."

Slate's gaze flicked over him. "You'd better come with me. Your neck looks pretty bad. Reed can treat your wounds."

"He knows about herbs?" Gray Wing blinked at her.

"I told you last time I visited." Slate got stiffly to her paws and nudged him with her muzzle. "You're getting forgetful in your old age."

Gray Wing nudged her back. "Who are you calling old?"

Slate's whiskers twitched fondly. "Wait there." She limped back to the gorse and dragged something out from beneath one of the bushes.

Grouse.

Its pungent scent touched his nose as she carried it toward him. Its wings dragged along the ground, and Slate struggled not to trip.

"Let me help." Gray Wing fell in beside her and grabbed the bird's tail in his jaws. Feathers pressed around his nose, his warm breath billowing through them.

Side by side, they carried Slate's catch to Wind Runner's camp. The scratches on Gray Wing's neck stung like fire, but he held fast to the grouse. They'd fought hard to keep it.

Slate guided him along the secret passages that led to the clearing hidden in a wide patch of heather. As the trail narrowed, she tugged the grouse from him and pushed ahead. Gray Wing let go and fell in behind, slowing as the heather opened onto a small grassy clearing. Would Wind Runner welcome him? The last time he'd seen her, she had made it clear that her new home was closed to outsiders.

"Gray Wing!" Gorse Fur saw him first. The gray tabby tom clambered out of a heather nest and hurried across the grass. "How are you?" He paused, his nose twitching. "I smell blood. Are you okay?"

Slate dropped the grouse and pushed it beneath the heather. "I ran into a fox," she explained. "Gray Wing heard my screeches and came to help. Don't worry, we chased it off. It won't show its snout around here for a while."

Small ears poked up above the rim of Gorse Fur's nest.

"Who is it?" A kit clambered out of the nest and came charging across the clearing.

"Moth Flight!" Wind Runner sat up in a nest a tail-length away. "It's too cold to be out of your nest. And Dust Muzzle will freeze on his own!"

"No I won't!" A second head bobbed up.

"You're supposed to be sleeping." Wind Runner meowed with annoyance.

"We can sleep later!" Dust Muzzle climbed out of Gorse Fur's nest and raced after his sister.

Wind Runner's eyes shone in the dark, widening as they reached Gray Wing. She hopped out of her nest. "It's you!"

"I'm sorry to disturb everyone." Gray Wing dipped his head.

Wind Runner flicked her tail happily. "It's good to see you." She tasted the air. "You're hurt!"

"Just scratches." Slate shrugged.

"Slate lost a piece of her ear." Gray Wing told her.

Wind Runner sniffed at Slate's wound. "Reed had better look at it." She called over her shoulder. "Reed? Are you awake?"

"How can any cat sleep with this noise?" A silver tabby tom was stretching in his nest.

Gray Wing felt soft fur brush his forepaws. A tail flicked past his nose. He looked down. "Moth Flight? Is that you?"

"Of course it's me." Moth Flight had grown. She was bigger than Dew Nose but still had her kit fluff. She gazed at Gray

Wing with bright green eyes. "Who are you?"

"I'm Gray Wing."

Moth Flight tipped her head. "You dug the graves for my sister and brother," she mewed, "when we lived in the hollow."

Gray Wing nodded, his pelt rippling uncomfortably as he saw grief glisten briefly in Wind Runner's eyes.

She shifted her paws. "Moth Flight, take your brother back to the nest. You can speak to Gray Wing once it's light. He has wounds that need treating."

Reed had crossed the clearing and was already sniffing at Gray Wing's neck. "I'd better put some herbs on those scratches before they turn bad."

Gorse Fur grunted. "Fox bites are as sour as a badger's."

"I can help you, Reed!" Moth Flight offered.

"Me too!" Dust Muzzle pushed past his sister. The tom-kit's gray pelt glowed in the moonlight.

Moth Flight pushed him away. "I offered first."

Wind Runner growled. "*Neither* of you is helping," she told them firmly. "Go back to the nest and sleep."

Moth Flight eyed her mother. "Can we have a bite of grouse first? It's the best catch we've had in ages."

Wind Runner gave her a stern look. "In the morning."

Moth Flight turned and flounced back to the nest. "If I starve to death before dawn, it'll be your fault."

Dust Muzzle ran after her. "At least we can look forward to a meal when we wake up," he mewed eagerly.

As the kits climbed back into their nest, Gray Wing scanned

the camp. The cold wind hardly penetrated the little hollow among the heather bushes. The cats had built deep nests in the shade of their branches. It was far cozier than the hollow had been, but when the kits grew into nests of their own, it would be cramped.

Reed peered at the scratches on Gray Wing's neck.

Gray Wing nosed him away. "Treat Slate's ear first."

The gray she-cat was acting as though her injury weren't bothering her, but Gray Wing could sense her stiffness. She was brave, but she must still have been shocked by the ferocity of the fox's attack. *If I hadn't been there, it could have killed her.*

He pushed the thought away. He was not going to lose another cat.

"It's a clean bite." Reed sniffed at Slate's ear. "It will heal neatly, but I'll make some ointment to stop it from getting infected." He sat back on his haunches and tipped his head sympathetically. "It's a shame it got your good ear."

Gray Wing blinked through the darkness and noticed that the tip of Slate's other ear was torn at the top. He'd never noticed before. "They're a better match now," he meowed encouragingly.

Slate's whiskers twitched. "Is that meant to be a compliment?"

Heat spread beneath Gray Wing's pelt. "I—I just meant…"

Reed padded between them. "I'd better make some ointment."

As the silver tabby crossed the camp, Gray Wing gazed

into Slate's eyes. "I only meant that you look fine," he murmured shyly.

"Thanks." Slate dipped her head.

Wind Runner paced around them. "How's your new home, Gray Wing? Slate told us about the cats splitting up. I was surprised you'd choose that dank old forest. I thought you were a moor cat to your bones."

Gorse Fur—who had hung back while Reed checked their wounds—leaned forward. "Tall Shadow must be happy."

"She is," Gray Wing purred. "The pine forest is peaceful and sheltered."

"Slate told us that Thunder has gone to live with his father," Gorse Fur went on. "Do you think the forest will be big enough for *both* of them?"

Wind Runner's ear twitched. "Hush, Gorse. They're Gray Wing's kin."

Gray Wing shrugged. "Clear Sky's changed, and Thunder has matured. . . . I'm sure they'll be fine."

Gorse Fur sniffed. "A tabby doesn't change its stripes."

A shadow moved at the far edge of the clearing. A gray-and-white she-cat ducked out from beneath the heather and padded toward them. "Who's this?" She eyed Gray Wing suspiciously.

"He's an old friend, from the hollow," Wind Runner explained. She dipped her head to the she-cat. "This is Minnow, Reed's mate."

Gray Wing nodded a greeting. "I'm Gray Wing. Pleased to meet you."

"*This* is Gray Wing?" Minnow's gaze flickered over his pelt. She sounded surprised. "I thought he'd be bigger."

"Wind Runner!" Moth Flight's mew sounded from Gorse Fur's nest. "We can't get back to sleep with every cat talking."

Wind Runner sighed heavily.

Gorse Fur nodded toward the sky, which was lightening beyond the heather. "It's nearly dawn," he mewed softly. "They might as well be up and running around. I can take them out of camp and show them the moortop . . . ?"

Wind Runner glared at him. "You know I don't want them out there until they're big enough to take care of themselves."

"They'll have me," Gorse Fur pointed out.

"I'll go with them," Minnow offered. The she-cat was small, but Gray Wing could see hard muscle beneath her gray-and-white pelt.

Moth Flight and Dust Muzzle were already scrambling out of the nest.

"*Please* can we go?" Moth Flight reached Wind Runner first and raced around her. "We'll never learn to take care of ourselves if we stay in camp the whole time."

Dust Muzzle stared gravely at his mother. "I'll make sure Moth Flight doesn't get into any trouble," he promised. "I won't leave her side."

"Please!" Moth Flight looked from Wind Runner to Gorse Fur. "We'll stay close to Gorse Fur and do everything he tells us."

Gray Wing saw Wind Runner's shoulders droop. "Okay,"

she meowed. "But don't stay out long. That fox might still be around."

Gray Wing lifted his chin. "I think we gave it a pretty good scare."

"We'll watch out for it!" Moth Flight raced for the camp entrance.

Dust Muzzle dashed after her. "Wait for me."

Gorse Fur lifted his tail happily. "They'll be fine," he reassured Wind Runner, and ducked into the heather tunnel.

Minnow followed. "Will you be here when we get back?" she called over her shoulder to Gray Wing.

"I don't know." Gray Wing glanced at the pale sky pushing back the stars. His campmates would be worried about him.

As Minnow disappeared, Reed trotted across the clearing, a leaf folded between his jaws. He dropped it on the grass and pawed it open. A thick paste was smeared over it. "I'll treat your ear first." He bent and lapped up a tongueful of the paste and began to wash it into Slate's ear tip.

Slate winced. "Are you sure that will help?"

"My mother used it on me," Reed told her when he'd finished. He puffed out his chest. "And look how healthy I am."

Gray Wing purred. He liked this friendly tom.

"Your turn." Reed turned to him. "Lift your chin." He dipped his tongue in the ointment again and, as Gray Wing stretched his nose toward the sky, began lapping it into the scratches around Gray Wing's throat.

Gray Wing was surprised by the tom's gentleness. The

ointment stung as it met his wounds, but Reed's tongue was fast and light. As the silver tom finished and backed away, Gray Wing wrinkled his nose. "I don't recognize that scent."

"It's dried oak leaf and marigold," Reed told him. "I collected the marigolds near the river in greenleaf. They dry well in the sun and keep their strength."

"I'll tell Pebble Heart about it," Gray Wing meowed.

"Pebble Heart." Reed's eyes shone. "Slate's told me about him. She says he's a natural healer. I'd like to meet him."

"I'm sure you will, one day." He glanced at Slate. "I should get back to him. He'll wonder where I am."

"Share some prey first," Slate suggested. "The grouse will feed all of us."

Gray Wing's belly felt hard with hunger.

Wind Runner lifted her tail. "Please stay." She padded to the heather wall of the camp and hauled out the grouse. "It's a long time since we've seen you." She tore off a wing and tossed it to Gray Wing.

It landed at his paws, its scent flooding his nose. "Okay." His campmates would know he was experienced enough to look after himself. He leaned down and took a mouthful of sweet flesh from the thickest part of the wing.

Wind Runner tore the bird into pieces, laying some aside for Minnow, Gorse Fur, and the kits, and shared the rest with Reed and Slate.

As Gray Wing ate, dawn pushed up from the distant mountains, sunshine breaking over the heather. The moor seemed to open beneath its warmth, releasing its fragrance into the breeze. Relishing the scent, Gray Wing sat up and licked his lips, his belly full.

Wind Runner had already finished and was washing her paws with long steady laps of her tongue. Reed padded to the edge of the clearing, where early sunshine was pooling, and lay down.

Slate pawed the last scraps of her meal toward Gray Wing. "Are you still hungry?"

"Save them for the kits." Gray Wing felt self-conscious about eating other cats' prey.

Wind Runner looked up. "Eat it," she urged. "You look thin."

Gray Wing suddenly realized that the moor cats looked as well as the last time he'd seen them. "Is hunting good here?"

"Not bad, despite leaf-bare and the sickness," Wind Runner purred. "Don't forget we have the tunnels, so there's hunting even when it snows." She narrowed her eyes, curiously. "Don't you miss it?"

"I miss the wind and sky. The dampness in the forest affects my breathing. But I have to stay with Pebble Heart and Tall Shadow." He paused, sadness tugging in his chest as he remembered his quarrel with the black she-cat. "Though I'm not sure Tall Shadow feels she needs me anymore. She accused me of trying to take over as leader. She said I'm not as strong as I used to be."

"I'm sure Tall Shadow didn't mean it. She just wants her new home to feel like *hers*." Wind Runner's tail twitched over the grass. "I felt the same way when we moved here."

Slate sniffed. "If she'd seen you fight off that fox, she'd know you're as strong as any cat!"

"Tall Shadow will always know that she's lucky to have you." Wind Runner licked a paw and ran it over her ear.

Gray Wing shifted his paws self-consciously. They were being too kind. He changed the subject. "How are you, Wind Runner?" The last time he'd seen her, she'd been grieving the loss of a second kit.

She met his gaze. "Moth Flight and Dust Muzzle are strong and bright. Our home is safe and warm. And now we have Reed, Minnow, and Slate. They're good hunters." She dipped her head to Slate. "And good company for the kits." She blinked slowly. "I guess I'm happy, even though I never thought I could be after all that I lost. Is that wrong of me?" She looked at Gray Wing with round, anxious eyes.

Gray Wing returned her gaze softly. "It's not wrong," he reassured her. "I thought I would never be happy after I lost Turtle Tail. But life goes on, and I can see new paths ahead of me." He snatched a look at Slate, who was eyeing him thoughtfully. "I think it's our duty to be happy, despite all that we've lost."

Wind Runner purred. "That's what Gorse Fur says. He seems to approach every new day as though it's his first and his last." She pricked her ears at the sound of paws pattering over the ground beyond the camp wall. The heather shook as Moth Flight and Dust Muzzle burst into the clearing.

"It's so big out there!" Moth Flight exclaimed.

"Gorse Fur took us to the top of the moor and showed us Highstones!" Dust Muzzle stared at Gray Wing. "Did you really travel all that way from the mountains?"

Gray Wing padded forward and nuzzled the kit's head. "It was a long, hard journey."

"I want to make a journey like that one day," Dust Muzzle exclaimed. "I want to go farther than I can see."

Moth Flight stared at her brother. "Leave your *home*?" She turned to her mother. "We should stay here and defend what's ours, shouldn't we?" Her eyes flashed fiercely.

Wind Runner lifted her chin proudly. "Yes."

Gorse Fur padded into camp. "Minnow's gone hunting," he announced. "She found a fresh rabbit trail. I might follow her and help."

Wind Runner stood and stretched, curving her spine until her tail trembled. "I'll come with you."

"When do *we* get to hunt?" Moth Flight asked.

"You've had plenty of excitement for one day." Wind Runner shooed her daughter away with her tail.

Reed lifted his head and gazed across the clearing. "Come and soak up some sunshine with me," he called to the kits.

"That's boring," Dust Muzzle complained.

"Let's play hunt the mouse!" Moth Flight screwed her eyes shut. "Quick, hide while I'm not looking."

"Don't leave the camp, you two!" Wind Runner ordered as Dust Muzzle wormed his way between the stems of the heather wall. She glanced at Gray Wing. "You'll stay awhile, won't you? I'd hate for you to leave while we're gone."

Gray Wing tipped his head. "I don't know. Pebble Heart will be missing me."

"He'll be fine. He must be full-grown by now." Wind Runner glanced at Slate. "You'll persuade him, won't you?"

Before Slate could answer, Wind Runner darted into the heather tunnel after Gorse Fur.

Gray Wing tucked his paws closer. The meal had made him sleepy and the scratches on his neck ached. "I should really be getting home," he murmured halfheartedly.

"Do as Wind Runner asks," Slate urged. "Stay and rest. Just for a while."

Gray Wing gazed at her through half-closed eyes. It was cozy here, and the old scents of the moor mingled with Slate's warm fragrance. He yawned. "I guess it wouldn't hurt to have a little nap before I leave."

CHAPTER 9

Clear Sky hung his chin over the edge of the branch and gazed at the camp below. Satisfaction washed beneath his pelt as he watched his cats. Acorn Fur lay in the weak leaf-bare sunshine that filtered through the branches, while Birch and Alder batted the tip of her tail between them. Every now and then she whisked it up into the air, and one of the young cats jumped for it, purring loudly.

Nettle and Thorn shared tongues among the roots of the beech, while Owl Eyes and Sparrow Fur picked through the prey pile.

Sparrow Fur pawed a mouse from the top and lifted her tail proudly as a small shrew showed beneath. She stepped away and eyed her campmates hopefully.

Cloud Spots crossed the clearing toward her. "What's fresh?"

"This shrew." Sparrow Fur nodded toward it.

"Did you catch it?" Cloud Spots's eyes twinkled.

Owl Eyes snorted. "You know she did! She's been boasting about it since we got back from hunting."

Cloud Spots licked his lips. "I love shrew."

Owl Eyes hooked out a mangy starling. "What about something with feathers?"

Sparrow Fur glared at him. "He wants *my* prey, not yours." She nudged her shrew toward Cloud Spots, who took it and carried it to the beech, where he settled beside Nettle and Thorn.

"*I'd* like the starling," Pink Eyes called from the holly bush where he was sunning himself beside Quick Water.

Quick Water raised her head. "Can I share it with you?"

Pink Eyes sat up. "Of course."

Owl Eyes picked up the starling in his jaws and bounded across the clearing. He dropped it at Pink Eyes's paws. "Sorry it's a bit scrawny."

"It's leaf-bare." Pink Eyes shrugged. "I'm happy we have any prey."

Owl Eyes glanced toward the bramble wall. "Blossom's patrol will be back soon. They'll have more."

Quick Water sniffed the starling. "This will be enough for us."

Clear Sky could see beyond the brambles from his perch in the oak tree. There was no sign of Blossom's patrol. He'd sent her out with Lightning Tail just after dawn. He'd sent Leaf out with Sparrow Fur and Owl Eyes a little later, and Leaf had already gone back out again to gather moss. Two hunting patrols should bring back enough prey to feed all the hungry bellies in camp.

He peered beneath the yew. Where were Milkweed and her kits? They'd seemed so frail when they'd arrived that he'd given them Birch and Alder's cozy nest, tucked deep under the dark, green branches. Birch and Alder had happily made new nests in a gap in the brambles.

As he searched the shadows, two pairs of eyes flashed beneath the bush. Milkweed's ginger-and-black pelt moved behind them. Clear Sky had found them on his border. His heart had ached to see them. The kits looked as scrawny as Fluttering Bird had been, while Milkweed had the same haunted look that used to darken Quiet Rain's eyes. He'd invited them to join his group even before Milkweed asked. But when she had given him Gray Wing's message, he'd felt a flicker of hope. Perhaps his brother was seeing sense in bringing all cats together after all.

A twinge of regret tugged at Clear Sky's belly. If only the other cats understood. They could be here now. More hunters would mean more food. Everyone would be safe, just as Fluttering Bird wanted.

Leaf-bare will be here for moons. It had brought him Milkweed, Thistle, and Clover. More hard frosts and snowfalls might help the moor cats and river cats realize they could not survive alone. And the pine forest might not turn out to be the prey-rich home Tall Shadow had dreamed of. *They'll see sense eventually.*

Star Flower's golden pelt caught his eye. She slid out from behind the oak and skirted the edge of the clearing. Stopping beside the yew, she stooped to look under the branches. "Hi, you two." There was a teasing purr in her mew as she called to Thistle and Clover. "Who wants to race me to the prey pile?"

Thistle and Clover scrambled eagerly into the light.

"There's prey?" Clover blinked.

"I told you I smelled mouse," Thistle told his sister.

"Milkweed said we shouldn't take prey unless it's offered." Clover's eyes were wide with worry.

Star Flower lifted her tail. "I'm offering."

Clear Sky snorted. Star Flower was acting as though it was her prey to give away! She'd hardly been here longer than the kits. She hadn't even been on the hunting patrol that had brought it back. She had lost none of her arrogance.

"Line up next to me," she told the kits as she crouched. "When I twitch my ear, *run*. The first cat to the prey pile gets first pick of the prey."

Thistle and Clover huddled beside her, their short tails flicking with excitement.

Milkweed squeezed out behind them. "Don't pick the best prey," she warned. "The hunters should get it."

Star Flower flashed her a look. "Don't teach them to take less than they deserve. They need to grow strong—one day, *they'll* be hunters."

Milkweed glanced around the camp, her gaze flicking nervously over the other cats. "I guess." She clearly did not feel comfortable depending on others for her food.

Star Flower twitched her ear, and Thistle and Clover sped away, their small paws pattering over the cold earth. Star Flower trotted after them, arriving a few paces behind as they skidded to a halt beside the prey pile.

"I got here first!" Thistle mewed.

"But I'm closest." Clover had stopped a whisker away from the mouse that Sparrow Fur had knocked from the pile. She snatched it in her jaws and began to drag it back toward Milkweed.

Thistle growled. "That's not fair."

"Don't you like mouse?" Star Flower asked, her eyes shining.

"Yes, but I want—"

Star Flower didn't let him finish. "Then go and help your sister carry it back to Milkweed."

The mouse had snagged on a jutting root at the edge of the clearing. Clover was tugging at it, her face crumpled with effort.

Thistle hurried toward her and, grabbing the mouse's tail in his teeth, unhooked it from the root. Clover blinked at him gratefully and they headed back to Milkweed, carrying the mouse between them.

As Star Flower sat back on her haunches and watched them go, Clear Sky narrowed his eyes. Thunder was watching the golden she-cat from beneath the oak. There was a glow in the young tom's gaze. *Was I wrong to let him bring her back to camp?* Clear Sky shifted his paws uneasily. The other cats had accepted her, but they still eyed her with mistrust.

On the night of her arrival, Leaf and Lightning Tail had followed Clear Sky out of camp and questioned his judgment.

"She's a traitor," Leaf had growled.

Lightning Tail had paced, frowning. "She lied to Thunder last time. She'll do it again."

Clear Sky had met their gazes steadily. "Thunder's no fool," he told them. "And what would she lie about? There's no cat left for her to betray us to. One Eye is dead. She has no one else. Would you have left her to fend for herself all leaf-bare?"

"Yes." Lightning Tail had kicked at the fallen leaves with a forepaw.

"Don't you think I have a *reason* for taking her in?" Clear Sky had argued. "Having her close means we can keep an eye on her. That way, if she *is* our enemy, we'll know it before she can harm us."

Leaf had tipped his head thoughtfully. "I guess."

Lightning Tail had curled his lip. "I'm watching her every move. *Especially* around Thunder."

Clear Sky's thoughts flicked back to the present. *Do they trust her yet?* Star Flower had shown nothing but loyalty so far. She'd hunted well, and had taken a damp nest among the beech roots without complaint. Lightning Tail had kept his word, watching her like a hawk and barging into any conversation she had with Thunder. But now Lightning Tail was out hunting, and Thunder was gazing wistfully at the golden she-cat. *He still cares for her.* Clear Sky moved on his branch as Star Flower stretched out her forepaws languorously, arching her back until her hind legs trembled. *She knows Thunder's watching her.* Clear Sky saw her gaze flick over her shoulder for a heartbeat before she picked a mouse from the prey pile and padded toward the yew.

Thunder turned hurriedly and began washing his tail as she passed.

I should have a talk with him, Clear Sky thought. *He's young. Feelings may cloud his judgment.* He got to his paws. *I'll do it later.* He knew that he'd need to pick the right moment if he wanted Thunder to listen to his warning.

Right now, he planned to patrol the borders of the forest. He wanted to find out whether any of the cats from the moor, pine forest, or river were hunting close to his scent lines. *Hunger will drive them to my prey-rich woods eventually, and we'll be together, just like Fluttering Bird wants.*

The bright skies had brought a fresh chill to the forest. He stepped toward the trunk and, scrabbling down from branch to branch, leaped down into the clearing. He tasted the air, wondering whether the fine weather would be warmed by rain or hardened by snow. The wind, tainted by the must of decaying leaf litter, gave no clue.

He padded around the edge of the clearing, nodding to Milkweed as he passed. Star Flower had settled beside the black-and-ginger queen and was sharing her mouse with Thistle, while Clover snatched bites from her mother's. Milkweed glanced up at Clear Sky, her eyes round with silent thanks. Her kits were sleeker already, though they'd only been here a few days. They would grow into good hunters.

Clear Sky dipped his head. "Would you like to join the next hunting party?" She might feel easier about taking prey if she'd helped hunt it.

Milkweed blinked eagerly. "Yes, please!"

"Can I go too?" Thistle looked up from his mouse.

"Not yet," Clear Sky told him. "But you can practice some

moves in camp." He glanced at Birch and Alder. Acorn Fur had rolled onto her side and was sleeping. The two young cats were pacing restlessly behind her, clearly looking for something to do. "Would you like to teach Thistle and Clover some hunting moves?" Clear Sky called.

Alder hurried over. "That would be great!"

Thistle sat up excitedly and licked his lips. "Can we start now?"

"Why not?" As Alder led Thistle toward the center of the clearing, Clear Sky headed for the bramble. He paused beside Pink Eyes and Quick Water, who were still chewing on the starling. "I'm going to check the borders," he meowed. "Keep watch on the camp."

Pink Eyes sniffed. "You should choose a cat with better eyesight."

Quick Water nudged the old tom. "No cat hears or smells better than you."

"I trust you won't miss anything." Clear Sky dipped his head.

Quick Water eyed him curiously. "Why are you patrolling the borders?" she asked. "I thought you welcomed strangers now."

"I still like to know who's coming and going," Clear Sky told her. He padded to the bramble wall and ducked through the gap between the branches.

Outside was cold. An icy wind whisked between the trees. No prey stirred, and he guessed that the tiny creatures of the forest were tucked deep in their warm burrows. Perhaps he should send out a hunting patrol at night as well as in the day. Mice and voles ventured out when the moon was high, but so did the owls and foxes that preyed on them. And the air would be too cold to scent anything but ice.

He followed the trail to the gully. One good rainfall and the narrow channel in the forest floor would be brimming with water, but for now it was dry. He hopped into it and headed toward the great sycamore.

He paused suddenly, the fur along his spine pricking as though it felt some creature's gaze. Was he being followed? He stopped and listened for paw steps. A blackbird shrilled overhead. Far away on the moor, a dog barked. He opened his mouth to taste the air—Lightning Tail and Blossom had passed this way, their stale scent carried away by the breeze rippling over him, heavy with the scent of the pine forest, but nothing else.

Clear Sky shook out his fur and picked his way farther along the gully, telling himself that he was just being jumpy.

As the woods rose to one side, he hopped out of the gully and began to climb the slope toward the sycamore. As he neared the top, a fresh scent touched his nose; not all prey was in its burrow. The thick layer of leaf litter beneath the sycamore, crawling with tasty bugs, must have tempted something from its shelter. He opened his mouth and tasted the musky scent of a vole.

Stiffening, he dropped into a hunting crouch and drew himself forward, one paw step at a time, toward the crest of the slope. As the earth flattened, he scanned the forest floor.

The ancient roots of the sycamore snaked into the ground. Movement flickered beside one of the gnarled stems. Clear Sky froze. The vole was snuffling at a seed pod, its tiny ears twitching.

He fixed his gaze on it, forcing his tail to stay still as he crept forward. His heart quickened as he closed in. The vole had picked up the seed pod and was nibbling at one side. Three tail-lengths from it, Clear Sky narrowed his eyes, judging his leap. If he pushed hard enough, he could land square on the vole and pin it against the sycamore root. His fur rippled along his spine. Bunching his legs beneath him, he waggled his hindquarters. Then he leaped.

Dead leaves fluttered out behind him. The vole turned at the sound, its eyes widening in terror. Fast as lightning, it scuttled out of sight. Clear Sky landed clumsily, thumping against the sycamore root.

"Mouse dung!" he hissed, frustration flashing though him.

Leaves rustled behind and he turned.

Star Flower was standing at the top of the slope. Her lustrous tail was high and her eyes glittered with amusement. "Nice try."

Heat flooded beneath Clear Sky's pelt. "You scared it off." He straightened angrily. "It probably smelled your scent."

She padded closer, her tail swishing. "At least *something* did."

"You were *downwind*." Clear Sky grunted. Was she *trying* to embarrass him?

"Perhaps I could give you some tips." She stopped a tail-length away. "I've been hunting here all my life."

Clear Sky climbed onto the root and sat down. "I don't need tips, thanks. I'm a great hunter." He lifted a paw and began washing it.

"I know that." Star Flower rounded the end of the root, where it plunged into the earth, stopping on the other side. "But you weren't born in a forest. You don't have the same feel for it as me. Leaf and Nettle share an instinct. You've seen them hunt. You must have noticed how they can blend into the woods in a way you'll never be able to."

Clear Sky stopped washing. "*That's* why I took them into my group," he said, his chest puffing with pride. Any cat could hunt, but few had the sense to recognize and use the skills of other cats. He leaned toward Star Flower. "Perhaps I should give you some tips about leadership."

Her green eyes glowed with a challenge. "Perhaps you should."

Clear Sky snorted. *Proud young cat!* "What are you doing here anyway?"

"You looked lonely, leaving the camp by yourself," she told him.

"I don't get lonely," Clear Sky snapped.

Star Flower eyed him for a moment. "Really?" She padded forward until she was just a whisker away from him.

He hopped down from the tree root and faced her. "Go back to camp and leave me alone."

"It's too . . . *cozy* in camp. I'm not used to being around so many cats. For most of my life, it was just me and One Eye."

"Surely you had littermates?" Clear Sky bristled with

irritation the moment he spoke. He'd allowed her to draw him into a conversation.

"They died with my mother." Her green eyes showed no expression.

Clear Sky's paws pricked uneasily. Did she feel no grief? "How did they die?"

"I don't know." Star Flower shrugged. "I was too young to remember, and One Eye refused to ever speak of them."

Clear Sky strode past her and gazed away between the trees. He wasn't going to feel sympathy for this cat. This was probably how she had won Thunder's affection. "That must have been hard for you," he meowed coldly. "But every cat holds some tragedy in their heart."

"Like you." She moved closer until her thick pelt brushed his.

Clear Sky flinched away and glared at her. "Go back to camp."

"We're more alike than you think." Her green gaze seemed to burn into his.

"We're nothing alike," he snapped. "I've never betrayed any cat."

"I'm not sure Gray Wing would agree with that," Star Flower pointed out. "Or Thunder. Or Jagged Peak." She paused. "Or Rainswept Flower."

Claw Sky could feel his claws extended, digging into the earth. How dare she remind him that he'd killed a cat he'd grown up with?

He had been trying to make amends for it every day since.

Star Flower lowered her voice. "I *understand* you, Clear Sky.

You've had to make hard decisions to protect the cats in your care. And sometimes it's meant doing things you've regretted." She held his gaze. "If I could take back some of the things I've done, I would."

He blinked. Was she *sorry* for her betrayal?

Her eyes glimmered as though lit by starlight. Her dark pupils looked like flowers. To Clear Sky, it was almost like the five petals of the Blazing Star seemed to shine in her eyes.

"I know you don't trust me," she murmured. "I don't deserve your trust. But I will try to show you that you can count on me. Once I choose my allies, I am willing to die for them. For all my mistakes, I never betrayed my father. And, if you trust me, I will never betray you."

Clear Sky fought to drag his gaze away, but he was caught in the green depths of her eyes. *I will never betray you.* As her words echoed in his mind, his heart ached with hope. Could it be true? Had he finally found a cat who had complete faith in him? Who would follow him without question through thick and thin?

Wind rattled the branches overhead, breaking the spell. Clear Sky turned away. "Go back to camp, Star Flower," he meowed firmly. "If you want to earn my trust—and the trust of the other cats—then you'll have to work for it. Help Milkweed groom the last of the fleas from her pelt. Get fresh moss for Pink Eyes's nest. His fur is thin, so he feels the cold more than most cats. Make sure Thistle and Clover never go hungry again." He faced Star Flower, searching her gaze. Would she obey him?

She dipped her head. "Okay." Then she turned and headed back through the trees. As she disappeared down the slope, sunshine reached through the branches like claws and raked her golden pelt.

Clear Sky stared after her, unable to move—he felt as though his paws had grown roots. His tail twitched.

Perhaps he'd been wrong about her. There was more to Star Flower than met the eye.

CHAPTER 10
✤

Thunder stretched in his nest and blinked sleep from his eyes. It was morning on a new day, but there was no sunlight in sight. Thick gray clouds washed the camp with drizzle. A fat drop of water splashed onto his muzzle. With a shiver, he hopped out.

"You're awake at last," Owl Eyes huffed as he landed beside the young tom.

He was sitting on the edge of the clearing, watching Birch and Alder train Thistle and Clover.

"Is it late?" Thunder searched the clouds beyond the tree-tops for some sign of the sun.

"Clear Sky's already sent out hunting patrols." Owl Eyes didn't pull his gaze from the young cats. "It's their second day training."

Birch and Alder circled the clearing, their paws pattering softly over the muddy earth. Thistle and Clover crouched at the center, their fur plastered against their thin frames as they concentrated on their hunting crouches.

"Keep your tail down!" Alder told Thistle.

"Tuck your hind paws tighter under you," Birch called to Clover.

Clover frowned. "But that makes it harder to jump."

"It will feel that way to begin with," Birch reassured the ginger-and-white kit. "But once you've gotten the hang of it, you'll be able to jump farther. And the farther you can jump, the less stalking you'll have to do."

Owl Eyes's tail flicked irritably behind him. "What's wrong with stalking?"

Ignoring the gray tom, Clover narrowed her eyes and bunched up her hindquarters. "Is that better?"

"Great!" Birch lifted his tail. "Now jump."

Clover hurled herself forward. As she pushed off from the ground, her hind paws slithered on the mud, and she fell sprawling onto her belly.

Thistle purred with amusement. "You look like you're trying to swim!"

Clover whipped around and glared at him. "*You* try it, mouse-brain!"

Thistle clamped his mouth shut and leaped. He sailed across the clearing and landed neatly, a muzzle-length from Birch. Purring loudly, he looked at the ginger tom. "How was that?"

"You're going to be a great hunter," Birch told him proudly.

Clover snorted and dropped onto her belly again, tucking her hind paws tightly beneath her. Grunting with effort, she leaped. This time, she landed skillfully, controlling her skid as her paws hit the wet earth. She blinked at Alder. "Better?"

"*Much!*" Alder congratulated the kit.

Owl Eyes sniffed. "I still think you should be teaching

them how to stalk, not to jump."

Alder glanced at the gray tom. "Clear Sky asked *us* to train them, not you."

Birch joined his sister. "You're just in a bad mood because he chose Sparrow Fur for the second hunting patrol."

Owl Eyes flattened his ears. "I hunt better than she does in the rain," he muttered. "Sparrow Fur doesn't like getting her paws wet." He stalked across the clearing and curled down among the roots of the beech, his pelt spiked from the rain. Miserably, he shoved his nose under his paw and closed his eyes.

I should be out on patrol, Thunder thought, tearing his gaze away to scan the camp. Where was Clear Sky?

He recognized Cloud Spots's voice beneath the yew.

"Chew these leaves, Milkweed."

Thunder's nose twitched at the smell of tansy.

"It's just a slight sickness in your chest," Cloud Spots was saying. "The leaves should clear it. Send Clover for more if you still feel bad later."

The long-furred black tom came out from beneath the yew and padded to the short, steep bank beyond the oak. Brambles spilled over the muddy overhang beside the hollow where Clear Sky made his nest. They smelled like a pungent meadow. Cloud Spots slid behind them. He'd been collecting herbs for days and stashing them among the prickly stems.

"Thunder!" Clover called to him. "Watch me jump!"

Thunder looked as she crouched and leaped across the clearing.

He'd been pleased that Clear Sky had taken the starving family in—even happier when he'd heard Milkweed pass on Gray Wing's message. Perhaps Clear Sky and Gray Wing's relationship was gently mending. But it was strange that Gray Wing had been on the moor. He'd gone to live among the pines with Tall Shadow. What had driven him back to his old home?

"Well?"

He realized Clover was staring at him expectantly. "Very good," he told her.

Clover purred. "I can jump as far as Thistle now."

"No you can't!" Thistle lifted his tail indignantly.

Birch stepped between the kits. "Why don't we practice stalking, like Owl Eyes suggested?"

Owl Eyes's ear twitched, but he didn't lift his muzzle from beneath his paw.

Thunder caught Birch's eye. "Where's Clear Sky?" Perhaps it wasn't too late to persuade his father to let him join a patrol.

Birch glanced at the branch that overhung the clearing. That was where Clear Sky liked to sit and watch over the camp. It was empty. Birch shrugged. "Perhaps he's gone to make dirt."

Thunder padded to the bottom of the oak. His father's scent was still fresh on the bark, which meant he probably hadn't gotten far. Thunder leaped up the steep bank and padded over the wet grass beyond. "Clear Sky?" he called.

The bracken at the edge of the camp rustled and Clear Sky slid out. "What is it?"

"I'd like to join one of the hunting patrols," Thunder told him. "Which way did you send them? I'm sure I can catch up."

"I want you to stay here." Clear Sky marched past him and paused at the edge of the slope. "Someone needs to watch over the kits."

"They've got you, and Birch and Alder," Thunder argued. "*And* Owl Eyes."

Clear Sky turned his head. "If you wanted to be on a hunting patrol, you should have woken earlier."

Was his father punishing him for sleeping late? "I'm sorry. I'm still used to the light on the moor. In the forest when it's cloudy, it's sometimes hard to tell day from night."

"No other cat here has that problem." As Clear Sky jumped into the clearing, Lightning Tail and Leaf pushed their way through the camp entrance. Thick wads of moss dangled from their jaws.

Lightning Tail dropped his soft, green bundle. "There's enough to line two nests here," he told Leaf.

Leaf spat out his moss. "We'll never get it dry in this weather."

"Let's spread it out beside the holly," Lightning Tail suggested. "The ground catches the sun there. If the clouds clear, it'll dry in no time."

Thunder turned to look pleadingly at Clear Sky. "Lightning Tail and Leaf are here now," he pressed. "Let me go hunting. Even if I don't catch up with the patrols, I can hunt on my own. It's leaf-bare. We need all the prey we can get."

"I need you to stay. *I'm* going on border patrol." Clear Sky met his gaze. "Besides, I don't want cats hunting alone."

Thunder blinked. "Why not?"

"All prey should be shared," Clear Sky told him briskly. "If we hunt together, then we will be less tempted to keep our catch to ourselves."

Thunder bristled. "You don't trust us?"

Clear Sky lifted his chin. "Of course I do. But it's my duty as leader to keep you from temptation."

Thunder glared at him. *Why do I keep forgetting how arrogant he is?* He didn't argue. Instead, he lowered his tail obediently. "If you're going on patrol, let me come with you. You've changed the borders so many times, I'm still having trouble telling the old markers from new. Perhaps you could help me."

This wasn't true; he could easily tell the difference between a stale scent and a fresh one, but he was desperate to make up for oversleeping. If he flattered Clear Sky, his father might let him join the patrol.

Clear Sky whisked his tail. "If you haven't learned that by now, you never will," he grunted. "I'm patrolling alone. Every cat needs solitude from time to time." Before Thunder could object, he marched toward the bramble entrance. Thunder watched him go, uneasiness worming beneath his pelt. Clear Sky had never wanted solitude before. Why now?

As his father pushed his way out of camp, Thunder hurried across the clearing toward Lightning Tail.

"I want you to watch the camp," he whispered quickly.

Lightning Tail was spreading his strips of moss over the wet earth with a paw. "Why?"

"Clear Sky asked me to do it, but I want to follow him."

Lightning Tail looked up. "Why? Where's he going?"

"He says he's going to patrol the borders," Thunder breathed. "I wanted to come but he's *ordered* me to stay in camp."

Lightning Tail shrugged. "Perhaps he wants to be alone."

"That's what *he* said," Thunder conceded. "But I'm following him anyway. What if he runs into a fox or a dog?"

Lightning Tail's whiskers twitched teasingly. "You're just being nosy."

"That's not true," Thunder snorted.

Lightning Tail straightened up. "Then I'm coming with you."

"*Now* who's being nosy?" Thunder teased.

Leaf looked up from his scraps of moss. "What are you two whispering about?"

"We need you to guard the camp," Thunder told him. "We're going out on patrol."

Leaf shrugged and smoothed a wide piece of moss with his paw. "Okay."

Thunder hurried toward the bramble wall, Lightning Tail at his heels. He ducked through the entrance tunnel, his mouth open as he tasted for Clear Sky's scent.

Instinctively, he looked toward the gully his father had led him along on their last patrol together, but Clear Sky's scent drifted from the other direction. Thunder followed it. Keeping low, he brushed past a clump of bracken and slid beneath a branch.

"He's heading for the river," Lightning Tail whispered from behind.

Thunder's tail twitched. There was a boundary at the river's edge. Clear Sky didn't patrol it very often. He believed that the river, which flowed between River Ripple's marshes and the oak woods, was enough to keep inquisitive rogues and kittypets from crossing into their territory.

Perhaps he was hoping to find some new recruits, just like he'd found Milkweed, Pink Eyes, and Blossom. Was that the purpose of his patrols? As Thunder pushed through a stretch of long grass, he wondered again at the change in his father. The leader who had fought so hard to defend his borders was now happy to open them to any cat.

The thought cheered him, and he leaped the last few clumps of grass and began to follow the forest floor as it sloped upward. He hurried onward watchfully. He didn't want Clear Sky to see that he'd followed him. Once he'd caught up to his father, he would only make his presence known if there was trouble—an unfriendly rogue or a hungry fox.

"Can you see him?" Lightning Tail fell in beside him as they neared the top of the ridge.

"No, but he can't be far ahead." Clear Sky's scent trail was fresh, his paw prints easy to make out on the damp forest floor. Beyond the crest, flattened grass showed where Clear Sky had bounded down to the river. Thunder scanned the slope, looking for Clear Sky's pale gray pelt. He could see the river glimmering beyond the trees, but no sign of his father other than the trail of crushed grass. He broke into a run, leaping down the slope, slowing only as he approached the tree line. The river flowed beyond, babbling lazily as it washed the stony bank.

Lightning Tail pulled ahead and peeked out from the trees. "He's not on the shore," he hissed over his shoulder.

Thunder pointed his nose downstream. "His scent leads that way, along the river."

"He must be heading for the flat rocks," Lightning Tail suggested.

The flat rocks were large boulders that rose above the river farther downstream. The first time Thunder had come to live with his father, they'd sunned themselves there, relishing the warmth of the sun-blanched stone. Now he sniffed the grass, picking up Clear Sky's scent. "Let's see," he told Lightning Tail. "Come on."

Keeping to the shelter of the trees, he headed for the boulders. The rain had eased, and sun was breaking through the thick, gray clouds. Before long, light glimmered beyond the trees as sunlight flashed on the rain-washed stone.

Thunder stopped and tasted the air. Clear Sky's scent was stronger here. He peered out from the trees at the wide expanse of stone. A light breeze whispered through the tree-tops above him, and the river gurgled somewhere far below the edge of the rocky outcrop.

"There he is!" Lightning Tail's whisper sounded in Thunder's ear.

Stiffening, he followed his friend's gaze.

Clear Sky was sitting in the middle of the flat rocks, his

ears pricked. He was scanning the forest that crowded the edges of the stone, tail twitching excitedly. Thunder narrowed his eyes. Had Clear Sky spotted prey?

A familiar mew sounded from the trees beyond. "So, you decided to take me up on that hunting lesson?"

Thunder froze as Star Flower stalked from the trees and crossed the stone. She stopped just in front of Clear Sky and raised her bushy tail. The sun's rays flashed through the clouds and turned her golden pelt to fire.

Lightning Tail stiffened beside Thunder. "What's *she* doing here?"

Thunder didn't answer. Jealousy was scorching through his chest as he watched the she-cat weave around Clear Sky. A low growl rumbled in his throat. *No wonder he didn't want me to patrol with him.*

"I'm not here for hunting lessons." Clear Sky blocked Star Flower's path.

She stopped, her eyes glittering playfully. "Then why *are* you here? I invited you to meet me so I could teach you the ways of the forest."

Clear Sky brushed around Star Flower, his eyes never leaving hers. He stopped close to her muzzle. "You don't need to teach me anything," he meowed. "I've learned all I need to know. And I've learned it the hard way."

"I told you," Star Flower purred throatily. "We have more in common than you think."

Clear Sky half closed his eyes. "Perhaps we do."

Star Flower let her tail slide beneath Clear Sky's chin.

Thunder curled his claws deep into the soft earth, imagining its softness flowing beneath his muzzle. She had used the same gesture when talking to him.

He stared at his father, willing Clear Sky to step away from the treacherous she-cat. But Clear Sky stood still while Star Flower padded slowly around him.

"You were going to give me some lessons in leadership," she murmured.

"Not yet." Clear Sky's eyes flashed. "Before you can lead, you must learn how to follow."

He's encouraging *her!* Rage surged beneath Thunder's pelt. Then fear. He knew better than any cat how Star Flower could turn against those she pretended to care for. She'd once convinced him that she wanted to join his group—that she wanted to be his mate. But she'd only been spying for One Eye. She'd told him she truly cared for him, but only after One Eye had died.

The anger burned in his belly. Why had she told him that? When she'd reappeared last half-moon, a tiny hope had sparked in his heart that she'd returned to the forest for him.

He watched, his pelt bristling, as Star Flower lay down, her tail swishing over the stone. She looked up at Clear Sky, her radiant green eyes catching the light. "Enjoy the sunshine with me."

Thunder turned away and marched through the forest, growling under his breath.

Lightning Tail bounded after him. "Thunder!"

"I should have known," Thunder snarled. "She never felt anything for me."

Lightning Tail barged across his path. "Wait!"

Thunder glared at him. "Are you going to say that you told me so?"

Hurt sparked in Lightning Tail's gaze, and Thunder felt instantly guilty. "I'm sorry." He hung his head.

"I'm just glad you saw this before you did something mouse-brained like telling her you loved her." Lightning Tail suddenly leaned closer. "You didn't, did you?"

"No!" Thunder snapped. "I'm not *that* dumb."

Lightning Tail glanced back toward the rocks. "It looks like Clear Sky is."

Thunder's heart lurched. He'd been so wrapped up in his own feelings, he hadn't considered his father. "She's using him!"

"What for?" Lightning Tail's eyes darkened with worry.

"Because she can," Thunder growled bitterly. "Because he's the leader, and becoming his mate would give her power and influence."

"But he knows she's treacherous," Lightning Tail reasoned. "He must realize what she's doing and why. Perhaps he's just seeing how far she's willing to go."

Thunder nodded slowly. Clear Sky's main goal had been bringing the cats together, not finding a mate. "Of course. He's letting Star Flower play her stupid games, making a fool of herself." He stared blankly at Lightning Tail, his gaze clouding. *Was that all it was with me too? A stupid game?* Pain seared his heart. He shook out his pelt, fighting grief. "Leave me alone, Lightning Tail. I need to think."

Lightning Tail stared at him anxiously. "You're not going back there to confront them?"

"No." Thunder retuned his friend's gaze solemnly. "Clear Sky can make his own decisions. I don't want anything to do with Star Flower." He saw Lightning Tail's fur smooth.

"Don't stay out too long," the black tom urged.

Thunder dipped his head. "I just need to clear my thoughts."

He watched Lightning Tail head away until he was no more than a shadow moving through the wilting undergrowth. Making for the river, Thunder broke from the trees and gazed over River Ripple's marshes. The reeds stirred and bent in the breeze. A gust whipped Thunder's whiskers against his cheeks. As he glanced downstream to where the boulders rose above the water, a deep ache twisted his heart.

I really thought she had come back for me. *But there's only one cat Star Flower cares about, and that's Star Flower.*

CHAPTER 11

❧

The weak leaf-bare sun was sliding toward the treetops before Clear Sky returned to camp.

Thunder had been watching out for him. His pelt twitched with annoyance as his father padded across the clearing and jumped past his nest among the oak roots onto the short steep bank beyond. He'd been trying to ignore the anger churning in his belly all afternoon, but he couldn't push Clear Sky and Star Flower from his thoughts.

He swallowed back a growl as Thorn nudged past him.

"Sorry." The gray she-cat dipped her head. "I'm heading for the prey pile, but the camp's a bit crowded."

Thunder snorted. "Is it worth the effort?" He glanced at the meager pile of fresh-kill. Three mice and a squirrel weren't going to feed so many mouths. It was mouse-brained of Clear Sky to keep every cat in camp when there was a whole forest full of prey.

Thorn picked her way past Pink Eyes and Quick Water, who were lounging beside the holly bush. She nodded politely to Milkweed, who sheltered beneath the yew, coughing from time to time. Cloud Spots crouched beside the sickly queen, chewing leaves into a pulp, while Thistle and Clover scrambled through the branches above them.

Lightning Tail was sharing tongues with Acorn Fur while Birch and Alder badgered them with questions about life on the moor.

"Did you really hunt in rabbit tunnels?" Alder's eyes were wide.

Lightning Tail shrugged. "I preferred hunting above ground."

Acorn Fur shivered. "Not me. I liked the shelter of the tunnels—there's no wind to ruffle your fur."

"But how could you see what you were doing?" Birch asked.

"With our whiskers, ears, and noses, of course," Acorn Fur told him.

"I never got a chance to hunt in the tunnels." Sparrow Fur sprawled sleepily at the edge of the clearing while Owl Eyes paced around her. "I was too young."

"Now we never have a chance to hunt *anywhere*!" Owl Eyes flashed a look at Clear Sky. He was clearly still angry that he had spent the day in camp.

Blossom wove past him. "I'm sure Clear Sky will let you hunt tomorrow."

"Yeah, right." Owl Eyes didn't look convinced.

Thunder felt a flash of satisfaction. Clear Sky's dumb hunting rules were ruffling fur among his campmates. They weren't even effective. He glanced at the prey pile again. Nettle and Leaf were lying like guards beside the pitiful collection of fresh-kill, eyeing their campmates warily.

Clear Sky called from the bank. "Thunder! Are both hunting patrols back?"

"Can't you tell?" Thunder snapped. The camp was overflowing with cats!

Clear Sky narrowed his eyes. "Is something wrong?"

Lightning Tail flashed Thunder a warning gaze.

It's not the time to confront him about Star Flower, Thunder thought, puffing out his chest and heading for his father. Leaping up the muddy bank, he landed beside Clear Sky and gave a curt meow. "It's not working."

"What's not working?" Clear Sky tipped his head.

"Sending out two hunting patrols each morning and then wasting the rest of the day with everyone cooped up in camp." Thunder felt righteous anger rising in his chest. "It's mouse-brained."

The fur bristled on Clear Sky's shoulders.

"Look at that prey pile." Thunder nodded toward it. "Most cats will go hungry tonight."

Clear Sky padded away from the edge of the bank, moving closer to the bracken. "Keep your voice down," he cautioned. "We've already discussed hunting. You know why I have to organize it so carefully."

"Because you don't trust us." Thunder followed his father out of hearing of their campmates. "But that doesn't explain why you only send out two patrols a day. I could be hunting right now. If you're scared that I'll eat half my catch, send Leaf and Nettle with me to keep watch." He snorted. "It would give them something to do. And what about Owl Eyes? He's been desperate to go hunting all day, but instead he's had to stay here, and tonight he'll sleep with an empty belly. I bet he's starting to wish he'd joined Tall Shadow's group—they probably hunt from dawn to dusk." He stared straight into Clear Sky's piercing blue eyes, hoping he'd touched a nerve. How could his father be so dumb? Dumb about hunting, and even *dumber* about Star Flower!

What a rabbit-brain!

Clear Sky returned his gaze steadily. "Do you want to hunt the forest dry in the first moon of leaf-bare?"

"No!" Thunder hissed. "But if you send out smaller groups and send them out regularly, we could hunt the *whole territory*. If we take a little from everywhere, we'd have more to eat. No cat would be stuck in camp, and the prey would last through to newleaf."

"I see you've thought about this." Clear Sky's ears twitched irritably. "Maybe *you* should be leader." There was sarcasm in his mew.

Thunder scowled at him. "On the moor, Tall Shadow and Gray Wing treated me like one of the leaders."

"This isn't the moor," Clear Sky snapped. "We do things differently in the forest. This group has *one* leader, and that's me. On the moor, no cat knew who was in charge. Every time there was a problem, you had to gossip like a bunch of starlings before you actually did anything about it. Here, my cats trust *me* to make the decisions. I don't need your advice."

Rage bubbled up from Thunder's belly. "You need *some cat's* advice!"

Clear Sky eyed him, suddenly cautious. "Are you really this angry about hunting patrols?"

"I saw you!" Thunder blurted. "You didn't go on patrol—you went to meet Star Flower."

Clear Sky's hackles lifted. "I ordered you to stay in camp."

"I'm not as easy to boss around as Owl Eyes." Thunder held his gaze. "What were you doing with her?"

"It's none of your business." Clear Sky bristled.

"You know she can't be trusted," Thunder warned. "She might make promises, but they're all lies. She only cares about herself." He leaned closer. "You trusted her father, and look where *that* got you."

Clear Sky flinched as though Thunder had clawed his muzzle.

Thunder backed away. Had he gone too far? "I'm only warning you because *I* fell for her lies once before," he meowed quickly. "I don't want to see her betray you the way she betrayed me. I'm thinking of us all. Trusting Star Flower will not end well."

Clear Sky's gaze suddenly softened. "I know she hurt you, Thunder."

Hope flashed in Thunder's chest as he saw sympathy in his father's eyes. "Does that mean you'll stop seeing her?"

Clear Sky looked past Thunder toward the clearing. "Take Owl Eyes and go hunting."

"Will you stop seeing her?" Thunder pressed.

"I'll think about what you've said." Clear Sky avoided his gaze. "Go hunting. That's what you wanted, wasn't it?"

Frustrated, Thunder leaped into the clearing and crossed the camp toward Owl Eyes.

"Thunder." A throaty mew caught his ear.

He turned to see Star Flower ducking into camp. He halted as she padded toward him and narrowed his eyes. "What do you want?"

Her golden pelt glowed in the afternoon light. "I smelled your scent by the flat rocks this morning."

"So?"

Her green eyes narrowed. "What were you doing there?"

"Why do you care?" Bitterness stung Thunder's throat. "Have you been following me?"

"I was following *Clear Sky*," Thunder growled. "I was worried about him being out in the woods alone."

Star Flower gave an amused purr. "I think Clear Sky is old enough to take care of himself, don't you? Besides, he wasn't alone. He had me."

Rage surged beneath Thunder's pelt. "Stay away from my father," he hissed.

Star Flower blinked. "Why? We get along so well and—" She paused, her gaze suddenly softening. "Oh, Thunder. I'm so sorry."

Thunder shifted his paws, his pelt burning. He looked away. "What for?"

"I didn't know you still had feelings for me," she gushed. "I thought you stopped caring for me when you found out who my father was."

Thunder stiffened, surprised to find hope pricking in his

chest. Was that regret in her mew? Did she still care about him?

"We were never meant to be together, Thunder." Star Flower shook her head sadly.

The ground seemed to move beneath his paws.

"I thought you understood that," she went on. "You and I are so different. Clear Sky and I have much more in common. I understand him. I know why he's so tough and ambitious. And *I* don't judge him for it—I admire him."

Thunder curled his lip. "You just like him because you think he's like *your* father," he hissed. "Well, he's not. He's far better than that fox-heart. You're pathetic, always looking for some cat to make you feel good about yourself. When are you going to learn to stand on your own four paws?" Tail lashing, he called to Owl Eyes. "Come on. Clear Sky wants us to go hunting."

Leaf looked up sharply. "Can I come?"

"Why not?" Thunder marched toward the entrance. He could take any cat he liked—he didn't need Clear Sky's permission. And Leaf would be in a far better mood if he had a chance to flex his claws on prey instead of moss.

He ducked through the bramble wall, Leaf on his tail.

Owl Eyes burst out after them, his pelt pricking with excitement. "Where should we hunt?" He gazed around the woods happily. Clouds were bubbling overhead as the sun sank behind the trees.

"There's a beech copse beyond the sycamore," Leaf suggested. "The nuts will attract prey."

Thunder nodded. "You lead." He wasn't going to be like Clear Sky and insist every cat follow in his paw steps.

Leaf bounded away and leaped the gully. Owl Eyes chased after him, tail high. Thunder broke into a run, relieved to feel his paws pounding the forest floor. The anger that had been pulsing beneath his fur melted as he raced after his campmates. Leaf charged up the slope and hared past the sycamore. Owl Eyes, smaller and lighter, moved fast through the forest. He zigzagged easily between the undergrowth, veering around a bramble and ducking beneath a jutting branch. Thunder kept a tail-length behind, wincing as a thorn snagged his thick pelt and leaping over the branch instead of ducking under. He could feel power surging into his paws as they thrummed over the earth. Wind streamed through his whiskers. Ahead, the beech copse showed among the other trees. Dark orange leaves clung to their branches, making the forest here glow like Star Flower's pelt.

Thunder pushed the thought away, skidding to a halt where Leaf and Owl Eyes had stopped beside a swath of bracken. Leaf nodded toward the forest ahead. The ground was littered with beechnuts. Roots showed just above the soil, winding over one another to make a low forest of nooks and shadows. It was a perfect spot for prey.

Thunder nodded to Owl Eyes. "Go around to the far side of the copse," he whispered. "If we flush out the prey, it'll run toward you."

Owl Eyes nodded and quietly picked his way around the trees.

Thunder dropped into a crouch and watched the tangle of beech roots.

Leaf squatted beside him, his mouth open as he tasted for scents. His muzzle twitched. "Thanks for letting me come," he murmured. "I'm sick of waiting in camp for some other cat to bring me food." He glanced sideways at Thunder. "How did you persuade Clear Sky to change his mind?"

"I just suggested it would be better to send out more patrols," Thunder answered lightly.

"Of course it is!" Leaf snorted. "What's the point of us all sitting around when the prey pile's half-empty?" The gray-and-white tom shook his head. "Clear Sky's gone soft since the battle."

Thunder snapped his head around. Was Leaf being disloyal?

Leaf's ear twitched uneasily. "I mean, he's still *Clear Sky*," he backtracked. "But all this talk of uniting and taking in sick, half-starved cats . . . It's not how he used to be." Leaf tucked his paws tighter under him.

Thunder shifted to rebalance himself. He could hear prey rustling the leaves between the beech roots. Owl Eyes's pelt showed in the shadows beyond. "Clear Sky's just doing what the spirit cats asked of him," he whispered to Leaf. "*They're* the ones who want us to unite."

"*Spirit* cats don't get hungry." Leaf gazed ahead, his eyes flicking one way, then the other, as he scanned for prey. "Why don't *they* look after the sick and the weak? Here in the real world, strength is the only thing that counts. What's the point in hunting for cats who can't hunt for themselves? They just sap the strength of the whole group."

Thunder glanced at his campmate. *Does he really believe that?* Of course, strength was important. But surely it was possible to be strong *and* look after the weak? "Everyone has their own strengths," he pointed out. "No one hears as well as Pink Eyes. And Jagged Peak has grown tough and practical because he's had to fight every paw step of the way."

"He may be tough, but can he *hunt*?" Leaf meowed darkly. "You've forgotten how long leaf-bare is. There are lean moons ahead, and it's not so easy to be softhearted when your belly's empty."

Thunder flexed his claws. Leaf was sounding like Clear Sky in the days before the battle. "All we have to do is persuade Clear Sky to change the hunting patrols. Then there'll be enough prey for all of us. You'll see."

A tiny shape scuttled through the leaves and darted over a root.

Mouse! Excitement surged through Thunder's muscles. Before Leaf could move, he raced for it. The mouse was heading for a gap where the root burrowed into the earth. Leaping, Thunder hooked it with a claw. He landed awkwardly, bending his other forepaw beneath him. Pain flashed through his flank as he hit the root, feeling the wind knocked from his body.

Squeaking, the mouse wriggled free of his grasp.

Leaf barged past and slammed his forepaws down hard on the ground. "Got it!"

As the black-and-white tom spoke, leaves exploded a tail-length away. Thunder jerked up his head and saw a rabbit racing away between the trees. They must have startled it when they caught the mouse. He struggled to his paws, his flank aching where the root had bruised it. His injured paw folded limply beneath him. *Mouse dung!*

"It's okay! I've got it!" Owl Eyes's triumphant yowl rang through the trees. He was on the rabbit's tail. He lunged fast and caught it between his forepaws.

Thunder shook out his weak paw until the pain eased. The scent of fresh-kill touched his nose.

Leaf paced around him, tail high. The mouse dangled from his jaws. Owl Eyes trotted toward them, the rabbit swinging beneath his chin.

"I told you!" Thunder purred. "With enough hunting patrols, there'll be prey enough for everyone."

Thunder led the way into camp, his fur fluffed with pride. On the way back, he had spotted a squirrel rummaging beneath the sycamore. He'd caught it as it tried to scoot up the trunk. Now he crossed the clearing and dropped it on the prey pile. "No hungry bellies tonight," he meowed loudly, scanning the camp for his father. Clear Sky had to see now that more hunting patrols would keep the group well fed.

Lightning Tail hurried to meet him, his gaze dark.

"Where's Clear Sky?" Thunder asked.

Lightning Tail scowled. "He left the camp," the black tom growled softly. "With Star Flower."

Thunder bristled. Clear Sky had ignored his warning. *He just sent me hunting to get me out of the way!* Blood roared in his ears. "Did he say when he'd be back?"

Lightning Tail glanced toward the bramble entrance, keeping his mew low. "All he said was that he'd be back later."

Then I'll wait. Trembling with rage, Thunder swallowed back a growl. *I have something to tell him. Something he will not want to hear.*

CHAPTER 12

❧

Clear Sky pounded down the slope, swerving between the trees. The ground had dried since the morning's rain, but the leaves were still slippery underpaw, and he skidded as he dodged around a bramble spilling across his path.

Star Flower was ahead. He could see her golden pelt glowing as she ran like a patch of sunshine moving between the trees.

Digging his claws into the soft earth, he regained his balance and pushed harder. He reached the bottom of the slope a moment after Star Flower.

"Do you still think you know the forest better than I do?" Her words came in gasps as she caught her breath. "I bet you've never been here before."

"Yes, I have," Clear Sky puffed.

Wilted ferns clumped between slender rowans. Beyond them, he could see a grassy clearing. *Have I been here before?* He narrowed his eyes. *Of course!* He recognized the wall of rocks on the far side of the clearing. As he padded into the clearing, wet grass brushed his paws. It was getting late, and dew glittered in the late sunshine. If the skies remained clear, it would turn to frost.

Star Flower stopped beside him as he gazed at the sun dipping behind the rocks. Its orange rays melted on top of the stones for a moment before disappearing. Clear Sky felt chilly shadows swallow him. "Come on." Chasing the setting sun, he leaped onto a jutting stone. He scrambled from boulder to boulder until he reached the top.

Star Flower looked up from the clearing below. "Watch out for the snakes."

"Snakes?" Clear Sky peered over the edge, his pelt prickling.

"They hide in the crevices between the stones." Star Flower leaped nimbly after him. He watched her, expecting any moment for a snake to dart from a gap and bite her.

She stopped beside him, her whiskers twitching as she met his anxious gaze. "Don't worry. One Eye taught me how to kill snakes."

Clear Sky blinked at her in surprise.

"Have you ever killed one?" A mischievous glint flashed in her eye.

"I've never had to."

"You should try it." She shrugged. "They don't taste bad, especially in the middle of a long leaf-bare. One Eye would bring me hunting here when there was no other prey in the forest. Snakes are sluggish when it's cold. Easy to catch, if you can find them."

Clear Sky stared at the she-cat, his tail twitching. What other secrets of the forest did Star Flower know? With this wily she-cat at his side, who knew what he might achieve. She might be able to help him work out a way to unite all the cats. Sunshine warmed his back. They had escaped the shadows below and caught up to the setting sun, which glittered between the trees as it slid toward the far horizon.

Star Flower wove around him. "So?"

"So, what?" Had he missed something?

She stopped, her muzzle close to his. "Have you decided to trust me yet?"

Clear Sky shifted his paws. "Thunder thinks that I shouldn't."

Star Flower's green eyes softened. "Poor Thunder," she murmured. "I'm sorry that I hurt him. But he's a young cat. He'll get over it."

"Do you think?" Clear Sky searched her gaze hopefully. He'd never met a cat like Star Flower before; she was clever, tough, and self-assured. A strange, strong urge to be with her pressed in his chest.

But what about Thunder?

He's a young cat. He'll get over it.

Star Flower's warm breath washed his muzzle. He nudged her cheek with his nose. Should he ignore Star Flower just to please his son? *Does he really want me to be alone?*

"We should get back to camp," Star Flower murmured. "It'll be dark soon, and the others will be worried about you."

Clear Sky nodded slowly. He didn't want to leave the last warm rays of the sun and return to the chilly clearing. But he was leader. He had a duty.

He leaped down the rocks, warily eyeing the gaps between the stones for snakes. He landed in the grassy clearing with a grunt of relief. Star Flower's pelt brushed his as she landed beside him.

She led the way home, her tail swishing through the shadows. Twilight seeped through the forest as the sun disappeared. As they neared the camp, he smelled the familiar scents of his campmates. He nosed his way through the bramble and padded into the dim clearing.

"Back off, Leaf!" Blossom stood face-to-face with the black-and-white tom, her ears flat. Behind her, Milkweed was shielding her kits while Leaf eyed them angrily.

"They ate my mouse!" Leaf snarled.

"It's not *your* mouse," Blossom challenged.

"*I* caught it!" Leaf's eyes blazed.

"And Owl Eyes caught the rabbit!" Blossom nodded at the carcass lying between Acorn Fur and Thorn. "But he was happy to share it."

"Only because Thunder let him have the squirrel!" The fur lifted along Leaf's spine. "All I've had is half the shrew Nettle caught this morning."

Clear Sky hesitated. *Why are they arguing over prey?*

Star Flower nudged his shoulder with her nose. "Stop them," she murmured.

Clear Sky shot her a warning glance. He didn't need her

telling him how to handle his cats. "What's going on?" He glared at Leaf.

Leaf turned on him. "I'm starving while *they* eat my catch!" He flung a hostile look at Milkweed. "What has she brought to the group apart from two hungry kits and a cough that keeps everyone awake?"

Milkweed's eyes narrowed to slits. Beside her, Thistle arched his back and hissed, while Clover ducked, wide-eyed, beneath her mother's belly.

Blossom showed her teeth. "They need food more than you! Can't you see that? They're half-starved!"

"Then they should have gone hunting today, like *I* did!" Leaf spat back.

Clear Sky pricked his ears. Leaf wasn't on today's hunting patrols. "Who said you could hunt?"

"Thunder did."

Clear Sky flashed a look at his son. "I told you to take *Owl Eyes.*"

Thunder's eyes were dark. A chill ran along Clear Sky's spine. How had the mood in the camp turned so sour? He turned back to Leaf. "*I* organize the hunting patrols."

"Leaf-bare is here!" Leaf lashed his tail. "We've already had snow, and the days are still getting shorter. The sickness killed half the prey, and we're feeding cats who can't yet hunt for themselves." His gaze flashed to Birch and Alder.

Birch puffed out his chest indignantly. "We'd hunt if we got the chance!"

"Exactly!" Leaf turned back to Clear Sky. "Every cat should

be out hunting, or at least *learning* to hunt. We shouldn't be sitting in camp hungry while prey roams the forest."

Clear Sky curled his lip. "Our prey is gorging on leaf-fall fruit, growing fat and strong again. If we hunt it while it's still recovering from the sickness, we risk destroying it forever." He looked around at his campmates.

Blossom stared at him nervously. Pink Eyes dropped his gaze. Acorn Fur and Lightning Tail exchanged glances.

Clear Sky stood up tall, looming over Leaf. "You think with your belly, not your head," he snarled. "Which is why I'm leader and you're not. If you're not happy here, then leave! Go back to living as a rogue. I only want cats here who *want* to be here!" He backed away, his tail lashing as silence gripped the camp like a hard frost.

Thunder broke it. "You're right." He stepped forward, his shoulders square. "Cats should only be here *if they* want *to be*. So I should leave."

Shock scorched through Clear Sky. *Leave?* He stared at his son. Numbness spread up from his paws until he could hardly feel the chill of the night settling over the camp. "Why?" he rasped.

"I can't stay another day trapped in a camp and watching cats I care about go hungry just because you order it."

A murmur rippled around the camp. Owl Eyes shifted his paws, while Pink Eyes nodded slowly.

Anger burned in Clear Sky's belly. "I don't let my cats gorge themselves into a stupor for a *reason*. I want the prey in this forest to last until newleaf. I want enough to share when Gray Wing and the others decide to join our group. If we hunt too much now, there'll be nothing left. Just wait. You'll see I'm right."

Thunder's eyes flashed. "That's all you care about, isn't it?" he snarled. "Being *right*! You'd sacrifice every cat in this camp just to prove you're the smartest cat in the forest."

"That's not true—"

"It *is*!" Leaf's hiss surprised Clear Sky. "Thunder's right. You don't care about preserving the prey. You just want to look clever."

Clear Sky dug his claws into the cold earth. How could any cat believe that, after everything he had done for them?

Thunder spoke. "I won't disturb you, or hunt near your camp. I'll live somewhere else in the forest—but I can't be a part of your group anymore."

"I'm going with him!" Leaf lashed his tail.

"Me too!" Lightning Tail stepped forward.

Clear Sky's thoughts whirled. What was happening? He wanted to *unite* the cats, not drive them apart.

Owl Eyes nodded to Thunder. "Can I come too?"

"And me." Cloud Spots glanced anxiously toward Milk-weed. "I'll leave my herbs for your cough."

Thunder was staring at the cats gathering around him, his eyes wide with surprise. "Y-you can come if you want," he stammered.

Owl Eyes gazed hopefully at Sparrow Fur. "Are *you* coming?"

Confusion sharpened the young she-cat's amber gaze for a

moment. Then she dipped her head. "No, Owl Eyes. I made my decision to join Clear Sky and I'm sticking with it."

"I'll come with you." Pink Eyes padded toward Thunder.

"You?" Clear Sky wondered if he was dreaming. "But I took you in. I fed you. I thought . . ." His words trailed away. *I thought you were my friend.* Grief stabbed his chest like gorse thorns. He struggled to steady his breathing. What was going on? *I'm losing control.* His heart pounded in his ears so that he hardly heard his own raspy mew. "Thunder, can we speak in private?"

Thunder nodded and padded past his campmates. Smoothly, he leaped onto the steep bank. Clear Sky scrambled after him and followed him toward the bracken where they'd shared words just this morning. How had everything changed since then?

"What are you doing, Thunder?" He desperately searched the young tom's gaze.

Thunder's wide, white paws glowed in the fast-fading light. "I thought, when I came here, that I could help you lead. But you're not interested in my opinion. You always ignore my advice. It's pointless, me being here."

Clear Sky's ear twitched. Thunder was whining like a spoiled kit. *Help me lead? What makes him think he's so important?* "Did you think you'd get special treatment because you're my son?"

Thunder's eyes widened. "No! I was no cat's son on the moor, but the cats there respected me."

"So you're abandoning us because you're not getting the

respect you deserve?" Clear Sky couldn't keep scorn from his mew.

Thunder thrust his muzzle close. "I'm *leaving* because I don't want to watch you make any more dumb decisions."

"I've *explained* why I won't let my cats hunt more prey."

"That's not the dumb decision I meant." Thunder's eyes flashed with rage.

Clear Sky drew in a sharp breath. "You mean *Star Flower*."

"You should banish her from the forest," Thunder snarled. "She's nothing but trouble."

"Stop acting like a kit who's upset he can't get first pick from the prey pile!"

"I'm not!"

Clear Sky snorted. "I'm your father. You can't tell me who I can take as a mate any more than you can tell me how to lead my group."

"That's the problem, Clear Sky." Thunder lashed his tail. "I can't tell you *anything*. You think you know it all. But you don't! You can't tell good from bad. You never could. But you're so determined to be 'right,' you'll twist everything to prove it. If you mistook a fox for a rabbit, you'd keep calling it a rabbit while it tore out your throat, just because you'd rather die than admit that you were wrong."

"That's not true!" Clear Sky snapped. "If Star Flower had chosen you instead of me, you wouldn't be leaving. You're blinded by jealousy."

Thunder lowered his voice to a hiss. "But Star Flower would *never* choose me. *I'm* not enough like One Eye." He turned, his tail whipping past Clear Sky's muzzle, and leaped back to the clearing.

Clear Sky's chest tightened. *He thinks I'm like One Eye?* Stiff with shock, he watched Leaf, Pink Eyes, Cloud Spots, Owl Eyes, and Lightning Tail gather eagerly around his son. With a flick of his tail, Thunder led them out of camp.

Grief dragged at his bones, as heavy as water. *I just wanted my kin near me.* Jagged Peak and Gray Wing were in the pine forest. Thunder was leaving. His eyes misted. *I'm sorry, Fluttering Bird. I've failed you, and now I'm alone again. Somehow, I always end up alone.*

A familiar scent touched his nose. "Star Flower?"

Paws scuffed the earth beside him, and he turned to see her green eyes shining through the darkness.

Her soft gaze met his. "It's been a tough day." She reached forward and brushed her cheek with her muzzle. "But don't be sad. A few troublemakers have left, that's all. This is your chance to build the loyal, strong group you always wanted. Let Thunder go if he wants. His only ambition is to fill his belly. He will never be the leader that you are."

Clear Sky let her words lull him. She wove around him, her thick pelt warming his. Icy weather was coming. He could smell it on the wind. Let Thunder find a new camp as leaf-bare tightened its grip. He still had a loyal band of cats. He rubbed his muzzle into the soft fur of Star Flower's neck.

At last, he had a mate worthy of him.

CHAPTER 13

❧

Thunder padded stiffly from the camp. He was acutely aware of the cats following at his heels. He was responsible for them now—all of them. His heart pounded in his chest. *Am I doing the right thing?*

His father's words rang in his ears. *If Star Flower had chosen you instead of me, you wouldn't be leaving. You're blinded by jealousy.*

Was that true?

No! It was far more than that. He couldn't live where he wasn't listened to—and he couldn't watch Clear Sky let cats go hungry. Did his father truly believe that their prey would not last through leaf-bare, or was he just flexing his claws because he enjoyed ordering cats around?

Lightning Tail fell in beside Thunder as he headed for the gully. "Why didn't you tell me you were planning to leave?"

Thunder avoided his gaze. "It was a quick decision." Numbly, he slithered into the gully. Rain had washed through it and the earth was soft. Mud seeped around his paws.

Lightning Tail landed behind him. "Where are we going?"

Thunder felt the cold night air pierce his fur. "I'm not sure." He glanced over his shoulder. Leaf, Cloud Spots, and

Pink Eyes were following, Owl Eyes on their tail. His heart pounded harder. *Gray Wing believed in me,* he reminded himself. *I can do this.*

The gully wound toward the sycamore slope, and he leaped up it, following the path he had carried prey along earlier that day. The forest was dark, the moon hidden behind clouds. As they climbed the slope, he stretched his eyes wide, picking out shapes among the shadows. An owl screeched in the distance, and Lightning Tail pricked his ears.

"There must be prey around," the black tom murmured.

"We can hunt in the morning," Thunder told him. "We have to find somewhere safe to sleep." If owls were looking for prey, foxes would be too.

"Thunder!" Owl Eyes called from behind.

Thunder heard fear in his mew and stopped. "What's wrong?"

Owl Eyes was staring back down the slope, his pelt bristling. "We're being followed."

Thunder stiffened. Had Clear Sky sent a patrol after them? He dashed past Leaf and Cloud Spots and stopped beside the young gray tom. "Can you see anything?"

Owl Eyes shook his head. "I heard voices."

Thunder tasted the air. There were no strange smells. Just the scents of the camp drifting through the damp forest. "You're imagining it." He began to head back to Lightning Tail.

A hiss sounded from shadows below. A twig cracked.

"Who's there?" Thunder unsheathed his claws.

"I'll take a look." Leaf barged past him, ears flat. Growling, the black-and-white tom raced for the gully.

Thunder watched him go, his ears twitching uneasily.

Cloud Spots's pelt brushed his. "Has Clear Sky come after us?"

"Why would he?" Lightning Tail paced around them. "He said we could go if we wanted."

Cloud Spots snorted. "But he's *Clear Sky*, remember? He can't be trusted."

Pink Eyes was staring silently into the darkness. The half-blind cat's mouth was open as he tasted for scents.

Thunder saw his ears twitch. "What—"

"Hush!" Pink Eyes leaned forward, his pelt bristling.

Thunder's belly tightened.

"Stop him!" Pink Eyes growled sharply.

"Stop who?"

"Leaf!" Pink Eyes raced forward, bounding down the slope.

Alarm flashed through Thunder. He sped after the white tom. A shriek exploded from the shadows ahead. A long, low yowl sounded in reply.

Thunder leaped past Pink Eyes as they reached the gully, and jumped down into the muddy ditch. He smelled fear-scent as he spotted Leaf's black-and-white fur. The tom was hissing at a she-cat. Two small shapes huddled at her side.

Milkweed!

As Thunder pushed past Leaf, the queen bared her teeth.

"What are you doing here?" Surprise rippled through Thunder's fur.

Milkweed crouched in the gully, Thistle and Clover on either side. She eyed Leaf accusingly. "We want to come with you, but *he* told us to go back."

Leaf bristled beside Thunder. "They can't hunt, and she's *sick*! Let Clear Sky look after them."

"How dare you!" Milkweed lashed out with a forepaw and sliced her claws over Leaf's muzzle.

The tom hissed, eyes flashing with rage in the darkness.

Thunder pushed between them. "Milkweed and her kits can come with us if they want to," he growled.

"They'll make us weak." Leaf's tail whisked over the mud.

"I want to come with you so I can *help*!" Milkweed snapped. "Clear Sky kept promising I could hunt, but he never sent me out with a patrol."

Thunder gazed at her sympathetically. "Are you strong enough to hunt?"

"Of course I am!" Milkweed snapped. Her ribs still showed through her pelt. "I've got kits to feed. *Their* hunger will drive me even harder than my own." She flashed a look at Leaf. "*He* only wants to fill his *own* belly. He doesn't belong in a group!"

Leaf bristled. "That's not true!"

"Your only loyalty is to yourself," Milkweed hissed.

"Be quiet! Both of you." Thunder looked from one to the other, and then at the kits. Thistle was watching with narrowed eyes. Clover was growling, teeth bared. "Leaf proved his loyalty when he chose to come with me," he told Milkweed. He turned to Leaf. "And Milkweed's right—she has kits to raise, which means she has more to fight for than any of us."

Leaf shifted his paws. "She's been coughing since sunup, and she's skinnier than a leaf-bare rabbit," he grunted. "I bet she can't even run."

Milkweed hopped out of the gully and leaned back to grab Thistle by his scuff.

He mewed indignantly as she hauled him out.

Clover scrambled up by herself. "We'll be able to hunt soon!" she hissed at Leaf. "One day you'll be old and stiff and grateful for the food we bring you."

Thunder felt a flash of pride in the feisty young kit. "Come on." He jumped up the slope and beckoned to the kits with his tail. "We need to find somewhere to sleep."

Leaf pulled himself out of the gully and stalked up the slope. "We should have just carried on walking," he grumbled as he passed Pink Eyes.

The white tom ignored him, his gaze on the kits. "Hurry up, Thistle." He whisked his tail encouragingly.

Thistle galloped toward him, Clover at his heels.

Thunder fell in beside Milkweed as they followed the kits up the slope. He glanced sideways at her. "I thought you were happy with Clear Sky."

"I'm grateful he took us in," she answered. "But I never liked depending on other cats to feed my kits. I want to hunt."

"You will," Thunder promised. He fluffed his fur against the chill. Finding enough prey to last through leaf-bare was going to be their biggest challenge—but first they had to find somewhere to make camp.

They caught up with Owl Eyes, Cloud Spots, and Lightning

Tail. Leaf was already heading past the sycamore while the kits scampered after Pink Eyes.

Lightning Tail blinked in surprise at Milkweed as she padded past him wordlessly, following her kits.

Thunder caught his friend's eye. "I thought I was going to be spending the night alone in the forest."

"Tough," Lightning Tail purred. "You're stuck with us."

Thunder felt a surge of affection for his friend. He'd been relieved when the black tom had stepped forward and offered to go with him. He fell in beside him now, and together they headed up the slope.

As the night deepened, the air grew colder.

"My paws ache," Owl Eyes muttered as they began to climb yet another slope.

Above, the clouds had cleared to reveal a star-speckled sky, and Thunder could feel frost settling over the woods. He'd lost track of how far they'd come. This part of the forest was unfamiliar: small, bare clearings followed by woodland brambled so thickly that it was hard to find a trail through. Where could they rest? The clearings were too exposed, the brambles too sharp to burrow beneath.

"Thunder!" Leaf's call sounded from ahead.

Thunder bounded forward, skidding around Cloud Spots and Milkweed as they nudged the weary kits on.

"Careful!" Leaf cautioned as Thunder neared. "It's a steep drop."

Thunder scrambled to a halt, sending a shower of grit spraying ahead of him. He heard it rattle over stone and land far below. Leaf was staring down into shadow, and Thunder followed his gaze. The land dropped away into a small ravine. Moonlight pooled at the bottom, lighting a clearing ringed by bracken and trees.

Leaf lifted his chin. "Do you think we could get down there?"

Thunder surveyed the cliff. It was rocky, but there were enough ledges and jutting boulders for them all to jump down. "With a little help, even the kits could make it," he meowed.

Lightning Tail caught them up and gazed into the ravine. "It looks like there's plenty of shelter."

Thunder jumped down onto the nearest ledge, relieved to find it solid beneath his paws. Excitement fizzed in his belly. "Tell the others to hurry," he called up. They could rest here for the night and explore the area more in the morning. *And hunt.* His belly rumbled at the thought. The undergrowth was so thick below, there had to be prey.

He led the way down, jumping from ledge to ledge, checking that the others were following each time he stopped. Before long, he landed on soft earth. A wall of prickly gorse blocked his way, and he sniffed along the base as Lightning Tail and Leaf guided Pink Eyes, Cloud Spots, Milkweed, and her kits down the cliff.

Owl Eyes landed clumsily beside him. "This is great!" His round eyes shone in the moonlight.

"It *would* be if I could find a way past this gorse," Thunder muttered.

"Here!"

Thunder looked up. Owl Eyes was already squeezing under a gap in the spiny bush. Thunder followed, the thorns scraping his spine. He wriggled out the other side and gazed ahead. Grass circled a bare earth clearing where a large boulder stood, glittering with frost. Brambles and bracken crowded the edge, and trees stood like guards against the forest beyond.

Hope flared in Thunder's belly. Could this be their new home?

Lightning Tail squeezed from under the gorse. "We can rest for the night over there!" He nodded toward a thick clump of bracken. He crossed the clearing and began to trample the stems until he'd hollowed out a den.

Thistle and Clover burst from beneath the gorse and raced toward the black tom.

"Is this where we're sleeping?" Clover looked at him with round eyes.

"I want to sleep near the edge so I can listen for foxes," Thistle announced.

Milkweed nosed her way into the clearing, Cloud Spots and Leaf on her tail.

Pink Eyes followed, tasting the air. "No cat scents here," he murmured. "Do you think Clear Sky knows about this place?"

"Let's hope not." Thunder felt a prickle of worry. In the morning, they would mark new borders and organize hunting patrols. The scent of damp bracken filled his nose. Suddenly he felt tired, his paws like stone.

Leaf was already circling in the den. The black-and-white

tom flopped down wearily while Thistle and Clover huddled on the far side, eyeing him suspiciously.

Milkweed slid in beside them and lay down, curling her tail protectively around them.

Pink Eyes sniffed the edge of the den before settling, while Cloud Spots crouched next to Milkweed, his mouth open to taste the scents of their new home.

"Come on!" Lightning Tail nodded to Thunder from the edge of the den. "You must be exhausted."

Thunder nodded and followed Pink Eyes across the clearing. He waited for the white tom to pad into the bracken before settling down beside Lightning Tail. His paws were sore from walking, his belly hollow with hunger. His eyes stung with tiredness.

"Should one of us sit guard?" Lightning Tail asked.

"I can do it," Owl Eyes offered. "I can sit on the cliff top and look out for intruders."

Leaf's nose was twitching. "Perhaps we should hunt before we sleep."

Thunder looked around at the cats huddled together in the shelter of the bracken. "No cat is hunting or guarding," he told them. "There's no scent of fox or other cats. We can sleep safely until morning, and then we can hunt."

Murmurs of agreement stirred around him in the darkness.

One by one, his campmates closed their eyes.

Thunder gazed across the clearing, grateful they'd found shelter for the night. Beside him, Lightning Tail's breath softened into sleep. Thistle and Clover stopped fidgeting beside Milkweed. Leaf's eyes closed, and Cloud Spots began to snore gently.

These were *his* cats now. Anxiety jabbed in his belly. *How can I protect them all?*

Thunder gazed at the tall oak, squinting against the sunshine spearing through its branches. He could see a wide gap far up the trunk.

Owl hole?

He climbed over the roots, satisfied when he saw a pellet of bones and fur lying among them. An owl definitely lived here. Prey must be rich in this part of the forest. He padded across the shaded stretch of ground and headed down the slope beyond. It felt good to be hunting alone, away from the responsibilities of the camp. *If we hunt together, then we will be less tempted to keep our catch to ourselves.* Clear Sky's words rang in his head. How could his father believe he would eat before the cats in his camp had full bellies?

In the days that had passed since they'd discovered the ravine, they had made more nests among the bracken. The frost that had first come on the night they'd arrived had returned again and again. But sunshine pooled in the small, sheltered spot and warmed the camp by day. It had seemed foolish to look for another home. Milkweed had begun weaving brambles into a den for her kits in case snow came. She had also hunted, bringing back as much prey as Leaf. Her eyes flashed with satisfaction each time she dropped her catch among the other pieces of fresh-kill.

Pink Eyes had watched the kits while she'd been gone. Thunder was pleased to see how at ease the old tom was in his new home. He could hardly believe that this was the same cat who'd snapped at Birch and Alder for playing with his tail. Now, he would lie patiently in the sun-warmed clearing while Thistle and Clover clambered over him or played moss-ball nearby. From time to time he'd venture out of the ravine, hunting with Owl Eyes or helping Cloud Spots collect herbs. His delicate sense of smell could detect fragrant leaves so well hidden that they were unharmed by the frosts.

Yet the hunting wasn't easy. The sickness had clearly reached this deep into the forest. Prey was as scarce as it had been in Clear Sky's territory, and with kits to feed, finding enough each day was a challenge.

Worry itched beneath Thunder's pelt as he padded down the slope. Had Clear Sky been right about hunting the forest dry before newleaf? What if the prey ran out? He pricked his ears. Water chattered ahead. He could see the river glittering between the trees. He licked his lips, suddenly realizing how thirsty he was, and headed for the bank. The river was sluggish here at the boundary of River Ripple's marshland, lapping the edge of the forest.

As he neared, movement caught his eye. He froze. A sparrow was hopping among the roots of a rowan, digging its beak deep into the leaf litter to rummage for bugs.

Thunder dropped into a hunting crouch and pulled himself forward, paw by paw. He lifted his tail to make sure it didn't drag over the rustling leaves.

The sparrow lifted its head and gulped down a morsel.

Thunder paused, waiting until it plunged its beak back among the leaves.

He narrowed his eyes. The sparrow was only a few tail-lengths away. Could he risk leaping from here? *No need.* It seemed busy with its hunt for food. He drew himself forward a few more paw steps, his heartbeat quickening as the sparrow looked up and shook out its feathers. It hopped onto a root and glanced at the branches above.

It's going to fly away!

As the sparrow spread its small wings, Thunder leaped, stretching high to bat the small, brown bird down before it could flutter into the air.

The sparrow fell to the ground. Thunder lunged, killing it with a quick bite. It was thin, but it would feed the kits. He carried it to the river and laid it down on the sandy shore before he bent to drink.

Leaves rustled behind him.

More prey?

He turned, water dripping from his chin.

Two amber eyes watched from the woods.

Blinking against the sunshine, Thunder unsheathed his claws. He smelled tom. Tasting the air, he detected the odd scent of frost and stone. This cat wasn't from around here. He narrowed his eyes, glimpsing the dark shape of a black cat, and growled as the stranger's gaze flicked toward the sparrow. "Catch your own prey," he warned.

"That *was* my prey." The tom padded forward, his paws clumsily scuffing the sandy earth as he stepped from the trees.

Thunder's pelt pricked. "What do you mean?"

"I was stalking it when you caught it."

Unease flashed through Thunder. He hadn't even realized he was being watched. He needed to be more careful on this new territory.

But the tom did not seem angry. Thunder suddenly saw how his pelt hung off his skinny frame, and how his shoulders jutted like twigs beneath his fur. He recognized the look of hunger hollowing the cat's eyes and glanced guiltily at the sparrow. "I didn't realize." Should he give up his catch? What about Thistle and Clover? They were hungry too. "Where are you from?" Thunder tipped his head. Was this cat from Twolegplace?

"We come from far away." The tom stared boldly now at the sparrow as it lay on the bank, hope sparking in his dull gaze.

We? Thunder scanned the forest edging the river, shifting his paws uneasily. Were there more cats watching him?

"We come from the mountains," the tom went on.

Interest sparked in Thunder's belly. When he was a kit, Gray Wing had told him stories of the journey he and some of the others had made from the mountains. From what Thunder could remember, it had been a long, dangerous trek. No wonder this cat looked so worn out. "How many of you are there?" he asked.

"I'll show you." The tom headed back into the shadow of the trees.

Thunder hesitated. Was this a trap? He could see the tom's pelt moving like a shadow between the trunks. *No.* They could have attacked him on the bank and taken his catch.

He picked up the sparrow and followed.

Beneath the trees once more, it took a moment for his eyes to readjust to the gloom. He halted and scanned the forest. The black tom was climbing over a fallen trunk, heading for a glade near the owl's tree.

Thunder hurried after him, leaping the trunk and weaving his way past the stumps of shriveled ferns. The tom was already climbing the far side of the glade. He stopped beside a long-dead beech tree. A split in the trunk showed a hollow inside. The tom whispered something into the shadows; as Thunder approached, he saw two blue eyes blinking in the darkness, and smelled the scent of a she-cat. She carried the same tang of frost and stone as her companion.

"Who's this?" The she-cat glared from her nest in the hollow trunk.

The tom dipped his head. "I don't know. I found him drinking by the river."

"Does he know them? Has he seen where they—" The she-cat began to cough, her frail body shuddering with each desperate hack.

The tom leaned down and began to lap her flank, trying to soothe her.

Thunder smelled the stench of infection and crept closer.

The she-cat's gray, speckled pelt was matted, her bones showing even sharper through her fur than the tom's. She crouched, trembling as her coughing eased, and Thunder saw a blackened wound at the top of her hind leg.

He dropped the sparrow. "You're injured."

"It's nothing," she rasped.

"I know a cat who could give you herbs to help it heal," Thunder offered. Should he get Cloud Spots?

"It will heal by itself," the she-cat muttered.

Thunder nosed the sparrow toward her. "Perhaps a little food will give you the strength to recover more quickly." This she-cat was old, far older than her traveling companion. White specks of fur showed around her muzzle.

She blinked at him in disbelief. "You'd give me your prey?"

"It was your friend's prey, really," Thunder told her. "He spotted it first."

The black tom blinked at him gratefully. "Eat it, Quiet Rain." He pawed the sparrow closer to the she-cat.

"This is the first kindness we've met since our journey began," Quiet Rain murmured.

Thunder dipped his head. "Prey has been scarce since the sickness."

"What sickness?" Quiet Rain lifted her head sharply, anxiety showing in her blue gaze.

"It has passed now," Thunder reassured her. "But it killed much of our prey before leaf-bare."

Quiet Rain glanced at her companion. "Sun Shadow and I thought we were coming to a land of plenty," she mewed bitterly.

"It will be, once newleaf has brought the woods and moor

back to life," Thunder promised.

Sun Shadow gazed at the sparrow hungrily. "How long will it be until 'newleaf'?"

Thunder felt a jab of pity for the skinny tom. Then curiosity rippled through his pelt.

She called him Sun Shadow.

Didn't Tall Shadow once have a brother called Moon Shadow? He'd died on the journey from the mountains. Could this be another littermate?

Quiet Rain ripped a mouthful of flesh from the sparrow. "What's your name?" she asked, chewing noisily.

"Thunder," he replied, wondering if she could read his thoughts.

Quiet Rain's eyes narrowed as she exchanged a glance with Sun Shadow. She swallowed, a feather clinging to her whiskers as she turned back to Thunder. "Have you met a cat called Gray Wing?" she asked, her mew tight with pain. "Or Jagged Peak? Or Clear Sky?"

Sun Shadow leaned forward. "Have you met Moon Shadow? He's my father."

Thunder's belly tightened. These cats were from the Tribe! What could he tell them? They had come so far to see their Tribemates. "I know Tall Shadow," he told them cautiously.

Sun Shadow's eyes shone. "She's my father's littermate!"

"And what of Gray Wing?" Quiet Rain's eyes lit up. "Clear Sky? Jagged Peak?"

Thunder's tail trembled. "How do you know them?"

"I am their mother."

Thunder searched for words. How could he tell this old she-cat that her sons now lived more as rivals than as litter-mates? Memories of the great battle crowded his mind.

"Well?" Quiet Rain stared at him expectantly.

"Gray Wing and Jagged Peak live on the far side of this forest with Tall Shadow," he told her, thinking he could lead them to the pines. He wasn't eager to return to his father's camp yet, so he did not mention Clear Sky. "I can take you to see them."

Quiet Rain struggled to her paws, her eyes glistening. "Are they well?"

"Yes."

"What about my father?" Sun Shadow leaned forward eagerly.

Thunder avoided the tom's gaze. "Tall Shadow knows more than me," he mumbled. "She can tell you everything when you reach her camp."

"We must leave!" Quiet Rain stepped over the half-eaten sparrow, her paws trembling.

Sun Shadow glanced at her anxiously. "You should rest for a while first."

Thunder nodded. "It's a long trek," he told her. "Finish your meal. We can go when you've got your strength back."

CHAPTER 14

❧

Thunder watched Quiet Rain return to her meal. Worry jabbed his chest. Each bite seemed to pain her. Her ears flattened as she chewed, and she winced with each swallow. Was she strong enough to make the journey? The pines were beyond the Thunderpath.

Doubt gnawed at him. *Perhaps I should take them back to my camp?* He nudged Sun Shadow aside. "I think Quiet Rain's wounds need treating before we leave," he hissed. Cloud Spots would know what to do.

"She won't wait for that," Sun Shadow whispered back. "Not now that she knows her sons are near."

"But she's so weak."

"She made the journey from the mountains, didn't she? It can't be much farther to the pine forest."

Quiet Rain jerked up her muzzle. "What are you two whispering about?"

Thunder met her gaze. "You should come back to my camp to rest, and let Cloud Spots help you." He hoped the mention of her old friend from the mountains might convince her, but

Quiet Rain only paused for a moment, then returned to her meal.

"I don't want to waste any more time," she mewed, having clearly said all that she wanted to on the matter.

Thunder exchanged looks with Sun Shadow.

"Don't bother arguing," the black tom murmured. "Once Quiet Rain has made up her mind, it stays made up."

Thunder gazed between the trees. He was a short run from the ravine. He should at least warn his campmates that he was heading for Tall Shadow's territory. They'd worry if he was late returning to camp. He dipped his head to Sun Shadow. "I must tell the others that I'm leaving."

Distrust sharpened the tom's gaze.

"It's okay," Thunder reassured him. "I'll come back."

"Alone?" Sun Shadow narrowed his eyes.

"Alone," he promised. The long journey had clearly left these cats wary. Who knew what cruelty they'd witnessed? "My campmates are busy hunting." Thunder kept his mew reassuringly light. "I'll be back soon."

Leaving the mountain cats crouched at the foot of the beech, he bounded between the trees. His paws thrummed over the frozen earth as he headed for the ravine. Cutting between brambles and leaping fallen trees, he raced until his chest hurt, only slowing as the slope steepened toward the camp.

"Thunder?" Milkweed's call surprised him before he reached the top.

He slowed to a halt, scanning the thick undergrowth until he caught sight of her ginger-and-black pelt. She stared at him from a patch of wood sorrel, its leaves closed against the cold. "Are you hunting?" Thunder asked.

Milkweed rolled her eyes. "No," she mewed sarcastically. "I just felt like a stroll."

Thunder's whiskers twitched. Now that her kits had a safe den and she could hunt once more, Milkweed showed as much spirit as any cat. The hunger she'd suffered still showed in her thin frame, but her eyes were bright and her cough had cleared. "Have you caught anything yet?" he asked.

"I buried a mouse back near the brambles." She nodded over her shoulder. "I'll dig it up on the way back to camp. What about you?" Her nose twitched curiously and she stiffened. "You smell strange."

Thunder whisked his tail. "I found two cats from the mountains," he told her. "They're looking for their kin."

Milkweed tipped her head. "Their *kin*?"

"Gray Wing, Jagged Peak, and Tall Shadow." He didn't mention his father's name. He didn't want to explain why he was taking them all the way to the pines. "I promised to show them the way."

"But why?" Milkweed blinked. "You have your own cats to look after now."

"These cats are starving and one of them is sick," he told her. "They need my help."

Milkweed gazed at him softly, nodding once. "Of course."

"Can the group spare me?" He glanced at the sky. The sun was climbing. It would be dusk before he returned.

"How long will you be gone?"

"I'll be back by tonight," Thunder promised.

"I guess we can hunt without you," Milkweed told him.

Thunder shifted his paws guiltily. "I *have* to go."

"It's okay." Milkweed padded from the sorrel. "We followed you because we trusted you to do the right thing. And if you are helping these mountain cats, it must be the right thing."

Gratitude flooded beneath Thunder's pelt. He gazed warmly at the mottled queen. "Thank you."

"You'd better get back to them," Milkweed prompted. "It sounds like they need you."

As Thunder turned, she called after him. "If you find any prey on your travels, bring it back to camp."

"I will!" Thunder whisked his tail as he headed back to Sun Shadow and Quiet Rain.

They were waiting for him, eyes bright with hope. Sun Shadow paced in front of the beech while Quiet Rain peered from the hollow trunk.

He could hear her rasping breath as he neared. "We'll skirt the edge of the forest and cross the moor," he told them as he stopped beside Sun Shadow. A journey through the forest would be too arduous for such weakened cats—leaping gullies and fallen trees would exhaust them.

And we might meet Clear Sky.

He pushed the thought away. "Follow me."

He headed for the river, leading them out from the shelter of the trees and onto the sandy shore.

The sun glittered on the water as a freezing wind whisked over it. Thunder felt it through his thick fur. He glanced at Quiet Rain and Sun Shadow. They padded side by side, keeping their paws clear of the water. "Are you cold?" he asked.

Quiet Rain caught his eye. "Cold? In *this* wind?" She snorted. "We come from the mountains, remember?"

"Of course." Thunder's whiskers twitched. Quiet Rain might walk with a limp and need to stop to cough every now and then, but there was nothing wrong with her tongue.

They walked in silence as the sun crossed the sky, the sand turning to pebbles beneath Thunder's paws. He tensed when he caught the scent of Clear Sky's markers, tainting the breeze. They were passing his father's territory. He glanced nervously into the forest, searching for movement among the trees. A blackbird chittered in the branches, but there was no sign of a patrol. Thunder was suddenly thankful that Clear Sky kept his cats confined to camp. He quickened his pace. He could see where the forest ended and the river bent toward the gorge. They could leave the shore and forest behind and head straight onto the moor.

"Not so fast!" Quiet Rain croaked. He glanced back, realizing that the mountain cats were falling behind.

He hurried back and took a spot beside Quiet Rain, shielding her from the forest while Sun Shadow flanked her other side. The sooner they were past Clear Sky's land, the better.

"Tell me about the mountains," he meowed softly, one ear twisted toward the woods.

"You must know of it already if you know Gray Wing and Tall Shadow," Quiet Rain answered. "Surely they've told you stories of their old home?"

"They've told stories," Thunder agreed. "But I don't know how much is real and how much imagined."

"What did they tell you?" Quiet Rain asked.

"That the snow fell so thick and so fast, it could drown a cat caught out in a blizzard," Thunder told her.

"That much is true." Quiet Rain flicked her thin tail. "Did they tell you about the eagles that can carry off a full-grown tom? And the drops so sheer, and valleys so deep, that if a stone fell, you would not hear it land?"

"What did you hunt?" Thunder only knew that hunger had driven Gray Wing and the others to the moor. "Are there mice and voles in the mountains?"

Sun Shadow purred. "There are mice everywhere. And in the warm season we can hunt the lower slopes for rabbits and small birds."

"What do you hunt when the snows come?" Thunder asked, wondering how these cats could ever survive the rocky crags.

"Whatever we can," Sun Shadow told him. "Sometimes we find the carcass of a deer left by a sharptooth."

"A *sharptooth*?" Thunder's pelt lifted along his spine.

"They're giant cats," Sun Shadow told him. "They are rare, but *far* more deadly than eagles."

"Why do you stay there?" Thunder asked.

Sun Shadow shrugged. "It's our home."

Thunder didn't understand. "But it sounds so cold and prey-poor."

"Stoneteller found it," Sun Shadow explained.

Thunder remembered Gray Wing and Clear Sky talking about Stoneteller. "Is that your leader?"

"She is more than a leader," Quiet Rain rasped. "She is ancient, and speaks with the ancients who died before her. She tells us what is and what will be."

Thunder could only blink. These certainly were strange cats.

Sun Shadow went on. "Long ago, she journeyed from far away, and the mountains were the first place to welcome her."

Welcome her? Thunder didn't comment. If these cats thought snowy mountains full of eagles and sharptooths were welcoming, they were even stranger than he'd thought.

Pebbles swished beneath their paws. The shore widened and the forest thinned beside them as the river curved away toward the gorge. Thunder could hear the faint roar of water where the river tumbled down between the cliffs. He could see the stepping-stones that crossed from the moor onto River Ripple's marshes.

Stones turned to grass as they climbed toward the moor. Wind streamed through his whiskers and he smelled the scent of heather. For a moment, memories swamped him. He was hunting with Lightning Tail, veering across the windblown grass as his friend drove a rabbit toward him. Hawk Swoop was calling them back to camp. Acorn Fur was pacing sulkily at the entrance to the hollow, complaining that they'd left her behind.

"Thunder!" A familiar call jerked him back into the present. He turned his head.

River Ripple's silver pelt showed on the shore behind them.

"Who's that?" Sun Shadow's pelt bristled along his spine. Quiet Rain flattened her ears.

"Don't worry." Thunder hailed the river cat with a flick of his tail. "He's a friend."

River Ripple bounded from the shore and hurried up the grassy slope after them. He slowed and stopped a few paces behind, his gaze flashing from Quiet Rain to Sun Shadow.

Quiet Rain's eyes narrowed to slits. "You smell of water," she hissed.

River Rippled dipped his head. "I live beside the river."

Quiet Rain wrinkled her nose. "What cat would live beside water?"

"The fishing is good," River Ripple told her.

Quiet Rain's gaze flicked along his sleek, plump flank. "You catch *fish*?" she gasped. "How?"

"I swim."

Quiet Rain turned to Sun Shadow, her eyes wide. "What kind of place have we come to?"

"A place like any other." River Ripple's mew was polite. "Where are you heading?"

"To the pine forest." Thunder jerked his head toward the distant horizon.

"Why cross the moor?" River Ripple padded to his side.

"You could have cut through the forest."

Quiet Rain narrowed her eyes. "Is that true?"

Thunder stiffened. River Ripple didn't know that he'd left Clear Sky to set up his own camp—and he didn't want to explain now. Quiet Rain might demand he take them back to meet her son. "Sun Shadow and Quiet Rain are weak from their journey from the mountains. I thought the moor would be easier to cross."

River Ripple's gaze glittered with interest. "You come from the mountains?"

"We come in search of kin," Sun Shadow told him.

Thunder added quickly, "I'm taking them to Tall Shadow's camp." He nodded toward Sun Shadow. "This cat is Moon Shadow's son."

River Ripple dipped his head. "Moon Shadow was a fine cat."

Sun Shadow stiffened. "He . . . *was* . . . ?"

River Ripple caught Thunder's eye. "You haven't told him."

Thunder lifted his chin, looking solemnly at the black tom. "Moon Shadow was killed. He died bravely saving his friends from a fire."

Sun Shadow swayed on his paws. "My father!"

Quiet Rain ducked in beside him, pressing her thin shoulder to his. "We always knew they were taking a risk when they left the mountains."

"But I wanted a chance to know him." Sun Shadow's mew was thick with grief.

Thunder stared at the ground, his pelt hot. "I should have told you before. I'm sorry."

Quiet Rain's mew hardened. "What about the others?"

Thunder tried to drag his gaze from the grass, his heart pounding. *What can I tell them?* So many were dead. This wasn't the time to share such sorrow. They still had to cross the moor. "Gray Wing and Jagged Peak are fine," he told her softly. Then he mumbled, "So is Clear Sky."

River Ripple wove past him and faced Quiet Rain. "There is much to tell you. But this is not the place. Let us lead you to Tall Shadow's camp, where you can rest." He caught Thunder's eye. "I'll accompany you."

Thunder felt relief wash his fur. River Ripple understood that these cats needed shelter far more than they needed to hear the truth. As the silver tom headed onward, the mountain cats followed him wordlessly. Sun Shadow's tail dragged along the ground, and Quiet Rain's breath rattled in her chest as the slope steepened.

River Ripple slowed and put his shoulder against hers. "We're nearly at the top."

Sun Shadow fell in beside Thunder. "How long ago did he die?"

"Many moons." Thunder kept his gaze fixed ahead. He wished he could ease the tom's grief, but he didn't know how.

"Did you know him well?"

"I was young."

"But you know Tall Shadow and Gray Wing?"

Thunder's pelt prickled uncomfortably. "Yes."

Quiet Rain glanced at him. "What about Jagged Peak and Clear Sky? How well do you know them?"

"Well enough." Thunder's mew thickened. "I'm Clear Sky's son."

Quiet Rain stopped and stared at him. "Clear Sky's son!" Delight flooded her gaze. "Where is he? Where's Bright Stream?"

Thunder faced her, puzzled. "Bright Stream?"

"Your mother!" Quiet Rain meowed. "Clear Sky and Bright Stream were destined to be mates."

"Bright Stream died on the journey from the mountains." The words blurted from Thunder's mouth before he could stop them.

Quiet Rain's eyes clouded. "She died *too*?"

"An eagle carried her off," Thunder mumbled, guilt clawing at his heart.

"She left the mountains, only to suffer a mountain cat's fate!" Anger tinged Quiet Rain's mew. "Who's your mother then?" Her gaze scorched Thunder's.

"Storm," he answered quietly.

"She is Clear Sky's mate?" Quiet Rain held his gaze.

"She was."

"*Was?*" Quiet Rain stared in disbelief. "*More* death?"

Thunder could only nod.

"Why did we ever come here?" Quiet Rain pulled away from River Ripple and limped to Sun Shadow's side. "This is a place where cats come to die!"

"Not all cats." River Ripple's gentle mew carried on the wind that was gusting over the moortop and tugging at the cats' fur. "It is a place where prey is rich and the greenleaf is long and warm."

Thunder purred his agreement. "Gray Wing and Jagged Peak love it here. And Jagged Peak has kits now."

Quiet Rain lifted her head. "Kits?"

"Storm Pelt, Dew Nose, and Eagle Feather," Thunder told her, relieved to have some good news for the older she-cat.

Quiet Rain mewed approvingly. "Good, strong names."

"Hawk Swoop had kits too." River Ripple nudged her gently onward. "Let me tell you about them."

Thunder felt a wave of gratitude toward the river cat as he steered the old she-cat across the moor, chattering easily.

They passed the rim of the four trees hollow and followed the moor as it sloped toward the Thunderpath. Beyond, the pines stood like a great dark wall, their tips scratching the pale sky.

Thunder stopped on the grass area at the side of the Thunderpath and gazed along the straight, black track. There were no monsters to be heard, but the foul stench in the air told him one had passed by recently. "We must be careful crossing here," he told Sun Shadow.

Quiet Rain snorted beside River Ripple. "Do you think we haven't seen plenty of these stinking tracks on our journey already?"

Thunder stepped back and let the she-cat approach the Thunderpath's edge with Sun Shadow. She glanced both ways, then scuttled across it like a mouse. The black tom bounded after her.

Thunder padded to River Ripple's side. "Do you think all mountain cats are as prickly as these two?"

River Ripple purred. "I'm sure they're just tired from their journey." He glanced along the Thunderpath, then darted across. Thunder chased his tail, pleased that there were no monsters.

Sun Shadow and Quiet Rain were waiting beside the pines, staring at the shadows beyond.

"Which way?" Sun Shadow asked.

"I'm not sure." Thunder glanced hopefully at River Ripple. "Have you been here before?"

River Ripple shook his head. "Slate's visited. She told me Tall Shadow made her camp deep in the pine forest."

Thunder looked at the brambles crowding between the straight, dark trunks. "That might be hard to find."

River Ripple padded into the shadows. "We won't fail," he promised.

"You must know their scents," Quiet Rain sniffed. "Smell them out! In the mountains, a kit can track a mouse in the snow!"

"Tracking scents in a pine forest might be harder than tracking scents in snow," Thunder warned. The tang of pine-sap swirled around them. He opened his mouth, searching for the familiar taste of his old campmates. *Please let us find the camp soon.* Quiet Rain's eyes were dull with exhaustion, and her limping stride was getting worse. She needed to rest.

"Come on." River Ripple beckoned the mountain cats forward and led them past a rotting log. Pelt pricking with unease, Thunder headed into the forest. What would Tall Shadow say when she saw her old friends from the mountains? And how would she break the news of the rift between Quiet Rain's sons—and the deaths of so many of her Tribemates?

CHAPTER 15
♣

Thunder brought them to a stop at the edge of a clearing so Quiet Rain could catch her breath. He peered through the brambles and felt his heart surge with relief: he could see Tall Shadow inside, meowing something to Holly. *We've found their camp!*

The black she-cat pointed with her tail at a prey pile. The two mice and scrawny blackbird would surely not feed all her cats. Thunder felt his pelt prickle with sympathy. It seemed that every group was having trouble keeping their cats well fed.

Then Thunder noticed the shelter Holly stood beside: a large den woven from the brambles at the far end, with a high, arched roof. *What an ingenious shelter,* Thunder thought. He wondered if he could re-create something similar for his own cats.

Thunder felt a warmth spread through his pelt. Tall Shadow's cats were making their new camp into a *home*. The shelter of the pines was surely safer and cozier than the hollow on the moor.

If they can do it, so can I.

He turned to Quiet Rain. "Can you continue?" he murmured.

"Of course I can," the old she-cat hissed.

Thunder led the others through the brambles, which rattled as they stepped into the camp.

Tall Shadow hurried forward to greet him, her nose twitching, likely at the unfamiliar scents of Quiet Rain and Sun Shadow. As she stared, puzzled, at the strangers, Mud Paws and Mouse Ear appeared behind her, their pelts bristling uneasily.

Holly drew up alongside her leader. "Who is this?" she asked.

Before Thunder could answer, Quiet Rain stepped forward and met Tall Shadow's gaze. Her speckled pelt might have clung to her bones, but she stood tall and proud. Tall Shadow seemed to sense her authority, her eyes narrowing nervously as Quiet Rain gave her a gaze that was almost . . . *familiar.*

Then Tall Shadow's eyes widened.

"Don't you know me?" Quiet Rain's mew was thick with emotion.

Tall Shadow leaned forward and sniffed, her pelt seeming to bristle with excitement. "Quiet Rain? Is that you?"

Holly shifted beside her. "You *know* this cat?"

Quiet Rain purred, her chest crackling. "She knows me well." She lifted her muzzle as Tall Shadow bounded forward and wove around her. Thunder felt relief tingling in his skin as her gaze flicked to the second cat.

"You must be Moon Shadow's kit! You look so much like him. You . . ."

Tall Shadow's words trailed off, her eyes shutting tight as if to stifle the ache in her heart. The loss of her littermate clearly still hurt her, but she shook her head clear of it, her face filling with delight to gaze upon his son.

Sun Shadow gave a solemn nod.

Thunder saw Tall Shadow freeze. He stepped forward, leaning close to her ear. "They know about Moon Shadow and Bright Stream," he murmured, "but that's all I've told them of their old Tribemates."

Quiet Rain was glancing around the camp, her eyes glistening with hope. "Where is Gray Wing?"

Tall Shadow hesitated.

"What's wrong?" Quiet Rain jerked around to stare accusingly at River Ripple. "Is that why you kept prattling like a magpie all the way here? Are you hiding more sorrow from us?"

River Ripple gazed steadily back at her but said nothing.

Tall Shadow gripped the earth with her claws. "Gray Wing isn't here at the moment." She looked to Thunder. "Have *you* seen him?"

Thunder frowned at her. "Why would I have seen him? He lives here now."

Holly's ears twitched. "He left the camp a few days ago."

"He's *missing*?" Quiet Rain blinked at Thunder. "You said he'd be here!" She scanned the clearing again. "Are Clear Sky and Jagged Peak *missing* too?"

Sun Shadow's spine fur stood on end. "What else are you hiding from us?"

Tall Shadow looked desperately at Thunder. Sun Shadow's bony flanks were quivering, while Quiet Rain swayed on her old, weak legs.

Thunder's tail drooped. *I've only succeeded in bringing them more grief.*

Paws pattered toward them. "I smell infection." Pebble Heart was hurrying across the clearing. He stopped beside Quiet Rain and began sniffing at her pelt.

She flinched away. "Who's this?"

"Pebble Heart," Tall Shadow told her. "He has the power to heal."

"I know herbs that might help you," Pebble Heart mumbled modestly. He sniffed Quiet Rain's pelt once more, stopping as he reached the blackened wound on her hind leg. "Is this your only injury?" he asked.

Quiet Rain snorted. "The only one worth mentioning."

"It needs a poultice," Pebble Heart told her. "I'll make you one. Please rest while I do. And eat. You will need strength to fight this infection. It's gone deep." He nodded toward the prey pile, then hurried toward his den.

Quiet Rain watched him go. "At least there's one cat who's honest."

"We are all honest!" Tall Shadow bristled, meeting Quiet Rain's gaze with a fierce one of her own. "Pebble Heart is right. You need to rest. There is much you need to know, but I'm not telling you anything while you look like you might fall over at any moment."

Thunder looked at the old she-cat, wondering how she'd

react to Tall Shadow's bluntness. Then a purr sputtered in Quiet Rain's throat. "You have your father's temper."

"And I see where Clear Sky got his spirit." Tall Shadow headed for Pebble Heart's den. "Follow me."

Thunder stayed close to Quiet Rain as she approached the den—just in case her tired legs gave way.

Quiet Rain sniffed. "It smells of sap!"

Tall Shadow halted beside the den entrance. "Pebble Heart is mixing herbs to treat your wound."

As she spoke, Pebble Heart slid out, a leaf folded in his jaws. He dropped it beside Quiet Rain. "Lie down, please."

She glanced at him warily, but followed his order and careful lowered herself onto the ground.

Thunder could see relief soften the old cat's face as she rested.

Pebble Heart unfolded the leaf with his paw, then lapped up some of the green pulp inside and began to wash it into Quiet Rain's wound.

She winced, but made no sound.

"Will it heal?" Sun Shadow leaned forward.

"In time," Pebble Heart murmured between licks.

Tall Shadow signaled to Mud Paws and Mouse Ear with a flick of her tail. "We'll need more prey."

Mouse Ear nodded. "We'll hunt."

"I found a stash of beechnuts while we were out this morning," Mud Paws meowed. "Where there are nuts, there are squirrels."

The two toms crossed the clearing, brushing past River Ripple as they headed out of camp.

Tall Shadow stepped away from Quiet Rain and Pebble Heart, coming to stop at Thunder's side. "Thank you for bringing them here."

Thunder shrugged. "She wanted to see you and Gray Wing."

Tall Shadow's whiskers twitched with worry. "If you see any sign of Gray Wing, please tell him to come home."

"I will." Thunder dipped his head.

At the edge of his vision, he saw River Ripple shifting his paws impatiently. "I must get back to the island. The others will wonder where I am."

Tall Shadow's green eyes brightened with hope. "Did you accept Dappled Pelt and Shattered Ice into your group?"

"Of course." The silver tom purred. "They were welcome and have settled in well. Night and Dew have been teaching Dappled Pelt to swim." Thunder shuddered at the thought. "She caught her first fish yesterday. She might have been born in the mountains, but she moves like an otter in the water."

"Did you say Dappled Pelt?" Quiet Rain's raspy voice called across the clearing.

"She and Shattered Ice live with River Ripple now," Tall Shadow called back.

"Mountain cats living beside *water*?" Quiet Rain blinked as Pebble Heart worked on her wound.

"Don't forget, we were raised behind a waterfall." Thunder

saw Tall Shadow's eyes glaze over at the distant memory. "Perhaps Dappled Pelt missed the sound of it lulling her to sleep."

Thunder's heart suddenly felt heavy. So many cats had made so many choices—from long before the time he was born. Each time they did, it brought changes to the cats, to the groups, to the camps . . . huge changes—new lines of territory, and occasional death. Not all the choices had been good ones. Would Quiet Rain be able to understand all the quarrels the cats had had? How would she feel, seeing the grave beside the four trees—the grave where so many of her Tribemates now lay?

River Ripple turned. "I must go."

"So must I." Thunder glanced at Tall Shadow. "Can you take care of them? Do you have enough prey?"

"We'll find enough," Tall Shadow promised. "We are quickly learning the best places to hunt among the pines. And in the quiet of the forest, prey is easy to hear. It may be scarce, but we're good hunters."

River Ripple gave a respectful nod before he headed for the entrance.

Thunder turned to follow, but stopped when he heard his father's mother call once more across the clearing. "Don't go, Thunder! Tell me more about Clear Sky. Has he found a new mate?"

Thunder hesitated, his paws suddenly feeling mud-sodden. "Stay," Tall Shadow whispered. "Just long enough to reassure her that he is well."

Thunder held her gaze, uncertain of how to respond.

Before he could, the bramble wall shuddered as Jagged Peak padded in.

Holly hurried to greet him. "You're back!"

Quiet Rain pushed herself to her paws, nudging Pebble Heart away. "My son!"

Jagged Peak paused, eyes wide. "Quiet Rain?" Joy lit up his gaze and he hurried to greet her.

Quiet Rain's gaze flicked instantly to his injured hind leg, which dragged behind him. "What happened?" she gasped.

"An old injury." Jagged Peak halted. "I fell from a tree. It's not important."

Quiet Rain stared at him, disappointment clouding her gaze. "You're *lame!*"

Jagged Peak stiffened, the fur ripping along his spine. Thunder's paws tingled with dread—Jagged Peak never liked other cats treating him as weak, but would he admonish his mother the way he had Gray Wing?

Holly growled. "He has a slight limp," she told Quiet Rain sharply. "That's all. He can hunt and think as well as any cat and—"

Excited mewls cut her off. Dew Nose raced into camp, dragging a vole, while Storm Pelt and Eagle Feather crowded around her.

"It's my turn to carry it!" Eagle Feather complained.

Jagged Peak turned on them sternly. "Behave yourselves! My mother is visiting from the mountains."

Dew Nose dropped the vole and stared at the ragged she-cat. "*That's* your mother?"

Storm Pelt raced to Holly's side and sheltered under her belly. "That cat smells funny."

Eagle Feather padded toward Quiet Rain, his nose twitching. "Why have you come here?"

Quiet Rain glared at Jagged Peak, bristling. "Is this how you raise your young in this land of soft earth? I would never have allowed such rudeness."

Holly's eyes flashed with rage. "Perhaps that's why your sons left."

Quiet Rain glared back. "How dare you?"

Jagged Peak stepped between them. "My kits are lively," he told her. "But they have good hearts and will make fine hunters one day."

Quiet Rain ignored him and turned to Thunder. "I wish to see my other sons," she meowed. "Where is Clear Sky?"

Thunder dropped his gaze. "He's in the forest."

Quiet Rain's eyes widened. "We found *you* in the forest. Why did you bring us all the way here?"

"I will take you to him when you're stronger," he mumbled.

Quiet Rain jerked her gaze to Tall Shadow. "And what about Gray Wing?"

"I told you," Tall Shadow meowed irritably. "We haven't seen him for days."

"If Gray Wing is missing," Quiet Rain growled, "you must find him. I came here to see my kin."

Thunder saw Tall Shadow staring at the she-cat. *Please don't fight,* he willed them both. *Quiet Rain is just a concerned mother, that's all.* The mountain cat was also tired and hungry, and carrying a wound that looked painful.

And there was still more grief for the old cat to face.

Tall Shadow seemed to come to the same conclusion as Thunder. She turned to face him.

"Find Gray Wing, please."

CHAPTER 16

Wind tugged Gray Wing's fur. Clouds, heavy with snow, were pushing over Highstones, yellowing the pale blue sky. They'd reach the moor by nightfall.

A shrew dangled by its thin tail from Gray Wing's jaws. Ahead of him, Gorse Fur ducked into the heather, Minnow just behind him. Gorse Fur had only a vole. Minnow's lapwing had been half-dead from hunger when she caught it. There wouldn't be much flesh on its bones.

Gray Wing wondered whether to stay out longer. If snow was coming, the prey pile should be high. But what was the point? They'd hunted half the day for this meager catch.

Gray Wing followed the others along the sheltered trail that led to Wind Runner's camp. He'd hoped to bring back a rabbit, but the rabbits were hidden deep in their burrows. They must have smelled the snow before he did.

Mews sounded along the heather tunnel.

"Gorse Fur!"

"Minnow!"

Gray Wing glimpsed Dust Muzzle pushing alongside Gorse Fur.

"Can I carry your vole?" the young tom begged.

"What did you catch?" Moth Flight stopped in front of Gray Wing. The excitement in her gaze faded as she spotted the shrew. "No rabbits?"

Gray Wing shook his head sadly and nudged her along the trail until they popped out into the sheltered clearing.

Wind Runner was pacing the far end, her gaze flicking toward the thickening clouds.

Reed stood near her, sniffing Slate's injured ear. The fox bite had healed quickly in the days since the attack, but Reed was still careful to keep checking for any sign of sourness in the wound.

Gray Wing dropped his shrew. "Is Slate okay?" he called to the silver tabby.

"Her ear will be fully healed in another quarter moon," Reed answered.

Slate ducked away from him. "I wish the fox had torn out a lump of fur instead." She shook out her pelt irritably. "At least fur grows back."

"Gray Wing, can I put your shrew on the prey pile?" Moth Flight's mew snapped him from his thoughts.

"Yes." He glanced at the empty patch of grass. Dust Muzzle was already dragging Gorse Fur's vole toward it. Minnow padded past him and dropped her scrawny lapwing. Moth Flight grabbed Gray Wing's shrew and raced over to place it on top.

Gray Wing was glad he could help the moor cats hunt. But he felt guilt pricking his belly. Surely his campmates in the pine forest needed help too?

Gray Wing's not as fast as he used to be. Jagged Peak's words rang in his ears, and once more he remembered his argument with his brother and Tall Shadow.

You've been giving orders since you came back to camp! Did Tall Shadow really believe that? Perhaps he should return to clear the air. And yet it still rankled that he'd been accused of being weak *and* of trying to take over as leader. *Make up your minds!* Tall Shadow and Jagged Peak seemed ready to criticize everything he did. Here on the moor, he was accepted as he was. Wind Runner was grateful for the prey that he caught. Slate seemed to enjoy his company, settling down beside him each night so they could talk before they slept and shared their warmth. And, away from the dampness of the forest, his breathing had eased. He felt as though the wind had reached deep into every part of him: he could run faster, breathe more deeply, and sleep more soundly.

Pebble Heart would be worried about him, though. Now that Sparrow Fur and Owl Eyes had moved to Clear Sky's camp, the young tom must feel alone. *And I miss him.* Gray Wing's chest tightened as he remembered Pebble Heart's soft, solemn gaze.

I should go home.

Slate crossed the clearing toward him. Her thick gray fur rippled as she walked.

Maybe tomorrow.

"Was that all there was?" Slate nodded toward the prey pile.

Gray Wing met her gaze apologetically. "We were lucky to

find that. Snow's coming, and most of the prey has taken to its nests."

Slate sighed. "Just when we need it most."

"I'll go out again later," Gray Wing offered.

"I'll come with you."

"We could try the tunnels." Gray Wing hadn't ventured underground yet. He'd never shared Acorn Fur's love of hunting in the dark. But they might unearth a rabbit's nest.

Slate's eyes glittered with unease. "I've never hunted underground."

"We won't go deep," Gray Wing promised. His gaze snagged the scoop in her ear where the fox had ripped off the tip. A dark scab edged it.

Slate dropped her gaze. "How bad is it?"

"You look a bit like an owl," Gray Wing teased.

Slate lifted her muzzle sharply. "At least I can still hear." She stared pointedly at Gray Wing's ears. "It's a wonder you hear anything at all. You have so much fluff in your ears, I'm surprised mice don't make nests in them."

Gray Wing nudged her playfully and she began to purr.

"Wind Runner!" Dust Muzzle's anxious mew sounded across the clearing. "I can hear paw steps."

Reed tasted the air, his muzzle high. "A forest cat's heading this way."

Fur bristled along Gorse Fur's spine. Wind Runner padded cautiously toward the camp entrance.

Minnow dropped into a defensive crouch. "Can you tell who it is?"

Gray Wing opened his mouth and let the breeze bathe his tongue. He recognized the scent at once. "It's Thunder."

Wind Runner pricked her ears. "What's he doing on the moor?"

Gorse Fur narrowed his eyes. "I thought I smelled his scent while we were out hunting."

Minnow nodded. "Me too. Near the four trees. And I smelled more than one cat."

Wind Runner blinked at the gray-and-white she-cat. "Rogues?"

Minnow shrugged. "They smelled strange."

The heather shivered as paw steps headed along the tunnel. Thunder poked his head into the camp. "May I come in?" He glanced at Wind Runner.

Wind Runner dipped her head. "You are welcome."

Thunder slid out from the heather, his orange-and-white pelt bright against gray leaf-bare branches. "Gray Wing! You're *here*!" His eyes lit up. "I've been tracking your scent."

Gray Wing tipped his head. "Why?" Surely his own campmates should have been hunting for him, rather than Thunder.

"Tall Shadow sent me."

Gray Wing shifted his paws, feeling suddenly guilty. "Is she okay?"

Worry sparked in Thunder's gaze. A chill ran down Gray Wing's spine. *Slash!* Had he attacked the camp? He'd assumed that Fern's plan to distract the vicious rogue had worked.

"She's fine." Thunder's tail twitched. "Everyone's fine."

"Then why did Tall Shadow send you?" Gray Wing frowned, puzzled.

"I found some strangers in the forest," Thunder explained hesitantly. "They were looking for Tall Shadow, so I took them to her camp."

Gray Wing leaned forward, curiosity pricking his pelt. Why did Thunder seem so wary? *Strangers?*

"They want to see you."

Slate shifted beside Gray Wing, her pelt bristling. "Who are these strangers?"

Wind Runner tipped her head. "Where are they from?"

Thunder stared at Gray Wing. "They're from the mountains."

"The *mountains?*" Gray Wing's thoughts whirled. Had the Tribe followed the Sun Trail? He remembered his dream of the empty cave behind the waterfall. *But they wanted to stay among the peaks.* Had something terrible happened to drive them from their home?

Thunder lowered his voice. "It's Quiet Rain."

My mother! Gray Wing's heart quickened. The journey from the mountains had been difficult for the young and healthy cat he used to be—Quiet Rain would surely have found it even more trying. "Is she okay?"

"She's weak and hungry, and carries a wound, but Pebble Heart is taking care of her," Thunder told him. "She came with a cat named Sun Shadow."

"Moon Shadow's son . . ." Anxiety fluttered in Gray Wing's

belly. What was she doing here? "I must go to her," he meowed, heading for the heather tunnel.

"Wait!" Slate called. "Who's Quiet Rain?"

Gray Wing glanced back at her. "She's my mother!" Why hadn't he been in the forest to greet her? He shouldn't be here on the moor. He had duties and responsibilities at home. As he shouldered his way through the heather tunnel and burst out onto the grass beyond, he felt his breathing shorten. His heart pounded in his ears.

"Wait for me!" Paws thrummed behind him as he raced across the moor.

Thunder caught up with him, panting. "Slow down!" he puffed. "She's not going anywhere."

"I should have been there." Gray Wing struggled to speak, fighting for breath.

Thunder swerved across his path. "There's no use getting there so out of breath that you can't even speak to her."

Gray Wing halted. "You're right." His chest wheezed as he spoke.

"Let's walk." Thunder fell in beside him.

Tiny flakes of snow spiraled from the sky as dusk fell. There would be snowfall by morning.

Padding slowly, Gray Wing let his fur smooth, relaxing until his breath began to ease. "Is Quiet Rain's wound dangerous?"

"I don't know," Thunder answered. "Pebble Heart says it will take a while to heal."

"Is Clear Sky with her now?" If Thunder had found Quiet

Rain and Sun Shadow in the forest, he must have taken them back to Clear Sky's camp first.

Thunder kept his gaze fixed ahead. "No."

"He didn't travel to Tall Shadow's camp with her?"

"He doesn't know she's here."

Gray Wing frowned, puzzled. "But *you* know?"

"I took them straight to Tall Shadow."

Gray Wing could hear stiffness in Thunder's voice. Something was wrong. "Why not take them to Clear Sky?"

"We argued," Thunder mewed softly. "I left Clear Sky's camp days ago. I've set up my own."

Gray Wing's heart sank. Would Clear Sky and Thunder ever reconcile? Before he could ask, Thunder changed the subject.

"Tall Shadow says that Sun Shadow looks exactly like his father." He lowered his voice. "I told him Moon Shadow had died."

Gray Wing glanced at him. "That must have been hard, for you and him."

"He was looking forward to knowing his father." Was that bitterness in Thunder's mew? "They know about Bright Stream too, but Tall Shadow didn't want to tell them anything more. Not until your mother is stronger."

Gray Wing glanced across the moor toward the four trees hollow, where the graves of so many of their friends lay. What would Quiet Rain say when she found out? He slowed, suddenly realizing how much news there was to share with her and how little of it was good.

What will she say when she finds out how we've fought among ourselves?
As worry wormed beneath his pelt, his forepaw scuffed a hard
vine in the grass. Pain shot through his leg as the vine tightened around it. Instinctively he tried to tug himself free, but
the vine gripped harder, digging into his flesh.

Thunder leaped back, fur on end. "What's wrong?"

"Something's caught me!" Panic flashed through Gray
Wing, spiraling as he tried to pull his paw free. Pain scorched
up his leg as the vine snared it harder.

"Hold still!" Thunder darted forward, examining his paw.
"It looks like a vine from a Twoleg fence."

Gray Wing could smell blood and looked down to see the
fur darken around his paw.

Thunder sniffed along the thin tendril. "It's tied to a stick."

Gray Wing fought against the blinding pain as Thunder
gripped the stick between his jaws and tried to haul it from
the ground.

He groaned with effort, then fell away, growling. "It's stuck
fast. I can't move it."

Gray Wing saw him glance warily across the moor. He
guessed what Thunder was thinking. "Foxes will smell my
blood." *And come looking for an easy meal.* Fear hollowed his belly.
I'm trapped like prey!

"Stay calm." Thunder paced around him. "We'll find a way
to get you out."

"How?" Gray Wing tugged his paw again, gasping as the
vine cut deeper.

"I know." A mew sounded from the heather behind them.

Gray Wing jerked his muzzle around and saw Fern padding across the grass toward them.

Thunder showed his teeth. "Who are you?"

Fern paused and tipped her head. "Gray Wing knows me."

"She's Fern," Gray Wing rasped.

Fern circled them, leaving a wide berth between her and Thunder.

Thunder's gaze was suspicious, his orange pelt bristling. "You know how to free Gray Wing?" he growled. "How? Did you set this trap?"

Fern purred with amusement. "Don't be dumb! It's a Two-leg trap for rabbits. If I knew how to set it, I'd never go hungry again." She rolled her eyes at Gray Wing. "I can't believe you were mouse-brained enough to walk into it."

Gray Wing gritted his teeth. "Just get me out!"

"You have to stop struggling," Fern told him. She gave a warning look to Thunder, then ducked down beside Gray Wing's paw. "Hold still."

Gray Wing forced himself to keep still, breathing fast against the pain.

"This might hurt a little," Fern warned. "I have to get my teeth around the vine to loosen it."

Gray Wing nodded and braced himself.

He shuddered as he felt her small teeth slide between the vine and the wound in his leg. She wriggled her head, and he gasped as pain flared through him like lightning. Suddenly, the vine loosened. Fern jerked her head away and Gray Wing slid his paw easily from the trap.

Relief swamped him as the worst of the pain receded. But the wound stung like fury, and he felt blood seeping into his fur. He put weight on his paw, relieved to find it solid beneath him. "Nothing broken." It was only a flesh wound. It would heal.

Thunder stared at the scarred she-cat. "Who *are* you?"

Fern caught Gray Wing's eye.

"She's just a rogue." He shrugged.

Fern's eyes flashed. "'Just a rogue'?" she snorted. "I'm the rogue who lied to a murdering tom just to save your friends."

Gray Wing's ears pricked. "You spoke to Slash?" he asked eagerly.

"I promised I would, didn't I?" Fern lifted her chin. "I told him about the prey and he went to look for it, just like I said he would. He's such a greedy fox!"

Thunder's eyes were wide. "Who's Slash?"

"He's another rogue," Gray Wing told him. "He sent Fern to spy on us."

Thunder narrowed his eyes at her. "You're a spy?"

"Leave her alone," Gray Wing told him sharply. "Slash is as cruel as One Eye. It took a lot of courage to lie to him."

Fern puffed out her chest. She looked like a scrawny pigeon. Gray Wing realized that she was skinnier than ever.

"Have you been hunting in the hollow?" he asked.

"Yes." She shrugged wearily. "But there wasn't much prey."

"Come back to my camp," Gray Wing meowed. "When Slash finds out you sent him looking for prey that isn't there, he won't be pleased. You'll be safer with us, and you can share our prey."

Thunder eyed him. "Tall Shadow might have something to say about that."

"Not when I explain what Fern has done for us." Gray Wing began to pad toward the pines. They loomed against the darkening sky, and snow was falling thicker. Pain shot through him with each paw step, but he ignored it.

His mother was waiting for him.

Fern trotted after him. "Can I really come with you?" She sounded like a nervous kit.

"Yes."

Thunder fell in beside her. "Why did Slash want you to spy on Gray Wing's camp?"

Fern shrugged. "He doesn't like to share his land with other cats."

"This isn't his land," Thunder growled. "If it was, we'd have seen him before. Where does he come from?"

"We used to live as strays in the Twolegplace. But Slash got bored of eating Twoleg waste and decided there would be richer pickings out here." Fern gazed across the fast-whitening moor. "Slash doesn't like to admit when he's wrong."

"Why do you stay with him?" Thunder's gaze flicked over her knotted fur and scars.

Fern stared ahead. "I have no one else."

"Not even kin? Surely—"

Gray Wing cut in. "Leave her alone, Thunder."

Thunder shrugged. "Okay." He nodded toward Gray Wing's paw. "How does it feel?"

"It hurts," Gray Wing told him. Pain throbbed where the vine had sliced through his flesh. "But Pebble Heart will know which herbs will soothe it."

They headed down the slope toward the Thunderpath. Monster tracks sliced through the slush covering the smooth black stone. Gray Wing pricked his ears, listening for monster growls. He heard nothing through the muffling snow, and there was no sign of eyes flashing in the distance.

"Come on." He limped across the Thunderpath, relieved to smell pinesap as he reached the other side.

Fern's black pelt was dotted with flakes. Snow speckled Thunder's whiskers. A fresh flurry whirled around them, and Gray Wing ducked between the straight, dark trunks into the shelter of the forest.

Thunder led the way to the bramble camp. Fern stayed close to Gray Wing, pressing closer as they neared.

"Are you sure this is a good idea?" she whispered as the ring of brambles loomed ahead of them.

Familiar scents filled the air. "You'll be fine," Gray Wing promised her. Skirting the camp wall, he followed Thunder through the entrance. He scanned the wide clearing. "Quiet Rain?" His heart swelled with excitement.

Mud Paws looked up from the prey pile, where Mouse Ear was sifting through the day's catch. Tall Shadow and Jagged Peak sat in the shelter of the camp wall, their heads close as they shared words.

Tall Shadow spotted Gray Wing. "You're back!" Relief flooded her mew.

"I'm sorry I stayed away so long."

As Gray Wing dipped his head, Dew Nose's voice sounded from the large den at the far end of the clearing. "Holly, can we play in the snow?"

"Tomorrow," Holly's voice answered. "It's time to sleep now."

Gray Wing blinked, impressed at the den she'd built while he'd been away.

Another den jutted from the side of the camp wall. Gray Wing opened his mouth and tasted the sharp tang of herbs billowing from it.

"Gray Wing?" An old mew rasped from beside it. Lying on the ground, her speckled gray pelt camouflaged against the snow-flecked needles, was Quiet Rain.

Gray Wing hurried toward her, wincing at the pain. Joy flared in his chest. He'd thought he'd never see her again— but here she was, in his new home! She struggled to get to her paws as he neared, but slumped back weakly. She was so thin now. Thick green pulp was smeared on the top of her hind leg. Her eyes shone as they met his, but he could see exhaustion in their blue depths. "Where's Sun Shadow?" He glanced around for the young tom.

"He's sleeping," Quiet Rain told him. "It's the first time he's had a full belly and a safe nest for quite some time."

Gray Wing blinked anxiously at his mother. "Are you okay?" The tang of the herbs filled his nose.

"I'm here," she murmured. "That's all that matters."

Emotion tightened Gray Wing's throat. He thrust his muzzle against Quiet Rain's cheek.

She relaxed at his touch, and his pelt rippled with pleasure as he breathed in the scent of her. For a moment he was a kit again, nuzzling beside her belly in the warmth of their mountain nest.

Suddenly, she pulled away. "I smell blood!" Fear lit her gaze as she saw Gray Wing's injured paw. "What happened to you?"

"I got caught in a Twoleg trap."

Her blue eyes clouded. "Why did you ever come to this place?" Her wail was thin, like the mewl of a kit. "There is nothing but death and danger here! You should have stayed in the mountains!"

CHAPTER 17

❧

Thunder watched Gray Wing lean close to Quiet Rain, trying to comfort her with soft purrs as flakes of snow drifted through the thick pine canopy, settling on their pelts. She'd wailed like a kit, though Thunder couldn't make out her words. Perhaps sleep and good forest prey would ease the old she-cat's distress.

He dragged his gaze away and surveyed the camp. *Should I leave now?* Unease spiked in his pelt. Mud Paws and Mouse Ear were staring suspiciously at Fern. Tall Shadow's gaze flashed in the half-light. Jagged Peak's pelt was rippling across his shoulders. He should stay until he knew she'd be welcome here.

Fern shifted beside him. "Maybe I should go."

"Just keep your fur flat and look friendly," he whispered.

"That's easy for you to say," she hissed back. "These cats know you."

Tall Shadow was the first to approach. She padded across the clearing, chin high. "Who's this?"

Fern dipped her head. "I'm Fern," she meowed politely. "Gray Wing said I could come back to the camp with him."

Tall Shadow's ears twitched. "*Did* he?"

Fern glanced at the entrance. "I can leave if you like."

"No." Tall Shadow's gaze moved slowly over the black she-cat. "If Gray Wing said you could come, he had a reason."

Jagged Peak limped toward them. "Has Gray Wing been rounding up strays?"

"I'm a *friend*." Fern's eyes sparked indignantly.

Should I tell them about Slash? Thunder glanced at Gray Wing. *No. Let Fern tell them if she wants. Or Gray Wing. It's none of my business.*

Holly padded from her den, exchanging looks with Mud Paws and Mouse Ear as she passed them.

Storm Pelt and Dew Nose raced behind her, Eagle Feather at their heels.

Fern silently met Holly's curious gaze as the she-cat stopped in front of her. Thunder could feel her trembling.

"Her pelt's all knotted!" Dew Nose scrambled to a halt.

"Is she another mountain cat?" Storm Pelt asked.

"What are those scars?" Eagle Feather paced around Fern, sniffing her pelt.

Holly flicked her tail angrily. "Be polite! This cat is a visitor, and your elder." She dipped her head to Fern. "I'm sorry about my kits. They speak before they think."

"They have spirit," Fern meowed stiffly. "They will grow into fine hunters."

Holly puffed her fur out proudly.

Jagged Peak narrowed his eyes. "You say you are a friend. Can you prove it?"

Holly glared at her mate. "This poor cat is half-starved! Let her prove her friendship once she's rested and eaten." She nodded toward the prey pile. "Mud Paws dug up a mouse nest today, so there's enough for all of us. Come and choose one." She beckoned to Fern with a flick of her tail.

"Yes," Tall Shadow agreed. "Eat and rest, Fern. We can talk in the morning."

Jagged Peak rolled his eyes. "Are we going to take in every stray that walks into camp?"

Thunder curled his claws into the snow. "Why not? Strays are no less loyal than mountain cats." He thought of Milkweed and Pink Eyes. They brought prey home whenever they could. Even Leaf, despite his temper, hunted for his campmates before himself.

Jagged Peak snorted and turned away as Holly led Fern to the prey pile.

Dew Nose, Eagle Feather, and Storm Pelt bounced after them.

"I can help groom the knots from your pelt, Fern," Dew Nose squeaked.

"I'm great at catching fleas," Storm Pelt boasted. "Do you want me to catch yours?"

Fern glanced at the kit. "I'm not sure I *have* fleas."

"But if you do, I'll be able to get them," Storm Pelt assured her.

Holly stopped at the prey pile, swung a mouse from the top, and dropped it at Fern's paws. "Take this and find a sheltered spot. You look like you haven't eaten in days."

Fern gazed at her gratefully, then snatched up the mouse and carried it to the camp wall, where she settled onto the snow-flecked ground.

Dew Nose scampered after her.

"Let the poor cat eat in peace!" Holly called.

"I will! I promise." Dew Nose flopped down beside Fern and stared at her as she ate.

Thunder glanced toward at the heap of fresh-kill. Snow dusted the top. He licked his lips and looked hopefully at Tall Shadow. "Can you spare some prey for me? I haven't had a chance to hunt today." *I gave the one catch I made to Quiet Rain.*

"Of course." She blinked at him kindly. "I haven't thanked you for bringing Gray Wing back to us."

"That's okay." Thunder hurried across the clearing, his belly growling. "He wasn't hard to find."

At the prey pile he grabbed a mouse and, crouching, gulped it down in a few bites. As he swallowed, he watched Gray Wing sitting beside Quiet Rain. What must it be like to see his mother after so long? He wondered, with a pang, how he'd feel if Storm suddenly padded from between the trees.

"I want to see Clear Sky!" Quiet Rain's querulous mew sounded across the clearing.

Gray Wing's gaze swept around and stopped at Thunder. "Will you get your father?"

Thunder froze, the mouse suddenly sitting heavy in his belly. "Now?" Dusk had given way to night. Beyond the forest, the snow would be falling heavily.

"You only have to cross the Thunderpath," Gray Wing pressed.

But I don't want to see Clear Sky yet! Fur bristled along Thunder's spine. He pushed himself to his paws and glared at Gray Wing. "Can I speak with you in private?"

Gray Wing straightened and padded toward Thunder. "What's wrong?"

Thunder lowered his voice. "I told you I left Clear Sky's camp," he hissed. "That wasn't easy to do. I'm not going back this quickly."

"I'm not asking you to live with him again." Gray Wing's gaze hardened. "Just to *get* him."

"Send some other cat!" Thunder glanced around the camp. Mud Paws and Mouse Ear were sharing tongues. Tall Shadow was sitting in the clearing, watching Fern as she ate beside Holly and the kits. Pebble Heart was sniffing at Quiet Rain's wound, while Jagged Peak paced outside his den.

Gray Wing flattened his ears. "Quiet Rain is your kin—she is kin to all of us. Clear Sky is your father. You should be the one to tell him."

"No!" Thunder growled. "I've spent all day taking cats from one camp to another. I'm tired."

"Stop acting like a kit!" Gray Wing snapped. "Clear Sky will want to know that Quiet Rain is here. He'll be grateful you told him. It might put an end to your conflict."

Thunder glared at Gray Wing. "And what if I don't want to put an end to it?"

"There's no time to sulk!" Gray Wing lashed his tail. "My mother is sick. Her wound is serious. You can quarrel with your father another time. Go and get Clear Sky while Quiet Rain's still well enough to talk."

Thunder stared at Gray Wing. Was Quiet Rain that ill? "Okay," he growled. "I'll go." Ignoring the frustration hardening in his belly, he headed for the camp entrance. At least he'd had something to eat.

Clearing the camp, Thunder hurried between pines creaking under the weight of snow. He scanned the shadows until he reached the Thunderpath. It cut a dark gorge between the neat pines and rambling oaks. No fresh monster tracks showed in the thick snow, and he crossed the path easily and slipped into the forest beyond.

Irritation still itched beneath his pelt. Gray Wing *could* have sent someone else. Thunder veered off the path to Clear Sky's camp, heading instead for the ravine. He had his *own* cats to take care of—and he'd made a promise to Milkweed that he'd be back by nightfall. He'd check on them; *then* he'd visit Clear Sky.

By the time he reached the top of the ravine, his paws ached. Snow swirled into the small valley and settled on the brambles and gorse below. He scrambled carefully down the slippery stones, landing with a soft thump in the snow at the bottom.

"Thunder!" Lightning Tail's happy mew greeted him as he squeezed beneath the gorse. "Where have you been?"

"Didn't Milkweed tell you?" Thunder crossed the clearing.

"Yes, but we thought you'd be back before now."

"It took longer than I thought." Thunder glanced around the snowy clearing. Milkweed was peering from the den she'd woven for her kits. He could see Clover's and Thistle's eyes shining in the darkness beside her. Pink Eyes crouched at the edge of the clearing, chewing on a scrawny starling.

Leaf bounded across the camp, a squirrel dangling from his jaws. He nodded to Thunder as he passed.

"It looks like you've had good hunting today," Thunder called after him.

Lightning Tail puffed flakes from his nose. "Pink Eyes smelled the snow coming, so we've been hunting all day. It might be our last chance for a while." He flicked his tail toward the prey pile, which was nearly as full as the one at Tall Shadow's camp.

Leaf carried the squirrel to Milkweed's den and dropped it at the entrance.

Thunder blinked. Was he actually taking food to the queen and her kits?

"Thanks, Leaf." Milkweed blinked gratefully from the shadows and hauled the squirrel into the brambles. "Do you want to come in and share it?"

"If there's room," Leaf answered.

Leaves rustled as Milkweed and the kits squeezed together and Leaf slid inside.

Thunder glanced at Lightning Tail.

Lightning Tail shrugged. "I think he feels guilty for saying she couldn't hunt. She brought back as much prey as he did today." He flicked his tail toward the prey pile. "You must be hungry. Have something to eat."

"I ate at Tall Shadow's camp," Thunder told him.

The bracken rustled beyond the prey pile. Owl Eyes nosed his way through, shaking snow from his muzzle. "Thunder! You're back!" He hurried across the camp.

"But I have to leave again," Thunder explained. "I have to get Clear Sky and take him to Tall Shadow's camp. One of the mountain cats is his mother, and she wants to see him."

Cloud Spots had pushed through the bracken now. He looked at Thunder, blinking in surprise. "Quiet Rain came all the way from the mountains just to see him?"

Thunder shrugged. "She wants to see Gray Wing and Jagged Peak too."

Lightning Tail swished his tail over the snow. "I'll travel to Clear Sky's camp with you."

Thunder shook his head. "I want you to guard the camp. There might be hungry foxes around."

"Then Lightning Tail should go with you," Owl Eyes urged. "We'll be okay. Pink Eyes can smell a fox as far away as the moor, and Leaf and Milkweed will help me protect the kits if there's trouble."

Thunder stared into the young tom's eager eyes. "Okay."

"You can trust me to keep the camp safe." Puffing out his chest, Owl Eyes trotted away and sat down beside Pink Eyes.

"We should leave now," Thunder told Lightning Tail. "Clear Sky's mother is sick. We can't waste time."

Lightning Tail stared at him. "Why did you come back here first?"

"I promised Milkweed I would." Thunder avoided his friend's gaze.

But the black cat had clearly guessed that Thunder was reluctant to return to his father's camp. "Don't worry," he mewed, nudging Thunder's shoulder with his nose. "We'll just tell Clear Sky about Quiet Rain and escort him to Tall Shadow's camp. It's the right thing to do."

"I know," Thunder muttered wearily. "I just wish some other cat could do it." He headed for the gorse and wriggled underneath. Thorns scraped his pelt and snow showered onto his muzzle as he emerged on the other side. He climbed the rocks to the top of the ravine, pausing to let Lightning Tail catch up, then headed into the forest.

They made the trek to Clear Sky's camp in silence. Thunder's ears were pricked for foxes. Lightning Tail's gaze was fixed on the forest floor as he picked his way over snow-covered roots and fallen twigs. By the time they reached the bramble wall that shielded Clear Sky's camp from the forest, Thunder was cold to the bone. He paused at the entrance and turned back to Lightning Tail. "Let's make this as quick as we can."

Lightning Tail nodded, and Thunder nosed his way into the camp.

The clearing was empty. Soft snores sounded around the edge.

"Thunder?" Acorn Fur sat up in her nest. "What are you

doing . . ." The young she-cat's mew trailed away as she caught sight of Lightning Tail. "Have you come back?" Hope flashed in her gaze.

"No," Lightning Tail told her softly.

Acorn Fur's ear twitched irritably. "Then why *are* you here?"

"We have a message for Clear Sky," Thunder told her.

Nests rustled around the clearing and eyes blinked from the darkness.

"Is that Thunder?" Blossom nosed her way sleepily from beneath the holly.

Alder and Birch hopped from their nests beneath the bramble. Nettle, Quick Water, and Sparrow Fur padded from the shadows into the snowy clearing.

"What do you want?" Birch eyed Thunder suspiciously.

"I hope you haven't come to recruit more cats," Nettle growled. "Because none of us are joining you."

Thunder narrowed his eyes and lifted his chin. "I'm just here to get Clear Sky." He'd been prepared for Clear Sky's anger, but not for the hostility of his former campmates.

Sparrow Fur padded forward. "How is Owl Eyes?"

"He's fine," Thunder told her. "I left him guarding our camp."

"What about Pink Eyes?" Blossom's tortoiseshell splotches stood out against the snow.

Lightning Tail moved beside Thunder. "He likes his new home. He's happy there."

"He was happy *here*," Alder muttered.

Thunder returned her gaze. "So why did he leave?"

Lightning Tail stepped between them. "We didn't wake you for gossip."

"We came to get Clear Sky," Thunder glanced toward the oak roots where Clear Sky's nest lay. It was empty.

"He and Star Flower have made a nest up in the bracken." Acorn Fur nodded toward the steep mud bank and the shadows beyond.

"Clear Sky!" Thunder raised his voice. He stiffened as the bracken rustled and Clear Sky's gray pelt showed in the shadows.

"What do you want, Thunder?" Clear Sky stopped at the top of the bank.

Thunder stared at him. "Quiet Rain has come down from the mountains. She is in Tall Shadow's camp. She wants to see you." He watched Clear Sky's eyes widen, satisfaction at his father's surprise rippling through his pelt. "I promised Gray Wing I'd get you. You need to hurry; she's sick." As he turned and headed for the entrance, a soft mew sounded beside Clear Sky.

"Wait, Thunder." Star Flower was calling him.

He stopped. "What for?"

"This is a shock for your father. Won't you show him a little kindness?"

Like the kindness he's always shown me? Bitterness rose in Thunder's throat, but he was aware of the other cats' gazes on him. "Okay." He waited as Clear Sky scrambled down the bank.

"How sick is she?" Clear Sky stopped beside him.

Thunder avoided his gaze. He didn't want to feel sorry for

his father. "She's half-starved and has a wound on her hind leg. Pebble Heart's treating it, but he says the infection has gone deep."

Star Flower jumped down the bank. "I'm coming with you."

Thunder stiffened. The she-cat smelled different. And there was a gentle glow in her eyes, which he'd never seen before.

"Please stay here," Clear Sky told her gently. "It's cold. You should rest. You're expecting our kits."

Shock stabbed like icicles into Thunder's chest. *Expecting his kits!* He dug his claws into the snow, trying to hide his disbelief. "Clear Sky's right," he growled. "You should stay here. Besides, this isn't your concern—Quiet Rain is *our* kin, not yours."

Acorn Fur stepped forward. Her eyes flashed in the dark. "What's done is done, Thunder. Don't be cruel."

Thunder glanced at her. *What do you know about cruelty? Your mother didn't die when you were a kit. Your father didn't send you away.*

"Come on," Lightning Tail murmured in his ear. "We're wasting time."

Thunder faced Clear Sky. "Are you ready to leave?"

Clear Sky's tail trembled. "Yes."

By the time they reached Tall Shadow's camp, the snow had pierced the pine canopy and was falling in heavy clumps onto the forest floor. An icy wind sliced between the dark trunks. Thunder ducked through the bramble entrance, relieved to reach the shelter of the high camp walls.

He waited for Clear Sky and Lightning Tail to follow him through.

The clearing looked deserted. The cats must have taken to their nests to escape the cold. Only Gray Wing lay in the open. He was curled into a ball outside Pebble Heart's den. Snow flecked his pelt. He leaped to his paws as soon as he saw Clear Sky and hurried across the camp to meet him.

Clear Sky spoke first. "Why has Quiet Rain come? Did something happen in the mountains?"

Gray Wing shook his head. "She came to see us. She's weak and sick from the journey." He nodded toward Pebble Heart's den. "She's waiting for you."

Thunder watched his father hurry across the clearing and disappear into the bramble den.

"Thank you, Thunder." Gray Wing's breath stirred his ear fur.

Thunder drew away from the gray tom. Gray Wing's harsh words from earlier still rang in his mind. *Stop acting like a kit!* Anger pricked beneath his pelt. "You asked me to get him, so I got him," he snapped. He'd spent all day doing what every cat had asked of him and now he was tired. All he wanted was to return to his own camp and sleep among cats who actually cared about him.

"I'm sorry." Gray Wing's mew was soft.

Thunder looked at him in surprise.

"I was too hard on you earlier," Gray Wing admitted. "But I was worried, and I needed Clear Sky to see Quiet Rain before she . . ." He stopped, his gaze glittering with fear.

Did Gray Wing think his mother was dying?

Paws scuffed the snow behind Gray Wing. Jagged Peak was heading toward them.

"There's prey, if you want it," he told Lightning Tail, nodding toward the pile, now covered with snow. "We've fed every other stray in the forest. You might as well share our catch too. Help yourself."

Lightning Tail caught Thunder's eye. "Will you be okay?"

"Of course." Thunder flicked his tail. "Go and eat. It's not often you get offered prey that you haven't hunted." He watched Lightning Tail cross the clearing, then looked back at Jagged Peak. "Is Fern okay?"

"She's sharing our den."

"And Sun Shadow?"

Jagged Peak nodded toward the camp wall. Thunder could make out a dark shape huddled beside Mud Paws and Mouse Ear in a nest of pine branches. "He ate two mice and fell asleep. He hasn't moved a whisker since dusk."

Thunder nodded, satisfied. "Quiet Rain has all her sons around her now. Once Lightning Tail has eaten, we will return to our camp."

"Don't you want to wait and see how she is?" Jagged Peak asked. "She's your kin, too."

Thunder snorted. "Clear Sky's hardly my kin. Why should Quiet Rain be any different?"

Jagged Peak's eyes glittered in the darkness. "It's easy to be angry, Thunder. But anger achieves nothing except heartache.

Have some pity. This must be hard for Clear Sky."

Only because he'll have to admit to her how much trouble he's caused.

Gray Wing moved beside him. "It's hard for all of us."

Jagged Peak nodded solemnly. "We came from the mountains in search of a good, safe home. That's what Quiet Rain expected to find when she got here—but all we have to tell her are stories of battle, sickness, and death. This isn't what any cat wanted."

Thunder glanced at Pebble Heart's den. What was Clear Sky saying to his mother?

Suddenly, the camp wall shivered. Thunder blinked in surprise as Star Flower padded through the bramble entrance.

Seeing her, Gray Wing let out a low growl and Jagged Peak arched his back with a hiss.

Thunder stepped forward. "What are you doing here?"

Star Flower brushed past Gray Wing, ignoring the hostility flashing from the tom, and stopped at the edge of the clearing. "I was worried about Clear Sky."

"He told you to stay in camp," Thunder muttered.

She narrowed her eyes. "I do as I please, not as I'm told." Unease rippled through Thunder's pelt when he noticed Jagged Peak's fur bristling along his shoulders. Star Flower had taken a big risk coming here. The last time any of these cats had seen her, she had just betrayed them to One Eye.

He moved closer to her. "You should leave," he hissed in her ear.

"I'm staying," she snapped.

Jagged Peak glared at the she-cat. "Why do you care about Clear Sky?"

"I'm his mate," Star Flower told him. "And I'm expecting his kits. I have a right to be at his side when he needs me."

Thunder felt the air crackle with tension as she met Jagged Peak's gaze.

"Gray Wing! Jagged Peak!" Clear Sky thrust his head from Pebble Heart's den. "Quiet Rain wants—" He stopped as his gaze reached Star Flower.

She returned it, her luminous eyes like stars in the gloom.

Clear Sky tugged his gaze away. "Quiet Rain wants to talk to us." He nodded to Jagged Peak and Gray Wing and ducked back inside.

As the two toms hurried toward the den, Tall Shadow sat up in her nest. "Is Quiet Rain okay?"

Star Flower crossed the clearing toward her. "She wants to speak with her sons."

Tall Shadow stared at Star Flower in amazement.

Before she could speak, Star Flower swished her tail. "I'm here to help Clear Sky. I'm his mate now."

"And you're carrying his kits." Pebble Heart padded out into the snow and stared at the golden she-cat.

She blinked at him. "How did you know?"

"I know the scent of a queen," Pebble Heart told her. He nodded to Gray Wing and Jagged Peak as they passed. "Try not to wear Quiet Rain out," he told them softly.

Thunder's belly tightened as he watched them slip into the den. What would they tell her about their new home? He backed closer to the shelter of the camp wall as the thickening snow obscured the far end of the camp. Had Quiet Rain expected to find her sons united in a peaceful land rich with prey? Thunder felt a wave of pity for the old she-cat. How would she feel once she knew the truth?

CHAPTER 18

❧

"Tell me!" Quiet Rain glared from the shadows at the back of the den. "What happened to my friends?"

Dread opened like a chasm in Clear Sky's belly. *How can we tell her?* He swallowed, his mouth dry. Beside him, Gray Wing and Jagged Peak shifted uneasily on their paws.

"Why is every cat acting like I've interrupted the burial of a Tribemate?" Her eyes blazed. "You are my kin. We should hide nothing from each other! Where are the other cats who traveled with you from the mountains?"

Jagged Peak dipped his head. "Dappled Pelt and Shattered Ice live beside the river now."

"I know *that*!" Quiet Rain trembled as she raised herself on her forepaws.

"Quick Water lives in the forest with me," Clear Sky offered. "Acorn Fur too."

Quiet Rain eased herself back onto her belly, her breath fast from the effort of moving. "Who is Acorn Fur?"

"One of Hawk Swoop's kits." Clear Sky throat tightened as he realized what her next question would be.

"Hawk Swoop?" Hope already flashed in Quiet Rain's eyes. "Where is she?"

Clear Sky dropped his gaze. "She died."

Quiet Rain recoiled. "H-how?"

Gray Wing and Jagged Peak exchanged looks.

Quiet Rain growled. "This is like plucking feathers from a pigeon! *How* did she die?"

Clear Sky glanced at his brothers. They stared at their paws. "There was a battle." Clear Sky's mew thickened.

"With whom?" Quiet Rain demanded.

Jagged Peak lifted his chin. "With Clear Sky."

Confusion clouded Quiet Rain's gaze. "Who fought Clear Sky?"

Gray Wing flattened his ears. "I did."

"We all fought," Jagged Peak put in.

"I don't understand." Quiet Rain's eyes glistened with distress. "You fought *each other*?"

Jagged Peak blinked slowly. "When we first arrived from the mountains, we lived in one group. But some of us wanted to live on the moor and some in the forest. So Clear Sky took some cats to the forest with him, and we stayed on the moor. And we lived in peace until—"

Clear Sky's heart quickened. Was Jagged Peak planning to blame him for the battle? He interrupted. "I decided it was best to divide our new land up so each group hunted different parts."

"You made *borders*!" Jagged Peak flashed him an accusing look.

Gray Wing lifted his head. "It seemed sensible at first."

Quiet Rain narrowed her eyes. "At *first?*"

"Clear Sky kept moving his borders," Jagged Peak told her.

Gray Wing's ears twitched. "We had to defend what we had."

"So you *fought?*" Quiet Rain blinked in disbelief. "Were words not enough?"

"We tried to talk," Gray Wing explained.

Jagged Peak snorted. "When we met to discuss territory, Clear Sky's group attacked ours."

Quiet Rain's gaze flashed to Clear Sky. It seared him like flames and he flinched away. "Is this true?"

"It . . . it was a mistake," Clear Sky mumbled. "I wanted to make sure that my group had enough land to hunt in."

Quiet Rain's gaze didn't waver. "You tried to take your brothers' land; and when they wouldn't give it up, you attacked them?"

Gray Wing stepped forward. "We *all* fought with each other," he insisted.

"We had no choice," Jagged Peak growled.

Quiet Rain's ragged fur lifted along her spine. "Who else died in this battle?"

"Jackdaw's Cry," Gray Wing mewed softly. "And Falling Feather."

Clear Sky stiffened. Would Gray Wing tell Quiet Rain that the brother and sister had killed each other? His breath caught in his throat as Gray Wing went on. "The rogues fighting with us were more vicious than we expected. They were willing to fight to the death."

Relief washed Clear Sky's pelt. *Thank you, Gray Wing.*

"Did one of these rogues also kill Turtle Tail?" Quiet Rain demanded.

Gray Wing's eyes clouded. "She was killed by a monster before the battle." His shoulders slumped. "It was an accident."

"And Shaded Moss?" Quiet Rain's mew weakened.

"Another monster," Jagged Peak told her.

"Rainswept Flower?"

Clear Sky froze as his mother spoke.

Rainswept Flower! Guilt hollowed his belly as he remembered his killing blow. He glanced desperately at Gray Wing and Jagged Peak. *Don't tell Quiet Rain the truth. . . .*

Jagged Peak's eyes glittered in the shadows. Fear flooded Clear Sky's pelt as the gray tom lifted his muzzle.

"She was killed in the battle." Gray Wing flashed a warning look at Jagged Peak.

Quiet Rain's gaze sharpened. "Why are you looking at each other like that?" She narrowed her eyes. "What are you hiding from me now?"

Clear Sky stepped forward, trembling, and raised his chin. It would be better for Quiet Rain to hear it from him. "*I* killed her," he confessed.

"*You?*" Quiet Rain stared at him.

Clear Sky forced himself to go on. "I was mad with rage. I wasn't thinking straight."

"You *killed* your Tribemate?" Quiet Rain's gaze fixed on him like a hawk's.

"It was a battle," Gray Wing meowed softly. "None of us were thinking straight."

Quiet Rain jerked her head around. "Get out, Gray Wing!"

Gray Wing flinched.

"Jagged Peak, too." Quiet Rain dragged her gaze back to Clear Sky.

As Gray Wing and Jagged Peak slunk from the den, Clear Sky backed away from his mother, his heart twisting. Disgust burned in the blue depths of Quiet Rain's eyes. "I'm sorry," he whispered.

Outside, he could hear Star Flower's anxious mew. "Where's Clear Sky?"

"He's still talking to Quiet Rain," Gray Wing told her gently.

"What about?" Worry sharpened Star Flower's voice.

"What's it got to do with you?" Jagged Peak huffed.

Star Flower hissed. "He's the father of my kits!"

Clear Sky longed to flee the den and press his nose deep into Star Flower's fur. Instead, he dragged his gaze back to meet his mother's.

Her scrawny body was trembling. Fever glistened on her muzzle. Froth showed at the corners of her mouth. Should he call Pebble Heart? But fury was burning in her eyes, stronger than any sickness.

"I did not think I could raise a kit to kill his Tribemate," she hissed.

"You don't understand what it was like!" Clear Sky felt the words rise from his throat like the pitiful wail of a kit. "We were in a strange land where the rules of living were very different from what they'd been in the mountains. We had no Stoneteller to advise us. I thought I was doing the right thing!"

"To turn on your kin and your Tribemates?" Quiet Rain snarled. "To *slay* them?"

Clear Sky leaned close to his mother. "I made a mistake," he groaned desperately. "You have to forgive me. You're my mother."

Pain sliced his nose as Quiet Rain lashed his muzzle with her paw. He ducked away, staring in disbelief at her. This was the cat who had suckled him at her belly; she had watched him bring back his first prey to the cave with eyes shining with pride. Now she stared at him with cold eyes.

"I'm sorry." The words choked in his throat.

"You are no kit of mine." Quiet Rain curled her lip. "Get out of my sight. I never want to see you again."

Clear Sky blinked at her, hoping for a heartbeat that she would hear her own words and realize how cruel she was being. "Forgive me," he breathed.

"Never." Her eyes were round with rage.

Clear Sky turned and fled from the den, shocked as snowflakes whipped his muzzle. He squinted through the whiteness, his gaze blurring with grief.

Star Flower's scent bathed his bleeding nose. Her amber eyes shone through the storm, their irises glittering like stars.

He blinked at her, numb with shock.

"Come with me," she murmured gently.

Clear Sky was vaguely aware of Gray Wing and Jagged Peak watching him from the clearing. Tall Shadow was no more than a shape in the swirling snow.

"There's a hollow in the brambles over here," Star Flower soothed. "We can rest there until the morning."

"I want to go home," he mumbled.

"We must stay."

Clear Sky felt her warm flank against his and let her guide him across the snow.

As they neared the brambles, she nudged him softly. "Wait here."

He stared blankly as she hollowed snow from beside the prickly camp wall, digging a den in the shelter of its stems. When she'd finished, she hopped from the shallow dip and nosed him forward. "We'll be warm in here."

His paws scuffed over the snow and slid into the earthen hollow.

Star Flower slipped in beside him. "Lie down."

He dropped to his belly, his paws buckling, and she curled around him, wrapping her tail over him as though he were a kit. Her gentle purr throbbed against his trembling flank; her warmth slowly seeped through his pelt. Like snow melting, his thoughts cleared. "Am I a monster?" he whispered hoarsely.

"No." Star Flower's whisper was firm. "You're a hero and a leader. You make the tough decisions that other cats fear.

There is no shame in that."

His heart ached, and he pressed hard against Star Flower. He felt her tongue lapping his cheek. Closing his eyes, he let the warmth of her lull him into sleep.

I hope that she is right. . . .

CHAPTER 19

Thunder blinked open his eyes, surprised to find himself waking in Tall Shadow's camp. Early rays of sunshine sliced through the canopy. Hushed mews sounded around the clearing. *I sent Lightning Tail home.* The memory flooded back. Last night, he'd watched Gray Wing and Jagged Peak emerge, shaken and wide-eyed, from their mother's den and had changed his mind about leaving. Clear Sky and Quiet Rain did not feel like his kin, but Gray Wing and Jagged Peak did. If Quiet Rain was to die, he could not let them mourn alone.

She can't *die.* Not after such a long journey to see her sons. It wouldn't be fair.

He had sent Lightning Tail back to their camp, worried about leaving Leaf and the others alone too long in a territory they hadn't yet fully explored. Who knew what might be lurking between the trees there?

He heaved himself to his paws, stiff from sleeping beneath a frosty bramble, and shook out his fur. The snow had stopped, but thick drifts banked one side of the camp, and the clearing glittered white.

He recognized Clear Sky's fur half-hidden in a nest dug

beneath the camp wall. Star Flower's golden pelt glowed beside his father's. The pair was still sleeping. A pang of jealousy pricked his belly, but he pushed it away. Star Flower had made her choice.

"Thunder!" Eagle Feather's excited mew rang from Holly's den. His small face peeked out. "We're going to make snow tunnels. Do you want to help?"

Dew Nose pushed past her brother and plunged into the snow. Then she bobbed up again and struggled toward him.

"I'm too big for snow tunnels!" Thunder called out.

Storm Pelt scrambled from the den and followed Eagle Feather as he chased his sister. "You could pretend to be a fox and try to dig us out!"

Thunder purred, then glanced guiltily toward Pebble Heart's den. There was a sick cat in the camp—perhaps he should tell the kits to be quiet.

Eagle Feather reached him and shook snow from his whiskers. "I'll start tunneling. You try to find me." He dived into a deep drift and disappeared.

"Give us time to hide!" Dew Nose called, scooting deep into the snow after her brother.

"Wait for me!" Storm Pelt scrambled after them.

The camp entrance rattled, and snow showered from the brambles around it. Thunder turned to see Jagged Peak pad into camp, a wren in his jaws. He crossed the clearing and dropped it outside Pebble Heart's den, then headed for his own. Wasn't he going to go inside and check on his mother?

Thunder was momentarily distracted by muffled purrs

from beneath the snow. He thought he should pull the kits out before they froze. Stepping toward the sound, he pricked his ears. He could hear Dew Nose whispering.

"Stay still or he'll guess where we are."

His whiskers twitched with amusement. Plunging his muzzle into the snow, he grabbed the first scruff he felt and plucked Storm Pelt out.

The kit swung into the air, spraying snow.

Jagged Peak halted, his eyes widening as he saw Thunder. "What's going on?" he demanded.

Thunder dropped Storm Pelt into a shallow patch. "The kits are tunneling."

Jagged Peak bounded across the clearing. "They'll freeze! Or drown! Or both!" He began digging through the snow with his paws.

"Ow!" Dew Nose squealed as he unearthed her.

Eagle Feather struggled to the surface, his head popping out. "What's wrong?"

Jagged Peak stared at him sternly. "Whose idea was this?"

"Mine." Eagle Feather stuck his nose in the air. "It's fun!"

"It's *dangerous.*" Jagged Peak swished his tail with annoyance. "Stay out of the deep snow and find something useful to do."

"It's not fair. We were only playing!" Eagle Feather struggled to the surface and padded away, his indignant swagger spoiled as every paw step plunged deeper into the snow.

Dew Nose bobbed after him. "Let's think up another game."

"We could practice hunting!" Storm Pelt followed.

Jagged Peak eyed Thunder sternly.

"I was watching them," Thunder told him.

Jagged Peak frowned. "Sometimes you have to say *no*."

Thunder felt a prickle of resentment. He'd been *rescuing* the kits! But he dropped his gaze and shrugged. "I guess." Jagged Peak had a lot to worry about. It wasn't surprising his temper was short these days.

The kits had crossed the clearing and stopped near Tall Shadow. The camp leader was gazing apologetically at Mouse Ear and Mud Paws. "Will you go hunting again today?" she asked them. "I know you hunted for everyone yesterday, but the others are"—her gaze flicked to Pebble Heart's den—"*distracted* right now."

"I just caught a wren," Jagged Peak called across the clearing. "And Gray Wing's out stalking."

"But we have extra mouths to feed." Tall Shadow nodded toward Holly's den. "Don't forget, Fern's with us now."

"I'll hunt with them." Sun Shadow's mew made the camp leader turn. The young tom was stretching in the wide nest of pine branches. He looked brighter than when Thunder had found him yesterday, his pelt sleek from a wash and his eyes shining. He bounded into the clearing and padded toward her. "I'm starting to get the hang of forest hunting."

"Good." Mud Paws greeted him with a nod. "The more paws the better."

"If there's any prey out today, it should be easy to spot against the snow," Mouse Ear meowed.

As Thunder wondered if he should offer to help, snow crunched outside the camp and Pebble Heart ducked through the entrance. A wad of browning stalks dangled limply from his jaws.

He stopped as he reached Tall Shadow and placed them carefully on the snow. "I wish we'd come to the forest in greenleaf," he meowed ruefully. "I can see spots where herbs would have been thick only a few moons ago. But there are only these left now." He prodded the straggly stems with a paw. "I'm not sure it'll be enough to help Quiet Rain."

Sun Shadow's eyes clouded with worry. "Is she worse?"

Pebble Heart met his gaze steadily. "The journey weakened her, and the infection may now have burrowed too deep for me to treat it with mere poultices. I'm hoping that chewing a few of these old nettle stalks might help her fight it from the inside."

Dew Nose hurried forward. "I can take them to her."

Tall Shadow shooed the kit away with her tail. "Go and play," she murmured distractedly. She stared at Pebble Heart. "Are there any herbs left in the hollow that we could get?"

"There should be." Pebble Heart nodded.

Mud Paws narrowed his eyes thoughtfully. "We can collect them while we're out hunting," he offered.

"Okay." Tall Shadow flicked her tail. "But be careful not to hunt on Wind Runner's land."

"We will," Mud Paws promised. He shook out his pelt and headed for the entrance.

Mouse Ear trekked through the snow after him, Sun Shadow at his heels.

The kits scampered through the snow in their wake, stopping as the toms disappeared through the camp entrance, and stared wistfully after them.

"You look tired, Pebble Heart." Tall Shadow tipped her head to one side.

Thunder dragged his gaze from the kits. He suddenly noticed the exhaustion in the young tom's eyes. Pebble Heart must have been up all night taking care of Quiet Rain. "I'll take the nettles to her while you rest." He sniffed them. They were little more than rotting stalks. "Does she just have to chew them?"

Pebble Heart's tail drooped. "It might be hard to persuade her. She's not an easy cat to care for."

Thunder lifted his chin. "I'll do my best." He leaned down and grasped the nettle stems, relieved that the frost that had wilted them had also stolen their sting.

He carried them across the clearing and ducked into Pebble Heart's den. The darkness inside was warm, but the air smelled sour with infection. Swallowing back queasiness, he crossed the earth floor to the heather nest where Quiet Rain lay. She didn't move as he neared, but lay limply on the dry fronds. Heat pulsed from her pelt, and he dropped the nettle stems in front of her muzzle.

"What do you want?" Her mew took him by surprise and he jumped backward. She lifted her head heavily, her nose wrinkling as she sniffed the stalks. "What are these?"

"Nettle stems. Pebble Heart says you have to chew them. They'll help your body fight the infection in your wound."

Quiet Rain pushed the stems away with a paw. "I thought that cat was a healer, not a poisoner."

"He went out in the snow to collect them for you," Thunder pressed. "The least you could do is eat them."

Quiet Rain met his gaze. "If he'd brought them for you, would you eat them?"

Thunder looked doubtfully at the stems. "I'm not sick."

Quiet Rain snorted, then coughed.

Thunder watched her body shake, helpless against the convulsions. "Just *eat* them!" he growled sternly. He wasn't going to let her die. Not after she'd come so far.

Quiet Rain's coughing eased, and she eyed him with interest. "I'll eat one if you do."

Thunder's claws itched with exasperation. "Okay." He leaned forward, snatched a stem, and began to chew it. Bitter juice burst onto his tongue and he fought the urge to gag.

Quiet Rain let out a throaty purr. "Not all that tasty, I see?"

"It's your turn now." Thunder wasn't going to let her off. "Unless you're scared of a bit of nettle."

He saw spirit flash in the old cat's cloudy gaze. She stretched her muzzle forward and grasped a stalk between her teeth. Chewing, she screwed up her eyes, and then she swallowed. "Do you eat a lot of nettles here?"

Thunder's whiskers twitched. "Just because we live in a forest doesn't mean we're rabbits!" He nodded to the two remaining stems. "You might as well finish them now that you've got the taste in your mouth."

Satisfaction warmed his pelt as she swallowed the stalks. "See?" he commented as she finished. "That wasn't so bad."

"Yes, it was," she grunted. She closed her eyes, her face stiff as though fighting pain. When she opened them again, she let out a long, slow breath. "Let's hope they work."

Thunder sat down beside her nest and tucked his tail over his paws. "What you need is to get up and go hunting. All this lying around isn't good for any cat," he teased.

"If only I could." Quiet Rain eyed him quizzically for a moment. "It's hard to believe that Clear Sky's your father. Even as a kit, he didn't have much sense of fun. He was always too busy wishing he was somewhere else."

"Is that why he left the mountains?" Thunder was surprised by his own curiosity. He didn't want to be talking about Clear Sky, but he couldn't help wondering what his father had been like as a kit.

"Yes." Wistfulness clouded Quiet Rain's gaze. "Jagged Peak was the same. But Gray Wing only left because I sent him away."

"Why did you do that?" Thunder blinked at her.

"Jagged Peak left without permission. I thought he was too young for such a journey, so I sent Gray Wing to take care of him." She seemed to be staring far into the distance.

"And you knew they wouldn't return." Thunder felt a pang of sympathy for Quiet Rain. "You must have been worried."

She shook her head. "I knew Gray Wing would protect

Jagged Peak—that once he'd found him, he wouldn't leave him. And I knew Jagged Peak would be too stubborn to turn back."

"Why did you stay behind?"

"The mountains are my home," Quiet Rain told him. "I was born there. And now that I've left them, I wish I hadn't. This land may be green and prey-rich come greenleaf, but it only seems to make trouble. It set brother against brother. In the mountains we had so little; there was nothing to fight over." Grief washed her gaze. "We would never have *killed* one another over land. I can't believe Clear Sky murdered his Tribemate."

Thunder felt a stab of sympathy for his father. "It wasn't like that," he argued. "He made a mistake. He was only trying to protect what was his."

"He killed a cat who'd helped raise him!" Quiet Rain fought back a cough, her voice breaking.

"And he will never forgive himself." Thunder realized that he was actually defending Clear Sky. "He learned from his mistake and he'll never let anything like that happen again."

Quiet Rain watched him, her gaze curious. "You must love your father very much."

Love him? Before Thunder could answer, he heard paw steps crunching outside. Opening his mouth, he tasted the scents of Clear Sky and Star Flower. Fur brushed against the bramble den.

"She doesn't want to see me again." Clear Sky's whisper sounded through the wall.

"Don't be mouse-brained," Star Flower answered him sharply. "She's your mother and she's sick. I just wish I'd had a chance to talk to One Eye before *he* died. But I didn't. You must make your peace with Quiet Rain before—"

"Before what?" Quiet Rain cut her off. Her old ears were as sharp as Thunder's. "Who's out there, planning my death?"

Star Flower padded through the entrance. She locked eyes with Quiet Rain, then slowly dipped her head. "I didn't mean you were going to die. I just wanted Clear Sky to understand how important the time we have with our kin is."

Quiet Rain's gaze slipped past her toward the entrance. "Well, come in, Clear Sky."

Thunder moved aside to let his father slide into the den.

Clear Sky crouched in front of his mother. "I thought you didn't want to see me again," he murmured miserably.

Star Flower snorted. "She *won't* if you whine like a kit."

Quiet Rain's whiskers twitched with amusement as she blinked at Star Flower. "Who are you?"

"I'm Clear Sky's mate. My name is Star Flower."

Quiet Rain's gaze flicked between her and Thunder. "What do you two see in this fox-heart?" she asked, glancing at Clear Sky, who pressed his belly to the earth.

"Get up!" she snapped at him. "These two deserve better than a sniveling piece of prey."

Clear Sky straightened. Thunder felt a wave of pity for his father. He had never seen him look so defeated. Suddenly, he realized where Clear Sky must have inherited his arrogance— and his cruelty. "Don't be too hard on him, Quiet Rain," Star

Flower murmured softly. "A lot has changed for him this past moon. He's only recently learned that I'm carrying his kits."

"You are?" Quiet Rain blinked, then turned to Thunder. "You'll have siblings."

Thunder's mind whirled. Star Flower's kits would be his kin. *But I live in a different camp now.* He would never truly know them.

A mew interrupted his thoughts.

"Quiet Rain?" Gray Wing was outside the den. "May we come in?"

"Who's *we*?" Quiet Rain narrowed her eyes against the light as she peered toward the entrance.

"Me and Jagged Peak."

"Very well."

As Gray Wing and Jagged Peak filed in, Thunder shuffled closer to the edge of the den, the bramble wall jabbing at his cheek.

Gray Wing dipped his head to Quiet Rain. "How are you this morning?"

"I've been better," Quiet Rain grunted. She looked at Gray Wing's injured leg. He'd washed the blood from the fur, but a ring showed where the Twoleg trap had dug in. "How's your leg?"

"Sore, but I can still hunt. I just caught a shrew in the forest."

"*I* caught a wren," Jagged Peak chimed in. "I can get it for you if you're hungry."

Quiet Rain shuddered. "No."

"But you must keep your strength up," Gray Wing urged her. "If you don't eat, you'll never get well."

Jagged Peak frowned at him. "Don't nag her. She's sick."

Clear Sky nudged between them. "If she wants food, *I'll* get it."

"She doesn't want food," Jagged Peak snapped. "Haven't you upset her enough already without bullying her now?"

"I wasn't bullying her!" Clear Sky bristled. "I was offering her food."

"Be quiet!" Star Flower shouldered her way between them. "Your mother needs rest. More than that, she needs to see that her kits can get along without *fighting!*"

Thunder blinked at Star Flower, a realization hitting him like icy water. Perhaps Star Flower would have been the wrong mate for him, in the end. She was ruthless and cunning in a way that Thunder couldn't ever be. But she was just what Clear Sky needed—a smart, no-nonsense cat who wasn't afraid to speak her mind. With Star Flower's reason to curb his temper, Clear Sky might become the strong leader he always wanted to be.

And perhaps he'll be a better father to her *kits than he was to me.* Sadness twisted Thunder's heart, but he ignored it. *I'm not a kit anymore. I'm a leader. What's past is past.*

"Quiet Rain?" Jagged Peak's anxious mew jerked him back into the moment. The tom was sniffing his mother's matted pelt.

Quiet's Rain's eyes were closed, her flanks trembling with each breath.

Thunder stiffened. "Should I go and find Pebble Heart?"

Gray Wing turned to him with wide, anxious eyes. "Perhaps she's just sleeping—"

A shriek cut him off. "My kits!" Holly wailed from the clearing, her cry sharp with fear. "Where are my kits?"

CHAPTER 20

The kits! Clear Sky was first out of the den. The numbness, which had clung to him since Quiet Rain had clawed his nose, melted. He skidded to a halt beside Holly. "When did you see them last?"

Her eyes were wide with panic, scanning the camp as though she might have missed something.

Clear Sky thrust his muzzle closer. "Holly, answer me. When did you see them?"

She froze and met his gaze. "This morning . . . when I chased them from the den. They'd been begging me to let them play in the snow. Fern was still sleeping. I just wanted some peace."

"I shooed them away from Thunder and told them to go and find something useful to do." Jagged Peak stood a tail-length away, guilt brimming in his blue eyes.

"Don't blame yourself. This is no cat's fault," Clear Sky told them sharply. "But we must find them, quickly. They could freeze in this snow."

Thunder and Gray Wing stopped beside Jagged Peak.

Star Flower padded past them. "Where should we look?"

Clear Sky's mind whirled. This forest was wide, and every tree looked the same. It would be easy to get lost among the straight, dark trunks.

Tall Shadow ducked in through the camp entrance. "I can't pick up any scent of them near camp," she puffed. "The wind is too brisk. And there's no sign of paw tracks. Only the ones Mud Paws, Mouse Ear, and Sun Shadow left."

Thunder's eyes lit up. "They might have gone after them!" He began to pace. "They watched them leave. They might have followed in their tracks. They have such small paws; it would be hard to see their prints in churned-up snow."

Tall Shadow nodded. "In that case, they'll be heading for the moor."

Jagged Peak started for the camp entrance. "I'll follow the tracks."

"I'll come with you," Holly told him.

Thunder swished his tail over the snow. "I'll head for the oak forest, in case Mud Paws went that way first."

"Let me come." Star Flower stared at the orange-and-white tom. "I grew up in the forest, and I can show you every hiding place."

"Why would they be hiding?" Thunder argued.

"When they realize how cold and hungry they are," Star Flower countered, "they'll find a sheltered spot and wait for help."

"Okay."

Clear Sky blinked as Thunder nodded and headed out of camp after Star Flower. *They're working together!*

Tall Shadow lifted her muzzle. "I'll check the Thunder-path," she growled darkly.

Clear Sky's belly tightened. She wanted to search for small bodies in the snow. "Where should I look?" he asked.

Tall Shadow stared at him. "You?" She sounded as though she hadn't expected him to join the search.

"Of course!" he growled. "Do you think I'd sit on my tail while three kits were lost in the snow?"

"Search the pines," Gray Wing told him. "I'll come with you."

Clear Sky glanced at his brother's injured paw. "You can't travel fast," he pointed out. "And someone should stay with Quiet Rain."

"She has Pebble Heart," Gray Wing argued.

Tall Shadow pointed her muzzle toward the nest of pine branches. Pebble Heart was curled deep in the middle, sound asleep. "He's exhausted, Gray Wing. I think you should stay."

Gray Wing gave a frustrated sigh, but then nodded slowly. "Okay."

"Besides," Clear Sky chimed in, "someone should be here if the kits find their own way home."

The entrance to Holly's den rustled. Clear Sky saw a black she-cat pad out, blinking sleep from her eyes.

"What's going on?" she yawned.

Clear Sky narrowed his eyes. Was Tall Shadow taking in rogues too? This one seemed scrawny. Scars marked her flanks.

"Fern, you're awake." Gray Wing padded toward the black she-cat. "How are you?"

Fern glanced anxiously around the clearing. "Where is everyone?"

"Holly's kits are missing," Gray Wing told her. "They're looking for them."

Fern's eyes widened. "Dew Nose and Eagle Feather?"

"And Storm Pelt," Tall Shadow added. "Jagged Peak and Holly are heading for the moor. I was about to check the Thunderpath."

"Let me come," Fern begged. "I know their scent better than any cat. I've been sleeping next to their nest all night."

"Are you ready now?"

"Yes." Fern raced for the camp entrance, kicking up snow. Tall Shadow bounded after her.

Clear Sky met Gray Wing's anxious gaze. "We'll find them," he promised.

Gray Wing glanced up at the canopy. Blue sky showed beyond. "Once the sun sets, the forest will freeze."

"They'll be back in their nests by then." Worry jabbed beneath Clear Sky's pelt. *I hope I'm right.* There was so much territory to search. But surely the kits couldn't have gone far? "I'd better go." He padded toward the entrance and nosed his way out of camp.

The forest floor was white. Snow piled at the roots of the tall pines. Clear Sky tasted the air. He could smell Tall Shadow's scent leading toward the Thunderpath. Jagged Peak's and Holly's were already stale, but he could see the churned snow where they'd headed for the moor. He made his way away from their tracks, breaking fresh snow as he trekked deeper into the pine forest.

Scanning the ground, he narrowed his eyes. Small tracks broke the whiteness between the trees ahead. Had the kits passed this way? He broke into a run, reaching the trail in a moment. His heart sank as he breathed in the scent of a squirrel. He could see its tiny paw prints at the foot of a pine, and the clumps of snow it had dislodged as it scooted up the trunk.

He moved on, keeping his nose low. Perhaps the kits' paw steps were too light to break the surface. The cold air had crusted the snow. They could have traveled over it, leaving no mark so long as they kept moving and the warmth of their paws didn't have time to melt the snow.

His own paws already ached from the cold. His heart quickened with fear. A small kit with nothing but fluff to keep out the chill would surely freeze fast in this weather.

"Dew Nose!" His call echoed between the trees. "Eagle Feather! Storm Pelt!"

The only answer was from a crow, which cawed as though amused by his fear. Its wings beat above his head, and he glanced up instinctively as it fluttered among the branches of a pine.

A small squeak sounded above him.

Clear Sky frowned, puzzled for a moment. It sounded like a kit, but why would it be all the way up in the tree?

Another mew rang from the pine branches.

He craned his neck. Could the kits have climbed to safety?

"It's coming closer!" Dew Nose's mew rang clear through the cold air.

Clear Sky froze as he glimpsed her splotchy brown pelt. The kits were clinging to a branch high above his head. Storm Pelt and Eagle Feather cowered behind her. On the branch above them, black feathers glinted in a shaft of sunshine.

The crow! Clear Sky's chest tightened. It was bigger than the kits. With a shudder he remembered watching crows on the Thunderpath, picking at fresh-kill on the stone, their long talons pinning the prey to the ground as they tore strips of flesh away with their strong, sharp beaks.

"Dew Nose! I'm coming!" Fear scorching beneath his pelt, Clear Sky circled the tree. His neck ached from looking up. The crow hopped down a branch and began to sidle toward the kits.

Eagle Feather let out a squeal of terror, shuffling backward.

"Stay away from us!" Dew Nose lifted a paw and lashed out with a hiss.

Storm Pelt cowered behind her, his belly pressed hard against the bark.

The crow only had to knock one of the kits from the branch to turn it into fresh-kill.

Clear Sky reached up and sank his claws into the pine trunk, relieved as he felt the softness of the wood. Hooking his hind claws in behind him, he pushed himself up. Groaning with the effort, he began to haul himself higher. His muscles burned. He paused to catch his breath. The lowest branch was still far above. His legs trembled, and heat washed beneath his pelt. Closing his eyes, he pushed himself higher. The bark scraped his cheek. *Don't let me fall!*

Suddenly, a rotten patch of bark crumbled beneath his forepaw. His claws lost their grip and he slipped. With a thump, his belly knocked against the trunk. Winded, he hung by three paws, fear spiraling in his mind. He pictured the earth far below and swung his free paw hard against the bark, sinking his claws in as deep as he could. Struggling to find his breath, he hauled himself up again, pushing with his hind paws and praying that no more bark would crumble.

Caw! Triumph sounded in the crow's cry.

Clear Sky gritted his teeth and pushed on. Looking up, he saw a branch within reach. Growling with effort, he dug his hind claws in deep and lunged upward. He swung his fore-paws toward the branch and grasped it. Pausing for breath, he hung between branch and trunk. Then, with a final grunt, he dragged himself up.

"Clear Sky?" Dew Nose's frightened mew sounded overhead.

He looked up. The kits were only a few branches above him. But the crow was just a tail-length from them, its beady black eyes glinting with excitement.

The next branch was within reach. He reared and flung his paws around it and hauled himself up. It was easy to scrabble onto the branch beyond. Another leap took him to the kits' branch. It trembled beneath his paws as he landed.

The crow snapped its head around, fear flashing in its gaze.

Clear Sky hissed. "Fly away unless you want to be my next meal."

The crow glanced back at the kits. With an angry shout, it unfolded its wings and soared from the branch. Clear Sky watched it swoop away between the trunks, its dark feathers black against the white forest floor.

"Clear Sky!" Dew Nose's mew was limp with relief. She stared at him with wide, frightened eyes.

Pity flooded beneath Clear Sky's pelt. He thought for a heartbeat of the kits Star Flower was carrying. What if this had been them? He pushed the thought away. It was too much to bear. A fierce, protective fire surged through every muscle as he stared at the helpless kits. *I've never felt like this before.*

Guilt flooded him as he thought of Thunder. *I should have cared about him like this.*

"Clear Sky?" Storm Pelt stared over his sister's shoulder. Eagle Feather clung to the bark behind her. They were close to the tip of the branch.

It was wide beneath Clear Sky's paws, but it narrowed to hardly more than a twig by the time it reached the kits, who were clustered like fledglings. It would never take his weight. If he tried to move toward them, it might break and send them all crashing to the ground. "You must walk toward me," he told them gently.

"My legs won't move!" Dew Nose stared at him, her eyes desperate with terror. She clung, belly down, like a mouse.

"I'll come first." Storm Pelt straightened behind her.

"Don't move!" Dew Nose shrieked. "You'll knock me off!"

Clear Sky pushed back the fear pressing in his throat. "Just dig your claws in hard, Dew Nose. The bark is soft, and if you hold on hard enough, nothing can knock you off."

She stared at him hopefully.

"Are you digging them in?" Clear Sky asked gently.

She nodded slowly.

"Good." Clear Sky looked at Storm Pelt. "Can you climb over your sister without falling?"

"I think so."

"That's not good enough," Clear Sky told him firmly. "You have to *know* you can do it." If he could just get one kit to him, it might give the other two enough courage to follow.

Storm Pelt met his gaze steadily. "I *know* I can do it."

"Good kit." Clear Sky's mouth dried as Storm Pelt began to clamber over his sister.

Dew Nose whined.

"Just hold on, Dew Nose," Clear Sky soothed. "You'll be fine." He kept his gaze fixed on Storm Pelt, who was wobbling as he padded over his sister's back. He paused on her shoulders, and Clear Sky's heart seemed to burst in his chest. He forced his mew to be calm. "Just jump onto the branch when you're ready."

Storm Pelt jumped.

The breath caught in Clear Sky's throat as Storm Pelt landed. The kit's paws slithered for a moment on the bark; then he dug in his claws and steadied himself.

"Well done!" Relief washed Clear Sky. "Now just keep

walking toward me." Blood roared in his ears as Storm Pelt approached slowly. "The branch is wider here," he encouraged.

Storm Pelt was less than a tail-length away. As he neared, Clear Sky leaned forward and grabbed the kit's scruff. Curling his claws deep into the bark to steady himself, he swung the kit behind him and placed him gently in the crook where the branch met the trunk. "You're safe there, as long as you don't move." Storm Pelt cowered in the shallow dip. Clear Sky turned back to Dew Nose, surprise pricking his paws as he saw Eagle Feather padding along the branch toward him. He waited until the kit was within reach, then leaned forward and, grasping his scruff, plopped him down beside his brother.

"Dew Nose." He faced the she-kit, forcing his mew to be as gentle as he could. She was still clinging to the thin branch, her eyes wide with fear. "Did you see how easy it was for your brothers?"

She nodded slowly.

"You need to uncurl your claws just enough to stand up," Clear Sky told her. "Then start walking toward me. You'll be okay. Kit claws are *really* sharp—sharper than thorns, I promise you. They'll dig into the bark and keep you safe. All you have to do is walk."

Dew Nose stared at him for a moment, then slowly pushed herself to her paws.

"Well done!" Pride surged in Clear Sky's chest. "Now walk." Hope and relief welled in his belly as Dew Nose put one trembling paw in front of the other. Her gaze was fixed on him, her ears flat against her head. "You're nearly there," he told her. She was almost close enough to grab. "Just a few more steps and—"

As he spoke, her forepaw slipped off the branch. Her chin hit the bark as she fell.

Horror scorched through his fur. As fast as lightning, he lunged forward and grabbed her scruff between his teeth. The she-kit swung down, jerking him toward the ground.

"Dew Nose!" Eagle Feather squealed behind him.

Pelt on end, Clear Sky dug his claws deep into the bark. *I've got her.* Forcing himself to stay calm, he straightened slowly, ignoring her terrified wails as she struggled beneath his chin. Carefully, he found his balance and lifted her, swinging her toward her brothers. Weak with relief, he dropped her between them.

Storm Pelt pressed his nose into his sister's pelt. "You're safe," he mewed.

Eagle Feather huddled against her. "How will we get down?"

Clear Sky looked at them, trying to steady his breath. "I can lower myself tail-first down the tree," he told them, keeping his mew light. His claws pricked at the thought of the weight that would be swinging from them. "You just have to cling onto my back like squirrel kits." He padded past them and straddled the trunk. "Climb on. There's room for all of you. This is going to be the most exciting badger ride you've ever had!"

CHAPTER 21

♣

"Clear Sky?" Quiet Rain *murmured, her* eyes closed.

Gray Wing leaned toward her and touched his nose to her cheek. "He's out looking for the kits."

Quiet Rain moved her head, groaning softly.

Gray Wing could see the black wound at the top of her hind leg. The flesh around it was swollen, fiery where it showed through her thin fur.

"Rest," he murmured.

But Quiet Rain was blinking open her eyes. "He's looking for kits?" she rasped.

"Jagged Peak's kits have disappeared," Gray Wing told her softly.

"He's too soft on them," she grunted. "No kit of mine would have strayed from the cave."

Gray Wing met her gaze softly. "*We* knew what dangers lay outside. The forest here is safer." Was he telling the truth? Slash was bound to return sometime. The lure of false prey would not keep him away forever.

"*No* place is safe for foolish kits." Quiet Rain lifted her head, her eyes dull with pain.

"We have three patrols looking for them," Gray Wing told her. "They will be found before they come to any harm."

Quiet Rain looked at him, kindness warming her blue gaze. "You were always the gentlest of my kits. I worried sometimes that you lacked Clear Sky's spirit and Jagged Peak's stubbornness. But you have the kindest heart. You always hope for the best." She shifted stiffly in her nest, wincing with pain, before she went on. "I knew you'd find Jagged Peak when I sent you after him."

"I only wish I could have returned to the mountains." Gray Wing remembered his frustration after he'd realized there would be no way back, that he would have to go on with Clear Sky to find their new home.

And we've never been able to agree on where that home even is!

"I knew Jagged Peak would insist on following Clear Sky—and that you wouldn't leave him until you knew he was safe." A broken purr sounded in Quiet Rain's throat.

"But I didn't keep him safe, did I?" Gray Wing murmured. "He's lame now."

"Was it your fault he fell from a tree?" Quiet Rain asked.

Gray Wing dropped his gaze. "No." It had been Clear Sky who'd pushed the young tom into climbing so high.

"Don't pity him," Quiet Rain rasped. "He has a mate and kits. He has prey to feed them and a good, strong den for them to shelter in."

Gray Wing felt his heart lift. Was Quiet Rain finally accepting that their new life was not as bad as she'd first feared? His heart twisted in his chest. *She must live until newleaf.* When she saw the green lushness and smelled the prey beneath every bush, she'd know they had done the right thing in coming here.

He realized that Quiet Rain was still gazing at him, a question in her eyes.

"What?" He blinked at her, puzzled.

"Why don't you have a mate?"

Heat flushed beneath his fur. "I *had* a mate," he murmured. The ache in his heart was still sharp when he thought of the loss that he had suffered. "Turtle Tail."

Quiet Rain's eyes brightened a little. "You noticed her at last."

"Yes." The ache tightened in his chest. "We were happy together, though I wish we'd had longer before she died."

"Did you have kits?"

"She was carrying someone else's kits when we became mates."

Quiet Rain blinked. "Whose?"

"A kittypet." Gray Wing dropped his gaze, trying to hide his bitterness at the memory of the arrogant, selfish tom. "Turtle Tail and I raised them together."

"Where are they now?"

"Sparrow Fur and Owl Eyes live in the oak forest. Pebble Heart has been caring for you."

"Pebble Heart is Turtle Tail's kit?" Quiet Rain's tail twitched. "Why didn't you tell me?"

"I didn't think to." So much else had been going on.

"Now I know why he looks to you whenever you speak, and with such fondness," Quiet Rain commented. "Does he know you're not his real father?"

"Of course."

"You must have raised him well to have inspired such affection."

Gray Wing dipped his head. "I hope so."

"You shouldn't spend the rest of your life mourning."

Gray Wing jerked up his head. "Who said I was going to?"

Quiet Rain looked at him fondly. "You should have a mate and kits of your own."

Paw steps sounded in the clearing. A young mew rang around the camp. "Holly! Jagged Peak? We're home!"

"The kits!" Gray Wing darted from the den.

Clear Sky was following Eagle Feather, Dew Nose, and Storm Pelt as they bobbed across the snowy clearing.

"Are they hurt?" Gray Wing asked.

"They're fine," Clear Sky told him.

"We climbed a tree!" Eagle Feather boasted.

Gray Wing noticed the lumps of fur sticking out from Clear Sky's pelt. "Have you been in a fight?"

Clear Sky glanced along his ruffled spine. A purr rumbled in his throat. "I had to climb down from a tree with three kits hanging off me." He winced, as though the memory stung.

"We were nearly eaten by a crow." Dew Nose stopped at Gray Wing's paws and stared at him proudly. "But it didn't get us!"

He frowned at her. "You shouldn't have wandered off. Holly and Jagged Peak are crazy with worry!"

"Where are they?" Storm Pelt looked around the clearing.

"I smelled their scent outside camp," Eagle Feather commented.

The pine nest rustled at the edge of the clearing. Pebble Heart was sitting up, blinking away sleep. "What's happened?"

Dew Nose bounded toward the young tom. "We've been climbing trees!"

Clear Sky snorted. "They were almost a meal for a crow."

"But you saved us!" Eagle Feather stared happily at Clear Sky.

Pebble Heart hopped from his nest and sniffed Dew Nose. "You're frozen."

Gray Wing suddenly realized that the kits were shivering. "We need to warm them up."

Pebble Heart nodded toward Quiet Rain's den. "Quiet Rain's fever will warm them, and they'll help cool her fever."

Dew Nose stared at Pebble Heart, round-eyed. "We can't go in there! She'll eat us up!"

Gray Wing's whiskers twitched with amusement. Quiet Rain *had* been bad-tempered since she arrived. But she seemed mellower now. And Jagged Peak's kits might boost her spirits. "She'll be pleased to see you," he promised. "But she's in pain, so you shouldn't climb over her or fidget."

Storm Pelt's teeth began to chatter. His pink nose tip was white with cold.

"Come on." Pebble Heart nudged Dew Nose toward his den.

Storm Pelt and Eagle Feather fell in beside them. "When will Holly be back?"

"I'll go and find her." Clear Sky eyed the kits sternly. "*And* the others. Every cat in the camp has been searching for you."

"You can scold them later," Pebble Heart told Clear Sky briskly. "Right now we must warm them up." As he nosed them into his den, Clear Sky headed out of camp.

Gray Wing followed Pebble Heart.

Inside, the kits lined up like owlets and stared nervously at Quiet Rain.

"Pebble Heart wants us to get warm," Dew Nose told her timidly.

Quiet Rain flicked her tail. "I hear you wandered off in the snow."

"We climbed a tree all by ourselves," Storm Pelt told her.

Pebble Heart padded forward. "Can they share your nest until their fur is warm?"

"Of course." Quiet Rain shuffled backward, pain showing in her eyes as she moved.

"We'll be careful not to hurt you," Eagle Feather promised.

"Thank you." Quiet Rain eyed him fondly as he climbed over the heather fronds and nestled beside her belly. Dew Nose followed, and Storm Pelt climbed in behind.

"You have your father's eyes," Quiet Rain told Storm Pelt.

"I don't," Dew Nose chimed in. "But Holly says I'm as smart as him."

"And what about you?" Quiet Rain asked Eagle Feather. "What do you get from your father?"

"I can climb trees," Eagle Feather told her. "But *I* don't fall out of them."

Quiet Rain's whiskers twitched. "He must be proud of you all." She wrapped her tail around them. "Tuck up tight and you'll be warm in no time."

Gray Wing felt memory sweep over him like a warm wind. *She comforted me and Clear Sky like that when we were kits.* The thought seemed to come from a different lifetime. Suddenly weary, he settled onto his belly and tucked his paws under him.

Pebble Heart's breath stirred his ear fur. "I'm going to go to the moor to see if I can find more of my old herbs," he whispered.

There was worry in his mew.

"Do you need them that badly?" Gray Wing glanced toward Quiet Rain, her muzzle resting beside the kits.

"Her wound is getting worse." Pebble Heart's mew was no more than a breath.

"Should I come with you?" Gray Wing began to move.

Pebble Heart touched his nose to Gray Wing's shoulder. "Stay with them."

As he slipped from the den, Gray Wing gazed at the kits. Their heads were drooping. Dew Nose rested her muzzle on Storm Pelt's spine. Eagle Feather tucked his muzzle under Dew Nose's shoulder. Bundled like mice in a burrow, they slipped into sleep. Beside their gentle snores, Gray Wing heard the rattle of his mother's breath.

Her eyes were still half-open, but unseeing.

Let Pebble Heart's herbs work! Gray Wing's chest tightened. *She can't have come all this way just to die.*

CHAPTER 22

Thunder's mew woke Clear Sky. Jerking up his head, he blinked at his son. *It's still night!* Moonlight filtered through the pines, reflecting in Thunder's gaze.

"What is it?" Clear Sky stiffened. "Why did you wake me?" He kept his voice low, conscious of Star Flower sleeping beside him.

"Pebble Heart sent me. It's Quiet Rain." Thunder's mew was tight with fear. "She's worse."

Clear Sky scrambled to his paws and hopped from the nest hollowed out beneath the bramble. Star Flower stirred in her sleep but didn't wake.

"Gray Wing's with her and I'm going to wake Jagged Peak." Thunder nodded to the bramble den, where the kits, warm and fed after their adventure, were now sleeping.

As Thunder padded away, Clear Sky tasted the air. The stone tang of ice had gone. Musty forest scents bathed his tongue. A thaw had set in—melting snow dripped from the canopy.

He padded through the slush toward Pebble Heart's den.

The young tom was waiting at the entrance. "I'm glad you decided to stay another night," he breathed as Clear Sky neared him. His eyes glittered with grief. "I thought I could save her"—his mew cracked—"but the wound . . ."

"You couldn't have done more." Numbness crept up from Clear Sky's paws until he could hardly feel the damp air or taste the pine-rich scents of the forest. *Quiet Rain is dying.* He stared into the shadowy den. *I must go in.* Every hair on his pelt trembled. *I can't.*

Paws splashed through the melting snow behind him. He caught Star Flower's scent just before her flank brushed against his.

He turned and stared into the depth of her luminous green eyes.

"She's waiting for you." Star Flower's breath warmed his nose.

He closed his eyes, his heart pounding with dread. Then, blinking, he padded into the den.

Gray Wing turned as he entered. The gray tom was crouching beside Quiet Rain's nest. "Pebble Heart's given her something to ease her pain." His mew trembled. "I'm not sure she can hear us."

Clear Sky gazed at his mother, who was little more than a scrap of fur in the heather nest. He had never seen her so weak. Even in the hungriest days on the mountain, she still seemed to glow with life, fighting for her survival and the safety of her kits. Now she lay limp, every drop of energy drained. Her flanks trembled with each halting breath. Her muzzle was crusty, and her closed eyes looked as wet as fresh wounds.

"Quiet Rain." Gray Wing leaned closer as Clear Sky crouched beside him. "Clear Sky's here now. You asked for him, remember?"

Clear Sky stiffened as Quiet Rain groaned.

She opened her eyes slowly. "You came to me."

"Yes." Clear Sky tried to keep the grief from his mew.

"I knew you would, my dear friend."

Friend? I'm your son. "It's me, Clear Sky." He moved his muzzle closer so she could smell his scent.

"It's good to see you, Shaded Moss."

She thinks I'm Shaded Moss!

The brambles rattled behind him as Jagged Peak hurried in. He slid next to Gray Wing. "How is she?"

"She thinks she can see Shaded Moss," Clear Sky breathed.

The fur rippled along Jagged Peak's spine. "Does she even know we're here?"

Gray Wing's shoulders drooped. "I don't think so."

"Shaded Moss." Quiet Rain's gaze fixed on Clear Sky.

Grief shuddered through him. *She doesn't know me.* He swallowed, fighting the urge to run away.

"This is the final part of the journey, dear old friend." Quiet Rain struggled for breath between words. Her ears twitched weakly, as though she was trying to hear something. "What was that you said?" A frown furrowed her brow. "Forgive him? But he killed a Tribemate! He drove his brothers away."

Clear Sky stiffened, heat washing his pelt.

Gray Wing glanced at him. "She doesn't know what she's saying."

But it's true. Sadness gripped his heart like claws, digging so deep he wanted to groan with the pain.

Suddenly, Quiet Rain's eyes closed and her head drooped.

Jagged Peak thrust his muzzle closer. "Is she—" The words seemed to dry in his mouth.

Clear Sky guessed what his brother was thinking and leaned forward, relieved to feel Quiet Rain's breath on his muzzle. "No."

As he spoke, her eyes slowly opened.

He flinched away, his heart lurching. There was sudden clarity in their blue depths. She was staring straight at him.

"It's me—Clear Sky," he told her. He didn't want her to call him Shaded Moss again.

"I know," she murmured. Her gaze flicked to Gray Wing, then Jagged Peak. "All my sons are here." There was satisfaction in her mew. "Don't be sad when I'm gone. It will be a relief. I have had a long life, and a good one. I've known hunger and cold, but I've known love too." She blinked softly at all three of them, her gaze coming to rest on Clear Sky. "And I forgive you, my firstborn. Shaded Moss has spoken to me. He explained . . ." Coughing took hold of her, racking her body until she convulsed helplessly on the heather.

"Quiet Rain!" Clear Sky leaned over her.

"Help her!" Jagged Peak called to Pebble Heart, who

lingered, wide-eyed, in the entrance.

"There's nothing more I can do," Pebble Heart murmured.

The coughing eased, and Quiet Rain rasped as she struggled for breath. "Shaded Moss told me."

"Told you what?" Clear Sky thrust his muzzle closer.

"Let her rest." Jagged Peak reached out his paw and placed it gently on her flank. "She must save her strength."

"Save her strength for what? She's *dying*!" Clear Sky trembled. "What did Shaded Moss say?"

"It was all foretold," Quiet Rain rasped. "You could not help what you did. It *had* to be that way. I forgive you, Clear Sky, and now"—she drew in a shuddering breath—"you must forgive yourself."

Clear Sky felt grief rush over him like a wave as Quiet Rain's eyes clouded and grew dull. Her head dropped limply onto the heather and her flanks fell still.

Clear Sky pushed himself to his paws and, leaning over Quiet Rain, closed her lifeless eyes with gentle laps of his tongue.

Forgive yourself. Her words rang in his mind. For what? His thoughts whirled. So much had happened! What was the crime he was supposed to forgive himself for?

Weak daylight was seeping into the den. Eagle Feather's mew rang across the camp. "The snow's melting!"

Small paw steps splashed across the clearing.

Jagged Peak got wearily to his paws and padded from the den. Gray Wing followed, his tail dragging over the earth.

Clear Sky gazed at Quiet Rain, his heart breaking. *If she'd never come here, I wouldn't have had to watch this.*

And yet a dark knowledge, deep in his belly, told him that these final moments with his mother would mark the rest of his life.

CHAPTER 23

❧

Thunder shuddered as a fat drop of water splashed onto his spine. The rainy day was giving way to night.

Beside him lay Quiet Rain's body. Clear Sky and Gray Wing sat on either side, stiff in the dying light, while Jagged Peak shivered next to Sun Shadow.

They'd spent the day sitting vigil beside Quiet Rain. Around them Mud Paws, Fern, and Mouse Ear had come and gone, bringing fresh-kill for the prey pile; Pebble Heart had sorted through the herbs he'd brought back from the hollow, while Star Flower stood by, helping where she could by wrapping the leaves he separated into neat bundles; Tall Shadow had crouched at the head of the clearing, solemnly watching over her camp. At sunhigh, the kits had crept quietly into the forest, Holly close at their heels. Through the afternoon, their excited squeaks sounded beyond the bramble wall of the camp, quickly hushed by their mother. They returned now, as dusk drew in.

"But *why* do we have to be quiet?" Dew Nose whispered as she led her littermates around the edge of the clearing.

"Out of respect for Quiet Rain," Holly hissed.

Eagle Feather sniffed. "No one asked her to come here and die."

"Hush!" Storm Pelt pawed his brother's tail sharply. "She was kind to us, remember?"

Thunder glanced uneasily at Sun Shadow. *What must he think?* But the black tom didn't blink, his eyes clouded with grief as he stared at the trees. Pity jabbed at Thunder's heart. *He came here to find his father, but now he is truly alone among strangers.*

Tall Shadow straightened. The sun was an orange ball beyond the pines, silhouetting the dark trunks with fire. "We must bury her."

Sun Shadow jerked his muzzle toward her. "Where? This is not her home."

"Her kin are here." Tall Shadow padded toward the young tom.

Sun Shadow returned her gaze silently.

Clear Sky lifted his chin. "She must be buried where we can all visit her grave."

Gray Wing nodded. "On shared territory."

"At the four trees?" Jagged Peak glanced at his brothers.

"She would be close to those she once knew," Tall Shadow murmured solemnly.

Thunder pictured the battle grave. Now there would be another grave beside it. The grave of a cat who had died in peace, among those who had loved her. "I'll help carry her there."

"Me too." Jagged Peak stood up.

Gray Wing got to his paws and stretched, wincing as his

injured forepaw slipped on the slushy ground.

Tall Shadow nodded to Mud Paws, who was washing in his nest. "Will you guard the camp while we're gone?"

Holly approached Jagged Peak. "Should we come with you?" She glanced at their kits, damp from playing in the snowmelt.

Jagged Peak shook his head. "Stay here."

"I'll come." Pebble Heart padded from his den. "I should help bury her, since I failed to save her."

Gray Wing brushed against the young tom. "She was *old*," he breathed. "It was her time."

Thunder straightened, realizing how stiff he was. He shook out his pelt, relieved to feel warmth flowing back into his paws and tail.

Star Flower crossed the clearing and touched muzzles with Clear Sky. "River Ripple should be at her burial."

Clear Sky frowned. "Why?"

"He is a leader, like you, Thunder, and Tall Shadow," she meowed. "You are all petals of the same flower, remember?"

"And Wind Runner," Gray Wing added, thinking of the camp on the moor. "Although . . . we are still giving her space."

Clear Sky looked thoughtful. "You are right. We should leave Wind Runner in peace. But the rest of us should be together," he mewed.

"I will get River Ripple," Star Flower told him.

Thunder felt a sudden flash of gratitude toward the she-cat, but he noticed that Clear Sky's pelt pricked uneasily.

"It's too far for you to travel," he argued.

Star Flower met his gaze. "Carrying kits does not weaken a cat; it makes her stronger."

"I'll go with her." Tall Shadow stepped forward.

Thunder blinked in surprise at the warmth in her mew. And yet, why not? Hadn't Star Flower been trying to make up for her betrayal in everything she did? She had not left Clear Sky's side, she'd treated his mother with respect, and now she was offering to get River Ripple for the burial. Was it possible that she'd earned their trust at last?

Clear Sky dipped his head. "Okay," he agreed. "We'll meet you at the four trees."

Tall Shadow headed for the camp entrance, waiting at the bramble tunnel while Star Flower touched muzzles with Clear Sky.

"Be careful," he whispered.

"I will."

As Star Flower turned and followed Tall Shadow from the camp, Jagged Peak leaned to push his muzzle beneath Quiet Rain. Thunder ducked to help, nosing the old she-cat's body onto Jagged Peak's shoulders and sliding in beside him. The first stiffness of death had left her, and she hung limp and cold between them.

Clear Sky led the way out of camp, Gray Wing following with Pebble Heart and Sun Shadow.

At the far edge of the forest, they paused.

Monsters roared along the slush-covered Thunderpath, spraying filthy, half-melted snow in great waves over the side.

"Wait here." Clear Sky nodded to Thunder and crept out

onto the grass. Through slitted eyes, he scanned the Thunderpath, ducking as another monster howled past. "There's a gap coming." He beckoned Thunder and Jagged Peak from the trees.

Thunder stumbled on the uneven grass, and Gray Wing slid between him and Jagged Peak, putting his shoulders beneath his mother's body.

"Stay close together," Clear Sky hissed.

Eyes flashed toward them, streaking them with light as the monster thundered past.

"Now!"

Thunder felt Clear Sky nudge him forward and hurried onto the slippery stone. He felt Gray Wing at one flank, Jagged Peak at the other. Together they carried Quiet Rain, stumbling to a halt as they reached the far side.

Thunder frowned at Gray Wing's wounded leg. Fresh blood was darkening the fur. "Can you manage?"

"She's not heavy," Gray Wing grunted.

Thunder caught his eye and saw grief glitter there. Quiet Rain had been half-starved when she died and weighed hardly more than a kit.

"Come on," Clear Sky urged from behind. "Let's get into the forest and away from this place." As he spoke, another monster thundered by, sending slush and grit spraying over them.

Thunder padded forward, trying to keep in step with Gray Wing and Jagged Peak as the ground grew uneven beneath his paws. Roots crisscrossed the path and brambles snagged at his pelt. He tripped twice, feeling Quiet Rain jerk as he stumbled. He felt relieved when Clear Sky led them from the trees onto the smooth grass slope that led up to the rim of the four trees hollow.

By the time they reached the top, Gray Wing was panting.

"Let Sun Shadow take your place," Thunder whispered.

The black tom had been eyeing Quiet Rain's body, distress showing each time Thunder stumbled or she began to slide from Jagged Peak's shoulders.

Gray Wing met Thunder's gaze with weary eyes and slipped from beneath Quiet Rain. "Will you help?" he asked Sun Shadow softly.

Sun Shadow dipped his head and slid in between Jagged Peak and Thunder.

Thunder lifted his nose toward Clear Sky. *He should have a chance to carry his mother to her final resting place.* "Do you want to take over for me?"

Clear Sky blinked at him gratefully, hurrying to take his place as Thunder slid from beneath her.

He left them and bounded into the hollow, his paws sliding on the muddy slope. At the bottom, he stopped beside the battle grave. Snow covered the ground, sheltered from the warm winds and sunshine. He scratched at the earth, surprised to find it still frozen beneath his claws.

How can we dig a grave here?

As he glanced around the clearing, searching for a spot clear of snow where the sun might have pooled, warm enough to soften the earth, bracken rustled on the far slope. He recognized Tall Shadow's black pelt moving through it. Star Flower's fur was camouflaged among the golden fronds, but he could smell her scent—and River Ripple's. A purr rumbled in his throat as the silver tom padded from the undergrowth.

River Ripple met his gaze solemnly. "I'm sorry to hear Quiet Rain died."

"It was her time," Thunder returned.

Tall Shadow padded from the bracken, Star Flower at her tail. "Have you chosen a burial spot?" She glanced across the clearing to where Jagged Peak, Sun Shadow, and Clear Sky were sliding Quiet Rain's body softly onto the ground.

"The earth is frozen," Thunder told Tall Shadow. "There's no way we can dig."

Pebble Heart was crossing the clearing, his gaze fixed on a large stone embedded in the earth. "If we can move this, we can lay her body in its place."

Thunder stared at the rock. If it was sunk deep enough into the ground to make a grave, how could they possibly dislodge it? "We're not strong enough."

Pebble Heart glanced at Clear Sky and Jagged Peak. "We will be if we work together."

Clear Sky jerked up his muzzle, his eyes shining. "I told you!" he exclaimed. "We need to unite."

Gray Wing eyed his brother darkly. "I thought you'd forgotten all that nonsense."

"Of course not. I—"

Tall Shadow interrupted him. "This is not the time to argue."

River Ripple padded past her and sniffed at the rock. "We need to loosen it first," he murmured thoughtfully.

Pebble Heart hurried to the edge of the hollow and grabbed a stick in his jaws. He carried it back and dug one end into the earth beside the stone. Holding it between his forepaws, he rocked it back and forth until it began to work its way down underneath.

River Ripple's eyes lit up. "I'll help." He got another stick.

Thunder could see that they were loosening the frozen earth around the rock to make enough space for it to move. He ran to the hollow's edge and rooted among the bracken for another stick. He found one sturdy enough not to crumble, and hurried back to the rock. Jabbing it into the dirt, he began twisting it with his forepaws, joy sparking in his belly as he saw the earth breaking around it.

"Push!" he called to Clear Sky.

Clear Sky placed his shoulder on the other side of the rock and heaved, grunting with the effort. Tall Shadow slid in beside him, pressing against the stone. Gray Wing and Sun Shadow joined them, their hind paws scrabbling against the ground as they strained at the stone.

Thunder hauled out his stick and hurried around to help them.

Pushing in between Gray Wing and Sun Shadow, he pressed his shoulder to the rock. He threw his whole weight against it, digging his claws into the earth and trembling at the effort.

With a sudden creak, the stone moved. Only a whisker,

but in that tiny movement they freed it from the earth's grip. Thunder sensed air flooding beneath it and pushed harder, feeling it shift.

Clear Sky grunted in triumph. Beside him, Sun Shadow trembled, and Gray Wing's breath came in gasps as they all heaved against the stone.

Gradually they began to rock it back and forth until Thunder felt it roll beyond the edge of its hollow. "Push!" he yowled.

As it tumbled to one side, Thunder's paws slid into the empty dip. He felt worms slithering around them and wood lice scuttling over his claws. Snail trails glistened on the brown earth. He hopped out and blinked at the others.

Sun Shadow lifted his gaze to meet Thunder's, his eyes shining. "Even in the cold season, there is life here. Quiet Rain would be happy to see this and to know that living creatures move around her even while she is dead."

"She's not truly dead while she's remembered." Thunder dipped his head. "She will be remembered here."

"And in the mountains, too." Sun Shadow nodded solemnly.

Clear Sky and Jagged Peak were heading for her body. They nosed it onto their shoulders and brought it to the graveside. Thunder stepped away as they let her tumble into the hole.

Pebble Heart hopped in after her. Carefully, he eased her muzzle onto her forepaws and wrapped her tail across her nose so that she looked as though she were curled in sleep. Then he scrambled out and got a bracken frond to place over her.

Touched by the young tom's kindness, Thunder padded to

the bracken and bit through a brittle stem. He dragged it back and laid it with Pebble Heart's. Sun Shadow got another, and then Gray Wing. Together they heaped a thick layer of golden leaves over her.

"We should replace the stone," Thunder murmured. "To protect her from scavengers."

Tall Shadow gave a small nod. "But first we must pay our respects." She looked at Gray Wing.

The gray tom gazed down at the golden stalks. "Quiet Rain," he whispered. "Thank you for loving us enough to let us go."

"Thank you for holding Fluttering Bird next to your belly for as long as she lived." Clear Sky's mew was thick with grief.

"Thank you for traveling so far to spend your last moments with us." Jagged Peak's eyes clouded as he stared into the hole.

Thunder lifted his muzzle and tasted the air. As he did, a drop of water splashed his nose. Then another. A moment later, rain pattered like countless paw steps over the frozen forest floor.

River Ripple put his paws to the stone and began to push. Thunder hurried to help. Clear Sky, Tall Shadow, and Sun Shadow joined him, while Star Flower hung back and watched, and together they rolled it back into place.

"We should go home," Tall Shadow called through the rain.

"Not yet." Sun Shadow was trembling. He crouched beside the rock, pressing his nose to the crack between stone and earth as though breathing in the last scents of his friend. With eyes closed, he grew still.

"He'll freeze!" Gray Wing looked in alarm at Pebble Heart.

"Let him grieve a while longer." Pebble Heart's mew sounded distracted. His gaze was drifting across the clearing, narrowing as though he saw something that intrigued him.

The rain fell harder. Thunder's pelt clung to his body, and yet he did not feel cold. Familiar scents were filling the hollow. He squinted as he saw shapes in the rain, ghostly outlines moving around the clearing.

The spirit cats!

His heart soared as he recognized Hawk Swoop. Shaded Moss stood beside her, and together they dipped their heads to a new spirit.

Quiet Rain!

The old she-cat's ghostly form moved with ease across the clearing. She reached out her muzzle to greet her old friends, her pelt sleek and her eyes as bright as though she'd never known pain.

Hawk Swoop wove around her. "Welcome, dear friend."

"Do you see now?" A mew rang across the clearing.

Thunder blinked as he saw a brown-and-white tabby she-cat calling to them. *Who is she?*

Clear Sky brushed him and hurried to meet the tabby she-cat. "Bright Stream!" Joy filled his mew.

His first mate. Thunder glanced toward Star Flower. Could she see the cat who had been carrying Clear Sky's kits when an eagle had killed her?

But Star Flower was oblivious to the spirit cats moving in

the clearing. She was watching Sun Shadow, her eyes filled with pity.

Bright Stream spoke again, "The past is the past. The future is fresh. You must forget all you have known, no matter how much you loved it, and choose paths that will carry you to a new dawn."

Clear Sky leaned forward to touch her muzzle, but the ghostly shapes were disappearing already.

Thunder jerked his nose toward River Ripple. "Did you see them?"

River Ripple purred. "Of course."

"What did she mean?"

Clear Sky turned on Thunder, his eyes glittering. "She meant what the spirit cats have always meant. We should be together. We must unite!"

Pebble Heart shook his head. "That's not what she said, Clear Sky," he mewed softly.

Gray Wing padded to the young tom's side. "He's right, Clear Sky. We must choose a *new* beginning."

"But . . ." Clear Sky's eyes were shining with a mixture of hope and grief. "Surely that means every cat should join together. . . ."

Thunder felt a twinge of pity. *Will he ever let this go?* "I have my own camp now, and my own cats," he told his father. "My future lies with them, not with you." His paws pricked guiltily at the flash of grief in Clear Sky's blue eyes. The hope was gone. Thunder dropped his gaze. "You will always be my father," he went on softly. "But you have to let us all be the cats we want to be. I can't come and live with you. I must find my own path." Hesitantly, he looked up at Clear Sky, surprised to find that his father's gaze was calmer now. Star Flower had crossed the clearing to stand beside him.

"Your father knows this, Thunder." She glanced at Clear Sky. "It is hard for him, but he understands."

Clear Sky nodded, his eyes brimming with emotion.

Throat tightening, Thunder dipped his head. "Take care of each other." As he turned to leave, he glanced at Quiet Rain's grave. Sun Shadow still lay beside it, his eyes closed. Had he even been aware of the ghostly cats in the clearing?

Thunder nodded to Gray Wing and Tall Shadow, then headed for the slope. It was time he went home. "Thanks for coming," he meowed to River Ripple as he passed.

He bounded up through the bracken, veering at the top to head into the forest. An owl called through the rain that pounded the trees. A wind was whipping their high branches, and they clattered as he passed. He raced on, certain of the path home, following the scents of the forest until he heard mews echoing up from the ravine. He halted at the top and gazed down into the camp. Shadows swallowed the bushes and dens. Rain glinted on the stones. He jumped down them, claws stretched to keep a grip on the slippery surface. At the bottom, he squeezed under the gorse, happiness surging through his fur as he smelled the familiar scents of his friends.

"Thunder!" Lightning Tail hurried to greet him, his black

pelt slick with rain. "We were just deciding whether to send out a search party."

"Not in this weather, I hope." Thunder stopped in the clearing. Lightning Tail was the only cat he could see. "Where is everyone?"

"In their dens!" Lightning Tail purred. "Haven't you noticed? It's raining!" He beckoned Thunder with a nod of his head and led him toward a large bush a few paces from the rock that towered at the end of the clearing. He ducked underneath and Thunder followed.

Beneath the low-spreading branches, paws had hollowed out the earth to make two nests. The rain pattered above them, but it was dry under here.

"Look." Lightning Tail nodded toward the gap they'd slid through. There was a clear view to the gorse entrance. "I thought this would make a good place to sleep. It's dry and we can keep an eye on who comes and goes."

Thunder purred. "Which nest is mine?" Only one of the hollowed dips was lined with moss.

Lightning Tail nodded toward it. "You can have mine tonight," he offered. "You must be tired. Tomorrow we can find fresh moss to line yours."

Outside, the gorse rattled. Thunder stiffened, peering at the gap beneath the spiny branches. Milkweed was squeezing her way through, a mouse hanging from her jaws. Leaf followed her into the camp, carrying a vole in his.

"Night hunting?" Thunder blinked at Lightning Tail.

Lightning Tail purred. "They left Pink Eyes in charge of the kits and slipped out at dusk."

"Together?"

"They haven't been apart since you left."

Thunder's heart swelled until he thought it would burst. Above him, rain battered the bare branches. But he was dry, and his campmates were content. Tomorrow he would roam the forest with Lightning Tail and bring back fresh-kill for *his* cats.

CHAPTER 24

❧

Gray Wing touched his nose to the rock that covered Quiet Rain's grave.

Behind him, Tall Shadow was saying good-bye to River Ripple. "Tell Shattered Ice and Dappled Pelt they are missed, but we are glad they're happy in their new home."

River Ripple swished his tail. "It's hard to believe I once lived alone on the island. I can't imagine life without my campmates now."

Gray Wing's pelt pricked along his spine. *Who are my camp-mates?* Tall Shadow and Jagged Peak? He had lived with them so long, it would seem strange to live without them. But the thought of returning to the dark pine forest filled him with gloom. Perhaps it was just the lingering grief of Quiet Rain's death. A bright morning, with sunlight piercing the canopy and pooling on the needle-strewn floor, might cheer him up. And Pebble Heart would be there, his determined gaze a comforting reminder of Turtle Tail.

"We should go." Clear Sky's mew called Gray Wing from his thoughts. His brother stood beside Star Flower, their pelts touching. "Come and visit often," he told Gray Wing.

"Especially when the kits come." His gaze flicked toward Star Flower, glowing as she returned it.

One Eye's daughter had shown such courage and loyalty to her mate. A pang of sorrow pricked Gray Wing's belly. Turtle Tail had once stood beside him like that.

You shouldn't spend the rest of your life mourning. You should have a mate and kits of your own. His mother's words rang in his ears.

"You will come to see the kits, won't you?" Star Flower leaned toward Gray Wing.

"Of course," Gray Wing answered distractedly.

He watched as Clear Sky and Star Flower padded side by side toward the forest.

Tall Shadow was nudging Sun Shadow to his paws. "Come with us," she murmured. "You'll catch a chill if you stay here in the rain."

Sun Shadow heaved himself to his paws, his eyes downcast.

Pebble Heart fell in beside the black tom, pressing his shoulder against his flank and guiding him toward the edge of the hollow. Jagged Peak followed, casting a final glance back at Quiet Rain's grave.

Tall Shadow fell in behind them. "Are you coming, Gray Wing?"

Gray Wing felt rain soaking through his pelt. It dripped from his whiskers and pooled at his paws.

"Gray Wing?" Tall Shadow's eyes narrowed.

"I'm coming."

A fresh wind sprayed fine rain into his face as he crested the top of the slope. It carried the scent of the moor, and he breathed it in, his heart aching.

You should have a mate and kits of your own.

Pebble Heart was guiding Sun Shadow along the edge of the hollow, following the slope down toward the pine forest.

His paws suddenly heavy, Gray Wing stopped. "I can't come with you."

Tall Shadow jerked around, her eyes wide. "What?"

Guilt rippled through Gray Wing's fur, but he had to speak the truth. "I can't live among the pines."

"But that's what you chose!"

"I chose it because I wanted to help you build a new home." He gazed solemnly at Tall Shadow. "But you're settled now. You don't need my help."

"Is this because I accused you of trying to take over?" Tall Shadow's tail twitched uneasily.

Jagged Peak stared at him. "We *need* you, Gray Wing."

"No, you don't." Gray Wing turned his head and gazed across the moor. "I can hardly breathe there. You were right. While I'm among the pines, I'm not as fast as I used to be, but up here the wind seems to rush through me, and I can run without losing my breath."

"Won't you be lonely?" Tall Shadow looked worried.

Gray Wing's chest tightened as he pictured Slate. "I hope not."

Pebble Heart's eyes shone through the darkness. He peeled away from Sun Shadow and faced Gray Wing. "You must follow the path you choose," he murmured softly.

"Do you mind?" Gray Wing searched his gaze, knowing

he would not leave Pebble Heart if the young tom still needed him.

"I want you to be happy," Pebble Heart mewed. "And I'll know where to find you if I need you."

"Where will you go?" Tall Shadow frowned. "Back to the old hollow?"

Pebble Heart didn't shift his gaze from Gray Wing. "He's going to Wind Runner's camp."

Gray Wing stared wordlessly back.

Tall Shadow glanced at Jagged Peak. "Of course." She dipped her head to Gray Wing. "We will miss you."

Jagged Peak padded forward and nudged Gray Wing's shoulder with his muzzle. "Come and visit the kits," he meowed. "They'll miss you."

Gray Wing nodded. "Take care of Fern." Guilt pricked his belly. He'd invited her to join him, and now he was leaving. But she'd be safe in Tall Shadow's camp—safer than she'd been with Slash. His belly tightened. "Be careful," he cautioned.

Jagged Peak frowned. "Of what?"

"Don't forget, the pines are still new territory. You don't know what other cats might claim it as their own." Should he warn them about Slash? *No.* Fern would know if the rogue had returned. She'd tell them all they needed to know. There was no need to worry them now.

Tall Shadow turned away, swishing her tail. "It's our territory now, and we'll fight for it if we have to." She padded toward Sun Shadow, nudging him forward. Raindrops glistened on her pelt.

Jagged Peak followed, and Gray Wing touched his muzzle to Pebble Heart's head. "I'm proud of you."

"I know." Pebble Heart ducked away and headed after his campmates.

Gray Wing turned toward the moor. He could see the clouds clearing, far beyond the moortop. Excitement rising in his belly, he broke into a run. Racing over the rain-slicked grass, he ducked into a swath of heather, enjoying the twisting path that sent him turning this way and that before it seemed to burst into an open stretch of moorside. He hardly felt the pain in his injured leg as he pounded on, smelling the scents of Wind Runner and her kits as he neared the camp. The rain had eased here on the moortop, and he shook the wetness from his pelt, relishing the wind that streamed through it. He was almost dry by the time he ducked into the heather tunnel that led to the camp.

Padding quietly into the clearing, he glanced around.

Shadows hid the edges. No cat stirred. *They must already be in their nests.* Should he head back to the moor and find a hollow to sleep in for the night?

"Intruder!" A shriek sent surprise flashing through his chest. Claws raked his cheek, then pierced his pelt as a cat leaped onto his back.

"Dust Muzzle! It's me!" He recognized the kit's scent and shook him off, wincing as the kit tore a lump of fur from his pelt.

"Gray Wing?" Dust Muzzle stared at him through the darkness. "What are you doing here?"

Heather rustled around him, and paw steps scuffed the grass.

"Gray Wing?" Wind Runner crossed the clearing.

Gorse Fur pushed past her. "Is everything okay?"

Minnow and Reed hung back in the shadows, their eyes glinting in the gloom.

"Everything's fine," Gray Wing told them. "But I can't live in the pine forest anymore. I can hardly breathe there, and I need to feel the wind in my fur again." He gazed hopefully at Wind Runner. Was she ready to take an old campmate into her new home?

"Then you are welcome here." Wind Runner purred loudly.

Moth Flight bounded from her nest. "Is Gray Wing coming to live with us?" She bounced around him, her eyes shining.

"Yes, I am." Gray Wing cuffed the kit playfully with his paw.

A warm smell touched his nose, making his heart speed up.

"Gray Wing?" Slate slid from the heather and met his gaze. "Are you really coming to stay for good?" She padded closer until he could feel her breath on his muzzle.

"Yes."

Dust Muzzle pushed between them. "Can you give me a badger ride?"

Wind Runner rolled her eyes. "It's time to sleep!" Starlight was glittering above them as the clouds eased away.

"Oh, *please!*" Moth Flight stared desperately at her mother.

"Let me take them out onto the moor." Gray Wing blinked

at Wind Runner. "The heather always smells best after rain."

Gorse Fur purred. "I wouldn't waste your time arguing." He nudged Wind Runner's cheek with his nose. "Let's go back to our nests and let them go roaming if they want to. The kits will be safe with Gray Wing."

"They're too big for badger rides," Wind Runner commented.

"That's Gray Wing's problem." Gorse Fur padded across the clearing.

"I'll come with you," Slate offered.

Gray Wing grunted as Dust Muzzle scrambled onto his back. Wind Runner was right. The kit was as heavy as a fat rabbit.

"What about me?" Moth Flight mewed.

Slate padded toward her. "You can climb on my back, but I can't promise to carry you for long." She swayed as the kit clambered up.

"Take us as far as the moortop," Moth Flight pleaded.

Gray Wing ducked through the tunnel. Dust Muzzle pressed himself low as the heather swept over their heads. Out on the moor, Gray Wing headed upslope. He wanted to see the view from the top.

His injured paw ached as he carried Dust Muzzle, but he didn't care. Slate caught up to him, Moth Flight balancing precariously on her back. She was frowning with the effort of carrying the young she-cat.

"Get off now, you two." Gray Wing shook Dust Muzzle

from his shoulders. "You can run to the top of the moor."

Dust Muzzle sprang onto the grass. "Come on, Moth Flight! I'll race you."

Gray Wing watched the two young cats streak away. He fell in beside Slate. "Are you glad I came back?" he asked, his mouth dry.

Slate shot him a teasing look. "What do *you* think?"

CHAPTER 25

Clear Sky curled tighter around Star Flower. It was moonhigh, and the she-cat was in a deep sleep, her golden pelt warm. Above them, stars showed between the branches of the oaks.

They had returned to camp after burying Quiet Rain. Acorn Fur and Nettle had hurried to greet him, wondering what had kept him away so long. When he'd told them of his mother's death, they'd brushed past him, showing their sympathy. Alder and Birch had brought him prey, two voles that they'd caught near the snake rocks.

Birch had narrowed his eyes when Clear Sky had given one to Star Flower. "We caught them for *you*."

Clear Sky glared at him. "We share prey in this camp."

Alder grunted. "When she disappeared, we thought she'd left again."

Clear Sky's hackles lifted. "She left you to be with me."

Had there been gossip while they'd been away? Had his campmates been discussing whether they could trust Star Flower? If only they had seen her loyalty and strength in Tall Shadow's camp, they'd know the answer was yes. She'd encouraged and comforted him selflessly. Tall Shadow and

Gray Wing had seen her devotion and treated her as an equal. Quiet Rain had admired her spirit. Even Thunder had begun to show her a grudging respect.

Grief jabbed Clear Sky's belly as he thought of his kin. For two nights he'd slept beneath the same trees as them. And together they had mourned Quiet Rain's death. *Why do they have to choose different paths from mine?*

He closed his eyes, breathing in the warmth of Star Flower's pelt, and let weariness pull him into sleep.

"Clear Sky."

A soft mew woke him.

He jerked up his head, blinking.

A silver she-cat stood at the edge of his nest, her eyes glittering in the starlight.

"Storm?" He kept his mew low. Star Flower stirred beside him but didn't wake.

What was the spirit cat doing here? He felt a flash of guilt. His hunger for power had driven Storm away while she carried his kits. Now he was nestled beside Star Flower, happier with his life than he had been with Storm. Had she come to reproach him?

"I'm sorry," he began.

Her eyes widened. "What for?" Her mew was rich with affection. "You have everything you want, and it pleases me to see you settled at last."

Clear Sky's throat tightened. "I just wish I'd given you happiness when I had the chance." Unwanted memories began to flit through his mind: Jagged Peak's accident, his quarrels with Thunder, the battle with Gray Wing. "I have let every cat down. Even Quiet Rain." He saw again the look of disgust his mother had flashed at him

"Clear Sky." Fondness filled Storm's gaze. "Forgive yourself."

That's what Quiet Rain told me.

"You've made mistakes," she went on. "But that is part of living."

"I've driven every cat away." Clear Sky gazed forlornly at her.

She nodded toward Star Flower. "Not *every* cat."

He dropped his gaze. "Star Flower understands me."

Silver light washed Clear Sky's nest, and when he looked up, Storm's pelt glowed like the moon. "The others understand you more than you think. You didn't drive them away—they had their own paths to follow, and they are right to follow them. You will see this, in time." She glanced up at the stars. "We are all where we belong."

"Don't you all belong with me?"

Storm purred. "Oh, Clear Sky," she murmured. "Do you really want your future filled with your past? It's time for you to look forward." She reached out a forepaw and laid it gently on Star Flower's flank. "Your future lies in here, with these kits. Take care of them."

Clear Sky felt a chill at his side and blinked open his eyes.

I was sleeping! Storm had been a dream. He turned to nuzzle Star Flower's belly, his heart filling with love for his unborn kits.

Star Flower! Where was she? The nest was empty beside him, the moss growing chilly where she'd been.

"Star Flower?" he called under his breath. Had she gone to make dirt? Unease pricking in his pelt, he clambered to his paws and hopped out of his nest.

He stood at the edge of the bracken and pricked his ears. "Star Flower!"

A wail sounded from the trees.

Was she hurt? Were the kits coming too soon?

He plunged through the bracken and raced between the trees. "Star Flower?" Ears pricked, he listened for another cry.

"She's over here." A nasty yowl rang from the gloom.

The claw of dread hollowed Clear Sky's belly. He jerked his head toward the voice.

Eyes gleamed from the shadows.

"Who is it?" he hissed.

Shapes moved between the trees. He recognized the glow of Star Flower's pelt. Around her clustered three mangy, scarred toms.

Clear Sky unsheathed his claws. "Let her go," he growled.

"She can leave if she wants." One of the toms stepped forward. He was a brown tabby with broad shoulders, torn ears, and half a set of whiskers. A flash of white fur showed across his front legs.

Clear Sky peered past him at Star Flower. Why wasn't she trying to escape? She stood meek as a kit between the ginger tom and his brown tabby ally. "Come to me, Star Flower. I won't let them hurt you."

She didn't move. Fear showed in her eyes.

"Star Flower always was sensible," the gray tom sneered.

"You *know* these cats?" Clear Sky stared in surprise at Star Flower.

"We grew up together." The gray tom threw a glance back at Star Flower. "I always thought she'd be my mate, but now she's carrying your kits."

Fury pulsed in Clear Sky's chest. "Who are you?"

"I'm Slash." The tom's eyes glittered with self-satisfaction. "An old friend of One Eye's."

Clear Sky's anger rose, roaring in his ears. "Star Flower is coming with me." He reared, hissing, but Slash leaped back and grabbed Star Flower. Hooking his claws into her shoulders he hauled her to the ground and pinned her there. The tabby and the ginger tom crouched on either side, their teeth bared.

Star Flower groaned, her eyes wild with terror.

Clear Sky froze. How could he fight them off without Star Flower getting hurt?

"That's better," Slash snarled. "It would be a shame to wound such a pretty cat . . . and with kits in her belly. The thought of harming them breaks my heart." His whiskers twitched cruelly.

The ginger tom hissed, his eyes gleaming. "Poor little kitties."

A chill ran along Clear Sky's spine. He met Slash's gaze, trying to hide the fear in his own. "What do you want?"

"I told you," Slash hissed. "Star Flower and I go back a long way. I was One Eye's closest friend."

Anger sparked in Star Flower's eyes. "Get off me!" She struggled, her paws slithering over the ground as Slash pushed her harder into the soggy leaves. "I never knew what One Eye saw in you!" she hissed. "You're not fit to say his name."

Slash's ear flattened. "Oh, really?" With a flick of his claws, he sliced her cheek. "Then why did you promise him that you would be *my* mate?"

"That was a long time ago!" Star Flower struggled harder.

Clear Sky felt panic rising as blood welled on her fur. He didn't understand what was happening. He just wanted it to end. "Stop! Tell me why you're here and what you want!"

Slash turned his head slowly toward Clear Sky. He let go of Star Flower and stalked forward, his lip curling. "Don't think we haven't noticed you mountain cats recruiting all the strays you can find." He tipped his head, his gaze menacing. "Why are you building such big groups? Everywhere we go now, we smell scent markers and see where you've been hunting."

"So?" Clear Sky tried not to look at Star Flower as she dabbed a paw at her cheek.

"This territory used to be ours," Slash snarled. "The strays caught prey and shared it with us. So we left them alone. Now they are part of your groups. They think they're safe. They think they don't need to share their catch with us any-more." He glanced back at the toms. "We're getting hungry, aren't we?"

"If you want prey, take prey!" Clear Sky growled. "There's enough food in the forest to feed three extra mouths."

"But we're not just three extra mouths." Slash's eyes narrowed to slits. "There are many of us. Rogues from the Twolegplace. Rogues from beyond the pines and the river. We're more than you could ever imagine."

"Then why have we never seen you before?" Fear wormed in Clear Sky's belly.

"You never had to," Slash snarled. "We only had to wander the edges of this land to collect enough prey. The strays who lived here knew how to keep us happy. They'd lay out fresh-kill for us to find. They'd leave the borders unhunted. There was no need to come looking for food here. But the strays hunt for *you* now. And we go hungry." He eyed Clear Sky with menace. "Why did you mountain cats have to come and spoil everything?"

"We were hungry," Clear Sky told him.

"That's not good enough." Slash paced around Star Flower, his sharp eyes flicking over her pelt. "We need to put things back the way they were."

"We're not leaving!" Clear Sky hissed.

"We're not asking you to leave." Slash paused beside Star Flower. Pushing his muzzle close to her injured cheek, he licked the blood from her fur with a long, lingering lap. "I just want to meet with the leaders of your groups so we can discuss how you might share your prey with us, like the strays used to." He glanced up at the sky. The moon was high and bright. "Tomorrow night, at this same time, I want to meet all the leaders on the sunning rocks beside the river."

Clear Sky stared back at him. What kind of leader would

obey these fox-hearts? "What if they don't agree?"

Slash's tail flicked sharply behind him. "I will kill Star Flower." He nodded to the tabby tom and padded away between the trees. The tabby grabbed Star Flower's scruff between his teeth and dragged her after Slash. The ginger tom followed, snarling at Star Flower's tail as her legs kicked in a futile attempt to free herself.

Clear Sky's thoughts tumbled over one another. Blood pulsed though his paws. He wanted to run after them and free Star Flower. But she might die.

So might the kits!

He felt sick.

The bracken rustled behind him.

He turned, fur bushing, as Quick Water slunk out.

"Were you watching?" he gasped.

She nodded, her gaze sharp.

"Why didn't you help?"

"Two against four?" Quick Water narrowed her eyes.

"Three against *three*!" Clear Sky hissed. "Star Flower would have fought beside us."

"Would she?" Quick Water looked unconvinced. "It sounded to me like she and Slash were pretty close once. And you remember how she betrayed us for her father. Why wouldn't she betray us for her father's friend, too?"

Rage pulsed through Clear Sky. "Didn't you see how he hurt her?"

"It could have been part of the act."

Blood roaring in his ears, Clear Sky lashed out with his paw and raked Quick Water's face. "Does *that* feel like an act?" he yowled.

Quick Water ducked away as blood shone on her muzzle. She glanced at him resentfully. "Clawing me won't make Star Flower loyal."

"She *is* loyal!" Clear Sky hissed. "More loyal than my own kin!"

"Only you believe that." Quick Water rubbed her nose with her paw. "Do you really think the other leaders are going to risk their pelts to save Star Flower? *No cat* will fight those mangy rogues to save a traitor, even if she *is* carrying your kits."

Clear Sky stared at the old she-cat. Where was *her* loyalty? Didn't she realize these rogues weren't just threatening Star Flower? They were threatening *every* cat! He pushed through the bracken, frustration burning in his pelt. Skirting the top of the mud bank, he barged past the bramble and stalked from the camp. The tops of the trees seemed aflame in the rising sun as he headed for the edge of the forest. Quick Water was wrong. The other cats *would* help. They weren't mouse-brained old fleabags like she was. They'd realize the threat facing them.

And they will fight for Star Flower.

They had to! Even if Clear Sky had to *force* them to fight.

No one threatens my kits and gets away with it.

DAWN OF THE CLANS
WARRIORS
A FOREST DIVIDED

BONUS SCENE!

Read on to see how Slate met Wind Runner . . .

PROLOGUE
❧

Slate skidded to a halt, panting, and gazed around, her ears pricked. The moorland stretched away from her in all directions, the short, springy grass dotted with clumps of reeds, gorse bushes, and outcrops of rock. Nothing moved in all the landscape.

"Cricket!" Slate yowled, her pelt prickling with worry. "Cricket, where are you?"

There was no reply, no glimpse of her brother's orange tabby fur.

I thought he was right behind me. . . .

Slate and her brother, Cricket, had been racing toward a big jutting boulder that reared up from the flat moorland in front of them. Slate had been winning, and when she'd glanced over her shoulder to see how close her brother was, he had vanished.

It was stupid of me to get so far ahead, Slate thought. *What if something happened to him? Cricket is always getting into mischief.* There were foxes and badgers on the moors, she knew, not to mention those aggressive cats who had appeared out of nowhere a few seasons before and settled down in huge groups as if they owned the place. What if Cricket had run into them?

Though they were littermates, Slate and Cricket were completely different cats. Slate had amber eyes and thick gray fur, quite unlike Cricket's orange tabby pelt. Cricket was lighthearted, always joking and playing around, while Slate was more serious and liked to plan ahead.

Once they had been part of a happy family. But the sickness that stalked the moor had taken their mother and their sister, leaving Slate and Cricket alone.

We only have each other, Slate thought. *I have to find him!*

"YAAAHHHHH!" Slate let out a terrified yowl as something heavy landed on her back and she felt four sets of claws digging into her pelt. Instinctively she hit the ground and rolled, sliding out her claws and bracing her muscles for a fight. But her attacker still clung on, and Slate heard bubbling *mrrows* of laughter coming from him.

"Cricket!" she spat. "You stupid furball!"

Cricket leaped away from her, and Slate scrambled to her paws to see him standing close beside her, his green eyes bright.

"You frightened me out of my fur!" she exclaimed.

"Yeah, I really got you." Cricket's tail curled with amusement. "You should have seen your face!"

Slate drew her lips back in the beginning of a snarl, then a moment later relaxed and swatted at her brother, brushing his ear with her claws sheathed. *I can't get angry with him. I love him too much.*

"We can't mess around all day," she meowed. "We need to hunt."

Cricket nodded vigorously. "My belly has never felt this empty."

"Come on, then. I bet I catch something first."

"We'll see about that," Cricket retorted.

The two cats split up. Cricket disappeared around a scatter of boulders, while Slate prowled across the moor, heading for the clumps of longer grass that grew around a pool. *That's a good place for prey to hide.*

Slate parted her jaws to taste the air, and picked up the scent of mouse. When she angled her ears forward, she heard tiny sounds of scuffling from the long grass and saw the stems twitching as a mouse pushed its way between them. Setting her paws down lightly, Slate crept up on her prey, then bunched her muscles for a pounce. Her paws slammed down on the terrified creature and she grabbed it in her claws.

Suddenly a yowl of alarm came from behind the boulders where Cricket had disappeared. Slate paused, her head raised, the mouse wriggling desperately in her grip.

Is Cricket playing another joke? she wondered. *I'll make him sorry if I lose this mouse and we don't eat today.*

Sniffing, she caught a trace of rank scent drifting toward her. *Fox!* Releasing the mouse, she spun around in time to hear another yowl as Cricket burst into the open from behind the clump of boulders. A big fox was hard on his paws, jaws wide to grab him.

My brother is not your prey!

Her heart thumping hard, Slate raced across the grass and hurled herself at the fox, swiping at its shoulder with her claws extended. The fox whipped around, faster than Slate had thought possible. She screeched as the fox's teeth sank into her ear and pain flooded her senses.

Slate pulled back, horrified to feel the tip of her ear tear away. For a couple of heartbeats darkness covered her eyes and her legs wobbled unsteadily.

When her vision cleared, Slate saw Cricket and the fox circling each other, both poised for the next blow. For a brief moment she realized how hungry the fox must be, now that the sickness on the moor had wiped out so much of the prey. *It needs food, just like us.*

Then she saw the blood pouring from her brother's shoulder, and any sympathy she might have felt for the fox vanished like dew under hot sunlight. She lunged again, raking her claws down its side, then leaped back out of range as the fox turned toward her, snarling. Cricket dashed up behind it, nipping at its hind paws.

Slate wanted to reach her brother so that they could attack together, but the fox was too wily for that. It kept its body between the two cats, attacking so viciously, so fast, to one side and then the other, that Slate and Cricket couldn't join up to fight side by side.

It could kill us, Slate realized, cold terror trickling down her spine.

She made one final attempt to dart around the fox, slashing it across the snout with both her forepaws as she lunged. For a heartbeat she thought she had made it past the bigger animal. Then searing pain tore across her belly, and she realized that she had left herself vulnerable to the fox's powerful claws.

Slate let out a shriek. Her paws slipped on her own blood and she collapsed onto her side.

"Slate!" Cricket screeched, a look of horror on his face.

For a moment he stood frozen, staring, as the fox swung back toward him.

"Cricket!" Slate choked out in warning, afraid that he was too shocked to defend himself.

But Cricket recovered just in time to meet the fox as it sprang toward him. He raised one paw and scratched the fox along the side of its face. The fox yowled in pain as Cricket's claws sank into its eye. It drew back, stumbling and shaking its head from side to side as blood streamed down its face.

It can't see out of that eye, Slate thought. *I can attack it from that side, slash its throat, and end all this.*

But as Slate tried to heave herself to her paws, she realized with horror that she couldn't move anymore. The blood from the wound in her belly was soaking the grass all around her. Dark mist was creeping up on her from every side.

A screech of rage reached her ears, seeming to come from far, far away. As her vision blurred, she made out a blocky shape—she couldn't even tell whether it was Cricket or the fox—hurling itself toward the other in a furious attack. Then the mist swirled around her, thicker and thicker, until with a defeated whimper Slate gave herself up to darkness.

CHAPTER ONE

Huge green eyes peered into Slate's and whiskers brushed across her face as she blinked groggily awake. With great effort she managed to raise her head, her torn ear aching with pain.

At her movement, the cat who was bending over her, a thin gray tabby tom, leaped back, startled. He looked vaguely familiar, but for the moment Slate couldn't remember where she'd seen him before.

"You're alive!" he exclaimed, relief in his voice.

Slate barely paid any attention to his words. She had spotted some fur lying in the grass just beyond him: the most familiar fur in the world. The orange tabby fur of her brother, Cricket. Slate closed her eyes, trying to block out the sight of her littermate's fur strewn in a mess of grass and blood.

"No . . ." she choked out.

The gray tabby followed her glance, and moved to stand between her and Cricket, fluffing out his fur to block her view. "You friend wasn't so lucky," he mewed, his voice soft and regretful. "I was out hunting and found you . . . and the remains of him," he added after a moment's pause. "The fox had gone by then."

Slate closed her eyes as grief washed over her like a cold wave, sweeping her away to drown in darkness. *Cricket gone . . . it's not possible.* She seemed to live the moment over again when she could have saved him, could have killed the fox or driven it off, if only she could have moved. *I failed my brother. It's my fault he's dead.*

The touch of a paw on her forehead roused Slate. She opened her eyes to see the tabby tom bending over her again, concern in his green eyes. "I'm sorry for your loss," he meowed, "and to be honest, you don't look too good, either. You've lost a lot of blood. I know a cat who can help, but you need to stay alive while I go to fetch him. Okay?" He blinked encouragingly. "Promise?"

Slate forced herself to nod in response, but she had no interest in staying alive. *What can the world possibly have to offer me now?*

"I don't mean to offend you," the gray tabby mewed, "but that wasn't much of a nod. I'm not sure I believe you." He thought for a moment, then went on. "Right, new plan. I'll send my mate and kits to keep an eye on you while I get help. They will make sure that no dangerous animals come near, too. Okay?"

This time he didn't wait for Slate to respond, just bounded off across the moor.

Slate knew the tom was being kind, but she wished he would just leave her alone. What did it matter if she died? She could join Cricket, then. She closed her eyes again, inviting the blackness to take her, sinking into it with a sigh of relief as her senses whirled away.

But Slate could not stay in the comforting darkness for long. She was roused by the sensation of being prodded all over by tiny paws. Forcing her eyes open, she saw two bright-eyed kits staring at her: a white she-cat and a gray tom.

"She's dead," the white kit mewed, sounding disappointed.

"She's not," the little gray tom retorted. "See, she's looking at you."

The white kit let out a gasp of excitement. "Her eyes are open!" Taking a step forward, she peered more closely at Slate and added, "Hello. Do you want to be friends?"

"Get away from her!" A sharp voice sounded in the distance; Slate couldn't see the cat it was coming from. "We don't know what kind of diseases that rogue might have."

Instantly the kits backed away and were replaced by a wiry brown she-cat; like the tom, she looked vaguely familiar to Slate. She halted several tail-lengths away and looked Slate up and down, her yellow eyes unimpressed.

Slate flexed her claws in annoyance at the she-cat's rudeness. *I don't know why I should care. All I want is to die in peace . . . but I'd like to claw that sneering look off her face.* She was offended, too, that the she-cat had called her a rogue.

Now I remember who these cats are, she thought. *They're part of the group Cricket was always complaining about.* Cricket had been outraged by the way these cats had appeared on the moor and settled down there and in the nearby forest, making it harder for the local cats to find prey. And they'd called the cats who had always lived here *rogues.*

"They want to fight all the time," Cricket had said scornfully. "They're violent prey-stealers, and I don't want anything to do with them."

Slate raised her head and glared back at the brown she-cat. "Hello," she meowed pointedly. "I can hear you, you know."

The she-cat narrowed her eyes. "So you're alive," she snorted, not sounding happy about it. "You don't have the sickness, do you?"

No, just this gaping wound in my belly, Slate thought. Aloud, she replied, "No, I don't have the sickness. My name is Slate," she added.

The brown she-cat whisked her tail. "I'm Wind Runner."

"And the kits?" Slate asked.

Wind Runner eyed her warily. "You don't need to know their names."

Lovely, Slate thought. *What a delightful cat to share my dying moments with.* She cast a disdainful look toward Wind Runner. The brown she-cat was ignoring Slate now, instead clawing up moss. When she had a mouthful, she trotted off with it in her jaws. A few heartbeats later she returned, with the moss dripping wet.

"Here," she growled, dumping the moss beside Slate's head. "Drink."

Slate stretched out her tongue and lapped at the moss. The water was cool and fresh, and Slate thought she had never tasted anything so delicious in her entire life.

While she was drinking, Wind Runner scraped together a bundle of grass, leaves, and more moss, and tucked it under

Slate's head to prop her up.

"What happened?" she asked brusquely.

Slate was bewildered by the contrast between Wind Runner's kind actions and the roughness of her speech. "It was a fox," she replied at last. "It attacked me and my brother, Cricket." Her voice shook as she added, "Cricket was killed."

Wind Runner looked stricken at the news. "I've noticed that fox lurking around the edges of our camp," she meowed. She turned toward her kits, who were play wrestling a little way away on the moor, and beckoned them with her tail. "Come closer!" she yowled.

The kits broke apart and scrambled to their paws. "You told us to get away from that sick cat," the white she-kit reminded her mother.

Wind Runner twitched her tail-tip in exasperation. "Come a little closer, then, but not *too* close," she meowed. "Do you have kits?" she asked, turning back to Slate as the kits scampered up.

"I've never seemed to have the time," Slate replied. She hadn't met a tom she wanted to have kits with, either, but she didn't feel like telling Wind Runner that.

She expected Wind Runner to say something comforting about how Slate would have kits someday, but instead the brown she-cat just snorted.

"You're lucky in a way," she continued after a moment. "Kits are exhausting. I haven't slept a single night through since they were born."

"They must be very needy, then," Slate mewed.

Wind Runner shook her head, her hard yellow gaze growing soft and affectionate. "No, it's my problem," she admitted. "I love them too much."

She's not unkind at all, Slate thought, rapidly revising her opinion of the she-cat. *Just tough on the outside—but there's more to her than meets the eye.*

Before she could say any more, the gray tabby tom reappeared, followed by a long-furred black tom with white on his ears, chest, and paws. He was carrying a bundle of leaves in his jaws.

"Oh, you've kept her awake," the gray tom meowed, bounding up to Wind Runner and pressing his muzzle to her shoulder. "That's great." Turning back to Slate, he added, "I'm Gorse Fur. Wind Runner's my mate. And this"—he waved his tail at the long-furred tom—"is Cloud Spots. He knows a lot about herbs and treating wounds, and he's come to help you."

Slate closed her eyes as Cloud Spots padded up and began to examine her. She was vaguely aware of him sniffing at her wound and touching her belly with gentle paws, but she kept drifting away into unconsciousness. This time, though, the darkness wasn't as alluring. Perhaps she wasn't going to join her brother in death yet after all.

Finally Slate came back to full consciousness to hear Wind Runner, Gorse Fur, and Cloud Spots talking together, the sharp tones of an argument in their voices. She opened her eyes and turned her head toward them, struggling to make out what they were saying.

"What did you expect?" Cloud Spots was asking Wind Runner. "That you'd just leave her lying here in the grass? She's lost a lot of blood. I've patched her wound with cobweb and put on a poultice of chervil to fight infection, but she's very weak. She needs watching."

"Then you should take her back to the hollow," Wind Runner snapped.

The hollow? What does she mean? Slate wondered, confused.

"I can't move her that far," Cloud Spots retorted. "Her wound would break open again. Wind Runner, *your* camp is just the other side of that gorse thicket."

Gorse Fur looked at his mate. "We could take her in," he suggested. "Just for a moon or so."

The fur on Wind Runner's shoulders bristled with annoyance. "We left the hollow to get *away* from other cats," she pointed out. "To protect our kits. And now you want to take in some flea-bitten rogue?"

"Excuse me!" Slate struggled to sit up, all her early dislike of Wind Runner rushing back. "I don't *want* to come to your camp. I've no interest in joining a group like yours."

"Why not?" Gorse Fur asked, his ears pricking up curiously.

"Because all you do is fight," Slate retorted, repeating what Cricket had said so often. "And you take prey from the cats who were born here."

"*We* were born here, thank you very much," Wind Runner put in.

Cloud Spots waved his tail, gesturing for silence. "Then what do you want to do?" he asked Slate. "Do you have kin who could look after you?"

An overpowering pang of grief for Cricket shook Slate from her ears to her tail-tip, but she did her best to hide it. She shook her head. "I'll look after myself," she responded, putting out all her strength to draw herself to her paws.

She tried to stalk off casually, but after a single step she felt as if her legs had turned to water. She collapsed, her head spinning. "Oh . . ." she murmured.

Gorse Fur bounded to her side. "We'll take her in," he meowed with a pointed look at Wind Runner. "We *have* to. Remember, she's some cat's kit."

Slate looked up at Wind Runner, who let out an annoyed growl, then shrugged in resignation. "All right," she told Slate. "But you *cannot* stay too long. We're not looking for more cats."

Slate glared at her. "I'm not looking to become one of your cats."

Cloud Spots's whiskers twitched in amusement. "Very well," he meowed. "Something tells me you two will have lots to talk about."

CHAPTER TWO

Slate crouched in a patch of sunlight, her paws tucked under her and her eyes slitted as she basked in the warmth. A half moon had passed since her fight with the fox, and the wound in her belly was healing well. But she didn't think that the wound in her heart, from the loss of Cricket, would ever heal. She still missed her brother every day.

A patter of small paws roused Slate and she opened her eyes to see the white she-kit, Moth Flight, scampering up to her. The little kit cast an approving glance over the rabbit bones scattered beside Slate's nest.

"You're eating better," she mewed.

"Yes," Slate agreed. "I'm feeling much stronger now."

Moth Flight's whiskers drooped sadly at her words. "That means you'll have to leave soon. My mother says you can only stay in our camp until you're strong again."

"I know," Slate responded.

Moth Flight lifted her voice in a wail. "But I'll miss you so much!"

"Maybe I can come to visit," Slate suggested, curling her tail gently around the white kit.

"It won't be the same," Moth Flight protested, leaning her head against Slate's shoulder. "You're the only one who will play with me. Wind Runner and Gorse Fur are too busy hunting all the time, and Dust Muzzle says I'm too silly."

"Maybe Dust Muzzle is right," Slate mewed. "But there are times when it's okay to be silly. It's part of who you are."

Moth Flight's only response was a sigh.

"So where is Wind Runner?" Slate asked, trying to change the subject. "It's almost sunhigh, and I haven't seen her or Gorse Fur today."

Moth Flight looked up at her, stretching her eyes wide in mingled excitement and fear. "They're tracking the fox!" she whispered.

"The fox?" At first Slate didn't understand.

"Wind Runner spotted it outside the camp just before dawn," Moth Flight explained. "And when she and Gorse Fur went to check it out, they found a dead stoat a little way across the moor, covered in fox scent."

"A stoat?" Slate asked, beginning to be worried. "That's a tough fighter for a fox to kill."

Moth Flight nodded eagerly. "I heard them talking about how the fox must be starving, because it's getting bolder. Look what it did to you!"

Slate nodded gravely. *Look what it did to Cricket!* she thought, but she did not speak the words aloud in front of the kit.

Before she could ask Moth Flight any more questions, Wind Runner appeared from behind the boulders that surrounded the camp, with Gorse Fur hard on her paws. Both

cats had serious expressions; Slate could guess what was bothering them.

As they approached Slate, Wind Runner flicked her tail
at Moth Flight. "Go and find Dust Muzzle and play," she
ordered. "We have to talk to Slate."

For a heartbeat Moth Flight seemed as if she was about
to protest; then she met her mother's fierce amber gaze and
bounded off.

"Slate, we haven't asked you any favors until now," Gorse
Fur began. Slate got the impression that his speech had been
carefully rehearsed. "But we *have* taken very good care of you.
We've kept you well fed, in spite of how hard it's been to hunt
since the sickness came, and—"

"That's true," Slate interrupted. "Are you saying that you
want me to go?"

"No!" Gorse Fur responded immediately, looking horrified
at the thought.

"Not *yet*," Wind Runner put in sharply. "But we need a
favor. We've seen the fox that attacked you, several times,
close to the camp," she continued. "This morning we found a
stoat killed just a few tail-lengths away. I'm afraid it won't be
long before the fox decides to try its luck with cats again. And
with the kits so young and vulnerable . . ." Her voice trailed
off.

"What are you planning to do?" Slate asked, mystified.

"We mean to kill it before it comes after us." Wind Runner's eyes and voice were full of resolve, and cold as a frozen
stream. "We need you to watch the kits tomorrow. We're

going to track it to its den and attack it while it sleeps."

Anxiety like clouds of dark mist rose around Slate as she listened to Wind Runner's plan. "You don't know what you're in for," she meowed. "This fox is *dangerous*. It killed my litter-mate!"

"But we have more experience in fighting than Cricket did," Wind Runner retorted, unmoved by Slate's warning.

Slate let out a snort. "Oh, yes, you group cats! Always play fighting. This is *not* like that." She didn't know how to describe to them how fast and vicious the fox had been.

Wind Runner's tail-tip twitched irritably. "We're grateful for your concern," she mewed, clearly struggling to bite back an angry response. "But all we need is for you to watch the kits."

Slate was not reassured. Gorse Fur looked anxious, as though her words had reached him. "If you and Wind Runner both go to attack the fox," she began, turning to him, "and if the worst happens, then you'll be leaving your kits all alone to fend for themselves." She faced Wind Runner again. "Do you want *that* to happen?"

Wind Runner sighed, her tail drooping. Slate realized that appealing to her love for her kits was what it took to make her listen.

"No," the brown she-cat meowed wearily. "But what else can you suggest?"

"Let me kill the fox." As Slate spoke, she realized that more than anything in the world she wanted to sink her claws into the vicious creature and see its life gush out. "That fox killed the cat I loved best." She spoke her final words through gritted teeth, with all the force of her hatred. "I want to be the one to kill it!"

Gorse Fur and Wind Runner exchanged a startled glance, as if they hadn't expected such a fierce reply. Then their gazes became more thoughtful.

"We can't let the fox keep coming around, getting closer and closer," Gorse Fur mewed. To Slate, he added, "Do you really think you can kill it?"

A strong sense of purpose flooded through Slate. Now she realized why she hadn't let herself die on the moor after Gorse Fur found her. *It was because I need to kill that fox!* "I *will* avenge my littermate," she assured Gorse Fur.

"I'll go with her," Wind Runner told Gorse Fur, authority in her voice. "I'm the stronger fighter. You stay with the kits."

Gorse Fur hesitated, then gave a reluctant nod. "Okay. But please be careful."

"We will," Wind Runner replied briskly. "Slate, we'll leave before dawn tomorrow. Better get a good rest before then."

"Wind Runner!" Dust Muzzle's voice rose from behind a rock. "Moth Flight bit my tail!"

Wind Runner heaved a sigh. "Kits!" With a whisk of her tail, she was gone.

Gorse Fur was left with Slate, his green gaze fixed on her. "Thank you," he meowed, his voice heavy with meaning. "You know," he added, "even if you kill the fox, I can't guarantee that Wind Runner will let you stay here."

"I don't want to stay here," Slate retorted, surprised.

Gorse Fur nodded and walked off.

As she watched him go, Slate realized for the first time that she wasn't sure she meant what she had said.

Slate felt a paw prodding her shoulder and opened her eyes to see Wind Runner standing over her.

"It's time," the brown she-cat meowed.

Stretching her jaws in a vast yawn, Slate stumbled to her paws. Overhead the stars were growing pale at the approach of dawn. She shivered in the chilly breeze that whispered over the moor.

"The fox was skulking around here again last night," Wind Runner continued as she led Slate between two boulders and out onto the moor. "I've picked up its scent."

"A rabbit without a nose couldn't miss that stink," Slate muttered as the rank smell caught her in the throat. "It should be easy to track."

Side by side the two she-cats followed the fox's trail across the moor. White mist wreathed over the ground, and the tough moorland grass was heavy with dew. The moisture damped down the fox scent, and sometimes they lost the trail altogether where the fox had crossed a stream, but they quickly picked it up again. The fox was heading directly toward the forest.

"That's where its den must be," Slate murmured, pausing and raising her head to survey the dark barrier of trees that lay ahead.

Wind Runner paused at Slate's side, shifting her paws uncomfortably. Slate turned toward her, aware that the brown she-cat wanted to say something but was finding it hard.

"We're both grateful to you," Wind Runner mewed at last. "But I'm not sure why you're doing this. You know we can't give you anything in return."

"I don't want anything," Slate responded. "Only to kill that fox."

Though she said nothing to Wind Runner, Slate admitted to herself that she didn't expect to survive the fight. She wasn't even sure that she cared. Killing the fox and protecting the kits—and yes, Wind Runner and Gorse Fur—would be enough. *It will be a noble death. And I won't have to go on trying to cope in a world without Cricket.*

But as they continued toward the trees, a tiny thorn of doubt still stuck in her heart.

The sky was milky pale with dawn by the time Slate and Wind Runner reached the forest, and a golden glow on the horizon showed them where the sun would rise. But shadows still lay deep under the trees. The fox scent led the two cats around a bramble thicket and then as far as a gaping black hole among the roots of an oak tree.

"It's in there," Slate murmured, gagging on the hot reek that flowed out of the den.

"Now what do we do?" Wind Runner twitched her tail angrily. "I don't mind chasing rabbits down their burrows, but I'm not going in there."

"We have to get the fox to come out," Slate meowed, thinking hard. "I know what to do. You go and hide in that clump of bracken."

Wind Runner hesitated as if she was going to ask a question, then gave a single lash of her tail and slid out of sight among the ferns.

Once she had gone, Slate collapsed on one side just outside the den. "Help me! Help me!" she whimpered. "I've hurt my paw. . . ."

She knew that the fox wouldn't be able to understand her, but she hoped that the pain and fear in her voice would be clear enough to entice it into the open. Her heart was pounding so hard that she thought the fox must be able to hear that too. *I've never been so scared.*

At first there was no movement in the black mouth of the den. But after a few moments Slate heard a scuffling sound, and a sharp snout poked into the open, sniffing. Then the fox's whole head appeared, its malignant eyes fixed on her.

Slate let out another piteous cry. But as the fox launched itself toward her, she rolled away and sprang to her paws, hissing defiance. In the same heartbeat Wind Runner exploded out of the bracken and hurled herself at the fox. Slate leaped in to attack it from the other side.

For a few moments the fox seemed bewildered, too surprised to fight back. But it quickly recovered, snapping at Wind Runner with all the viciousness Slate remembered.

Slate jerked back, too scared of getting her paws, or worse, her neck, caught between the fox's jaws to battle with it up close. She could see that Wind Runner shared her fear, darting in to rake her claws across the creature's pelt, then leaping back out of range. Slate concentrated, waiting until Wind

Runner had drawn the fox in one direction, then attacking from the other. She swiped at the fox's hindquarters, but it whipped around and snapped at her, forcing her back.

Slate waited until the fox turned away again. Then she lurched forward, stretching out her foreclaws to dig them deep into the fox's side, trying to open up a gash like the one it had made in her belly. The fox snarled and turned, stretching its jaws wide to snap at her. Slate ducked aside, wincing as she felt the fox tear out a chunk of her neck fur. She staggered backward, warm blood running down her neck, as Wind Runner threw herself at the fox again.

To her horror Slate saw the fox raise a forepaw and slam it across Wind Runner's head. Wind Runner let out a yowl of pain and tumbled to the ground, rolling over and over, her legs and tail waving helplessly.

As the fox loomed over Wind Runner, Slate recovered her balance and charged forward, expecting to draw her enemy away. But the fox did not react. Its eye on the side facing her was cloudy and half-closed. *It's the eye Cricket hurt,* Slate realized, remembering her brother's claws ripping at the fox's face. The fox couldn't see her attacking from the side because of its wounded eye.

That's the key to defeating it!

Slate took a deep breath, then flung herself at the fox from that side, keeping low to stay out of the way of its vicious jaws. As her claws sank into its fur, the half-blind fox turned to meet her, but Slate stayed out of its line of vision by attacking from under its jaws. She had a clear path to its neck, and plunged her foreclaws into the softer fur, tearing at the fox's throat with every scrap of strength she could muster.

Panicking, the fox thrashed and snarled, desperate to escape Slate's grip. Wind Runner scrambled back onto her paws and lunged at the fox from the other side. Together the two she-cats forced the fox to the ground, its struggles growing weaker.

Slate held on tight, ripping and tearing at the fox's throat until blood sprayed upward, splashing her muzzle. The feeling of triumph was all she had hoped for.

"That's for Cricket!" she snarled through clenched teeth.

As she watched the light die out from the fox's eyes, Slate became dimly aware of Wind Runner yowling urgently.

Another fox? she thought. *Does this one have a mate that's charging to its rescue?*

Slate released the fox and stepped away from it, trying to brace herself for another attack. She swayed on her paws, looking around for the new enemy. But all she saw was Wind Runner, staring at her with a look of horror in her yellow eyes.

"Your wound!" Wind Runner cried, gesturing toward Slate's belly.

Slate looked down and saw blood—a lot of blood—seeping from the gash in her belly. Cold fear washed over her as she sank to the ground, turning her head toward Wind Runner.

"Help me," she begged.

Blackness beckoned to her, coaxing her to sink down into its comforting depths. Slate fought against it, realizing that

she had been wrong when she thought she would be content
to give up her life in the fight.

I don't want to die. . . .

But the blackness was too strong for her. The echoing dark
was all around her, and Slate was falling, falling into a pit that
had no bottom, where the light of day would never come.

Slate felt the touch of a tiny paw on her forehead. She
opened her eyes to see a small white face with bright eyes, so
close to her that the kit's whiskers tickled Slate's ears.

"She's alive!" Moth Flight called. "I told you she wouldn't
die!"

Moth Flight pulled back, and Slate looked around to see
Gorse Fur, Wind Runner, Dust Muzzle, and Cloud Spots all
gazing down at her. She realized that she was back in her nest
in Wind Runner's camp.

Wind Runner took a pace forward and rubbed her cheek
against Slate's. "I was so afraid," she confessed. "You didn't
wake up, even when we dragged you home."

Cloud Spots appeared behind Wind Runner, his eyes warm
with relief. "I'm not surprised," he meowed. "I could tell when
I first met you, Slate, that you're a fighter."

Slate looked down at her belly and saw that Cloud Spots
had sealed her wound again with a wad of cobwebs. "Thank
you," she murmured. "Thank you all so much."

"It's the least we could do," Gorse Fur responded. "You
saved us from the fox."

"I couldn't have done it without Wind Runner," Slate

mewed. Turning to the brown she-cat, she went on, "I'm sorry I've gotten myself injured again. I wasn't aiming to stay in your camp forever. I'll leave as soon as I'm feeling stronger."

Gorse Fur and Wind Runner exchanged a glance. "Actually," Gorse Fur began, "we've been talking—"

"You can't leave!" Wind Runner blurted out suddenly, her eyes filled with emotion.

Gorse Fur nodded. "You're family now," he agreed.

"That is," Wind Runner added, twitching her ear, "if you'd ever want to become a *group cat.*"

Slate looked from the excited kits to Cloud Spots, to Gorse Fur, and finally back to Wind Runner. *Half a moon ago, I wouldn't have believed this was possible. But now . . .*

"I do," she meowed, warmth flooding through her from ears to tail-tip. "I want to be part of this family."

WARRIORS: POWER OF THREE

1

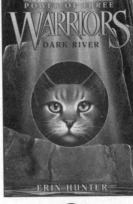

2

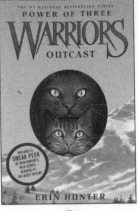

3

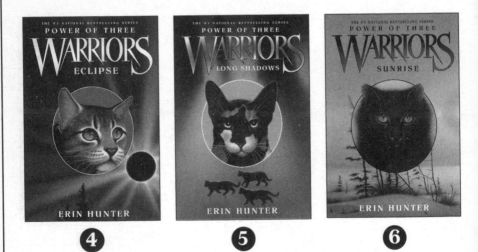

In the third series, Firestar's grandchildren begin their training as warrior cats. Prophecy foretells that they will hold more power than any cats before them.

NEW
LOOK
COMING
SOON

WARRIORS : OMEN OF THE STARS

In the fourth series, find out which ThunderClan apprentice will complete the prophecy.

NEW LOOK COMING SOON!

HARPER
An Imprint of HarperCollinsPublishers

www.warriorcats.com

WARRIORS: SUPER EDITIONS

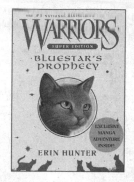

These extra-long, stand-alone adventures will take you deep inside each of the Clans with thrilling adventures featuring the most legendary warrior cats.